Praise for *Lights All Night Long*

"Formidably accomplished . . . Fitzpatrick sharply examines the cheapness of life while at the same time flagging up and homing in on various redemptive riches, from brotherly bonds to cross-cultural relations to the pursuit of justice. . . . Few debut novels are so tightly plotted and powerfully written. . . . A gripping, emotional journey."   —*Minneapolis Star Tribune*

"This vivid coming-of-age novel spools out an engrossing mystery amid a tender story about family ties and adopted homes."   —*Esquire*

"*Lights All Night Long* is that rare work of fiction that gathers page-turning momentum from its prose as much as its plot. Fitzpatrick's writing, accessible yet exquisite, relies on surgically precise metaphors for a lot of heavy emotional lifting. . . . Darkly beautiful, melancholic but not bleak, *Lights All Night Long* is storytelling at its finest. Fitzpatrick has written a compelling novel full of intimately portrayed, easy-to-love characters whose spoiled joys and resurgent hopes will linger with readers."   —*BookPage*

"*Lights All Night Long* is utterly brilliant and completely captivating. Lydia Fitzpatrick writes with cinematic clarity about life on margins of contemporary Russia and America. The result is one of the most propulsive, un-put-downable literary novels I've read in ages."
—Anthony Marra, author of *A Constellation of Vital Phenomena*

"A luminous debut . . . Fitzpatrick does so many things right in *Lights All Night Long*, it's hard to believe it's a debut novel. As a mystery, it's paced perfectly, with the novel moving seamlessly back and forth in time between Ilya's life in Russia and his new one in America. Fitzpatrick proves to be an expert in building suspense; it's hard not to read the book in a single sitting. . . . It's tricky to capture the specific, sometimes difficult language that brothers use to let each other know they care, but Fitzpatrick manages to do so perfectly, and it makes their relationship all the more beautiful and affecting. *Lights All Night Long* is both an expertly crafted mystery and a dazzling debut from an author who's truly attuned to how families work at their darkest moments. . . . An excellent novel from an author who seems to be at the beginning of an impressive career." —*Los Angeles Times*

"A slyly comic, knife-in-the-heart debut novel." —*O, The Oprah Magazine*

"The bonds of family and homeland—new and old—are tested in this sexy and pensive thriller." —*The Observer* (London)

"Fitzpatrick's remarkable debut novel is a coming-of-age narrative interwoven with a gripping mystery." —*Shelf Awareness*

"Beyond the brothers' crystalline characterizations, Fitzpatrick gifts her intriguing debut with elegant prose, affecting images, and rich settings." —*Booklist* (starred review)

"A poised, graceful literary debut . . . An absorbing tale imparted with tenderness and compassion." —*Kirkus Reviews*

"A glittering debut . . . The murder mystery is intricate and well-crafted, but the highlight is the relationship between the two brothers—the shy brainiac and the charming addict—and in the smoldering, seething resentment felt by young people. This is a heartbreaking novel about the lengths to which people go to escape their own pain, and the prices people are willing to pay to alleviate the suffering of their loved ones." —*Publishers Weekly*

"Brotherhood? Check. Murders? Check. Russia? Check. Corruption and betrayal? Check and check. This book has it all." —*The Skimm*

"Fitzpatrick's enthralling debut about a fifteen-year-old Russian exchange student in small-town Louisiana is difficult to stop reading once you start. Well-written. Well-paced. Memorable characters. In the best possible way, this novel is simply very gratifying." —*AM NY*

"For readers drawn to literary thrills, *Lights All Night Long* offers drugs, sex, and murder, but this supple, sparkling novel is really about tender souls navigating unfamiliar terrain and human bonds warm enough to thaw snowbanks. The indecipherable language of loss, love, and longing is normally impossible to understand. At last, thankfully, we have Lydia Fitzpatrick to interpret it."
—Adam Johnson, winner of the Pulitzer Prize for *The Orphan Master's Son*

"This intricate, capacious, startlingly inventive novel is so vivid, and rings so true, that its characters have taken up permanent residence in my imagination. What an accomplishment."
—R. O. Kwon, author of *The Incendiaries*

"A cross-cultural coming-of-age story that breaks your heart in the best way. Full of tender hopes and hard truths, Lydia Fitzpatrick's first novel marks the debut of a gifted storyteller."
—Maggie Shipstead, author of *Seating Arrangements*

PENGUIN BOOKS

LIGHTS ALL NIGHT LONG

Lydia Fitzpatrick's work has appeared in *The O. Henry Prize Stories, The Best American Mystery Stories, One Story, Glimmer Train,* and elsewhere. She was a Wallace Stegner Fellow at Stanford University, a fiction fellow at the University of Wisconsin–Madison, and a recipient of an Elizabeth George Foundation grant. She graduated from Princeton University and received an MFA from the University of Michigan. She lives in Los Angeles with her husband and two daughters.

Look for the Penguin Readers Guide in the back of this book. To access Penguin Readers Guides online, visit penguinrandomhouse.com.

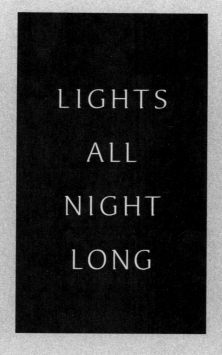

LIGHTS
ALL
NIGHT
LONG

LYDIA FITZPATRICK

Penguin Books

PENGUIN BOOKS
An imprint of Penguin Random House LLC
penguinrandomhouse.com

First published in the United States of America by Penguin Press,
an imprint of Penguin Random House LLC, 2019
Published in Penguin Books 2020

ISBN 9780525558750 (paperback)

THE LIBRARY OF CONGRESS HAS CATALOGED THE HARDCOVER EDITION AS FOLLOWS:
Names: Fitzpatrick, Lydia, 1982– author.
Title: Lights all night long : a novel / Lydia Fitzpatrick.
Description: New York : Penguin Press, 2019.
Identifiers: LCCN 2018034986 (print) | LCCN 2018038616 (ebook) |
ISBN 9780525558743 (ebook) | ISBN 9780525558736 (hardcover) |
ISBN 9781984877901 (international edition)
Classification: LCC PS3606.I8874 (ebook) | LCC PS3606.I8874 L54 2019 (print) |
DDC 813/.6—dc23
LC record available at https://lccn.loc.gov/2018034986

Printed in the United States of America
1   3   5   7   9   10   8   6   4   2

Set in Berling LT Std
Designed by Cassandra Garruzzo

For my family

We look at the world once, in childhood.
The rest is memory.

—*Louise Glück, "Nostos"*

LIGHTS
ALL
NIGHT
LONG

CHAPTER ONE

The air in the Baton Rouge airport tasted like toothpaste. Chemical-tinged and cold enough to give Ilya goosebumps, to make him wonder where he had left his winter coat, whether it was somewhere in the Leshukonskoye airport or wadded in the back-seat of Maria Mikhailovna's car or still at home on the hook that had given it a permanent hump behind the collar. Up ahead, through a set of glass doors, his host family—a man, a woman, and two girls—were holding a poster that said ILYA ALEXANDROVICH MOROZOV in cramped letters. His name was surrounded by hollow red hearts. The poster was too small to be held by four people, but they each gripped a corner determinedly. Ilya walked past them. He felt their eyes move over him, and then on to someone else, and all the while he kept his face vacant and slack.

Behind them was a row of baggage carousels, but only one was moving. Ilya stood by it and waited for his army duffel to emerge. The bag had been Vladimir's. It was the one Ilya and his mother had brought to the clinic, stuffed with gauze and ointment and a plastic bedpan. Now everything Ilya owned was inside—his clothes, a book of English idioms, his *Learn English: The Adventures of Mi-chael & Stephanie* tapes, and his tape player. The duffel was half

empty. He'd told Maria Mikhailovna that everything inside was
worthless, but still she'd written his name on a baggage tag in the
same careful letters that she used to correct his translations. Then
she'd swaddled it in plastic wrap, murmuring about what thieves
the baggage handlers were, about how Leshukonskoye was bad, but
Moscow was worse, and who knew about America. When the bag
finally circled, the plastic wrap was in tatters, clinging to the old
hammer-and-sickle pins that Vladimir had stuck in the canvas. Ilya
almost smiled, wondering what, if anything, they'd bothered to
steal. More likely they'd looked inside and known instantly that he
was too poor to steal from.

Ilya headed for the bathroom. He had to walk by the host family again, and he allowed himself a longer look this time. Maria
Mikhailovna had told him that they had three daughters, and all
winter he had imagined them: three girls, each more beautiful
than the last, like in a fable. But there were only two girls, knobby
and prepubescent, with long, lank hair and rabbity eyes. The man
was tall, the woman short, and they both had bodies like matry-
oshka dolls, like all of their weight had sunk into their hips and
asses. They weren't fit. They weren't tan. They could have been
Russian.

Outside the bathroom, Ilya fished in his pocket for a coin before
realizing that peeing was free here and that he didn't have any
American coins anyway. The stalls smelled like lemons. Each tile
was perfectly bright and white. He took a long piss. The family
would either wait or they wouldn't, and he didn't feel especially
tied to their decision. He pumped the soap dispenser a dozen times,
just to see if there was any limit to how much soap one could take.
There was not. The dispenser kept dutifully squirting pink gel until
his palm was full. He washed his hands, smearing soap all the way

up to his elbows, and he had to rinse for a long time to get rid of the suds.

As he pulled a wad of paper towels from the dispenser, a sonar noise filled the bathroom. A sound both underwater and electronic. Ilya pinched his nose and blew hard out of his ears, thinking that the noise was in his head, that his internal pressure might still be out of whack from the plane, but the noise gathered strength and resolved into a stuttering human voice. Ilya's English was good, but these words were hesitant and mangled. It took him a minute to realize that the voice was speaking Russian, not English, was hacking away at the same series of syllables, and that those syllables were his name. There was a pause, a static silence, then the voice asked him to come to the information desk by the Budget Rent-a-Car.

The family huddled under the orange fluorescence of the Budget sign. This time Ilya lifted a hand in greeting. As they recognized him, confusion tangled the adults' faces. The man gave Ilya an embarrassed smile and held out his hand, and Ilya could feel him pocketing his hesitation.

"Zdravstvuyte," the girls said, in unison, their tongues tripping over the silent "v."

The older girl stared at the poster as if it had betrayed her. "Did we spell your name wrong?" she said.

"I'm Cam Mason," the man said, "but you can call me Papa Cam."

"And I'm Mama Jamie," the woman said. Her hair was very yellow and cut in a banged bob, a style that Ilya had only ever seen on prostitutes and small children. They introduced the girls—Marilee and Molly—and as they waited for him to say something, their faces were so wide open, so vulnerable with hope. He knew the expression because he had imagined them having it, when he was vulnerable with hope too. But now Vladimir was in prison, and Ilya hadn't imagined the guilt these strange, smiling faces would call up in him. His throat narrowed, and because English felt like too much of a betrayal he said, in Russian, "I'm Ilya."

The airport doors parted with a sucking sound, and the heat rushed through them. It was wet, heavy, something to be reckoned with. Ilya's lungs could barely expand, and he imagined them sticking, their pumping slowing to a twitch and then stopping. He was momentarily terrified, but the Masons were unfazed. The girls each took one of his hands and led him across a parking lot. Papa Cam and Mama Jamie dropped back, whispering, Ilya guessed, about his lack of English.

Halfway across the lot, Papa Cam hit a button on his key ring, and a car honked in enthusiastic response. It looked like something an oligarch would own—black, with aggressive tires and tinted windows and enough rows that they could each occupy one. It was spotless except for a bumper sticker that read, LOVE, GROW, SERVE, GO!, the senselessness of which reminded Ilya of the Young Pioneers slogans that his mother and her friends would recite when they were drunk and feeling cynical and nostalgic. They all climbed inside and again the girls sandwiched Ilya. Papa Cam put on a pair of sunglasses that wrapped around his head and gave it the look of an egg that's been cracked by a spoon. He adjusted the rearview mirror until it was centered on Ilya's face.

"We're two hours from Baton Rouge, three hours from New Orleans, and a whole lot happier for it," he said.

As they sailed down the highway, the girls told Ilya their favorite colors, favorite foods, and favorite sports. Molly told him that she was seven and three-quarters, and Marilee told him that she was eleven, and he pretended not to understand a word. When they'd exhausted the topic of themselves, they took turns asking him what he ate for various meals in Russia and what sounds animals made in Russian and whether *American Idol* played in Russia. He nodded vaguely.

"Mama," Molly said, tugging on Mama Jamie's seat belt from behind, "you said he'd speak English."

"I know I did, sugar pie," she said. She twisted in her seat and reached out and touched Ilya's knee. "Did you take English in school?"

Ilya shrugged.

"He doesn't know a word," Marilee said.

"Shhhh," Molly said.

"Why?" Marilee said. "It's not like he can understand us."

He wanted to slap the girl, and he could feel the urge showing on his face, so he brought his hands up and hid his eyes in the cave of his palms.

"He might be tired," Mama Jamie said, "or shy." And when Ilya let his hands fall, she was giving him this huge and forceful smile, as though her smile alone might be powerful enough to drag him from his shell.

"He looks old. Like twenty. Or there could be something wrong with him." Marilee leaned forward and dropped her voice to a whisper. "Like from Chernobyl?"

It took Ilya a moment to understand her pronunciation of "Chernobyl," to feel its sting.

"Hey now." Papa Cam braked and flashed his eyes in the rearview. "Let's give him some peace and quiet, girls. He's traveled a ways to be with us."

"Life is hard there," Mama Jamie said.

"The life expectancy is only sixty-one," Marilee said.

Molly tapped his thigh with her pointer finger. She had become his favorite by default. "What about a rooster?" she said softly. "Do roosters in Russia go cock-a-doodle-do?"

Her eyes were dancing over his face, the sort of eyes that hid nothing. For a second, she reminded him of Vladimir, and he wanted to answer her, to give in to her the way he'd always given in to Vladimir, but the second passed, and Papa Cam turned the radio on to a news station, and the low voices lulled the girls into silence.

On either side of the road was swamp. Kilometer after kilometer of swamp, and Ilya had learned the word, though he'd never known the thing itself. It was beautiful. Shimmering and still, you thought, until you looked closer and saw long-legged birds sunning with their wings spread and fish leaving ringlets on the surface. Buzzards picked at carcasses on the roadside and their feathers ruffled as the car sped by them. The sun was hidden behind a low shield of clouds, but still everything was bleached by it.

Way out across the water, in a tangle of swamp trees, Ilya caught the flash of metal. He narrowed his eyes and tried to follow it, and then the pipeline pierced the thicket, shot across open water, and curved along the road. Before long it led to a refinery and its crown of smoke. There were the stacks and the cooling towers and the lengths of chainlink fence. It was just like the one in Berlozhniki, and Ilya imagined the pipeline snaking through land and water, connecting this place and the place he'd come from. Oil pumping through it like blood. He knew, though, that it didn't work that way.

"That's my office," Papa Cam said. He worked in human resources at the refinery. Maria Mikhailovna had told Ilya that, and that the Masons were getting paid to host him. "If they don't feed you, if they're treating you poorly, just call me," she'd said, in a burst of worry. "You can use a code word if you need to. How about 'Raskolnikov'? Just mention him like he's someone you know." At the time they'd been a third of the way through *Crime and Punishment*—an English version, poorly translated—and now it occurred to Ilya that they'd never finished it. Maria Mikhailovna had spared him the punishment part.

Papa Cam eased the car off the highway and onto a smaller one with traffic lights. There were shops now, fringing the swamp. Groceries and video stores and pizza places and a store with a sign saying, EVERYTHING'S A DOLLAR!, and through the windows Ilya could see that the shelves were completely full. There were gas stations, their crimson signs slashed by the white *E* of EnerCo. Each series of shops was larger than the town square in Berlozhniki, and they seemed to go on forever.

Ilya swallowed. He was exhausted. It had been two days since he'd left Berlozhniki. Thirty-six hours since he'd flown out of Leshukonskoye, but his stomach was still sour with the liquor he'd drunk there. Samogon, the man hawking it had told him, but it had tasted more like rubbing alcohol. He wanted to close his eyes, but when he slept he dreamt of Vladimir. For months—since the night of the Winter Festival—he'd been dreaming of Vladimir. On the flight to Moscow, he'd awoken to a stewardess's hand on his arm, her face bent over his.

"You were screaming," she'd said, her mouth tight, and then she'd moved off down the aisle.

Now Mama Jamie was pointing at something. "That's our church," she said. Up ahead, an ugly building rose out of a field. It was shaped like a pyramid, with two walls of concrete and two of glass. As they got closer, Ilya saw letters carved over the door. STAR PILGRIM CHURCH, they said, and otherwise he never would have

known that it was a church. There was no cupola, no cross—
Orthodox or not. Papa Cam slowed as they passed it and through
the glass Ilya could make out rows of seats, a shadowed aisle that
must lead to a pulpit.

"We go every Sunday," Mama Jamie said. "I think that's the
same—in Russia, I mean?"

Ilya stifled a snort. He imagined Babushka hearing her say that,
as though Americans had been the first to worship on Sundays.

"Is he Christian?" Marilee said loudly, like she was suddenly terrified to be sitting thigh-to-thigh with a heathen.

"I'm not sure, honey," Mama Jamie said. "But whatever he believes
is OK. Remember? We talked about that." Then she aimed another
invasive smile at Ilya. "We also have family dinner every night—all
five of us. Six now, with you."

Ilya knew this meant that there was another daughter, who
would, no doubt, be waiting at home with questions about communism and *American Idol*, but he let himself imagine that Vladimir would be the sixth at the table, that somehow Vladimir had
been able to come too, that he was with them now, in the back row
of the car, with his duffel under his head and his boots propped
against the window.

"Tell them to stop. We need some refreshments. I'm starving,"
he'd say, pointing at one of the convenience stores whose windows
were plastered with advertisements for lottery tickets and sausage
sandwiches. "I bet these places put the Minutka to shame. I bet they
have Doritos we've never even heard of. Did you see that sign? ALL
YOU CAN EAT! They've got no idea how much this Russian can eat."

Molly had fallen asleep with her mouth agape and her temple
bouncing against Ilya's shoulder, and Vladimir said, "The girls are a
bit of a disappointment, no? One's a bitch. And they're both a little

young. But just be patient, Ilyusha. Think of the long con. Trust me—the age gap will be a good thing down the road."

Ilya turned around, suddenly sure that he would see his brother's face, but the back row was empty. The leather was smooth and shining in the sun, and Ilya bit his lip to stop the burn in his eyes. The seams in the road ticked by, taking him farther and farther from Vladimir, and he could feel it in his gut, this growing absence, and, worse, he was sure that Vladimir, wherever he was now, could feel it too.

In the front seat, Mama Jamie was still talking about the family rules. She was saying something about praying every night. She put her hands together and bowed her head in supplication. "Pray," she said, dragging the word out so that each letter was a syllable.

Behind him, Vladimir belched. "We'll pray for your daughters to get hot," he said, and Ilya looked Mama Jamie in the eye and made his face as blank as a field of snow.

CHAPTER TWO

At the train station in Berlozhniki, a billboard stretched across the tracks. BERLOZHNIKI MINES RUSSIA'S FUTURE! it said, though the mine had closed decades earlier and in the winter, when the trains stopped running, there was no one to see the banner. On the town square, birds roosted on a concrete pedestal where a statue of Stalin had once stood, facing the labor camp, his overcoat unbuttoned as though he were expecting milder weather.

Two kilometers from town was a crescent-shaped complex of six huge kommunalkas, which had been built for the coal miners and their families. When the mine collapsed, the families stayed, without their miners. This was before perestroika, when living in a place was the closest you could come to owning it, and Ilya's family had lived there for half a century without ever believing it their own.

On the west side, the kommunalkas overlooked the remains of the mine, and, on the east, the remains of the camp, where the cells and the guard towers crumbled slowly, where crosses had been staked in the ground. In winter, snow fell, and people measured its depth by how much of the cross it swallowed. If it only reached the footrest, the winter would be mild. If it reached the higher crossbeam, the winter would be long. To the north, across the river, the refinery jutted into the sky, smoke heaving from its towers. Ilya's mother worked in the cafeteria at the refinery, and she moaned sometimes about the poison it was spewing and the cancers that were sure to result, but Ilya was mesmerized by it. Electricity in the kommunalkas could not be counted on, but the refinery's lights shone all night long. Like a city, like places Ilya had seen on TV. Moscow or Times Square or a space station. A patch of some other world stitched into Berlozhniki's horizon by mistake.

Ilya's family lived in Building 2, which was considered the best by practical people because it was closest to the road into town and the worst by spiritual people because in the '70s two brothers had jumped off the roof. Their apartment was one of a dozen on the eighth floor. All the floors were identical except for the color of paint used in the long, low hallways, so they came to be known by colors instead of numbers. Ilya's floor was zhelty, a bright yellow that had dirtied over time to mustard. At the head of each hallway was a shared kitchen—though most of the residents had acquired tiny electric stoves—and at the end of each hallway was a shared bathroom. Before he died, Ilya's father would wake in the middle of the night and trudge down the hall just to take a shit in peace. Vladimir had reported this fact to Ilya. All Ilya remembered of his father was a pair of dark, expressive eyebrows, and the thrill he'd get when his father flipped him over and pretended that a piece of candy had fallen out of his hair.

Their apartment was tiny: a bedroom that Ilya's mother and grandmother shared, and a living room where Vladimir and Ilya slept head-to-toe on a pull-out couch. The walls were crisscrossed with water pipes and studded with radiators. Above the couch hung a painting of a mother and child mushroom hunting that had been prized for its innocuousness long enough to become loved for its familiarity. There were striped curtains and a plaid tablecloth and mismatched floral cushions on each of the kitchen chairs. The woodstove was used for storage, and the red corner was papered with worker propaganda. When the shift occurred, Babushka had tacked a laminated icon right on top of Gorbachev's portrait. She'd only used one pin, so it could be quickly removed if things shifted again, but it had been there for Ilya's whole life: Jesus on the cross, the plastic clouded with grease, Gorbachev's birthmark half visible over the thorny crown.

Ilya was the younger son, without much to distinguish him from his brother but a chipped front tooth and a lopsided sag to his shoulders. The tooth was a mystery, but the shoulder sagged because his collarbone had broken during birth and never healed properly. He had been born in '93, when Yeltsin was impeached, and tanks were shelling the White House. His mother said that the doctor had been listening to Echo of Moscow, to Rutskoy as he pleaded with the air force to bomb the Kremlin, and that in the excitement of it all he'd gripped Ilya's shoulders a bit too hard with the forceps. She said that she could still hear the snap. "Like a nut cracking," she'd say, with the same wince every time, because Ilya's pain was intertwined with her own. But the kids in the kommunalkas had a different story: "Your mama's a bone breaker. Tight enough to crush a man," they whispered, until the day Vladimir overheard and threatened to crack each of their collarbones one by one.

When Ilya was little, he was happy to be like Vladimir. Happy to have the same buzz cut, to wear Vladimir's old snowsuits, which were too small in the waist and too long in the leg. Happy to time Vladimir skating up and down the Pechora on a knockoff Timex and to diligently log Vladimir's times in a notebook, though they never really improved. When he was little, Ilya treated school like Vladimir treated school: as time spent dreaming up things to do when not in school. He learned to read from Vladimir's comic books and hockey magazines, his chin hooked over Vladimir's shoulder. Ilya was an observer and a mimic, Vladimir a natural performer who never seemed to mind the force of Ilya's attention, though he did, from time to time, take advantage of it. Afternoons, when they were walking home from school, he'd ask Ilya to steal Fantas from the Minutka, and Ilya would stuff them under his sweater without a second thought. Once, ancient Anatoly, who worked the register, caught him and made him spend the day unloading beer crates as punishment. Ilya stole two beers to make up for the lost Fantas, and Vladimir accepted these as though they were his due.

When Vladimir and his best friend, Sergey, clung to the back of the #33 bus, the one that took the neftyaniki out to the refinery, Ilya clung to the back too. They would jump off just before the gates in snow that came up to Ilya's knees. Everything—the snow, their skin—was blue-tinged by the refinery's light. Vladimir and Sergey dragged sticks along the chainlink fence, which seemed so high that it even segmented the sky, and when they were far enough from the road, they took turns flicking matches through the fence and watching them burn little holes in the snow. They circled the refinery slowly, like sharks might, looking for a break in the fence, and inevitably Vladimir and Sergey began trading stories of Fyodor Fetisov, the oligarch who owned it all.

"Once," Vladimir said, "he took a bath in beluga."

"With two prostitutes," Sergey said.

"That each cost two million rubles a night," Ilya added, because this detail had stuck with him. Two million rubles was more than a thousand Fantas. Two million rubles could probably buy the Minutka and everything inside it.

"That's right," Vladimir said. "And they had on thongs made of gold."

"And diamonds for nipples," Sergey said. They all went silent for a moment at the power of this image. "He can do whatever the fuck he wants with them. Anything," Sergey said, with a cruelness that sometimes surfaced in Sergey and that made Ilya wish it were just Vladimir and him leaning against the fence.

"Where does he live? On the square?" Ilya said.

Vladimir and Sergey looked at each other and laughed.

"He doesn't live *here*," Vladimir said. "He's probably been here once, to cut the ribbon."

"No one lives here," Sergey said.

"Not even the prostitutes?" Ilya asked.

"Ilyusha," Vladimir laughed, "I like the way you think."

When it was too cold to be outside, Ilya and Vladimir watched movies. Vladimir was obsessed with American movies, and Ilya liked them because Vladimir did. The pure action movies were Vladimir's favorites—anything with Jean-Claude Van Damme or Bruce Willis, anything with roundhouse kicks and explosions and sparse dialogue—but he would settle for badly dubbed dramas or sitcoms with too-loud laugh tracks or whatever Kirill the cranky Chechen was hawking at the Internet Kebab. The movies were all a decade old. The tapes were all bootleg.

In *The Bodyguard*, the dubbing turned to Chinese five minutes in, and a wave of static washed across Whitney Houston's face. In *Die Hard*, the Russian had been added without removing the

English, so every line Bruce Willis said was a tangle of the two. One VHS was unlabeled, and Vladimir had bought it hoping that it was porn, but it was a Jean-Claude Van Damme movie, the title of which they never learned because the tape began at some point a third of the way in and ended right before the climax. Vladimir kept the VHSs stacked, according to genre, next to the TV, and when the VCR jammed, which it did with regularity, Ilya would hold the player's mouth open, and Vladimir would use Babushka's tweezers to unsnag the tape with a patience and attention that were rare in him.

He and Ilya spent whole winters sitting cross-legged on the carpet. They watched blood fly and cars wreck and buildings crumble. They knew the dubbed Russian by heart. When the power went out, and the VCR whirred to a stop, they recited the dialogue. *Kickboxer* was their favorite. Vladimir could enact the final fight scene perfectly.

"Like he trained for the Bolshoi," their mother would say.

"Oh, the Bolshoi," Vladimir would say with a swoon because their mother had a crush on Alexander Bogatyrev.

"I just mean," she'd say, "that if you can memorize this, you can memorize other things. Useful things. What's eight times six?"

And Vladimir would groan and say, "Mama, you're ruining it."

One afternoon, when Ilya was seven and snow was falling lazily outside and they were watching the unlabeled VHS for the millionth time, Ilya found himself mesmerized by Jean-Claude's lips, by the fact that he was speaking a totally different language. Halfway through the movie, the fighting lulled and there was a love scene. Vladimir had roamed out to the balcony to take a piss. On-screen, Jean-Claude's character was in bed with a blond woman. They were both so tan that Ilya thought they were a different race.

The woman's hair was in a lascivious halo around her face. The sheets vined up her body, covering strategic areas, though Vladimir was convinced that for a half second half of her nipple showed. She was asking Jean-Claude if he'd ever give up and settle down.

"Yebat 'ne," a husky voice said.

The Russian was ridiculous and the dubbing was off, so it took a second for Jean-Claude's lips to part in a silent "Fuck no." No sound came out, but Ilya could *see* the sounds he was making: the flash of his teeth against his lower lip with the "Fff," the slight grimace of the "ck," the pursed lips of that final "o," and Ilya found himself stringing the sounds together until he could hear Jean-Claude's voice clearly, as though he had whispered right into Ilya's ear.

"Fuck no," Ilya said softly.

It was English. He had said two words in English. Not only that: he knew what they meant. He looked to see if anyone had heard him, sure that the thrill he felt, a thrill like he'd cracked a code, was illicit. His mother was sleeping off her night shift, and Babushka was working the coat check at the Museum of Mining, and Vladimir had finished pissing and was doubled over the balcony railing spitting on the sidewalk.

The woman in bed was sitting up now, with the sheets clutched to her chest. Jean-Claude leaned over her.

"Yebat 'ne," the husky voice said again.

"Fuck no," Ilya said, his lips moving at just the moment Jean-Claude's did, and again that thrill twirled up his spine.

"What did you say?" Vladimir stood in the doorway, his cheeks pink from being outside and upside down. He was ten then, with this haze of hair on his upper lip that Ilya wanted badly for himself.

Ilya said it in Russian.

"No," Vladimir said. "You said it in English. Say it again."

"Fuck no," Ilya murmured.

Jean-Claude and the woman were kissing now, but in a minute the Chinese mob would kick down the door and shoot the bed with such vigor that feathers filled the air.

"You learned that? From watching their lips?"

Ilya nodded.

Vladimir clapped his hands. "Come here," he said. He went back onto the balcony, and Ilya followed him.

The balcony was the size of a shower stall and webbed with so many strands of laundry line that you had to crouch to get to the railing. When they did, Vladimir propped Ilya on the rail. The courtyard was a muddy expanse, scabbed with spring snow. One man trudged across it, coming from the bus stop with a bagged beer. Behind him, the refinery was the whole horizon, bright and pulsing.

"Yell it," Vladimir said. He had his arms around Ilya's waist. The metal rail was so cold that it felt as though it were burning Ilya's ass right through his pants.

"Go on," Vladimir said. "Yell it."

Ilya was quiet, and then Vladimir said the woman's line in Russian, "'Are you gonna give up?'"

"Fuck no," Ilya said, and his voice wasn't big enough to carry. The man with the beer kept trudging.

"Fuck no!" Vladimir yelled, and Ilya could hear the thickness of English on Vladimir's tongue, could hear how his own had been clear in comparison.

Ilya opened his mouth and this time he yelled it. The insides of his cheeks tightened in a rush of cold, and the man with the bottle looked up. If he could understand them, he didn't show it. Vladimir pointed at him just as he dropped his beer in a patch of slush and disappeared around the corner of their building.

"See," Vladimir said, "you already know more than that old fucker." He lifted Ilya down. "Jean-Claude wasn't born American."

"He wasn't?" Ilya said. He'd thought Jean-Claude the epitome of all things American.

"He was French. Or Dutch or something. But he's American now. He moved there. And you know who he brought with him?"

Ilya shook his head.

"His brother. They live in a mansion right on fucking Hollywood Boulevard." They ducked under a line of Ilya's underwear, which had been Vladimir's before him and had turned the color of concrete. Vladimir nudged Ilya toward the TV. "Go see what they say next," he said.

And because Ilya wanted that thrill again, and because Vladimir had told him to, he did. He spent the afternoon a meter from the screen, his fingers kneading the nub of Babushka's carpet. Behind him, Vladimir practiced choke holds on pillows, while Ilya listened to the Russian and moved his lips like the Americans. The little, sharp words were the easiest to mimic: the "nos" and "thanks" and "fucks." But as weeks and months passed, he learned to pause the videos, to play them in slow motion and tease out the vowels and cobble together longer words. Syllable by syllable he watched the way American tongues hit American teeth. There was a lot he didn't understand, but that seemed inconsequential next to the miracle of what he did.

CHAPTER THREE

The sun was still high as Papa Cam pulled onto a smaller street and sped up a rise into a cul-de-sac where a lone house bit a chunk out of the sky. It was as graceless as a kommunalka. Over one of its shoulders, Ilya could make out the refinery, so small that its lights had merged into one light. Its smoke melted into the clouds. The Masons' lawn was cut military short, but the lots on either side were full-grown with sawgrass.

"It was supposed to be a neighborhood, then the market crashed," Papa Cam said. He slung Ilya's duffel over his shoulder with a grunt and made his way up a brick walk to the door.

"We have it all to ourselves," Molly said in a rote, uninflected way, as though that were the party line.

Inside, everything—the walls, the furniture, the pillows, the countertops—was the color of tea made for a child, with lots of milk. The ceilings went up and up and up, and there seemed a determination not to divide space into rooms. The kitchen bled into the dining room, which bled into the den and the foyer, where the stairs curled into an open-air hallway. Mama Jamie gave Ilya a tour, using game-show host gestures, and the house did seem like something on TV. It was all polish; it lacked dimension, lacked the smells and sounds and smudges that were life in the kommunalkas. Ilya's duffel, in all of its dirtiness, suddenly seemed like the only real thing, and he wanted to grab it from the chair where Papa Cam had left it and run. He would head toward the refinery and figure things out from there, he thought, just as Mama Jamie reached out and took his arm. Ilya flinched, and there was this flash of fear in her eyes, as though he'd been the one to touch her. She looked at him and he looked at her, and his heart was beating so hard that he was sure that she could see it shaking his body. Then she smiled. And he was wondering how many times she would do that—let her good-will trump her instincts—when footsteps sounded in the hallway and a girl appeared at the top of the stairs. The third daughter. The *first* daughter, he thought, because she was the eldest. She was his age. Maybe a year younger. Her hair was dyed a shade close to white, which was more unsettling than attractive, but still there was something beautiful about her. Like the girls in Berlozhniki, she was all long, pale lengths: her shins, her wrists, her neck, which she was stretching now, with an arm crooked over her head and an elbow pointing to the ceiling. Her voice was long and pale too.

"Took you a while," she said, and it did not in any way mean that she cared. She let her arm drop and rolled her head gently and her eyes closed with the motion. She was wearing an enormous black T-shirt with cut-off jean shorts, and as she walked down the stairs toward him, the T-shirt consumed all of her shorts except the little white threads that hung down her thighs like icicles. Her sneakers were high-tops, spray-painted silver so that even the laces were crusty with paint.

"Ilya," Mama Jamie said, "this is Sadie."

Sadie looked at him for a long moment. "Welcome to Leffie," she said. "Home of the largest boudin ball ever cooked." She smiled.

A darting, furtive expression. Ilya tried to think what "boudin" meant and could not.

"It's not as bad as all that," Papa Cam said.

"True," Sadie said. "There's the corn festival."

"Ilya doesn't speak quite as much English as we were thinking," Mama Jamie said, "but he's going to learn fast. Immersion, right?"

"He doesn't speak *any*," Marilee said.

Sadie rolled her eyes—whether at Marilee or her mom or his lack of English, Ilya wasn't sure—and walked past them all into the kitchen. She opened the fridge door and disappeared behind it. Ilya thought that they would all migrate to the kitchen, that naturally they would follow her, but Mama Jamie just called, "Don't spoil your supper," and led Ilya upstairs, where the girls' bedrooms marched down the hall, one after another. Marilee and Molly opened their doors to reveal studies of pink and green—plaid, polka dots, stripes, flowers. There was not an inch that had been left unmolested. But when Ilya looked through the cracked doorway into Sadie's bedroom, it was spartan: a white quilt on a slim bed; a single pillow over which a slight, black cross hung; a wooden desk with a chair lumped in clothes. It looked temporarily inhabited, like there might be a suitcase somewhere out of sight. He wanted to linger, to open the door just a little wider, but Mama Jamie had moved on.

"This is our room," she said, presenting a carpeted kingdom into which Ilya could easily have tucked his entire apartment. "The door is always open."

"Well, not literally," Papa Cam said, "but you can always knock."

Ilya stared. He couldn't help it. The TV at the foot of their bed was as big as a door and as thin as a dinner plate. There was a sleek bureau with a dozen drawers, and on top was a silver tray bearing bottles of perfume and shimmery boxes. Through another door he glimpsed a bathroom with marble counters and two sinks in case Mama Jamie and Papa Cam ever wanted to wash their faces in concert. He tried to lock on to just one detail that he could give to his mother, something that she might use like currency with the other mothers in the kommunalkas, something about which she might say, "*This* is what it's really like there," but no one in the kommunalkas would talk to his mother now, with Vladimir in prison, and besides there wasn't any detail that wouldn't sting.

When they'd gone back downstairs, Papa Cam said, "I'm going to call Terry and see if we can't figure out this whole language situation. Maybe there's someone in Leffie who speaks Russian."

"Doubtful," Sadie said. She had a series of plastic containers open on the counter. She dabbed a finger into a beige puree, tasted it, and wrinkled her nose. "Is this old?" she said.

Mama Jamie ignored her and went on telling Ilya about the house. She pointed here and there. Bathroom, she said. Towels. Trash. Chores. Yard. Phone. Garage. Her lips did wild exaggerations of each word, and twice beads of spit flew off her tongue, propelled by the force of her enunciations.

"We have a pool," she said, "and if you don't know how to swim, Papa Cam can teach you. He taught all the girls. He had Molly doing freestyle—"

"I'm sure he knows how to swim," Sadie said.

Ilya knew little more than how to keep his head above water—summers in Berlozhniki were short, and between the mine and the refinery, the river wasn't so clean—but his throat caved in at the thought of Sadie in a bathing suit. A bikini. Topless, even, with sunglasses and a stomach piercing and a sweating Coke can in hand. It was a ridiculous fantasy, he knew, ripped in part from some advertisement he'd internalized, and it came barbed with the memory of nights, lying in bed, listening to Vladimir talk about girls. He couldn't think of any fantasy of his that hadn't been Vladimir's first.

"Terry's looking into it," Papa Cam said, coming back in from the deck. "He was stumped. He said Ilya's the best student in the whole town there, like some sort of language savant, at least according to his teacher there. He's going to get in touch with her."

Maria Mikhailovna. Ilya could see her pushing her glasses up her nose, nodding to the beat of his conjugations. He could see the tiny red notations she made in the margins of his homework, and the way she gripped her pen with one too many fingers. What would she say if she saw him now, after all her work, after all she'd risked, pretending not to understand a word of English?

Mama Jamie's smile was failing her. Worry puckered her mouth. He knew that this was the moment to speak up, to blurt out something in English, to say he'd been exhausted, scared. Any excuse would do, but he couldn't shake the idea that uttering a word in English would be letting go of something.

"Ilya, can you understand us?" Mama Jamie said. "Can you—"

"I'm out of here," Sadie said. She grabbed a backpack from a closet off the kitchen, and Mama Jamie and Papa Cam pulled their eyes off Ilya and looked at her.

"Where are you going?" Papa Cam said.

"Kayla's," she said. "The summer reading report's due Tuesday."

"And you've had how long to work on it—all summer?" Mama Jamie said. "It's Ilya's first night. We're going to eat soon."

There was a long silence that Ilya recognized. Even the little girls stared at Sadie with big eyes, and Ilya could see that she was like Vladimir had been. She was the one they worried about.

Sadie zipped up her backpack, which was encrusted with the

same silver spray paint as her sneakers. As she pulled it onto her shoulders, her hair got trapped under the straps. She gathered it at the nape of her neck and freed it, and her eyes met his. She had not been particularly nice to him, but still he had the distinct impression that she'd saved him somehow, that she'd interrupted Mama Jamie on purpose and bought him a little more time.

"Home by ten," Papa Cam said.

"Nine," Mama Jamie said.

"Later," Sadie said to no one in particular.

As Mama Jamie slipped a casserole into the oven, Papa Cam led Ilya out onto the deck to see the backyard. A grill was tucked into one corner. Mow lines checked the grass, which was encircled by a low brick wall.

"It's to keep out alligators," Papa Cam said, pointing at the wall. "Vicious, but they can't even climb a foot."

The pool was square and still, the water taking on a dark shine, like oil, in the dusk. Papa Cam seemed to have taken the idea of immersion less literally than Mama Jamie, or maybe he was more comfortable with silence. He leaned against the deck rail and let Ilya look for himself. Eventually he said, "It took us two years to get the pool built. For a while there I thought it just wasn't in God's plan."

Part of Ilya wanted to express his awe, but what he wanted to say more—the thing burning his tongue like acid—was that if God did exist then he was a motherfucker if the Masons' pool was part of his plan, was even a blip on his radar.

Ilya thought of his mother and Babushka, wondered what they were doing at that moment. He did not even know what time it was at home, whether they were sitting on the wooden bench in the hall of the police station, waiting for someone to talk to them, or whether his mom was halfway through her night shift, eating the boiled eggs on rye that Babushka packed her every evening. He couldn't imagine where Vladimir was. The only prisons he'd seen were on TV—American prisons—and he knew that wherever they were holding Vladimir would be worse. But then, suddenly, he could picture Vladimir: his back against a rough concrete wall, the kind that crumbled slightly under your fingertips. His lips were moving like he was praying, but of course he wasn't. He was reciting the lines from *Kickboxer*, the movie unspooling behind his eyelids, his fists clenching with the muscle memory of the fight scenes.

Behind him, Papa Cam flipped a light switch on the wall of the house, and the pool jumped into being. Turquoise and glowing, with a rim of blue tiles and a lone leaf resting on the bottom.

"There," Papa Cam said. His voice was exalted, and Ilya thought he might vomit.

For almost a year, since the night Maria Mikhailovna had knocked on their door, he had thought about America constantly. On some level he had imagined the wide, smooth streets, the car-size refrigerators, the tank-size cars, the carpets that went all the way from one wall to another. He had even anticipated the faith with which the Masons clicked their seat belts; the way Papa Cam had paid for the airport parking with a lazy swipe of his credit card; the fact that, in the one grocery store they'd driven past, there had been no lines. But he hadn't ever thought of this: in America, they light their pools. *This* was the detail for his mother. He imagined telling her. He could almost hear her silence, the quick suck of air through her teeth.

"Sometimes," Papa Cam said, "the girls like to swim at night."

CHAPTER FOUR

By the time Ilya turned eleven, he'd skipped a level at School #17, and there was constant talk of his promise. "He's sharp," one teacher said. "A prodigy," said another. They said that he might get a scholarship to Syktyvkar State or even to the Language Institute in Moscow. Convinced by his teachers of Ilya's aptitude, his mother and grandmother started to hope. For a little more money, for a table that didn't wobble, for a bigger apartment, for a car, but most of all their hope conjured his future: a degree and a good job in Moscow or St. Petersburg, neither of which they'd ever seen. They treated Ilya as tenderly as the brass samovar that came out from under the bed, from under its layers of felt, only for polishing. His grandmother mixed extra sour cream into his shchi. She scooped it onto his pelmeni.

"More smetana, Ilyusha?" she'd say. He'd watch the cream quiver on the end of her spoon and knew she'd give him all they had.

Vladimir noticed this favoritism—it was impossible not to. He teased Ilya about it. "Your big brain is oozing out of your ears," he'd say, or, "Study, smart-ass, study!" But sometimes when Ilya pulled out his pencil case and his textbooks, Vladimir would go quiet.

He'd shut off the TV and slink down to the stairwell where boys bounced tennis balls off the walls and smoked cigarettes.

Ilya started secondary school, and his new English teacher, Maria Mikhailovna, was a tiny woman with enormous glasses and a prodigious amount of hair that she wore in a thick, schoolgirl braid. Her husband was a policeman, so everyone regarded her with a bit of suspicion, but she herself was soft-spoken and sometimes seemed surprised to find herself at the front of the room and the center of attention. After Ilya's first week in her class, she asked him to stay behind and said, quietly, "You have a gift."

Ilya's eyes fell like sinkers. He was used to hearing things like this by now, but still he never knew what to say in return. "Take the compliment like a boss," Vladimir always told him. "Just say, 'No shit.'" But, as always, Vladimir's advice was only applicable if you had Vladimir's balls, and Ilya did not.

"Thank you," Ilya managed.

Maria Mikhailovna handed him a piece of paper. "Ask your mother to get what she can, and if it's any trouble, tell me."

He nodded. There was a Russian-English dictionary on the list, a book of idioms, a tape player, a set of tapes, and corresponding workbooks. He estimated the costs on his walk home, and the total was close to a week's groceries, but his mother smiled when he showed it to her. She handed Vladimir a stack of rubles and told him to take Ilya to the bookstore on Ulitsa Snezhnaya, which was the more expensive of Berlozhniki's two bookstores.

When they walked in the door, a tiny bell shook above them, and the shopkeeper looked at them and said, "Money on the counter." The shopkeeper was a sour sort, with permanently pursed lips, and Ilya could feel Vladimir bristling next to him, could feel how badly Vladimir wanted to slam the door, head across the square, and spend the money on a dozen VHSs at the Internet Kebab, but instead he cleared his throat and showed the man Maria Mikhailovna's list. When the total was more than their mother had given them, the shopkeeper allowed a smile.

"If I cancel the tapes you'll have enough," the man said.

"We're not canceling the tapes," Vladimir said.

"It's OK," Ilya said. "Maria Mikhailovna—"

"We're getting the tapes." Vladimir reached into the waistband of his jeans and plucked out a bill that was rolled thin as a straw. He handed it to the shopkeeper. "You do the math," he said.

"Of course I'll do the math," the shopkeeper said, and, once he had, he said, "It'll be two weeks at least."

Vladimir nodded, and Ilya followed him out the door. When it had closed behind them, Vladimir said, "Did you see his mouth? He looks like he's been sucking cock nonstop for a decade."

Ilya laughed, but Vladimir was not joking. His eyes had gone narrow and sharp. "You're not going to get anywhere, ever, if you let people like that push you around." He was walking fast toward home, his steps making a staccato rhythm of his words. "That guy wants the whole world to fail. You. Me. Himself even. Just so he can say he saw it coming."

"OK," Ilya said.

"Not OK," Vladimir said, ahead of him.

"Where did you get the money?" Ilya asked. He knew for a fact that Vladimir had spent his name-day money within an hour of receiving it, but Vladimir didn't answer.

Two weeks later, when they returned to the shop, the shopkeeper hefted a box out of the storeroom and slid it onto the counter. Ilya could see that everything was there. The tapes in a cellophane stack. The books pristine, their pages so bright and white that Ilya could feel the way they would cut his fingers.

"Thank you," Ilya said, but Vladimir, who lost his homework on a weekly basis, unearthed Maria Mikhailovna's list from his pocket.

"I'll check it," he said, and he began to match the books' titles to the ones on the list. Ilya knew that Vladimir meant to make a point, but his reading was a work in progress, his English abysmal, and it took him a long time to sound out each title. His lips moved, slow and labored, as though he were giving birth to each word. The shopkeeper pulled a toothpick from his pocket and began to flip it, end over end, between his teeth. He was watching Vladimir too.

"I have to piss," Ilya said, because he could feel the shopkeeper practicing insults with each flip of the toothpick.

"Hold it," Vladimir said. He moved his finger down the list and began sounding out and searching for the last title. Finally, he was done. He handed Ilya the tapes and stacked the books in his arms, and as Ilya followed him out the door the shopkeeper said, "Idiot."

Vladimir did not react. He did not stiffen. He did not get the furious flush that usually preceded a tantrum of some kind. It didn't seem as though Vladimir had heard the man, and so Ilya pretended he hadn't either. They brought the books home. And because of the books they had a meatless dinner for the tenth night in a row, and Vladimir said nothing about that or about the shop-keeper. But a few days later, Ilya walked by the shop alone and found the glass storefront splintered. The glass had held, but cracks radiated out from a crystalline patch in the center of the window. Ilya looked down, wondering what Vladimir had thrown, but the sidewalk was clean. Inside, the shop was dark and empty. Ilya put a finger to the point of impact and pushed, just gently, and it seemed to him as though the window bowed inward—a millimeter, no

more, but enough to make him whip his hand back. His fingertip
came away coated in tiny shards, one of which brought out a bead
of blood. Ilya sucked it, and then he looked up. The shopkeeper was
behind the counter. He had come out from the storeroom and was
watching Ilya through the cracks in the glass, and Ilya shoved his
hand in his pocket and hurried away.

The set of tapes was called *Learn English: The Adventures of Michael & Stephanie*, and Maria Mikhailovna assigned him an hour of
listening comprehension each night on top of his regular workload.
Michael and Stephanie were an American couple. They went to the
grocery store, to the beach, to the movies and the mall. All the
while they'd talk in slow, happy, somewhat stoned voices, and Ilya
would listen. Sometimes they'd ask him questions:

"What did you have for lunch today?" Stephanie would ask.

"Bread and cheese," Ilya would say.

"What is the weather like today?" Michael would ask.

"It snows," Ilya would say.

There were line drawings of Michael and Stephanie in the corresponding workbooks. Stephanie was decent looking, with pointy
breasts that made twin tents in her sweaters. Vladimir claimed that
she was good fodder for masturbation, and that Michael, who was
gangly and wore glasses, was not satisfying her adequately. Her
breasts excited Ilya, as did the pinch of her waist, but it was her
eyes that he loved. They were big and liquid and sad, despite all the
American fun she had.

In Maria Mikhailovna's program, Ilya's world narrowed. He was
only ever at school or at the kitchen table with his workbooks spread
before him. His ears were always bracketed by a pair of foam Delta

headphones that had come with the tape player. But somehow the world felt expansive. He'd close his eyes and listen through the static until Michael's and Stephanie's voices grew clear and large, and it was as though he'd opened a tiny, secret door onto an incredible vista. It was as though he were moving through the door, shutting it carefully behind him and breathing this new, perfect sort of air. Before long, he didn't even need to be listening to the tapes to be transported. Michael and Stephanie spoke to him constantly. Every time he looked at his watch, they told him the time in English. Every time he climbed the flights up to his apartment, they counted the steps in English.

"Uzhin gotov, Ilyusha," Babushka would say, and Ilya would hear Stephanie say, "Ilyusha, dinner is ready."

"What are we eating tonight?" Ilya would say, in English, and Babushka would look at him with the jolt of an old fear in her eyes. Then her face would soften, and she would say, "Even you can't make English sound pretty."

While Ilya studied, Vladimir gained his own sort of knowledge. He stole a carton filled with crisps from a truck broken down on the high road and sold them outside the school for ten rubles less than what crisps went for at the Minutka. He skated down the Pechora, smoked pot under the bridge, and broke his arm skating home. He watched porn over the stuttering connection at the Internet Kebab. He was held back a year in school and in his new grade, he got a girlfriend, Aksinya, who let him feel her breasts. He told Ilya that they were as small and hard as new potatoes. Aksinya gave Vladimir a hand job. Then a blow job. Each night, in bed, Vladimir reported all of these developments to Ilya with gusto, with hand motions, and for a while Ilya thought that he could do these things too, that he was making a choice to study instead. But one afternoon, when he was eleven, he went to find Vladimir in the stairwell of Building 4, where he and Sergey liked to bounce tennis balls against the wall and smoke cigarettes. Vladimir wasn't there. No one was. There weren't any balls or cigarette butts on the ground. The graffiti had been painted over, the floor had been swept, and Ilya got the same feeling looking at that clean concrete that he got when the swallows departed on cue each August, when the gray sky was full one moment and empty the next.

Snow was falling that afternoon, and his footprints were already soft at the edges as he followed them back across the courtyard to Building 2 and climbed to his floor. Babushka had recently struck up a friendship with Timofey Denisovich from down the hall, and they were playing prostoy durak at the table. Timofey was even more ancient than Babushka and had the sort of unkempt nostril hair that felt like an act of aggression. He and Babushka did not talk much, although sometimes Ilya would come home to find them humming songs from the Revolution or swapping sovok jokes.

"What's the latest requirement for joining the Politburo?" Timofey would say.

"Tell me," Babushka would say.

"You have to be able to walk six steps without a cane."

"No, two. Two steps is enough." Babushka would laugh, tears trickling from the corners of her eyes the way they did when she was happiest.

That afternoon they were quiet, though. There was just the click of cards against the table, and the hiss of air through Timofey's nose when Babushka laid down a strong suit.

"Where is Vladimir?" Ilya said.

Babushka looked at him with a smile left over from a card she'd played. "God knows," she said as though God really did. "Are you hungry?"

Ilya shook his head.

"I am," Timofey said.

"He is the one who needs to eat, not you. What are you doing all day? Not studying. We know that," she said, but she stood anyway, and got Timofey a plate and one for Ilya too.

And so Ilya spent the afternoon at home, as he always did, picking at a beef blini and paging through his *Handbook of Commonly Used American Idioms*. On the cover was an American flag, a baseball, and a hamburger. Idioms were messy, logic-less things, but each page of the book had been divided into two columns—on the left were the idioms, on the right their definitions—and usually Ilya loved this imposed order, the promise that if he learned a column a week he would know them all in a hundred and sixty-two weeks. He would know them all by the time he was Vladimir's age.

"Above all," he murmured.

"Ace in the hole," he said, but that day he couldn't quite make the words mean anything.

Vladimir was probably with Aksinya, cupping her new potatoes. Or he could be skating, but the ice wasn't thick yet, and Ilya looked and could see the shine of Vladimir's skates in the bin under the couch. Maybe he was clinging to the back of the #33 bus with Sergey, though Ilya didn't know if they even rode out to the refinery anymore. And then, as though Ilya had conjured him, Vladimir burst through the door. His boots were untied, the laces wet and whipping at his ankles, and there were two girls following close behind him.

"We saw Fyodor Fetisov!" he said. "We were up on the bridge and all of a sudden all these black cars roll out—one after the

other—and then this SUV that is—" Vladimir kissed his fingers
the way Italians did on TV when they saw a beautiful woman. "He
was going like one fifty. He almost hit us." Vladimir grabbed the
blini off of Ilya's plate and took it down in two bites, as though his
brush with death had left him famished. Then he said, in a softer
voice, "I touched his car. Just reached out and touched it."

Ilya could see it: his brother's fingers touching that perfect paint
job, the car shocking him with the import of the man inside.

"Bozhe moy," Babushka said. "Why do you do things like that?
You're going to get yourself arrested." She collapsed the fan of cards
in her hand into a neat stack and said, "Who are you?" to the girls.

One of them was almost too beautiful to look at, with long, dark
hair like the Nenets and blue eyes that were all Russian. "Aksinya,"
she said, and then, to Vladimir, "I don't know why you wanted to
touch his car. He's terrible. That's what my sister says."

"It's no business of ours," Babushka said.

"I'm Lana," the other girl said. She was blond, softer, with a gap
between her teeth that suggested a gentle stupidity.

"Lana Vishnyeva. I know your father," Babushka said, and Lana
nodded.

Ilya asked if they'd seen the oligarch's face, and Vladimir shook
his head. He said that the windows were as black as oil. "I saw
Maria Mikhailovna's husband through the windshield though,"
Vladimir said. "He was driving."

"Why's Fetisov here? He hasn't been here since—" Ilya paused.
As far as he could remember, Fyodor Fetisov had never been to
Berlozhniki.

"Some new pipeline project," Vladimir said.

"Because the billions he has aren't enough," Babushka said, her tone sharp, and then it softened, and she said, "Are you hungry, girls?"

Once Vladimir had asked her if she ever got tired of asking people if they were hungry, of feeding them. "There's nothing that makes me happier in the world than being able to feed a child," she'd said in that tone that old people used when they talked about the Great War, and Vladimir had rolled his eyes.

"I'm starving," Lana said, without any shame.

Aksinya nodded, and Babushka brought out more plates. Ilya cleared his books, and the prostoy durak game was put on hold. They crowded around the table, and the apartment got that feeling that it could sometimes have, like it was holding something golden and sweet, like it was filled to the brim with honey.

CHAPTER FIVE

From down in the basement, Ilya could hear the Masons eating dinner. The clink of dishes. Chairs scraping, water running, the occasional shriek of Marilee or Molly. He had yawned enough times during Mama Jamie's tour of the basement—the "rec room," she called it—that she had relented and allowed him to skip dinner and whatever other orientation activities she had planned.

The basement had a set of glass doors that framed a dark patch of earth under the deck where a few bikes were slumped in a pile. A ping-pong table stretched across half the room. The net had given up in the middle, the paddles peeled at the edges, and Ilya was comforted by these tiny signs of neglect. Over the bed, there was an enormous poster of a beach with footprints near the surf. The sky had been enhanced till it looked radioactive. The water was the color of Freon. It had something to do with Jesus, but Ilya wasn't sure what exactly. He had his own bathroom. "Feel free to flush the t.p.," Mama Jamie had said, and she'd ripped a few squares off the roll and flushed them herself to prove the power of American plumbing. Then she'd opened a shallow cabinet over the sink to reveal a toothbrush, toothpaste, deodorant, and shampoo, each in its own bright packaging. Ilya wished that he didn't need them—if he had left under different circumstances, his mom would have packed them—but he did.

In a little nook by the glass doors was a desk with a computer. The monitor was off, the screen the gray of a dead tooth, but still Ilya's stomach lifted and flipped when he saw it. He wanted news of Vladimir. He wanted, so badly, just to see Vladimir's face. As soon as Mama Jamie had retreated up the basement stairs, he pressed the button on the hard drive. For a long second there was nothing, and he thought it must be broken, aged out by the sleeker model in the den, but then the computer exhaled softly. Something inside began to spin. A weak green light flicked on, and the screen came to life. The background loaded: Papa Cam, Mama Jamie, and the girls on a beach. They were all in turquoise shirts and white shorts. Sadie's hair was a darker blond—her natural color, Ilya guessed—and now that he could stare at her unabashedly, he saw that there was something strange about one of her eyes. One pupil was slightly jagged, as though it had suffered a tiny explosion. Then the applications popped up. One covered Sadie's face, and Ilya pulled the mouse over to the internet browser and clicked.

First he checked his email, hoping for some sort of good news, but of course there was nothing but spam—ads for penis enlargements and hot American pussy and cheap flights to Lake Baikal. He couldn't log in to VKontakte without converting the keyboard to Cyrillic, and so he spent half an hour Googling keyboard conversions, and another half hour in the bowels of the computer settings, until, finally, the Roman letters on the keyboard called up his old, familiar alphabet. Then he logged in, typed Vladimir's name in the search box, and waited for his profile to load.

He'd last checked Vladimir's profile the day before Maria Mikhailovna drove him to the airport, and there were dozens of new posts since then:

Rot in Hell.

Even GOD won't forgive you.

I hope you get raped up the ass every day for the rest of your miserable life. That will = what you deserve.

Ilya forced himself to read each one, to wait until the sting had faded, and then to read it again. He moved slowly, deliberately, sounding out each word in the same way he did with his lists of English vocabulary. Pyotr Vladimirov, who lived two floors below them, had written *Genesis 3* without any additional explanation, and Pasha Tretiak, who had skated with Vladimir the one year he'd been on the School #17 team, had written *I always knew you were a sick fuck.*

One person had posted a picture of Vladimir superimposed over a picture of the devil—horns, tail, and all. Another had posted a picture of Olga Nadiova, the second girl killed, and written, *Why?*

Russians murdering Russians—this is capitalism, one man had written, and a political debate had unspooled in a dozen more posts.

You are why the death penalty exists.

If only Stalin were alive to deal with you.

They were the same things that people had spat at him and his mother and Babushka in the bathroom line; the same things that people had spray-painted on their apartment door.

"Why are you torturing yourself?" Kirill had asked him once, when he was paying for yet another session at the Internet Kebab. "Move on, bratishka. He *confessed.*"

Vladimir had confessed to all three murders. That was true. But

Ilya reminded himself, just as he had reminded Kirill, that Berlozh-niki was a gulag town, a place born of forced and false confessions.

He typed Lana's name into the search box. Her wall was filled with new posts too. Sympathy posts. There were images of bou-quets, of Jesus crying, of hearts broken, bleeding, weeping. There were notes too—*I miss you. I love you. You're somewhere better now.* All of it was the virtual equivalent of the flowers and cards and stuffed animals that had been left in the grove where she'd been killed, but Ilya was looking for something different. Some shift in tone, some strange specificity. That was the shape that clues took. He scrolled down and read for a half hour, until he reached posts that he knew by heart. There was nothing strange; in fact it was all so clichéd that it felt anonymous, even the posts from the people who'd known Lana best. *You were too good for this world,* her mother had written. *We'll never forget you.* But it felt to Ilya that they al-ready had.

Ilya clicked on the photos tab and scrolled through Lana's pic-tures. He started at the beginning, when she'd first created her account. In the first photo she was twelve or thirteen, in a teal sweatshirt with Madonna on it. Her hair was curled, glitter nestled in the creases of her eyelids, and her face was rounder than Ilya re-membered. There were pictures of her sipping from a carton of milk in the school cafeteria, sticking out a tongue to catch a snow-flake, onstage in a leotard at the House of Culture. Halfway through the pictures, the pink streak in her hair made its debut. Her makeup got heavier, her shirts lower cut. A cigarette appeared between her fingers and stayed, even as the background changed. There was Lana smoking in a dim apartment with green walls. Lana smoking in a swing on the primary school playground. Lana smoking in a nest of bedding wearing a black bikini and a too-big baseball cap.

Then came the picture from the Tower, which was not a tower at all, but the old gulag barracks, where kids went to do nothing good. There they all were: Lana, Aksinya, Vladimir, and Ilya made almost life-size by the Masons' enormous monitor. Ilya and Vladimir were in the middle, and Aksinya and Lana flanked them. Aksinya was kissing Vladimir's cheek, and Lana was kissing Ilya's cheek. Lana's fist was thrust out, flicking off the camera. Somehow the other photos had a doomed quality to them that reminded Ilya of the faded portraits of miners at the museum on the square, but this one was the worst to look at because Lana seemed so alive. Simply, defiantly alive, like she might tip forward, tumble out of the monitor, and start to dance. Like she had no idea what was coming.

Ilya hunched closer to the screen. The flash had been kind to Vladimir. It had erased the shadows under his eyes, the sore on his lip, the blackheads that speckled his nose. There were the thin, bright slips of his eyes. His mouth was open—what had he been saying?—and there were his teeth, the front two crossing at the bottom the way Babushka crossed her ankles when she sat. It was not the face of a murderer. A punk, sure. An idiot. An addict. But not a murderer.

Ilya opened a new email and typed Vladimir's address.

I know you didn't do it, he wrote.

Each blink of the cursor was a tiny jab of expectation. *That's it?* it seemed to say. *That's all?* Ilya clicked send. He'd sent Vladimir this same message dozens of times now. He knew it was a lost cause, a kopek in a well—Vladimir would probably never be allowed to check email again—but what else could he do?

Ilya pushed the chair back from the desk. Out the glass doors, through the gaps in the deck supports, he could sense more than see the pool's glow, as though there were a crack in the earth issuing cool light. He closed his eyes. The Masons' dinner noises had faded into the murmur of the TV. It was still early, but his body felt thick with tiredness. It was the time difference and the exhaustion of hearing nothing but English. It was looking at his brother's face.

Upstairs, the phone rang once, twice. Probably Terry, the American exchange coordinator, Ilya thought, telling the Masons to get him on the first plane out of Baton Rouge. Fine. He would go home. He imagined his mother, three days from now, turning at the sound of the apartment door. She'd have that look of fear that had become the new set of her face, and then the look would loosen into disappointment at the waste of him, home again. She would not have the energy even to yell, and at the thought of that, his eyes filled and he pressed the heels of his palms into them to keep from crying.

For as long as he could remember, he had been meant to leave Berlozhniki. He had *wanted* to leave. Now he wanted that old desire. He wanted to be that old self, the Ilya who would be upstairs with the Masons right now, sitting on the couch, speaking textbook English. He was the good kid, the perfect student, the big brain. How had this happened? he wondered, and of course the answer was right in front of him, in a thousand pixels: Vladimir. If it weren't for Vladimir, he could take all of this—America—as his due, but instead here he was, alone in a dark room, and he couldn't even feel properly sorry for himself because of course Vladimir was alone too, and somewhere way worse than this.

There were footsteps on the stairs, a wooden creak. Ilya wiped at his cheeks and stood. It would be Papa Cam, his face a study in apologetic firmness. "Ilya, I'm sorry," he'd say, "but you're going to have to go home." But the footsteps grew fainter rather than closer. They were outside, Ilya realized, and then there was Papa Cam in silhouette, gripping a long net. He paced the length of the pool, fishing for that one leaf.

Ilya pulled the shredded plastic wrap off his duffel and unpacked. All of his clothes fit in the dresser's top drawer. His tape player and *Michael & Stephanie* tapes were still in the pink plastic bag, buried beneath Vladimir's sweatshirt. He'd found the bag the week before he left. It had been the only thing in Vladimir's room at the Tower, its presence a mystery, a minor miracle. As Ilya pulled out the sweatshirt, it released a vinegary tang. He recognized the smell—Vladimir on his worst days, Vladimir sleeping it off—just as it dissipated, anesthetized by whatever industrial-strength cleaning agent Mama Jamie used to make the basement smell like a very clean toilet. All of the tapes were there. He had listened to them so many times that the cardboard covers had gone white and furry at the edges. The titles had worn off the spines. He stacked them in a neat row on top of the dresser along with the tape player and his book of idioms. In the bathroom, he scrubbed his face and underarms, pulled on his sweatpants, washed his underwear and undershirt in the sink and hung them over the shower rod to dry.

He wanted to listen to Michael and Stephanie as he always had at home, to let their soft, insistent repetitions fade into white noise, and so he plucked a tape from the top of the stack and climbed into bed. The sheets were perfectly smooth. Up the hill the pool lights went out, and the basement walls went black. In the dark the bugs sounded more aggressive, like they were planning an invasion. Babushka said that before the refinery, in the summer, the bugs in Berlozhniki were the loudest in Russia, and, by implication, the whole world. She said this like it was a point of pride, like the bugs could stand in for a town orchestra or opera, but after the refinery was built they went quiet.

Ilya slipped the Delta headphones over his ears and pressed play. He could feel his eyes closing in anticipation of their voices—it was the only moment of pure pleasure he'd had that day—but their voices did not come. He pressed the button again. Still nothing. He flipped the player over and popped open the battery compartment. It was empty. All four 286s stolen by some thug in Leshukonskoye who'd spent all his earnings on beer and couldn't afford batteries for his TV remote. So instead of Michael and Stephanie, Ilya rapped the words to "Dark City" softly, hoping that might soothe him. It was one of Kolyan's hits, an ode to gangster life that Vladimir had sung so often that sometimes it became the soundtrack to Ilya's dreams.

He was halfway asleep, giving in, too tired to dream, he hoped, but when he slept, he did dream. Of Vladimir in their kitchen. Naked, water dripping from his chin, his penis like a slug against his thigh, dried blood turning red as Babushka washed him. In the dream Vladimir's leg was just as it had been—the skin the color of onions cooked in grease, a long, thin chasm where his flesh parted to show bone. His lips were the turquoise of the Masons' pool. He was smiling, saying something sly, something about love that Ilya couldn't quite understand.

Ilya woke with a scream balled in his throat. His pulse jerked in his neck. He washed his face in the sink and went upstairs. The house was filled with the mechanical noises that at home would have been familiar and would have amounted to silence. The clock on the microwave read 2:07. He opened the fridge and stared at the jugs of juice, the tubs of lettuce and sticks of butter. Everything was in a weird container. The butter was too yellow, the lettuce too white. Ilya poured a glass of water from the tap, and it stank of iron and tasted of salt.

His mother had bought him a phone card at the Internet Kebab— sixty minutes, Kirill had said—and he used it to call her, thinking that her voice, at least, would be like home. Her phone was off, though, and her outgoing message was stiff and cheerful, was not really her at all. Still, he left a message saying that he'd arrived, and that the family seemed nice enough, but before he could say any- thing more, before he could ask after Vladimir or say that he loved her, the connection ended, and a computerized voice announced that his phone card was empty. Kirill had ripped them off, and the normalcy of this, after all they'd gone through, was like a little gift.

Ilya sat at the table, looking out onto the den and foyer and up to the hallway, which was high and dark and silent. He listened for the Masons' breathing. He wanted to hear a sigh or snore, some- thing to know that he wasn't alone. Then behind him, on the deck, there *was* a noise. A faint scratch, a scuffle. He turned in his chair, but the deck was empty, the window black and blank.

"Think of white paper," his mother used to tell him when he had nightmares, "paper, just white and empty," and he tried to, but still his pulse jumped like something trying to escape him. Sweat gath- ered on his lip. He kept seeing Vladimir half dead in the dream, and then it came to him what Vladimir had said: "Love is like a devil in the corner." One of Babushka's sayings. The sort that didn't actually make any sense when you tried to analyze it, but when you let your mind stay outside of it you understood.

There was the noise again. A louder scratch this time. A wet exhale. Ilya pushed his chair back, and it screeched against the tiles. On the deck, there was this white flash of movement back and forth, back and forth, like a hand waving. A puff of condensation bloomed on the glass. Ilya fought the urge to yell. Then the creature let out a high-pitched yip, the condensation faded, and he saw that it was a dog. It was up on its hind legs with its front paws on the glass. Its tail wagged steadily behind its head. He tried to remember whether the Masons had said anything about owning a dog and could not. At home strays ranged, loping across snowy streets and marking certain alleys as their territory. They could be vicious—many were part wolf—and they were routinely rounded up and shot in the square, but this creature seemed docile. Ilya opened the door a crack, and the dog cocked its head at him. It had white fur that curled in coy tendrils at the base of its ears and an air of indulged expectation that was not unlike Marilee's and Molly's.

"Otvali," Ilya said. And then, thinking the dog might be more apt to obey English, he whispered, "Go away, dog! Go!"

The dog stopped panting for a second, as though it were listening. It let its paws fall from the glass with a thud and wandered down the steps into the yard. It skirted the pool and picked its way across the grass slowly, as though it did not care for getting its paws dirty, and then it stopped by the alligator wall where a figure was standing. Ilya's insides went heavy and hard, like they were turning to cement. It's him, he thought, whoever killed those girls, and then the figure stepped out of the gloom, and Ilya saw that it was Sadie. She crossed the yard with the dog at her heels, and climbed up the deck steps toward him. She was barefoot, in the same black T-shirt, but with sweatpants underneath. Her silver sneakers dangled from one hand.

"'Go away, dog'?" she said. She let the dog in, slid past him, glanced up the stairs toward her parents' bedroom, and clicked the door shut behind her. "Don't look so shocked," she said. "I knew before."

"Will you tell?" he asked.

"I won't if you won't. But you should—for all our sakes—or else they're going to keep talking to you like you're deaf."

"You don't think they know?" For a moment, Ilya's stomach burned at the idea that they might. He imagined them explaining to their friends, *It turned out he does speak English—he was just pretending not to.* He imagined them thinking this strangeness the result of a disturbing Russian childhood or, worse, simply the result of being Russian, and then he remembered another of Babushka's sayings: embarrassment is a luxury. He remembered his mother on that wooden bench at the police station, the secretaries nakedly staring, looking for something in her that might explain Vladimir.

"They don't know," Sadie said. "They're innocents. Tell them and they'll forgive you. They love forgiving people." She said this softly, but with a scorn that made it clear that she did not love forgiving people and that she did not consider herself an innocent.

She walked past him into the kitchen and opened a cabinet that was stuffed with boxes of crisps and crackers and biscuits. "I get hungry at night. All the time. I'm growing. I can feel it happening sometimes—it's like cramps in my legs."

"You look completely grown to me," he said.

"Is that a compliment?" she said, and she gave a quick smile that slid across her face like a snake across a path. Like she was afraid to let it last. "Are you hungry?"

Ilya nodded. "I didn't eat dinner," he said.

"Mama Jamie might not forgive that." She pulled a box out of the cabinet with a picture of little girls in what appeared to be construction hats. "Girl Scout cookies," she said.

His heart was still thumping away, but his fear was no longer entirely unpleasant. It was exhilarating to talk to her. He'd never actually used his English with a native speaker, and it seemed as though she could understand him, that his words were not as clumsy as they felt on his tongue. And she was beautiful. Her hair was in a big knot on top of her head, and it made her face seem wider, younger. She looked like Snegurochka in the book of fairy tales that Babushka had read to them as kids, in the picture when she first comes out of the forest, when she's newly, magically made. Even the one shattered pupil seemed more like magic than a mistake.

"What happened to your eye?" he said.

She lifted a hand to it as though she'd forgotten. "Birth defect," she said. "Sometimes I forget it's there and I wonder why people are staring at me."

That was not what people were staring at, Ilya knew, but he liked her modesty.

She took a cookie out and snapped it in two with her front teeth. They were shiny with spit, and Ilya remembered Vladimir's leg. That wet bit of bone. The skin failing to cover it.

"Do you miss home?" she said. The question was a nice one, but her voice had a strange distance to it, like the idea of missing home was a curiosity. For her, it probably was.

"Yes," he said.

"The whole no-English thing—did you just feel like messing with us?"

"I wasn't in the mood," he said. He could hear how cold his voice sounded, and of course that wasn't the truth. But how could he explain to her that speaking English felt like cutting the last thread of a fraying rope? It was stupid, he saw now. An empty protest. As useless as the emails he sent Vladimir. What did it matter what he spoke? Russian, English, gibberish. He was still here, and his brother was still there.

She was looking at him with narrowed eyes. She had said something, and he had not heard her.

"What?" he said.

"I said, 'Don't you want to be here?'"

A few hours ago, the thought had almost made him cry, and he was afraid that he might, but instead he had the strange sense that he was solidifying, as though he were rejoining his old self, the one for whom this moment—a conversation alone in the middle of the night with an American girl—would have been an insane distillation of desire.

"I did," he said, "but then my brother—" If he told her the truth—that his brother had been arrested for murder, that his brother had *confessed* to murder—she would look at him the way everyone in Berlozhniki had started to, as though he were guilty by association, and, of course, she wouldn't think to ask whether Vladimir had actually done it.

"Your brother?"

"My brother died," he said, and he was surprised at how easy it was to say, and for a second he found himself thinking how much easier it would be. He fought the urge to cross himself, to knock on wood.

"I'm sorry," she said. She looked him in the eye. "But that doesn't mean you can be an asshole."

Heat rushed to his face. She took a handful of cookies and pushed the box across the counter toward him. "Church is early tomorrow. You should sleep. And tell them about your brother—they'll understand."

She walked past him again, closer this time, and she smelled like cut grass and something acrid too, like oil. The dog followed her, its nails clicking gently against the floorboards. As they started to climb the stairs, he saw that the bottoms of her feet were dirty. The cuffs of her sweats were speckled with bits of grass and her ankles were crisscrossed by thin pink scratches.

"Sadie," he said.

She stopped halfway up the stairs and looked at him, and the dog did the same. He hadn't asked her what she'd been doing in the yard. *I won't tell if you won't*, she'd said, and he hadn't even wondered what she meant.

"What were you doing?" He gestured toward the door.

"The dog had to pee," she said.

He nodded. It may have been true, but from the look of her pants, she'd been walking outside for a while, and there were her sneakers, dangling from her hand.

"How did you know? That I spoke English?" he said.

She hesitated. "You just have a look. Like you're listening. Most people don't have that, even when you're speaking their language." She smiled at him, a lasting smile this time, and then she climbed the rest of the stairs, and he watched the flash of her dirty heels as they disappeared into her bedroom.

CHAPTER SIX

Immersed as he was in his studies, Ilya did not notice exactly when Vladimir first started cutting school. Babushka shooed them out the door at the same time each morning, and they still walked together across the Pechora, up Ulitsa Snezhnaya, past the bookstore where the window had been replaced, past the little wooden church where their father and Dedushka were buried and where Babushka lit her candles, past the abandoned Komsomol headquarters to School #17. They parted ways at the front doors, and Ilya assumed that Vladimir went inside to his classroom just as Ilya did, but apparently he did not.

"Is Vladimir sick?" Maria Mikhailovna asked him one day. For the second year in a row, Vladimir was in her Introductory English class, a class that Ilya had skipped altogether. Not knowing what else to do, Ilya said that yes, Vladimir was sick. Then Aksinya and Lana started sneaking to Ilya's classroom. They'd stare in through the windows in the door, making Vs of their fingers and flicking their tongues between them. Ilya would ask to go to the bathroom, his face burning, and when he emerged, they'd giggle uncontrollably. Their hair was gauzy around their faces, the purple under their eyes somehow beautiful. They were always out of breath.

"Have you seen Vladimir?" they'd ask.

Every time Ilya hoped for a different question—something to do with him, not Vladimir. "We need help with our English paper," or "Let's go to the Internet Kebab," or "There's a party later, at the Tower." But it was always "Where's Vladimir? Where is that mudak, that asshole brother of yours?" and when Ilya didn't know, they'd leave him in the hall, clutching his bathroom pass.

Another teacher gave Ilya a folder labeled HOMEWORK FOR SEP-TEMBER to bring home to Vladimir. Ilya slipped it into his backpack and that night, once their mother had left for work, once Babushka had made up the couch for them and was snoring softly in the bedroom, he handed it to Vladimir.

"It's from Nikolay Grigorievich," Ilya said. "The math you've missed."

Vladimir opened the folder and flipped through the pages. He looked at them closely, not casually, as though they were written in a code he might be able to unlock if only he knew the key. Ilya thought of him at the bookshop, sounding out the titles from Maria Mikhailovna's list, and in that moment he wanted so desperately for school to be as easy for his brother as it was for him. Then Vladimir dropped the folder onto the carpet and began to undress for bed.

Ilya stared at it. "What should I tell him?"

Vladimir shrugged. "Tell him you gave it to me." He fell backward onto his pillow, pulled his socks off by their soggy toes, and said, "Let me tell you, Ilya, a vagina is an alarming thing to look at." Vladimir went on, detailing his latest exploits with Aksinya, and Ilya picked the folder up and slipped it back into his backpack.

The next afternoon, after he'd finished listening to *Michael & Stephanie*, after he'd done his translation for Maria Mikhailovna and all of the homework for his other classes, he began to chip away at Vladimir's math. He didn't do it out of loyalty, but out of this new anxiety that hit him sometimes like a fever. He was worried for Vladimir, worried when Vladimir was not home in the afternoons, worried even when Vladimir *was* home, was right next to him on the couch, watching one of Babushka's telenovelas with one hand stuffed in a bag of crisps and the other stuffed down his pants.

It took Ilya a week to do all the makeup work. All those lines and figures. All those neat totals. He'd had to teach himself the basics of trigonometry, and when he finally presented it to Nikolay Grigorievich, the teacher said, "I'm afraid that ship has sailed."

Vladimir began skipping dinner too, and Babushka would groan and say, "The boy never eats," or, "He's with that girl. The one whose parents are dead, and the sister who's a you-know-what."

"Aksinya," Ilya would say, because he loved saying her name, and because the fact that such a beautiful girl liked Vladimir seemed to him something to be proud of.

Ilya's mother would bite a radish in half and make a bitter face and say, "What am I supposed to do? Put him in a straitjacket?" And it was true that there was little she could do. She worked the night shift, slept during the day. She was with Vladimir and Ilya for only two exhausted hours in the evening and one exhausted hour in the morning.

"He'll be fine," Timofey would say, his nostril hairs twitching. "Just give him some time. He's running around. It's what boys do."

Then they'd all look at Ilya with this awkward sort of appreciation, because of course he would never do the things that boys do.

Every once in a while, after Ilya was already in bed, half asleep, listening to Michael and Stephanie, Vladimir would poke his head through the door and say, "Ilyusha, I'm sleeping at Sergey's tonight," or "Night, night, bratik. I won't be home until late." His breath would be a beery fog, and behind him, in the light of the hall, Ilya would see Sergey and Aksinya and Lana, their hands clamped over their mouths to keep from laughing, to keep from waking him, as though he were a baby. Vladimir would click the door shut, and he would hear their voices echo up the stairway. And there were times—and this is what Ilya would remember—when he would simply not let the worry in, when he would not wonder where Vladimir was going or what Vladimir was doing, when he would stretch his legs out and revel in the expansiveness of the couch. It felt decadent and very adult to be sleeping alone, to have two pillows. The refinery lights sparked on the ceiling, and he would imagine that they were city lights, and that he was in his own apartment, in Moscow or St. Petersburg, and that in the morning he would be heading to work, not school. Those nights, Ilya slept like the dead, but he'd wake and, in just the way your tongue finds the tender spot where you've bitten your cheek, his mind would find Vladimir.

One morning in October, as Ilya, his mother, and Babushka were eating syrniki with cream and apples, Vladimir walked in the door of their apartment wearing a tracksuit and smelling dank. He pulled a term card out of his pocket and slid it onto the table, right between Ilya's plate and his mother's. The card was filthy. It had been crumpled, stepped on, and partially incinerated—as though Vladimir had used it to roll a cigarette, lit it, and then thought better of it—but Ilya could still make out Vladimir's grades: a neat column of ones. Ilya gasped. No one got ones. Ones were like zeros, just a place for the scale to start, the end of a ruler.

Their mother was in her work clothes: a hairnet, blue smock, and rubber clogs. At first she did not notice the card. She had a magazine next to her plate and was flipping the pages impossibly fast. She was angry—either because Vladimir had been out all night, or because she hated her job, or because Babushka had recently announced that she and Timofey from down the hall were romantically involved, and Ilya's mother had not been romantically involved with anyone for a decade. But after a minute she saw the card there on the table and snatched it up. Her eyes went shallow.

"Are you an idiot?" she said. "Or did you just not go?"

Ilya thought of the man in the bookshop. How many times in his life had Vladimir been called an idiot?

Vladimir slumped into his chair at the head of the table. Vladimir had told Ilya that it had been their father's chair, but Ilya couldn't picture anyone but Vladimir in it. "I'm an idiot," Vladimir said.

Ilya's mother nodded very slowly, and the precision of the gesture, its economy and patience, reminded Ilya of the way lions stretch backward before they pounce.

Vladimir tucked his chin into his chest and looked at the empty patch of table before him. "The teachers are bitches," he muttered.

"Ilya," their mother said, "has he been there?"

His mother had white spots on her cheeks. Under the table, Ilya could feel her foot shaking. This was another way the apartment could be, with the refinery's lights turning everything blue, like they were trapped in a cube of ice.

"Ilya?" his mother said.

"I don't know," Ilya said.

"You do know," she said, and the words came out crushed with anger. "Look at me, Ilya. How long since he's gone?"

Ilya looked at Vladimir. His hair was dirty. Little zits bridged his eyebrows, and his eyes were red-laced. He did not look worth protecting. Ilya thought of the folder of homework and how Vladimir had dropped it to the ground and the hours he'd spent on it and how Vladimir's teacher had said, *That ship has sailed*, and he wondered if Vladimir even wanted protection.

"Look at me, Ilya," their mother said.

Babushka was ripping a hunk of bread into tiny pieces without eating a bite. She cocked her head, considering Ilya. "What can he do? Tattle on his brother?" she said, just as Ilya blurted, "A month."

Ilya's mother pulled her hairnet off her scalp and crumpled it in a fist. It left a thin, red groove across her forehead. Next door, Tatyana Zemskova was vacuuming. Across the hall, the Radeyevs had the television turned up. Someone was climbing the stairs, making the burners rattle gently on the stove. Outside, Ilya could hear the snow collecting, a silence like a giant, held breath.

"Where's your term card, Ilyusha?" Vladimir said, with this clench to his voice that was usually reserved for their mother. "Let me guess: all fives again."

"Yes," their mother said, and her voice was just as hard, "all fives again."

Vladimir rolled his head around on his neck, sighed, and said, "You know I'm not good at school. I'll get a job. Aksinya's sister—"

"Is a whore," Ilya's mother said, and Ilya thought of the oligarch, the prostitutes with their diamond nipples and thongs of gold, of Sergey's voice when he'd said, "He can do whatever he wants with them."

"The whole generation has no morals," Babushka piped up. "Neither does yours," she said, with a look at Ilya's mother. "Maybe communism wasn't such a bad thing. We gave it up for what? Salami and blue jeans and—"

"Not tonight," his mother said.

"I just want to have some fun before I get shipped to Georgia," Vladimir said.

"You'll get shipped there even sooner if you drop out," she said.

Vladimir grinned, like he'd suddenly found something funny in the idea of conscription. He stood, snapped his legs straight, and held his right hand to his head in a military salute. "Can you imagine me in uniform?"

The longer he tried to stay stiff and still, the more he swayed. Babushka was clutching her podstakannik, staring up at him, and as Vladimir grabbed the edge of the table to steady himself, her tea sloshed onto the tablecloth.

"Bozhe moy," she said. "He's drunk before eight a.m." Her voice sounded dramatic, but they'd all seen Vladimir drunk. She just didn't want it to go unsaid.

"You go to school tomorrow or you're out," Ilya's mother said. "Out of school and out of here."

"Tomorrow's Sunday," Vladimir said. "I doubt they'd want me to show my face."

"Then sleep it off until Monday," she said. Her features had gone stiff—she was trying to keep herself from crying. Babushka had no such control. She put her face in her hands and splayed her fingers so that they could all see her tears. Ilya pushed his spine against the back of the chair, the pressure somehow holding him together. He didn't look at his mother. He tried not to listen as Babushka muttered choked little prayers. He understood that they weren't grieving over Vladimir's expulsion. They weren't grieving at the thought of conscription, of Georgia or Chechnya. They knew, as Ilya did, that it would be a miracle if Vladimir made it to eighteen.

That day Babushka left the dirty dishes on the table as a reproach to all of them. Their mother went to bed with a wrung-out look in her eyes, and Vladimir slept for ten hours straight. When it got dark, Ilya climbed into bed next to him and slid a *Michael & Stephanie* tape into his player. It had been nearly four years since

Vladimir took him to buy the tapes, and the Delta headphones were disintegrating. When he turned the volume all the way up, there was this high, quavering whine in the background.

"The cup is red," Michael said.

"The bowl is red and blue!" Stephanie replied.

It was a Level I tape—colors, meals, domesticated animals. Ilya had memorized it but still he liked to listen to it before bed. In it, Michael and Stephanie used only short, declarative sentences, each word a tiny, enthusiastic nail. They spoke slowly and never ventured out of the present tense.

Sometimes, Ilya had the feeling that the more English he learned the less Russian he spoke, as though the languages were worlds and he could only exist in one or the other. That night, he wanted that feeling, wanted very much to leave this world. That was why he'd chosen such an easy tape—so there would be no effort of translation, so that he could be transported—but Vladimir's feet were stuffed under his pillow, and they smelled of mushrooms and sweat, and the ridge of one of his shins pressed against Ilya's ribs, and he couldn't conjure the feeling. Instead he found himself waiting for the swampy tide of Vladimir's breath to wash over his face. He flipped the tape to the B-side and kept listening. Not long after eleven, when the Radeyevs' clock tolled endlessly, the quality of Vladimir's breathing changed, and Ilya realized that he was awake.

"Vlad," he said.

"Ilya," Vladimir said.

The refinery light was pouring through the windows, giving the ceiling the glow of the moon. Right over Ilya's head, there was a smudge that looked like a footprint, and Ilya liked to pretend that the footprint was Yuri Gagarin's, though he knew that Gagarin had never made it to the moon.

"What if I just stopped?" Ilya said.

"Stopped what?"

"Stopped studying. Stopped going to school." Just saying it gave him a pain in his sternum like there was a shard of glass lodged there.

"Why would you do that?" Vladimir said. He was yawning as he said it. He didn't understand Ilya's point yet, couldn't know that Ilya was remembering the two of them out on the balcony and the way Vladimir had held him and made him yell his first English words over the courtyard, or the way Vladimir had given the shop-keeper the extra money for Ilya's books.

"Why would *you*?" Ilya said. "You think I don't ever want to be lazy too?"

"No," Vladimir said. "I don't. I don't think it's possible for you to be lazy." Then he propped himself up on his elbows and looked down at Ilya. The radiator in the corner began its nightly orchestra: a rattle like there was a whole pocket of change in its pipes. And Vladimir smiled. "Are you threatening me?" he said.

"Just tell me you'll try," Ilya said.

"Or what?" Vladimir said.

"Or I stop too."

"What if I try?"

"Hollywood Boulevard. You and me. Vladimir and Ilya Van Damme."

"You fucking punk," Vladimir said, but his grin was huge. Each tooth lit up like a tiny candle. Ilya was joking, of course. In all the talk of Ilya's future, with all of the English he'd learned, no one had ever mentioned America. America was a place that existed only in *Michael & Stephanie*, in the television, in the Cold War corners of their mother's and Babushka's minds.

"Fine," Vladimir said. "I'll try."

CHAPTER SEVEN

That first morning in America, Ilya took the longest shower of his life in hot water that seemed as though it would never go cold. He used the toiletries that Mama Jamie had bought him—the toothbrush and toothpaste and deodorant—and then carefully returned each to its cardboard box.

"I do speak English," he whispered to his reflection in the mirror. "I'm sorry," he said, getting his inflection just right.

When he was sure that they were awake, he climbed the stairs. They were all at the kitchen table except Sadie. Molly was wearing a miniature ball gown and crown and had an arm plunged into an enormous box of cereal.

"I ate every marshmallow," she was saying. "Every single one."

Marilee was staring at the TV, transfixed by a cartoon of what seemed to be Jesus lugging his cross through an unpleasant throng. Papa Cam was in a bathrobe. Hair stuck up from the back of his head, and at the sight of this vulnerability, Ilya wanted to slink back down into the basement, but he thought of Sadie saying that they would forgive him. Mama Jamie turned in her chair and saw him. Her face had been shellacked with makeup. She'd been up for hours, waiting for him, he realized, as she said, "He's awake!"

Ilya took a step toward them.

"I'm sorry," he said, in English.

Papa Cam set a forkful of eggs down on his plate, and the eggs quivered in this way that made Ilya want to vomit.

"I do speak English," he said. "I'm sorry. I was in grief. My brother died." The Masons looked at each other across the length of the table. "I'm sorry," Ilya said again.

"No," Mama Jamie said, "you poor thing. Please don't apologize. I'm so sorry about your brother. We had no idea." She stood and opened her arms, and Ilya crossed the bit of carpet between them and hugged her. With her arms around him, she breathed deeply, as though her own calm might somehow osmose into Ilya, and Ilya felt each of her exhalations as a hot rush on his shoulder.

"What happened?" she said, when she released him. "If you don't mind my asking."

"He was sick," Ilya said. He thought of Vladimir in the clinic. He had not been sick exactly, but he certainly hadn't been well. And if he was convicted he might as well be dead.

"Was it cancer?" Marilee whispered.

Ilya looked at her. Her eyes were huge. "No," he said.

Next to her, Molly began to cry, and Mama Jamie scooped her up.

"Will his brother go to Heaven?" Molly managed. "If they're not Christian, will his brother get to go to Heaven?"

"He'll go to his own Heaven," Mama Jamie said, and Ilya saw Vladimir with a needle in his arm.

"Amen," Papa Cam said, and Ilya had no idea what the word meant. Papa Cam looked at him. Ilya expected to see mistrust in his eyes, but they were wet and shining with what looked to Ilya like a mix of pity and pride.

In the cartoon, Jesus had fallen under the weight of the cross, and the show ended with a preview of next week's episode: the crucifixion. Mama Jamie fixed Ilya a plate and told him that they'd be leaving for church in a half hour. She had to go upstairs to wake Sadie, and when Sadie finally came down, her eyes were small and sleepy.

"Ilya found his voice," Mama Jamie said. "The first miracle of the day."

"How many are you expecting?"

"More than you, it seems."

Sadie lifted the carafe of coffee up and sloshed it to gauge its fullness. "This is a miracle," she said, emptying it into a mug.

"You know I don't like you drinking that," Mama Jamie said.

Sadie slurped it.

"You shouldn't even need it. Lord knows you're not waking up early," Papa Cam said. "You don't drink coffee, do you, Ilya?"

"I drink tea," Ilya said. Sadie had changed into a pair of leggings that had a sheen to them and were printed with the galaxy. The Milky Way curved around her thighs, and the hubris of this was not lost on him. "Very strong tea," he said. "It's stronger than coffee."

"I'm sure it is," Mama Jamie said.

Sadie looked at him over the rim of her mug. Her feet were clean now, and if the dog hadn't been leaning against her shins, panting, he'd have believed that her standing out in the yard in the middle of the night had been a dream.

"I met your dog last night," he said, and he was not imagining Sadie's sudden attention, the way her head swiveled toward him.

"Dolly," Marilee said. "She's an idiot. Sometimes she walks into walls."

"Did she bug you?" Mama Jamie said.

"Bug me?"

"Wake you up?"

"No, she didn't wake me," he said. He looked at Sadie. She was looking at her feet, cheeks flushed, and he felt a stab of guilt for having said anything. "Do you know how to say 'idiot' in Russian?" he said to Marilee.

"I don't know how to say anything in Russian," Marilee said.

"Ee-d-ee-o-t," he said slowly, thinking of the shopkeeper at the bookstore on Ulitsa Snezhnaya and the way he'd flicked his tongue with the "t" as though he were spitting on the sidewalk. "Or 'durashka' if you want it to be a little nicer."

"Durashka," Marilee repeated, and her pronunciation wasn't as terrible as he'd been expecting.

"What a wonderful word," Mama Jamie said. "Durashka. We should call her that."

"That wouldn't be very charitable," Papa Cam said.

"She wouldn't even know the difference," Marilee said. "It's not like she ever responds to her name."

The dog let her body sink to the ground as though too weary to defend herself.

"Poor Durashka," Papa Cam said, and his pronunciation was terrible.

"Ilya," Molly said, "what was your brother's name? The one who died."

Ilya was quiet for a moment. Sadie looked at him, her face softer than he'd yet seen it. Somehow telling them Vladimir's name felt more like tempting fate than telling them that he'd died, as though, if given his name, fate might find a way to make the lie true. "Vladimir," he said, finally, and his voice was almost a whisper.

The Masons' church, Star Pilgrim, seemed to have been designed in defiance of the central Louisiana weather. The two walls of glass acted like a magnifying glass, taking the morning sun's light and focusing it into something capable of burning. Even before the service began, the congregation's faces dripped. Ilya's balls chafed in his jeans, and he tried to locate a bathroom where he could air them out, but Mama Jamie herded the girls and him into a pew at the back of the church.

"Is it always so hot?" he asked. He was between Sadie and Marilee, and he let the question float out into the viscous air.

"This isn't even that bad," Sadie said.

"Sometimes it's hotter, but if they turn the air too loud we can't hear the sermon," Marilee said, just as music began to blare over the loudspeakers and a tall, slab-jawed man strode to the pulpit.

On the way to Star Pilgrim, Papa Cam and Mama Jamie had explained to Ilya that their church was nondenominational. "We believe in Jesus and all, but we don't follow the rules of some of your more orthodox religions," Papa Cam had said, and from that— and from the fact that the girls and Mama Jamie were shawlless and showing a considerable amount of skin—Ilya gathered that their religion was some sort of watered-down version of Christianity. But nothing could have prepared him for a Star Pilgrim service. The pastor looked like a porn star. His teeth were opalescent; his shoulders strained at the seams of his shirt, which gleamed like sealskin. He stayed behind the pulpit for only a millisecond and then, as though the music were rippling through his spine, he began to shimmy back and forth across the stage and up and down the aisle.

Above him, a giant projector beamed a rainbow of light that hit the concrete wall and burst into images of mountain streams and sunsets and cuddling baby animals, the same sorts of images that had been posted on Lana's wall. Three colored spotlights swung to the beat of the music, and an overserious man with a video camera darted among the pews. "He's streaming," Marilee said when she saw Ilya staring. "When we're sick we watch Pastor Kyle from home."

Pastor Kyle's sermon was a mishmash of sound bites. He seemed more concerned with volume than with content. His voice was a power hose, blasting the congregation's brains. *Serve. Jesus. Amen. Spread. The. Word. Of. God. Amen.*

Pain began to prickle Ilya's temples. He could feel the sun scorching the back of his neck. Sweat trickled down his spine and into the gully between his buttocks, a sensation that could not have been less celestial, but then Ilya had never been much of a believer. Babushka was the only person in his family to have faith. Under communism, the church in Berlozhniki had been repurposed as the Museum of Atheism, and Babushka had not dared attend the covert services that other women held in their apartments, but after perestroika she made up for lost time. She'd spent the bulk of Ilya's life at the Church of the Ascension, with its dank nave and incense and the faded, golden ikony that braver families had hidden under their floorboards and in their mattresses. There had been one icon—a chipped, barely distinguishable Virgin Mary—which Babushka said had simply appeared at the church without being painted, and was a miracle. Ilya's mother always said that she didn't have time to believe in miracles, but that God could feel free to convince her.

Ilya had never had faith in anything except that knowledge

could be gained. Numbers in a column added up to something. If you stared at a word, if you sounded out the letters and visualized its meaning, it could be learned. And there was Vladimir. Vladimir, who could not be counted on for anything, who was untrustworthy in a million little ways, but who had still managed to inspire Ilya's faith.

As Pastor Kyle danced, Ilya turned these things over in his mind. He stood when the Masons stood. He held a hymnal and let Marilee flip to the right pages. The music grew softer, and then Pastor Kyle announced that it was time for testimonials. A woman took the microphone. She was plump with pinkish hair, and in a soft voice she admitted that in times of trial she turned to food rather than God. Then a kid Ilya's age mumbled that he had played a video game that was somewhat Satanic. A bookish man told the congregation that he had not gotten a much hoped for promotion. His coworker had gotten it instead, and the man had been angry. He was crying as he spoke, his glasses slipping on the damp planes of his cheeks. The hardest thing, he said, was that his anger and his jealousy—a jealousy so intense that it seemed almost sexual—had clouded his relationship with God. When he prayed, he felt like he was yelling under water, his words muffled and choked and inaudible to anyone above the surface.

Pastor Kyle nodded through transgressions large and small, a beatific smile on his lips, a muscle spasming gently in his jaw. When the last testimonial had been aired, he began to preach. He spoke of a direct line to God. No call waiting. No being put on hold. Then, through a transition that Ilya could not follow, he was describing the gates of Heaven, saying how quickly they would open for the righteous. He began dancing again—a sort of slow gyration, his eager hips leading him down the aisle.

"There are two kinds of people in this world," he said. His lips grazed the microphone. He was only a few meters from the Masons' pew, and then he stopped, and he looked at Ilya. "There are the Cains and the Abels. There are the believers and those that don't." He paused and smiled at Ilya as though he and Ilya were in on some joke. "We have someone new with us today, folks. All the way from Mother Russia, will you give it up for Ilya Morozov!"

The congregation began to clap around him. The man with the video camera hovered behind Pastor Kyle, and Ilya could see that the lens was trained on him.

"You're supposed to stand," Sadie whispered, and he looked at her, and she read the fear on his face and said, "Just for a second."

Ilya stood.

"Ilya," Pastor Kyle said, "is a top student in his town, which, as I understand it, is in the Siberian wilderness. Can you say 'hello,' Ilya?"

Pastor Kyle held the microphone out, and Ilya leaned toward it and said, "Hello," and his voice sounded sullen and small. He cleared his throat, was about to add that Berlozhniki was not in Siberia, when Pastor Kyle whipped the microphone back and said, "Ilya is here today in the good old U-S-of-A thanks to the generosity of EnerCo and the Mason family." There was another round of clapping. Papa Cam and Mama Jamie nodded, their cheeks pink, and Pastor Kyle waited for the applause to die down before saying, "But Ilya's family has suffered a tragedy."

Ilya stiffened. Beside him Papa Cam and Mama Jamie were flushed with attention. Ilya dug his fingers into his palms, tried to stem an anger that he knew was not entirely justified. He had lied, after all, had used their pity to gain their forgiveness, but still he couldn't believe how quickly they had told Pastor Kyle. Pastor Kyle, who was looking at Ilya like he was one of Jesus's lost lambs. Pastor Kyle, who, as he opened his mouth to speak, revealed a wad of something pink and bright between his molars. Bubble gum.

"Ilya's brother died not long ago, folks," he said. "And I was thinking there might be something we could do to help his family."

Around him, people were nodding. Someone a few rows behind him said, "Yes!" There was a basket weaving its way along the rows, and the ladies were reaching into their purses, and the men were leaning on one haunch to get to their wallets. Ilya let his hands loosen. He unclenched his gut. Maybe they *could* help, he thought. They would collect money, and he would send it home to pay for a decent lawyer or to bribe someone to tell them where Vladimir was being held or to cover travel expenses so that his mother could visit him. Ilya could feel the anger leaving him, could feel his face softening as though it were clay, losing its shape in the heat, and then Pastor Kyle said, "What do we do, when a family is in need? What is the thing we can *always* do to help one another no matter our circumstances?"

"Pray!" Marilee yelled from down the pew.

Pastor Kyle pointed a finger at her and clicked his tongue. "Bingo," he said.

He turned on his heel and headed back to the pulpit, and when he got there, he bent his head and closed his eyes and made his voice as low and lush as velvet. "Lord," he said. "We have a brother in need among us. We have a brother who is in *pain*, who is *grieving*, who has lost someone he loves, and we ask you to comfort him."

Pastor Kyle kept saying "brother," over and over. All around Ilya, heads were bowed. Rows and rows of people, their hair shining in the sun. Ilya could smell sweat distinctly. He could almost feel the force of their prayers, like they were leaving a wake as they sped up to an industrious American heaven where they would be answered with ease. Except the prayers were wrong. Misdirected. And Ilya was sure that they would come plummeting back to Earth in some new and twisted form, and so he closed his eyes and tried to redirect them.

Just give me a clue, he thought. Just something to prove he didn't do it.

He tried to picture Vladimir the last time he'd seen him—in the clinic with white sheets all around him. But instead he saw Vladimir in the picture from VKontakte. It was as though, in staring at that picture the night before, Ilya had burned it into his retinas, and now his imagination could project it onto his lids at will. Pastor Kyle's voice began to rise and crest, and then it was as though Ilya were *in* the picture. He was there again, at the Tower with Vladimir and Aksinya and Lana and Sergey. He could feel the bass coming up through the concrete floor, making his jaw chatter. A smile lifted his cheeks. All around him the pulse of bodies, dancing. The golden whip of a girl's hair. That chemical prick to the air. The soft hump of someone's ass hitting his. The slosh of vodka in the bottle as Aksinya took a swig. The crunch of glass under his sneakers. Lana was next to him, his fingers clammy on her waist. Her skin burning hot. Sergey was holding up Aksinya's phone.

"Not your best angle, Aksinya," Sergey said, and Aksinya held out her middle finger and flicked him off. Lana flicked him off too, and just as the flash clicked Vladimir said, "You have competition, Ilyusha." *That* was why Vladimir's mouth had been open in the picture, *that* was what he'd been saying. In the moment, Ilya had thought that he meant Sergey, that Sergey liked Lana, though Sergey had his own girlfriend. In the moment, he'd thought it was a joke because Lana was not his to compete for, but now he could see Vladimir's eyes, made even more narrow by his sidelong glance. He had not meant Sergey. He had been looking to the side, past Aksinya and Ilya and Lana. He had been looking *at* someone.

Ilya felt a hand on his wrist. Lana, he thought, but when he opened his eyes it was Sadie. Her nails ragged, the skin around them chewed pink and raw. She kept her hand on his skin for a second, and then she said, "I have to get up there."

Ilya looked to the aisle. Marilee and Molly and a troop of preteen boys were marching up toward the pulpit, and now Sadie squeezed past him. For a second her foot was between his. Her thigh brushed his. The opening chords of a song were twanging in the heat. At some point, while Ilya's eyes were closed, Pastor Kyle had moved from the pulpit to an electric keyboard. The kids gathered behind him, and Sadie joined them. Someone handed her a microphone. She looked at Ilya. That one eye was so beautifully broken, like something at the end of a kaleidoscope.

You'll know it when it happens, Vladimir had told him one night, when he and Aksinya were still a new thing. Vladimir had never been shy about talking about women—he was the sort to sing his love from the rooftops, too cool to be embarrassed. But Ilya had been embarrassed to listen. He had always been more squeamish than Vladimir, and, besides, it hadn't seemed to him like something he needed to know about, not yet anyway, not like participles and gerunds and contractions. But now he wished that he had listened, had asked, "So you know it when it happens, and then what?"

Up by the pulpit Pastor Kyle's hands were dancing over the keyboard. Sadie put the microphone to her mouth. He could hear her lips part, and then she began to sing.

"He's quite something, isn't he?" Mama Jamie said. They were backing out of their parking spot at Star Pilgrim. Pastor Kyle was standing by the doors to the church waving vigorously. Now that the service had concluded, he chomped openly on his gum.

"Mom has a crush on him," Marilee said.

Molly giggled.

"I think every mom in there has a crush on him," Sadie said. She was sitting next to Ilya. Her thigh was an inch from his. It looked like a loaf of toasted bread. Little blond hairs traversed it, catching the sun.

"I'm inspired by him, if that's what you mean," Mama Jamie said. "Did you like it, Ilya?"

The service, with its crackling acoustics and spastic light show, had seemed to him like a glossier version of the "karaoke club" that Pasha Kamenev ran in the boiler room of Building 6, the testimonials like the sad stories that Berlozhniki's half-dozen reformed alcoholics told over and over at their Tuesday meetings in the communal kitchen. Now, with Papa Cam scanning the radio stations and the car's AC blasting, even that moment when his memory of the Tower had crystallized seemed a bit ridiculous. More heatstroke than divine intervention. Ilya was sure that when he looked at the picture on VKontakte, Vladimir would be looking straight ahead, at no one but him.

"Church in Russia is more serious," he said, and then, realizing that that sounded like an insult, he said, "It's more fun here."

Papa Cam laughed. "Not always," he said. "I grew up Baptist, and let me tell you that is some serious worshipping."

"No dancing," Mama Jamie said. "No drinking. No coffee. No soda."

"You didn't have soda?" Molly said, incredulous. "Never, once, not any?!"

Papa Cam shook his head. "I was deprived," he said.

Postchurch, the Masons had planned an entire day of back-to-school shopping at a mall in Alexandria. The girls each got new outfits, new sneakers, new notebooks. Pencil cases and key chains and a calculator for Marilee that cost over a hundred dollars. Papa Cam hefted the growing collection of bags from store to store like a pack mule. In the Walmart, Mama Jamie sent Ilya and Papa Cam on a mission to get undershirts and underwear and socks, and Ilya wondered if she'd seen his drying on the shower rod down in the basement.

The options were paralyzing: sleeveless, V-neck, ribbed, briefs, boxers, each in their own plastic satchel. Mountains of them, drifts of them, the fabric as gleaming white as snow. So many that Ilya found himself staring at them blankly. Papa Cam threw a pack of boxers and short-sleeved shirts into their cart.

"Never hurts to stick with the basics," he said.

"Stick with the basics," Ilya repeated, just the way he used to with Michael and Stephanie when he wanted to commit something they'd said to memory.

"Quick study," Papa Cam said. "Do you know that one?"

Ilya shook his head. "Quick study," he said.

"Exactly." Papa Cam smiled.

On the way home they stopped at a place called Red's that served sandwiches as long as Ilya's forearm. They ate at picnic tables overlooking a stagnant stream with shit-colored water. The sandwiches,

Ilya learned, were called "po' boys" and the stream was called a "bayou," and the gray-green vines cloaking the trees were "Spanish moss." Ilya's English was not as perfect as Maria Mikhailovna had believed or as he had hoped. There were constant hiccups in the conversation—moments when the Masons' eyes flicked up slightly, as though they were searching their brains for his meaning—and he was so much slower than he wanted to be. English, as the Masons spoke it, was a rapid-fire slurry of slang and abbreviations and inter-ruptions. If he gave it his full attention, he could catch enough of what they said to cobble together an understanding, but he kept thinking about Vladimir's eyes in that picture and he'd lose the thread of the conversation, and then, by the time he uttered a word aloud, whatever he said seemed clunky and irrelevant. He would flush, embarrassed, and his eyes would find Sadie. Sadie, poking at her sandwich with a fork; Sadie, pulling apart the strands from a stray clump of moss and braiding them back together; Sadie, with her face half hidden behind a curtain of hair. She seemed separate from her family. Self-contained. He thought of her room—the empty walls, the spartan bed—and was not sure what to make of her. He thought of her standing in the dark by the pool. Sometimes she looked at him too, and if there wasn't necessarily affection there, there was at least a measure of curiosity. And she had touched his arm at Star Pilgrim. She had sat next to him in the car. Small things, sure, but taken together they began to add up.

By the time they got home that night, Ilya's head throbbed with the effort of understanding. His tongue was so exhausted that it had become a presence in his mouth. But still, when the Masons said "good night," he was able to answer "sleep tight." It was an expression that had long confused him, but from their smiles he could see that that, at least, he had gotten right.

In the months between Vladimir's arrest and his own departure, Ilya had tried to ask himself the sorts of questions that the police would have been asking had Vladimir not confessed. The questions that they *should* have been asking even though he had confessed. Three women were dead: Olga Nadiova, Yulia Podtochina, and Lana. In the movies, there was always one thing that connected the victims and that inevitably led to the killer, but Lana and Yulia and Olga were connected in a million messy ways. They were all women, all lower class, all somewhat attractive. They all liked to party. Olga and Lana had lived in the kommunalkas. Yulia and Olga had been seen together at Dolls, a club named after some infamous Moscow hot spot that no one had ever seen. Yulia had worked at the refinery, and so had Lana's dad, a welder whose cheeks were flecked with scars from flying sparks.

Of the three, Lana was the only one Ilya had actually known, and so he'd asked himself over and over whether there was anyone who had wanted her dead. He tried to imagine Lana at school, before she'd dropped out like Vladimir and Sergey and Aksinya. He tried to picture her in the hallway, tried to remember where her locker had been, which table she'd eaten at in the cafeteria, and who had sat next to her, but she'd been in a different grade, and Ilya had always been studying. Studying so much that he might as well have existed in a different world. He barely knew who her friends were, let alone her enemies.

One afternoon, desperate for information, he'd gone to see Aksinya at her sister's apartment. She'd answered the door in her coat, just home from somewhere, her eyes shiny with exhaustion or tears or drugs or all three.

"Ilyusha," she'd said, "Lana was like sugar. Simple, sweet. People made fun of her, but you couldn't not like her."

"But was there anyone who liked her too much?"

Aksinya shook her head. "Too much? She slept around. She wanted a boyfriend, but nobody was knocking down her door."

"Slept around?"

"Is that a big shock? She hooked up with you, right? So, yeah, she was scraping the bottom of the barrel."

"What about Sergey?" Ilya asked.

"For sure when we were younger. But not for a while I don't think."

Aksinya was beautiful enough to leave Berlozhniki—that was what people said about her—and Ilya had always wondered whether Vladimir loved her beauty more or her potential for flight, but since Vladimir's arrest there was this weariness to her. As though she weren't still young, as though she hadn't been young for a long, long time. She wouldn't ever leave. Ilya could see it: she'd marry some midlevel apparatchik, move into an apartment a little better than this one. She'd have kids and love them, but at night, she'd dream of Vladimir and the way that when he held her his laughter had shaken her body, had felt like it was coming out of her own mouth. Then she would wake up.

"And what about Vladimir?" Ilya asked, his brother's name like a lump in his throat.

"Don't say his name like that," she'd said.

"Like what?" he said.

"Like you-know-what," she said. "He didn't kill anybody. And he didn't sleep with my best fucking friend."

She'd shut the door then. It was the same thin plywood as his own door. He could have knocked again—she would have opened it—but he hadn't had any other questions to ask.

Now, in the Masons' basement, he logged back in to VKontakte. It had been ten hours since the church service at Star Pilgrim, and he was sure that he had imagined Vladimir's sidelong look in the picture, just as he'd imagined the heat of Lana's skin against his palm. As he typed in Vladimir's name, there was this leadenness to his lungs, the anticipation of a dead end. This was real life, he reminded himself, not a movie, not a telenovela where the murders were committed and solved within an episode. The image loaded, and there was Vladimir's mouth. It *was* open. He had been saying something—Ilya had been right about that—but his eyes were looking straight at the camera.

Ilya sighed and clicked Aksinya's tag in the picture. The photo was hers. It was the only one that she'd tagged from that night at the Tower, but now, as her profile loaded, he saw that it wasn't the only one that she'd posted. There were a dozen of the same shot, more or less, and Ilya clicked through them. In the first, Sergey's finger was on the lens, obscuring Vladimir entirely, but Aksinya looked gaunt and gorgeous, which must have been why she'd posted it. In the second shot, Lana's eyes were closed and so was Vladimir's mouth. The third photo was the one they'd all been tagged in, and then, as Ilya clicked to the next and the next, Vladimir's mouth opened wider. The pictures blurred until they were like a movie— the girls dipping inward to kiss Ilya and Vladimir's cheeks, their arms extending to flick Sergey off. Vladimir's lips split. His tongue hit his teeth. Ilya could hear him again, just as clearly as he had at the Masons' church. "You have competition, Ilyusha," and as Vladimir said it, his eyes shifted bit by bit by bit until, in the last photo, they were looking to the far left.

Ilya zoomed in on the photo until each of their faces was as big as his palm. He scrolled left, past Vladimir, past himself, past Lana.

There were people dancing all around her. The background was a
tangle of appendages whose owners were hard to identify, but on
the edge of the frame there was someone in the foreground. Someone walking past them, close enough for his shoulder to brush
Lana's. That was who Vladimir was looking at. The person was cut
in half. One shoulder, one leg, the shadowy suggestion of hair under
a baseball cap. Ilya zoomed in as far as the computer would allow.
The pixels fattened and blurred like cells in a petri dish, and then
they clarified, cell by cell, until the face resolved into one that
Ilya recognized. It was Gabe Thompson, the only American in
Berlozhniki. His baseball cap had an orange bear on it, and the hat
struck a chord in Ilya's brain, made his ribs clench his heart like a
fist squeezing tight.

He clicked on Lana's name under the photo, and her profile pictures loaded just as they had the night before. There, just before the
photo from the Tower, was the series of Lana lying on a bed in the
black bikini, which seemed, on closer inspection, to be a bra. Her
hair was wild, her makeup in half-moons under her eyes. She was on
her stomach, her breasts squished together so that a seam of cleav-
age halved the photo. The sight of all that skin tripped some sexual
circuit and heat rushed Ilya's crotch and then he thought, *she's dead*,
and just as quickly the feeling was gone, replaced by nausea as if he'd
drunk sour milk. She was wearing a baseball hat too. It was askew,
the brim tilting toward one cheek. The logo was only half visible,
but still Ilya could see that it was an orange bear, its fangs bared.

Since the midnineties Berlozhniki had played host to a trickle of
tourists, groups of Swedes or Brits decked out in snowsuits so new

and stiff that they barely allowed for movement. They'd check in to
the Hotel Berlozhniki, which was really more of a hostel, eat at the
pizza place on the square, and visit the Museum of Mining, where
Babushka would give them a chit for their coats. They'd tour the
museum's three rooms, have a coffee in its café, reclaim their coats,
and go gawk at the field of crosses that marked the camp's dead.
After thirty-six hours, two days at most, they'd leave, feeling sober
and superior, but Gabe Thompson had been in Berlozhniki for close
to two years.

He'd arrived alone, with money, and without, it seemed, any
plans to leave, and at first the town had welcomed him. The Cold
War was over, after all, and families had him over for supper. This
young, blond American in a parka and a too-big suit. The mayor's
wife baked him her famous kulich. He got a monthly discount at
the Hotel Berlozhniki, and the pizza place gave him a free pie, took
a picture of him eating it, and made a poster of it that said, AUTHEN-
TIC! AMERICA! PIZZA! The businesses on the square spruced themselves up—Anatoly at the Minutka was even spotted mopping—in
the hope that Gabe might be the vanguard of a new wave of tour-
ism that would drown Berlozhniki in rubles.

If Gabe seemed at all odd—and he did talk, occasionally, about
angels and a golden book buried on a mountaintop—it was attrib-
uted to the language barrier. Besides, everyone said, all Americans
are eccentric because look what they'd impeached their president
over: some funny business with a cigar. Then, one day, Gabe picked
a bench on the square, unzipped a duffel bag filled with pamphlets,
and began to preach about Joseph Smith and the Angel Moroni and
a dream mine. Ah ha, people said. Finally they understood. Gabe
had been sent to Russia to proselytize. With great disappointment

they began to ignore him, to give his bench a wide berth or else to take his pamphlets and use them to kindle their stoves. Anatoly let the Minutka return to its usual filthy state and joked to anyone who would listen about how only in America would people waste time mining dreams.

A year passed, Gabe converted no one, and everyone assumed that he would go back to the bosom of whatever church had sent him, but he stayed. He ran out of pamphlets, and still he stayed. Kids approached his bench on dares and asked him questions about saints in stumbling English, then giggled while he answered. From time to time he brought a bagged Baltika to the bench, and the babushka who cleaned his room at the Hotel Berlozhniki revealed that he had several each evening as well. The women of Berlozhniki found this development especially dispiriting. Their lives were filled with men who lined up at the kiosk for a beer before work, and now it seemed that this problem was not particular to Russia, that all across the whole, wide, enormous world, men were worthless. Some days Gabe didn't make it out of his hotel. Some days he sat on his bench, drunk, letting snowflakes melt on his cheeks. Sometimes he fell asleep there, and the police would leave him for a little while— everyone agreed that some gentle punishment was necessary—but they would always drag him back to his room before frostbite set in. And then there were the days when he seemed resolved to make a fresh start. His suit was clean and pressed. His face was puffy, but his eyes were clear and hard.

"I need to talk to you about God," he'd say, and people would shake their heads at him, they would cross the square, and his voice would rise, and he'd yell, "Give me a minute! It's not too late to be saved!"

Ilya was fascinated by Gabe, the only native English speaker for hundreds of miles, but he'd avoided him just as everyone else had. Though once, when Gabe was sitting on his bench asleep, Ilya and Vladimir and Sergey had seen a dog trot over to him, lift its leg, and piss on Gabe's shins. They'd stared, transfixed. They were only a few meters away, close enough that Ilya could see an angry red divot in Gabe's cheek, as though some insect had crawled out of or burrowed into his skin. They were close enough to shoo the dog, Ilya was thinking, just as Gabe's eyes opened. For a second he looked at Ilya calmly, and then he sensed the dog or felt its piss, and he began to yell. The boys scrambled away—the snow tripping Ilya, Vladimir grabbing his arm—and ran for the Minutka. Once they were safely inside, roaming the aisles under Anatoly's glare, Vladimir and Sergey started to laugh. They were screamed at, scolded, and cuffed with regularity. Disapproval was like a drug to them, but Ilya was terrified. He'd been able to understand what Gabe was yelling.

"Come on, Ilyusha," Vladimir had said. "He's just drunk."

Vladimir picked up an Alyonka bar and began to examine it as though he might purchase it. At the register, Anatoly's eyes narrowed. This was a cue to Sergey and Ilya to pocket something while Anatoly's attention was focused on Vladimir. Sergey slipped some caramels into his coat with his usual finesse, but Ilya did not. Vladimir put the Alyonka bar down. "What's wrong, Ilya?" he said.

"Are you afraid he's going to come piss on you? A revenge piss!" Sergey said.

"He said he'd kill us," Ilya said.

This had sent Vladimir and Sergey into another round of hysterics, and Ilya had forced himself to laugh with them until he realized that Anatoly was no longer watching them. He was looking out the window, the safety of his merchandise forgotten, and Ilya followed his eyes to the sidewalk where Gabe Thompson was standing, staring at them.

"Stop it," Ilya hissed, and Vladimir and Sergey quieted.

"Just our luck," Anatoly murmured. "The only American we get is insane."

Gabe didn't move. His stare pinned Ilya in place, gave Ilya the sense that his own stillness was ensuring Gabe's, that if he flinched, Gabe would spring into violent motion. So Ilya resisted the urge to hide behind the enormous case of birch juice to his left. He forced himself to look at Gabe's eyes, which were puffy and bloodshot and horrible, and then Anatoly picked up the shovel he kept by the door and stepped out onto the sidewalk.

"Shit," Vladimir whispered.

Gabe took a step toward Anatoly. Anatoly gripped the handle of the shovel and raised it off the ground—a half meter, maybe less. Ilya would have hit Gabe with it. He knew that with certainty, but maybe Anatoly had been born brave, or maybe because he'd outlived Stalin and Beria and communism and had little left to fear, he did not hit Gabe. Instead, he turned and rammed the shovel into the centimeter of snow that had fallen that afternoon. Metal screeched against concrete. It was not enough snow to shovel, but still Anatoly flung the dusting of it into the street, and Gabe turned and walked back across the square.

It had been terrifying—surely Ilya hadn't imagined that—but could Gabe have killed Lana and the other girls? Ilya wasn't sure. Gabe was fervent, which was a close cousin to crazy. He was a drunk, probably an addict, possibly, as Anatoly had said, insane. Yet he was in a picture with Lana on the night she'd died. And Lana had posted a sultry picture of herself in Gabe's hat like it was something to be proud of, like she wanted it to be recognized. At the thought, anger gathered, burning behind his eyes, and then another idea struck him: Berlozhniki was not the sort of place one chose to go; it was the sort of place you were sent. It had been part of the gulag. Prisoners had dug the mine. They had laid the train tracks and built the station and poured the roads that radiated from it. Everyone in Berlozhniki had assumed that Gabe had been sent there by his church on a conversion mission—but what if Gabe had not been sent to *do* anything, what if he'd been sent because of something he'd already done?

Ilya opened a browser window and typed Gabe's name into the search engine. He'd never heard the name Gabe before, and so he'd assumed that it was rare, but as the results loaded, he could see that it was not rare enough. There were hundreds of hits. There was an NFL player with the name, a reality TV star, a professor at a school in Ohio. A Gabe Thompson was in the *Guinness Book of World Records* for toenail length. Another had been in the Summer Olympics that year. Ilya clicked on the image results. He scrolled through page after page. None of the faces were familiar. None of them were him.

Babushka had saved Gabe's pamphlets. She was a hoarder by nature and too devout to throw out any image of Jesus, even if it was the paraphernalia of a ridiculous offshoot of Christianity. Instead, she'd cut out the sherbet-colored pictures—all of those angels and archangels—and pasted them to the windowpanes in her bedroom. In the summer, when the sun lit them from behind, they looked like stained glass, which had been her hope. CHURCH OF JESUS CHRIST OF LATTER-DAY SAINTS was stamped in tiny letters in the corner of each picture, and Ilya remembered sounding out those

words and puzzling over the meaning of "Latter-day," before decid-
ing that it must be a fancy way of saying "tomorrow." Now he added
the church's name to Gabe's in his search. Again there were lots of
hits. Congregations of clean-cut boys in suits and ties. Ilya scanned
the pictures until his eyes blurred, but again none of them were him.

Ilya cleared the search window. In its empty box, the cursor
blinked in synchrony, it seemed, with his heart. He typed Gabe's
name again, and this time he added the word "murder." There were
fewer hits this time: a dozen sullen-cheeked men in orange jump-
suits, and Ilya thought of Vladimir. But Vladimir wouldn't be in
orange; in Russia, prisoners wore black.

Upstairs there were footsteps, and Ilya looked at the clock on
the computer, thinking that it might be Sadie, that it was the middle of the night and that she was about to sneak out again, as she
had the night before. But it was much later—five a.m.—and the sky
was lightening. In a few hours, it'd be his first day of school in
America. He took one last look at the computer screen, at the violence in each set of eyes, and then he emailed Aksinya.

Did she sleep with Gabe Thompson? he wrote, and then, with a
throb of love for Aksinya because she had been Vladimir's or because she was beautiful but still wouldn't ever get to leave, he
wrote, *Please stay away from him.* He clicked send and fell into a
deep and dreamless sleep.

Chapter Eight

For a while that last winter, Vladimir did try. He came home for meals. He seemed generally sober. Some afternoons, he and Aksinya and Lana would lie on the carpet like three sardines in a tin, watching movies, while Ilya did homework at the kitchen table. Ilya even saw him at school—granted, he and Aksinya were disappearing into the custodial closet, but still, he was in the building. There had been no more questions from teachers about Vladimir's health, no more folders from Nikolay Grigorievich, and Ilya took all of this as a good sign.

That winter, Ilya's last in Berlozhniki, was one of the coldest in the books. Snow swallowed the crosses in the field by the Tower completely. It was rumored that the Pechora was frozen solid, surface to bed, with whole schools of salmon trapped in the ice. A Nenets man parked his sleigh outside the clinic, unharnessed his reindeer, and dragged it inside. It was alive, but one eyeball had frozen in its head. The doctor said there was a clink when he touched it with the scalpel.

Sometime in the dregs of November, a month after the first freeze and a month still to go until the New Year's festivities, a windstorm took down dozens of trees. Tatyana Andropova from Building 4 brought her dog out for a pee, and the dog was blown away like a tumbleweed. The doors to the stairwell were ripped off Ilya's building, and all the radiators in the kommunalkas rattled, sighed, and went quiet. Babushka took the old Chukovsky books out of their storage spot in the woodstove, dusted off the baffles and firebricks, and sent Ilya and Vladimir down to buy satchels of wood from Daniil Chernyshev, who was crazy and kept birch logs stacked floor to ceiling along his walls in case of just such an occasion.

The wind shrieked up the stairwell, the sort of wind that feels barbed, and there were enough people who were too frail or too afraid to leave their apartments that Ilya and Vladimir each made a couple hundred rubles shuttling between their floors with satchels of wood curled under each of their arms. The wind got stronger and stronger, louder and louder so that they had to yell to hear each other. Ilya's arms ached from carrying wood, but there was a giddiness to it all too, to the easy money.

"Motherfucker!" Vladimir said as they rounded the third-floor stairwell, headed down to Daniil's again. The wind pulled tears up out of his eyes toward his temples. "This is amazing. Watch this," he said. He stood at the top of the next flight, scooted his feet so that they were halfway over the edge of the stair, and leaned a couple of millimeters into the wind. It was strong enough to hold him. His jacket ballooned behind him. His jeans slicked to his legs. The wind rippled the skin of his cheeks like water. But then he got greedy—Vladimir had a tendency to get greedy—he stuck his chest out even farther, as though he were a figurehead moving over the waves. Ilya gripped the railing behind him.

"Try it, Ilyusha," Vladimir said, and at that moment the wind stopped and Vladimir fell. Down three stairs, then four, then five, all the way to the landing where he crumpled into a ball.

Ilya ran to him, thinking of what he'd broken and whether they'd have to go to the clinic and whether it would be open and whether it had electricity, and then Vladimir sat up and began to laugh. Blood was trickling out of his nose.

"You saw that, right?" he said. "The way the wind just stopped."

Ilya nodded. He wanted to say that if you leaned into the wind forever then it was bound to stop, that it was nothing personal, but then the wind began to whistle through the rungs of the railing, and then it was fully wailing again, the noise inhuman but seeming to speak of human pains, and Ilya wondered if somehow it was personal. Vladimir wiped at his nose and blood smeared across his cheek.

"Help me up," he said, and Ilya could barely hear him over the wind.

That night they pulled the table as close to the stove as they could. The backs of Ilya's calves burned, but his legs felt frozen in the center, like meat that's failed to thaw. The windows were blanketed against the cold, and, as the wind went on and on, as their kommunalka, squat as it was, began to sway, Ilya wanted to pull the blankets down so that he could see the storm and make sure that it hadn't taken on some new and terrible form.

The buses were not running to the refinery, and his mother had found a mostly empty bottle of peppermint schnapps, and she'd had a few shots and was ruddy with it, with all of them together at the table. As Babushka heated dinner, she prayed to St. Medard, who she said had once been shielded from a hurricane by a hovering eagle. He was a Catholic saint, but Babushka occasionally prayed to Catholic saints if there was one perfectly suited to the occasion.

"Even a saint's gonna get shat on, standing under a bird," Vladimir said.

"Hush," their mother said, with the requisite sharpness, but her eyes had this bubbliness to them, like kvass poured into a glass, that they got only from Vladimir.

After dinner Babushka dealt out seka, and Ilya divvied up a box of macaroni to use for bets. Babushka beat them all for the first five hands, but then Vladimir started to pay attention. He got three of a suit twice in a row, and soon he had to get a bowl to hold all of his macaroni. He was gloating, talking about becoming a card shark and joining the weekly game the dedki played in the kitchen.

"I'm gonna rake it in. Those old fuckers are so busy moaning about Gorbachev and Yeltsin and how at least before you could count on your 120 rubles that they won't even know what hit them," he said, when a knock sounded.

Under the wind, it seemed that the knock was far off, on some other door down the hall, but then it came again, louder and clearer.

For a second they were quiet. The candles on the table gave their faces new shadows, made them all look strange, but Ilya saw a familiar panic flash in Babushka's eyes. "You won't last long if it takes a knock on the door for you to know they're coming," she liked to say, or sometimes just "A knock on the door is never good."

"Maybe it's Timofey," Ilya's mother said.

"Wanting company," Babushka said. After three decades in the coal mine, Timofey couldn't stand the dark. He kept the lights on all night despite his tiny pension. "He's probably scared to death," she said, opening the door with a sly smile meant for Timofey.

Maria Mikhailovna stood in the hallway. She was wearing a militia coat with a long fur collar and a gold badge. The coat swallowed her whole and made her look like a child playing dress-up. It must be her husband's, Ilya thought, remembering that he was a policeman. Her nose was raw and running, and behind her glasses her eyes were leaking like Vladimir's had been earlier.

"Izvinitye," Babushka stuttered. "We didn't know. Ilya didn't—"

"Please." Maria Mikhailovna put up a hand. "Hello, Ilya. Hello, Vladimir," she said in her tiny voice. She was in a fur ushanka too, her braids trailing out of the ear flaps.

"Come in, Maria Mikhailovna," his mother said.

"Zdravstvuyte," Vladimir said, looking horrified, and then, in mangled English, he said something that sounded like "Good evening."

As soon as Maria Mikhailovna stepped inside, the wind slammed the door shut behind her. She had never been to Ilya's home. He had studied with her for almost four years now. He knew the way she sucked air through her teeth when she concentrated. He knew that she favored crisps over sweets and that she used a teabag five times before she tossed it. Each afternoon, she sat close enough for him to see the tiny brown hairs that lapped at the corners of her lips, but he had never imagined her here, and it seemed as though wires had been crossed somewhere. Characters from two different movies had been transposed and stranded in unsuitable settings.

"You were out in this awfulness?" Babushka said.

"It's terrible, isn't it? Dmitri drove me, and the wind was making the car wobble from one lane to the next."

"He's in the car?" Babushka said it like he might be dead.

"He has to make his rounds. He patrols the refinery," she said.

"Ah," Babushka said, "important duty," which was exactly what she said about any job at all, but in this case it happened to be true.

Maria Mikhailovna bent to take off her boots, and Ilya's mother said, "Keep them on, please. It's too cold. The heat's been off since this morning."

In a flash, Babushka cleared the cards and, ignoring Vladimir's protests, dumped the macaroni back into its box. She swapped the plastic tablecloth for a lace one, put a kettle on the stove, and produced a box of Malvina's, which were Vladimir's favorite biscuits and were supposed to have been a present from Babushka on his name day.

"I'm sorry to have interrupted," Maria Mikhailovna said as Babushka ushered her to a seat at the table. "But I couldn't wait."

"It's an honor," Babushka said, and Vladimir rolled his eyes.

What couldn't wait? Ilya wanted to say, but he felt a sudden shyness with her. There was always a textbook and a desk between them. A question or an answer. Now she was sitting at their table, and he couldn't imagine what had brought her here in this storm. Ilya had needed school supplies occasionally—new installments of *The Adventures of Michael & Stephanie* and, once, a computer program—but she'd just sent him home with a note.

"I've finished the translation," he offered.

Vladimir snorted.

"The translation?" Maria Mikhailovna was distracted, and for a second he wondered if she was here for him at all. Maybe she had come to talk about Vladimir. Maybe she had noticed the effort he'd been making of late, and she had some plan to help get him back on track. Maybe she would ask their mother if he had actually ever been sick, Ilya thought, and his stomach went sour, but Maria Mikhailovna just said, "Ah, the Pushkin. Good."

Babushka pressed a biscuit on her, and she nibbled at its corner and then set it down on her napkin, and Ilya could feel Vladimir staring at it like a wolf.

"You have been well, I hope," his mother said.

"Yes."

Ilya twisted in his seat. The women, it seemed, would drag this out. "Do I need new books?"

"No."

"He's performing well? Doing his work?" his mother said.

"Da. Very well."

"Good," his mother said. "He works hard."

"He gets that from you," Maria Mikhailovna said.

Ilya's mother smiled and shook her head. Maria Mikhailovna took another swallow of tea. "What brings me here tonight is an opportunity—a possible opportunity—and it could have waited, of course, until the storm is over, but *I* couldn't wait." She slid her lip between her teeth and then went on: "Gazneft has decided to sponsor an exchange program along with an American petrol company. One student from Berlozhniki is to be sent to a city in America. It's only for a year. A year of upper school. He'd have to take the boards early, of course, and he'd have to get above the ninetieth percentile, but I believe he's in that range, and it seemed—"

She hesitated, struck maybe by the silence of the room or by the force of the hope she was giving them. Babushka's hands shook on the table, and his mother reached for them and covered them with her own.

"It seemed," Maria Mikhailovna finished, "perfect for him."

"Could he be chosen?" his mother said.

"Who, me?" Vladimir said, with a tight smile, and they all turned and looked at him because they had forgotten—or at least Ilya had—that he was in the room.

"He has a chance?" his mother said. "Won't the spot be saved for someone?" She meant someone important. The mayor's son or the daughter of some refinery bureaucrat.

Maria Mikhailovna straightened in her chair. "In this, I have some influence. It's just a bit of luck really. Dmitri drives Fyodor Fetisov and mentioned to him that I teach at the school, and he's asked me to choose the Berlozhniki student."

Ilya's mother's eyes went huge and wet, and when she turned them on Ilya, the happiness in them was terrifying.

Vladimir got up from the couch, walked to the table, and shoved a Malvina in his mouth. "What city?" he said. "New York? Orlando? Florida?" He was chewing aggressively, all the power of his body collected in his jaw. "I'll do it. What are my chances?"

"Vladimir, go in the bedroom," their mother said.

Maria Mikhailovna looked at Vladimir. There was still a crust of dried blood under his nostril from his fall, and Ilya expected a look of disgust from her, but she smiled. "Third period is much more lively with you back, Vladimir Alexandrovich."

Vladimir let out a sudden laugh. "It's an exchange?" he said. "So you're saying that an American is coming *here*?"

"Not next year," she said, "but in the future, maybe."

"Of course," Vladimir said, "in the future, maybe."

"What would it cost?" Babushka said.

"It's funded, Mamulya. She already said that." His mother glanced at Maria Mikhailovna as though she and Babushka were failing some oral exam.

"Gazneft and EnerCo pay for everything. The flight and visas and everything."

"Everything." Babushka said it like it was a word she'd never heard.

"Ilya can stow me in his suitcase," Vladimir said. "I promise to behave."

"I need your approval before I can submit his name and register him for the boards," Maria Mikhailovna said.

His mother and Babushka nodded. Maria Mikhailovna nodded.

"Ilya?" Maria Mikhailovna said.

Ilya imagined himself in the big belly of a plane. His mother, his brother, the kommunalkas, the refinery, even, shrunk to a pinprick of light. A lesser star. Ilya didn't hear her say his name again. He didn't notice the candle sputtering out under the plastic icon or the way his brother's face was buckling. He had left. In his mind, he was up high and far away.

Maria Mikhailovna put a hand on his arm. "Would you like to go?"

Ilya looked at her. "Yes. I want to go," he said, just as Vladimir slipped out the door and into the storm.

CHAPTER NINE

Breakfast that first day of school was a chaotic affair. The kitchen reeked of bacon. The radio by the sink bellowed Christian rock, and Papa Cam sang along, cracking eggs with gusto. The microwave beeped and beeped, and the dryer churned, desperately fluffing things that had wrinkled overnight. Mama Jamie ripped tags off Ilya's and the girls' new book bags and cut crusts off their sandwiches and threw them in the trash. Babushka had always wiped the crumbs from her cutting board into the palm of her hand and eaten them. "The best bits," she called them, and when Vladimir and Ilya were little they used to fight over who would get them. He imagined telling the Masons this story. *Fighting for crumbs*, they would think, though that wasn't the point; his family was not that poor.

Sadie was sitting at the table, eating a slice of toast and staring out the sliding glass doors. Her lips were buttery. Her knees were tucked into another huge black T-shirt, and again Ilya had the sense that she was separate from them all. He wasn't deluded enough to think that they were together in their separateness, but at least they were similar for it. She was looking toward the refinery, and he sat next to her and said, "My home is so close to the refinery that it lights up our whole apartment."

She looked at him, but it took a second for her to focus on him, as though her mind were returning from some distance.

"There are houses like that here too," she said. "How'd you sleep?"

"You get accustomed to it," he said. "But at first people were awake all the time, and they complained. And Gazneft manufactured a study saying the lights would be healthy for us, make us less sad, since it's dark so much of the time."

"That's a new one," Papa Cam said.

"I meant how'd you sleep last night," Sadie said, and Ilya wondered if she could tell from his face that he'd barely slept at all.

"I don't like the dark," Molly said. She squeezed between Ilya and Sadie with a plate of waffles and began to systematically pour syrup into each of the waffle's tiny trenches. "That's why I have ten nightlights."

"Let me guess," Marilee said, from across the table, "your longitude is very far north."

Papa Cam emerged from a closet with what looked like a tripod. "Latitude," he said, and Ilya got the sense that even patient Papa Cam found satisfaction in correcting Marilee.

"In the middle of winter there are only a couple of hours of light each day," Ilya said.

Sadie smiled. "That sounds kind of nice," she said.

"In what way?" Mama Jamie said.

"If you don't know I can't tell you," Sadie said, and Mama Jamie wiped her hands on a dishcloth and said, "Photo time. Everybody to the fireplace."

Marilee, Molly, and Sadie groaned in unison.

"This is something we do every year on the first day of school, Ilya," Mama Jamie said, "and if the girls don't appreciate it now, they will later."

The girls slumped over to the fireplace, and Mama Jamie scooped up the dog, which they were now routinely calling Durashka, and climbed onto the brick fire skirt so that her head jutted above her daughters' shoulders. Molly's shirt was tucked into an inch of exposed underwear. A citrusy stain traversed the entirety of Papa Cam's tie, a rash had sprouted on Marilee's cheek, and the vacancy had not quite left Sadie's face. Ilya watched them arrange themselves, and they were not much to look at, but still he thought of his mother and Babushka alone in their apartment, and he felt a bit of bile rise in his throat because on top of everything else the Masons had each other.

"Why's he staring at us like that?" Marilee said.

"Nobody's looking any which way," Mama Jamie said.

"Yes he *is*," Marilee said, and Ilya looked at his feet because he knew that in this case she was right.

Papa Cam lifted an arm like some sort of lamed bird. "Front and center," he said.

"No, please," Ilya said. "I'll take the picture."

"No you don't!" Mama Jamie cried. "Get in here."

Ilya wedged himself under Papa Cam's arm, and Papa Cam clicked a button on a tiny remote, and a red light on the camera began to flash. "Timer's on," he said.

Next to him Marilee began to itch the rash on her cheek.

"Stop it," Mama Jamie hissed.

"I can't help it," Marilee said.

"Are you sure you set it?" Sadie said as the camera clicked, whirred, and went silent.

Papa Cam stared at the camera screen. "Well, we sure captured the real deal," he said.

"I didn't want to capture the real deal." Mama Jamie sighed.

"Ilya, do you want one of just you? To send to your mom? First day of school in a new country—can you imagine, girls? Ilya is brave, right?"

A picture of him here, safe, would soothe his mother.

"Yes," he said. "She'd like that."

His eyes were gritty with tiredness, but as Papa Cam crouched behind the camera, he tried, for his mother's sake, to look happy. "Cheese," he murmured. The flash blinked, then burst. Papa Cam showed him the photo, and he had expected to look as grim as the convicts online, but the flash had collected in his pupils and made his eyes look like the lights of a train pushing through a dark tunnel. It was a look of purpose. He told himself to temper his hopes. All the picture of Lana in Gabe's hat proved was that they had been involved. It wasn't enough, but still it was more than he'd had the day before.

Leffie High was a concrete slab hunched under a big sky. Behind it, playing fields stretched into the distance, and kids ran back and forth between the goals with a sort of grace, like birds rearranging in the sky. Sadie had her own car and, much to Ilya's delight, was in charge of driving him to and from school. She pulled into a parking spot between two pickups with huge, rutted tires. A melancholy rock song blasted from the radio—"Smashing Pumpkins," Sadie said, when he asked who it was—and she mouthed the words while dabbing something that smelled like coconut on her lips.

"It's familiar," Ilya said, though it was not.

"Oh yeah? They're big in Russia?"

"Very," Ilya said.

Kids surged around the car, headed for the front doors. They yelled hellos, shrieking over new haircuts and new outfits. The song ended, and Sadie said, "Ready?" softly, as though she were talking to herself more than to him.

Inside, the press of bodies, the thin clanging of lockers, the sheer energy of teenagers colliding were all familiar to him, but that made it all no less terrifying. Ilya watched Sadie's white hair slip through the crowd, and as she got farther from him, he began to sweat. Someone stepped on his foot. Someone else yelled, "The Russian!" He didn't realize that he'd stopped walking until he saw Sadie's slim shoulders sliding back through the crowd for him.

"You're famous," Sadie said, and when she saw his face, she said, "I'm just kidding. Everyone will get over it by tomorrow."

Sadie brought him to the principal's office first. "This is Miss Janet," she said, nodding at a woman behind a desk. The woman couldn't have been much older than his mother, but her skin had been sunned so that it crinkled like the brown paper lunch bag that Mama Jamie had given him that morning.

"And is this Ilya?" Miss Janet said, pronouncing the "I" like the letter.

"It's *Ilya*. He's supposed to see Principal Gibbons," Sadie said, and her pronunciation wasn't perfect, but still this heat seeped into Ilya's chest at hearing her say his name, at the fact that she'd bothered to correct Miss Janet.

"He's on a call, sweet pea," the woman said, "but you head on, and I'll take care of Ilya here."

Sadie paused at the door. "We have history together," she said. "So I'll see you then," and then she was gone, and Ilya was left alone with Miss Janet, who was baring too-white teeth at him.

"Russia, huh?" she said. "Now that is a far way to come."

The phone on Janet's desk rang, and she rolled her eyes in a conspiratorial way and ignored it. "I went to Alaska once. On a cruise. A long time ago. And at one point—I'll never forget this— the captain came on the loudspeaker and said that we were close enough to swim to Russia." The phone rang again, and this time she was moved to put a hand on the receiver. "Of course the water was too cold to actually do it but I just thought it was so exciting. Swim to Russia. Can you imagine?"

"Yes," Ilya said, and if she noticed the sarcasm in his voice, she didn't show it.

The phone rang once more, a door opened behind Janet's desk, and a small, powerful man said, "The phone. Please."

Janet looked back over her shoulder, unperturbed. "Principal Gibbons," she said, "this is Ilya from Russia."

"Ah ha," Gibbons said. "Come on back."

Principal Gibbons held out a hand to indicate a chair for Ilya, twisted a rod to shut the window blinds, and leaned against his desk. He had the body of a spetsnaz, like he'd know his way around a Kalashnikov. His skin looked buffed. It shone like the fruit had at the Walmart the day before.

"This is quite an opportunity for you," he said. He did not smile. "I hope you're ready to take advantage of it."

"Yes," Ilya said.

"The Masons are a fantastic family. And as I said, we're glad to have you—" A bell rang, and Gibbons tilted his head and waited for it to finish. "But there are rules and ramifications here. You will be held to the same standard as every other student. No diplomatic immunity, you understand?"

"I understand," Ilya said, wondering whether the man was always this aggressive. Gibbons picked up a folder from his desk. He opened it, though it seemed to be empty, then closed it again.

"I imagine that where you're from is pretty rough—"

Ilya tried to speak—not to disagree, because Berlozhniki was rough by any standard, but to say that that didn't mean *he* was— but Gibbons held up a hand. His fingers were incredibly thick and straight. "Whoa. Whoa. Let me finish. I *admire* the fact that you've gotten yourself here by hook or crook."

Hook or crook, Ilya thought. That was in his book of idioms. He understood the insult in "crook" but could not remember what "hook" meant in this context.

"That takes determination, and we like to reward determination here. In this country. So keep that in mind." Gibbons's hand was still in the air. It had not moved a millimeter. "How old are you?" he said.

"Fifteen."

"We've got you in sophomore classes for now. See if you sink or swim. Except English. And history. You'll be with the freshmen for those two. I'm assuming that American history was not part of your curriculum." A smile flitted across Gibbons's eyes. That word, "curriculum," was a test. He wanted to know how good Ilya's English actually was, and, as luck would have it, Ilya had understood that word perfectly.

"In Russia, Russian history is the standard curriculum," he said.

The smile leaked out of Gibbons's eyes. "OK, then. Let's get you integrated. First period began"—he looked at his watch—"two minutes ago."

Miss Janet printed out a schedule for Ilya and led him through the empty halls to his first class.

"Don't worry," she said when they got to the door. "Nobody's gonna bite."

In each class, Ilya was introduced as the EnerCo Exchange Student. The teachers were so careful to say "EnerCo" that Ilya knew the school must be getting some sort of payment for taking him on, just as the Masons were. In first-period math, Mr. Cammer trotted out some elementary Russian. In second-period biology, Mrs. Lareaux asked him to write his name on the board. He did so, using the Cyrillic alphabet, and when he stepped back and brushed the chalk dust off his palms, she had the look of someone lost in a maze.

"Oh, that's right," she said. "There's a different alphabet. Would you mind writing it in English too, so that we can read it?"

So Ilya carefully chalked the roman letters under each Cyrillic one and listened as, behind him, a dozen voices sounded out his name.

His new backpack was soon full of syllabi and textbooks. There were course calendars, course expectations. That was all as overwhelming as he'd expected, but he hadn't anticipated the force of attention: the questions, the smiles, the silences he was expected to fill. For fifteen years Ilya had lived with Vladimir, who lived for attention of any sort, and Ilya's personality had been shaped by Vladimir's need. Ilya was used to observing from the edges; he was used to going whole days without saying much of anything—except, of course, to Maria Mikhailovna or Michael and Stephanie—and now, when he entered a room, every face turned to look at him, and he wished that he'd brought his tape player, that he could listen to Michael and Stephanie and slip from this America into that other one.

It didn't help that he had worn the wrong things: his jeans were too skinny, his sneakers not nearly large enough nor bright enough.

Boys in America did not, it seemed, wear their T-shirts tight, and no one had a fringed haircut like his that tapered into spikes above his eyebrows.

By fourth-period history, he was desperate to see Sadie. He wanted to hear her say again that tomorrow they would have forgotten all about him. Luckily, the history classroom was next to his third-period class, so he was saved the embarrassment of asking some other straggler in the hallway for directions. When he walked in the door, he saw her almost immediately, in the far back corner, framed by an enormous poster of a nobleman in a wig that was the same color as her hair.

"Sadie," he said, and he was halfway to her, nearly across the room, before he realized that the seat next to her was taken by a boy who looked more like a man. The sort of man in cologne commercials. The sort of man whose abs had bristled on the packet of boxers that Ilya had opened just that morning. He was looking at Ilya now, and so was Sadie. They had been talking, Ilya realized, and had stopped when he said her name.

"Hi," Sadie said.

Ilya could feel himself flushing. Sadie was smiling, as was the man-boy next to her. All around Ilya the desks were filling up—and he could tell that he would be left standing, the odd man out, the perfect target—and he tried to remember where the closest bathroom was so that he could propel himself there and hide in a stall until the last bell had rung. And then he heard a voice say, "Before you take a seat, would you mind coming up here and telling us a little bit about Russia? About your city or town?"

Ilya turned to find a small, thin man with a beard to rival Father Frost's and the sleepy smile of a lizard on a rock.

"Mr. Shilling," the man said, "American history buff and, by necessity, teacher, at your service." He led Ilya to the front of the room. "So, Russia, tell us about it," he said, and a silence fell over the class, so thick that Ilya could almost feel it on his skin. They were all looking at him. He knew they wanted the dramatic things, the things that reaffirmed America: that his grandfather had died in the mine, that his father had died coughing it up, that his grandmother had spent a third of her life in lines; that after the currency collapse your life savings could buy you a pack of Optimas; that his brother was in prison for murder. Or maybe they wanted to know about the cultural tidbits: about Victory Day, and the ice sculptures, and the fact that they gave presents for New Year's, not Christmas.

"Let's start with where you live," Shilling said. "Russia is a big place, right?"

"Yes," Ilya said.

"What's your town called?"

"Berlozhniki," Ilya said.

"Where is that?"

"The northwest."

"OK," Mr. Shilling said, and when Ilya didn't offer anything further, he said, "Maybe it'd be easier if we let the class ask some questions, things they're curious about."

Ilya nodded.

"Please remember," Shilling said, turning to the class, "that your grades are partially based on participation."

A few hands went up, but not Sadie's. She was writing something in a tiny notebook. Actually, from the way her pen was moving it looked like she was drawing.

"What's the population?" asked a boy with glasses and a splash of acne on each cheek. When Ilya told him, he wrote the answer down in a notebook, which prompted a girl in the front row to ask if they'd be tested on this information. Mr. Shilling shook his head, and said that he hoped they'd pay attention anyhow.

"Was it part of the gulag archipelago?" a girl in the front row asked. She said the phrase—*gulag archipelago*—like it was the Latin name for some rare, carnivorous plant, like she should be congratulated on her recall.

"Yes," Ilya said.

"You ever meet a mail-order bride?" This came from the manboy, who was leaning so far back in his chair that its feet lifted off the ground.

Sadie rolled her eyes, but a few other girls giggled.

"Ignore J.T., please," Mr. Shilling said. "Let's try not to sink to the lowest common denominator."

Shilling pointed at a chubby girl with dark lipstick. "Chelsea," he said.

"Is the refinery privately owned? Or does the state own it?" she said.

It was an easy question, easier than the gulag one in theory, but it felt somehow accusatory, as though it were Ilya's fault that Yeltsin had dealt out the country's resources to his friends like a hand of seka, but as she asked it, the sun came out from behind a cloud and half soaked the classroom, and the light was like melted butter, was like nothing he'd seen before, as if they orbited a different star here, and home suddenly felt so far.

As his silence grew, the class's did too. They stopped moving in their desks, stopped cracking knuckles and chewing gum. Even J.T. had stopped fidgeting and was looking at him the way you look at a three-legged dog, with lots of pity and a little amazement. He thought of Aksinya saying, "Maybe over there you'll grow a pair." Of Vladimir saying that Ilya would be a boss, that he'd run shit. Of

Vladimir asking Maria Mikhailovna to send him instead. He thought of Lana sleeping with Gabe Thompson, and he knew why she'd done it: she'd wanted to be here too, and Gabe had been as close as she could get.

"This oligarch owns most of it," Ilya managed. His words were clipped, his voice terse. He sounded like some sort of demented robot. Vladimir, he knew, would be expansive. Vladimir would embellish, impress. He would not worry about the truth. "Fyodor Fetisov. An oligarch is someone who's rich. Dirty rich."

"Filthy rich," Mr. Shilling said.

"Filthy rich," Ilya said. "And this oligarch, once he filled a bathtub with caviar and two prostitutes."

Sadie looked up from her drawing.

"Hell yes!" J.T. shouted.

"And these prostitutes, they've got diamonds for nipples and thongs made out of gold. These are women so fucking beautiful that they cost millions of rubles a day, and he has them for as long as he wants, forever. All thanks to oil. We have a joke at home, that the oligarch's balls are filled with oil, instead of—I don't know the word—and when he's finished he takes a lighter—"

"OK, OK," Mr. Shilling said, and J.T. started to laugh. Next to him, Sadie was smiling. He looked at her, and for one triumphant second it was clear to him that she liked him. It was right there in her eyes. And then J.T. leaned across the aisle, cupped his hand over his mouth and whispered something in her ear, and it was just as clear to Ilya that J.T. was her boyfriend. Of course she had a boyfriend, he thought; why else did girls sneak out in the middle of the night?

"I'm not sure how those words translate," Mr. Shilling was saying, "but they're not really appropriate for school."

"Which words?" Ilya said.

"Mr. Landry," Mr. Shilling said, to J.T., "maybe you can tell Ilya after class, once you've finished whispering with Ms. Mason."

"Happy to," J.T. said with a smirk. Beside him, Sadie went back to her drawing.

J.T. did corner Ilya after class, to tell him that he was a badass. "You're a fucking oligarch," J.T. said, raising a fist, and, when Ilya did not raise a fist in return, he bumped it against Ilya's arm. Ilya wanted to hate him, but the force of J.T.'s enthusiasm was hard to deny. "Catch you later," J.T. said, and he spun off into the crowd, and when Ilya finally had a chance to look for Sadie, her desk was empty.

By the end of eighth period, Ilya was exhausted. His eyelids were a force to be reckoned with. It had been two nights now of little sleep. Five if he counted the nights he'd spent traveling. He hadn't taken a decent shit since arriving. He could only manage to expel these angry, fossilized pellets, and with so little output, eating had become uncomfortable. Plus, Sadie had a boyfriend, a boyfriend charming enough to charm even Ilya, though J.T.'s charm dissipated with time as Ilya roamed the halls trying to find his way back to his locker. In the end, he found the library and slumped in front of a computer monitor. It was the middle of the night at home, but he checked his email anyway, thinking that his mother might have stopped off at the Internet Kebab on her way to work. He had only one email, from Aksinya:

> Have you heard anything from V? I still don't know
> where he's being held or whether he's coming home for
> the trial. Your mom keeps fucking avoiding me and
> your grandma looks at me like I'm a ghost.

I don't know about Lana and Gabe Thompson. He's
been gone for a few months at least. Pavel said the
police sent him home, but Pavel wouldn't know his dick
from a toothpick.

Study hard, smarty. He needs you even more now.

—A

Ilya had no idea who Pavel was or whether the email was good
or bad news. Surely it was more than a coincidence that Gabe had
left Berlozhniki not long after Lana's murder. Ilya tried to remember the last time he'd seen Gabe and could not. Gabe had been part
of life's backdrop, like the nasty-tempered babki who ran the flower
kiosk in the summer and the ancient, one-armed dedok who bore
the flag in the Defender of the Fatherland parade each year. The
dedok who, Ilya had to admit, had been dead for several years before Ilya noticed. And the fact that the police had been involved
seemed especially hard to parse. Had they suspected Gabe too and
decided that getting him out of Berlozhniki was easier than reopen-
ing the investigation? Or had they just gotten tired of dragging
Gabe back up to the Hotel Berlozhniki every time the temperature
got below minus ten?

Why the police? Ilya wrote. He clicked send, hoisted his book bag
onto his shoulder, and went back into the halls in search of his
locker. Half an hour later, Miss Janet found him slumped against it,
waiting for Sadie to finish track practice.

"You'll get scoliosis if you keep sitting like that," she said, and
she ushered him to the front office and set him up at an empty
desk that had belonged to another secretary. "Principal Gibbons no

longer needed her," Miss Janet said, with this swell of pride in her voice.

Ilya was afraid that Miss Janet was the sort who would chatter nonstop, who sought out quiet types because they offered the least resistance to verbal barrages, but once Ilya opened his chemistry textbook and began a problem set, she unwrapped a sandwich swaddled in tinfoil, and they settled into a companionable silence that she broke only once, to say, "It must be so strange waking up here. Half a world away from home."

Home, Ilya thought. *The police sent him home*, which, of course, meant here.

"It is. It's very strange," Ilya said. He looked at Miss Janet, who was considering the last bite of her sandwich. "How would you find someone in America?" he said. He tried to keep his voice nonchalant, like finding this person was not at all crucial, like the prospect of it was not burning through his veins with the power of a drug.

"Find someone? Like in Leffie?"

Ilya nodded.

"You'd look online. In the White Pages," Miss Janet said.

"The White Pages?"

"Yeah, the White Pages, the Yellow Pages. They were actual books—I'm aging myself—but now they're databases." Miss Janet sucked the tip of a finger and dabbed, absently, at stray sandwich crumbs.

"But what if you don't know where he is?" Ilya said.

"Well, who is he?" Miss Janet said.

"He's this American who came to my town on a mission, only I can't remember where he's from."

"I guess you could search state by state," she said. "What kind of mission was it?"

"He wanted to convert us," Ilya said. He thought of Gabe, pleading with them for a minute of their time, for a chance to be saved, and the way that his pleas had gone from earnest to angry and had seemed, eventually, like rants.

"I figured that," Miss Janet said. "But convert you to what? Was he Baptist?"

Ilya shook his head, thinking of Papa Cam, who hadn't been allowed to dance or date or drink soda. "The Church of Later Day Saints," Ilya said.

Miss Janet smiled. "It's not 'later,'" she said. "It's 'latter,' like a ladder that you climb."

"Ladder. Latter," Ilya said, and out of habit his hand drifted to his back pocket, where he used to keep his notebook of unknown words, but he'd memorized all the words in it and left the notebook in Berlozhniki.

"So he's Mormon. I don't know much about Mormons, but I'm pretty sure there aren't any in Leffie," she said. She crushed the tinfoil into a tight ball and tossed it into the trash can under her desk. At home, they did not throw away tinfoil. Babushka rinsed it and hung it to dry on the laundry line, as did everyone else in the kommunalkas. And sometimes, when Ilya was walking home from school and the sun hit the balconies just right, the whole building seemed to sparkle.

Chapter Ten

Ilya woke the morning after the windstorm with the last bits of a dream melting in his mind the way sugar melts on your tongue. Had all of it—Maria Mikhailovna's visit, the exchange program, America—been a dream? The heat was back on. All of the candles had burned down to nubs overnight. Frozen wax puddled on the countertops and windowsills. Babushka was chipping away at it with a spoon and collecting the shavings in a pot. Ilya watched her for a moment, then he sat up.

"Is it true?" he said.

Babushka nodded. She put the pot on the stove, walked over to the couch, and sat on its edge. "When I woke up this morning, for the first time in my life, I was thankful that your grandfather is with God instead of with me. Do you know why?"

Ilya shook his head. She leaned over him, the way she used to when he and Vladimir were little and still got good night kisses. She was beautiful as grandmothers go. Her spine was straight, her eyes clear and blue. She did not have any of the terrible and obvious signs of age—the knobs and growths, the shaking—but still it scared him to really examine her. Her veins were too apparent. Loose skin fringed her jaw like melting wax and every once in a while her voice slowed as she spoke, as though her brain were limping toward the end of the sentence.

"Why?" he said.

"Because he wouldn't have let you go. America. Not in a million years. You suffer for a country, and either you find a way to love it or you go crazy. He found a way to love it. Even here." Ilya's grandfather had been in the camp for seven years. The day after he'd gotten out, he'd taken the son he'd never met fishing. The day after that he'd gone to party headquarters and begged for his membership to be reinstated. "But it's different now," she said. "It's allowed."

"Yes, it's allowed," Ilya said, gently. In theory he understood her awe, but it still seemed misplaced. The miracle wasn't that someone was allowed to go to America, but that *he* had been chosen. "I dreamt of flying there," he said, because a piece of the dream had come back to him. He'd been up in a plane, and the stewardesses' faces all came straight out of *Michael & Stephanie*. They were a rainbow of races, but somehow identical, just like Stephanie's friends, and they had taken turns offering him sodas and blankets and bonbons with the simple diction of the Level I tapes.

"Listen," she said, "you're smart—I know that, that you're smart and that you work hard—but you're lucky too. There aren't places for everyone in this world."

He knew what she meant, knew that she was thinking of Vladimir, who had left before Maria Mikhailovna, while the windstorm was still raging outside. Ilya winced at the thought. Worry seeped into his brain, and then annoyance, at the way his happiness always had to be alloyed by Vladimir.

He was still dressed in a half-dozen layers from the night before, and all of a sudden he felt clammy, suffocated. His tongue thick and furred in his mouth. He needed to wash his face and piss before Marina Kabayeva began her endless ablutions in the bathroom. He needed to get to school, to see Maria Mikhailovna and have the reality of it all confirmed, but he could see that Babushka hadn't gotten across whatever point she'd intended, or that, if she had, it hadn't had the desired impact.

"Babulya," he said, "what if I could go to university there? Get a job there. Bring you all over."

"Sure, with your grandfather haunting me the whole way." The pot of wax began to make wet, popping sounds on the stove.

"Go on," Babushka said. "You can't start being late now."

Ilya washed, dressed, and was out the door faster than he'd ever been before. The stairwell seemed strangely silent without the wind. The air was thin and too easy to move through. Outside, the storm had raked the snow, made hard ridges like ribs on its surface. On the road that ringed the kommunalkas, an old fir tree had split in two. It had been there for all of Ilya's life, and now its insides were exposed, a yellow so bright in all that white that it was unseemly, as though someone had dragged a highlighter across a blank page. The storm had rearranged the playground at the primary school. Snow splashed up the slide. The seesaw had been ripped off its mooring and flung into the parking lot and the swings were so twisted and tangled that they dangled out of reach.

Ilya took it all in with a new, distant sense of wonder. This world wouldn't be his for long, he thought, and another piece of his dream came to him: the plane had landed, and it was only when the stewardesses paraded down the aisle and up the gangway that Ilya had noticed that he was the only passenger. In the dream, this seemed natural to him, a source of pride even, like he was Fyodor Fetisov and the plane was his own private jet. He didn't have any bags, and he walked past row after row of empty seats toward the cockpit, which was empty too. The cockpit door was open, and Ilya could see panels of buttons and screens and the windshield, which was lit up by the shine of the American sun. For a second he'd basked in its glow, but then he'd heard a voice calling him from back down the aisle. And in one of those rare moments when your dream self listens to your rational self, he'd ignored the voice. It was speaking Russian, and he'd told himself he didn't understand it. He'd studied the glint of sunlight against glass and walked off the plane.

"What's wrong?" This voice was real and came from close enough to startle. It was Lana. She was in a miniskirt and heels. The girls all wore things like this despite the weather, as though their vanity were insulation enough, but Lana was visibly cold. Goosebumps brailled her thighs, and her cheeks were grayish-blue.

"Nothing. Actually I'm good," Ilya said. He wanted to tell her the news about America, but Maria Mikhailovna had asked them all to wait until after he'd taken the boards and the exchange was officially announced at the Winter Festival in March.

"Good for you," she said, her eyebrows pulling together like he'd said something unseemly. "Did Vlad walk you?"

He shook his head. There was a clump of what looked like eyelashes stuck to one of her cheeks. This was mysterious and slightly repulsive, one of those things about girls that Ilya filed in his mind for later exploration. She dug in her purse for a pack of cigarettes and lit one.

"So he's not in there?" She arched her neck in the direction of School #17. The wind had blown snow against the building, covering the front steps and the first-floor windows entirely. Ilya could already feel what the light would be like inside, the bottled-up, pinkish cast it took on when the snow was this high. It was late—three minutes until the first bell—and the stragglers were picking their way through narrow paths dug out of the snowbanks.

Ilya shook his head again.

"What about Sergey?" she said.

"I don't know," Ilya said. "Are you going?"

"I doubt it," Lana said. She ran a finger over her lips, as though she were thinking of kissing him or remembering kissing someone else.

"How do you say 'I love you' in English?" she said.

Ilya blushed. He wondered if somehow America had already seeped into his appearance and altered his aspect, whether it had made him noticeable to girls, lovable even.

"I love you," he said, in English.

"I love you," she said, sounding out the phrase with such unabashed awkwardness that he knew it was not meant for him. "Is that right?"

He nodded. "I'm gonna be late," he said, just as Sergey loped up.

"Let's get the fuck out of here," Sergey said.

Sergey was squat and meaty, his face perpetually sullen until something made him laugh and his cheeks dipped into folds like a puppy's. Ilya used to be comfortable with him, but they'd lost that ease recently. Or maybe it wasn't recent. Maybe it had been months since Ilya had seen Sergey laugh.

"Sure," Lana said, and then, to Ilya, "You better get in there." She took another drag of her cigarette, dropped it into the snow, and wobbled off with Sergey, her heels sliding and clacking on the icy sidewalk.

In preparation for the boards, Maria Mikhailovna began tutoring Ilya after school and during lunch. She had the same lunch every day—a row of sprats in a tin—and afterward her lips were shiny with oil and her breath smelled like Ilya imagined the ocean might. Everything she said came with this tiny puff of salt. Ilya was trying to master the defective verbs, the ones that did not have a past tense, and he found himself conjugating all the time: as he walked through the halls at School #17, as he brushed his teeth in the communal bathroom. *I can. I could. I must. I should.* He'd spit toothpaste into the sink and in the hallway someone would yell for him to hurry up, and he'd realize that his gums were bloody from brushing so long.

Vladimir had not been home since the night Maria Mikhailovna announced the exchange. Ilya was rarely home himself. Between school and tutoring, it was dark when he arrived at school and dark when he came home, and it was easy not to think of Vladimir as gone. His absence wasn't anything so dramatic. Plus, Ilya saw him around: sitting on a bench at the old bus stop with Aksinya straddling him, her butt pushing at the seams of her jeans; in the passenger seat of a car, sputtering off the square; smoking outside Dolls. Ilya didn't hesitate in these moments. He'd raise a hand, yell Vladimir's name, and Vladimir would wave back, would yell from the window of a car, "I'll swing by tomorrow," only he never did, and as weeks passed this tiny distance between them grew. Ilya would never have imagined it possible, but there it was, and the next time he saw Vladimir through the glass at the Minutka, he did hesitate, and instead of stopping, he walked a little faster until he'd rounded the corner toward home.

That winter, School #17 went electric with talk of a new drug. Rumors hummed in the halls. *Krokodil* the kids called it, and the cooler of them said it in English: *crocodile.* They said the high was like an endless orgasm, like all of your best dreams rolled into one. They said it was like living in your memories, like being back in the womb. They said you could die from one hit. That it turned your skin to scales. Some said a soldier, fresh off a stint in Chechnya, had brought the recipe to town. Some said Aksinya's sister's pimp had showed her how to cook it and that it was all the rage in Moscow. Others said that Sasha Blazhenov had invented it with nothing but the shit his mother kept under the kitchen sink.

Ilya learned of krokodil slowly. There was no moment when he didn't know and then did. For some kids, the Vladimirs and Sergeys and Aksinyas of the world, life developed quickly. A Polaroid shaken. A world clarified. But without Vladimir, knowledge of the nonacademic sort came gradually to Ilya, if at all. He had to rely on overhearing and observing—conversations snipped by the open and shut of the girls' bathroom; the grunts and nods and gestures of boys. When girls said it, their lips looped around the word. *Krok-o-dil*. Each syllable marked off like the tock-tick-tock of a clock. A word made for hand clapping, for dancing, for music with a beat. From boys, it came out as something sly, a long glint of a word like a knife glimpsed in a waistband.

The worst kids disappeared from school first, like they'd run through a sieve meant to separate them from what was worth keeping, and the teachers seemed more relieved than concerned. Ilya told himself it had nothing to do with him. Less than a year from now, he'd be in America. He'd pictured himself in that big-bellied plane so many times that thinking of it felt like remembering. He'd sit by a window, and as Berlozhniki grew smaller, he'd grow larger. He'd fill out his skin. Start to exist.

With Maria Mikhailovna, he practiced his idioms. *Go for broke. Good riddance. Grasping at straws.* He practiced ordering at an imaginary McDonald's. Over and over he said the word "extra-large."

"In America, you order an extra-large even if you're not hungry," Maria Mikhailovna said. "It's a custom."

"Hello, sir," she said. "What may I prepare for you to eat today?"

"I'll have an extra-large hamburger with an extra-large french fry, please," Ilya said. "And please an extra-large Coca-Cola." But that other word—krokodil—snuck in, hijacking his mind, and there was nothing he could do to stop it. He wanted, desperately, not to know or care. It was clearly the sort of thing one was better off not knowing about, but he knew that the kids disappearing were like Vladimir. If they had heard of krokodil, Vladimir had tried it. If they had tried it, Vladimir was hooked.

Aksinya and Lana were rarely at school, and then never. Aksinya left a coat of hers hanging on a hook in Maria Mikhailovna's classroom, and every day during tutoring, Ilya stared at it. He didn't know whether he wanted her to claim it or not. It was the same green as the larch trees, with a hood trimmed in fake fur and grime on the cuffs. It smelled of ancient cigarettes and mildew. He'd seen her in it dozens of times. He'd watched Vladimir unzip it. He'd watched her smoke in it, with the hood up and the fur edging her forehead like bangs. It was the only coat he'd ever seen her in, and they were deep in winter now—a bad winter; the snow had completely covered the crosses that ringed the camp—and Ilya couldn't think what she was doing without it.

Once, Maria Mikhailovna caught him staring at it.

"I think it's Aksinya's," she said. "She must have gotten a new one."

Ilya nodded. Maybe she had. Maybe the same man who pimped her sister kept her and Lana now too. He might buy them new coats and perfume and high heels—all the things girls wanted but didn't need. Those were the things Stephanie bought, in *The Adventures of*

Michael & Stephanie, when Michael took her to the shopping mall. But Aksinya was tougher than Stephanie, tougher than her sister. She wore a T-shirt with a pig roasting on a spit, and the pig had CAPATLISM carved across its belly. Spelled like that. Spelled wrong, but Ilya hadn't told her, nor had he thought it stupid. Plus, Aksinya loved Vladimir at least enough not to fuck other guys.

"Do you know where she is?" Maria Mikhailovna said.

Ilya shook his head. He could feel his eyes starting to burn, though he wasn't sure why. He thought of Babushka and the way she apologized for crying sometimes, saying that it wasn't her fault, that her eyes were just old.

"She'll be back," Maria Mikhailovna said. "She's too smart to give up for good."

Vladimir wasn't dumb, Ilya thought, but that hadn't stopped him from giving up on school. Or maybe that was the definition of being dumb.

"Ilya?"

She waited until Ilya looked at her to go on. "Why don't you come to dinner at my house? Saturday night? My husband would love to meet you. And we can celebrate."

"But I haven't passed the boards yet."

"I know," she said, "but this winter we need an excuse to celebrate, right? And you will pass them."

"OK," Ilya said.

"Good," she said, "that's settled," and she scooted a piece of paper over the expanse of desk between them. English contractions were typed in neat rows:

she's = she is
there's = there is

it's = it is

hadn't = had not

"What's the difference between a contraction and the possessive?" she said. He watched her lips move in the spastic way they did when she spoke English. Like the words were sharp and hard to maneuver. He thought of Lana's lips. How they paled in the cold. He imagined them opening, singing, "Krok-o-dil."

"A contraction," Maria Mikhailovna said, "and the possessive."

"A contraction is a combination of two words. And a possessive shows ownership."

"How do you form one?" She leaned back, and her glasses caught the overhead light.

"With a hook."

"A hook?" she said, smiling. She curled a finger, slashed the air with it.

"An apostrophe."

"Good. Now use 'there's' in a sentence."

There's a new drug, he thought. *There's* nobody left.

"There's America," he said. He'd have his nose against the window. He'd see it for the first time at night. The lights would be bright enough to blanken his mind, and he'd feel nothing but right.

"Again."

"There's nothing in the cupboard."

"Good," she said, "but you don't say the 'p' in cupboard. It's quiet."

Silent, not quiet, he thought, but he nodded and wrote "cupboard" in his notebook, the last in a list of words he'd practice that night. He'd say them over and over until his voice had smoothed out all the bumps, and sometimes as his mother wiped down the table, he'd hear her murmuring them too.

Later, when Maria Mikhailovna took one of her bathroom trips, Ilya yanked Aksinya's coat from the wall and stuffed it into his backpack. The backpack bulged, and fur sprouted from the zipper, but Maria Mikhailovna didn't seem to notice. When they'd finished for the day, she turned out the lights and locked the classroom. They walked through the school's empty corridors, and their footsteps sounded out a slow beat. It was strange, he thought, that she was the one person in the world that he spent the most time with. This tiny woman with the plain face and the pretty smile. They pushed through the main doors and out into the cold. It was four-thirty and pitch black. Maria Mikhailovna's glasses fogged, and she swiped at them with her mittens, smiling apologetically.

"So this weekend," she said, "we'll see you for supper."

It was around this time—December of Ilya's last winter in Berlozhniki—that a body was found in a snowbank on Ulitsa Gornyakov.

Seventy years earlier, prisoners had laid Ulitsa Gornyakov, pouring hot asphalt down the gentle slope from Berlozhniki, past the mines, to the camp. Over the years, through the Great War, through Brezhnev and glasnost, through seventy freezes, the asphalt had cracked and furled and canted until it jarred even the sturdiest of axles. Then the refinery was built, and the road was dug up. It was widened and smoothed so that two tankers could pass with a meter margin. Most of the roads in Berlozhniki disappeared under snow each winter, leaving the buildings lonely and illogical without their connections, but Gazneft cleared Ulitsa Gornyakov religiously, and the body was found by a plower named Mikhail Tukhachevsky early one morning.

Mikhail Tukhachevsky told the *Vecherniye Berlozhniki* that each type of snow feels different to the plow. There is snow that's crusted with ice, which makes the plow buck then dip, buck then dip. Wet snow is heavy enough to drive the plow toward the shoulder, heavy enough to have your forearms aching at the end of a shift from holding the wheel straight. And then there is pillow snow, Tukhachevsky said. Light and dry, easy as breathing. It had been pillow snow that morning, and so Mikhail Tukhachevsky had noticed the instant the plow took on weight, dragged left, and went light again. He climbed down from the cab and circled back behind the truck. In the red of his taillights he saw a woman's leg slanting up out of the snow. Straight up, he said, like a joke, except that she was barefoot, and so he'd known that she was dead. He dug for her face anyway, just to be sure.

Her name was Yulia Podtochina. If someone had not left the paper in the communal bathroom, Ilya would not have even read the article. If Yulia Podtochina had not worked at the refinery, he would not have taken much notice. There were a few deaths from exposure every year in Berlozhniki, drunks or junkies who got confused about where home was and wandered the wrong way. But Yulia worked at the cafeteria in the refinery: fitting the hot trays into their metal frames, wiping down tables, mixing the soda water and soda syrup in the machines, doling out pelmeni and cutlets to the neftyaniki. She had his mother's exact job, except that she worked the opposite shift. She slept while his mother worked; she worked while his mother slept. She was like his mother's shadow, in a way, and they were joined by that one moment each afternoon when their buses passed on Ulitsa Gornyakov, and each driver pressed the horn, and the two blasts were sharp and short in the cold.

She had been murdered. *Killed with violent intent,* the paper said, though how someone could be killed without violent intent, Ilya wasn't sure. There weren't any more details about her death, but the little Ilya read about her was a relief to him because it quickly became clear that she was nothing like his mother. Yulia Podtochina was young. Only twenty-four. She'd grown up in Arkhangelsk and moved to Berlozhniki two years ago. She was married to a childhood sweetheart who still lived in Arkhangelsk, working the ice barges. The paper had not been able to reach her husband for comment, and according to a cousin of Yulia's who lived in Berlozhniki, she and her husband hadn't seen each other in over a year.

One Friday after work, Yulia was supposed to meet up with this cousin—they were going to get a drink at Dolls—but when she didn't show, her cousin didn't worry. Their plans had been loose, and Yulia had friends at work, friends from her building, friends everywhere, it seemed, and her cousin figured that she'd found a better party. That Friday, she hadn't boarded the bus with her colleagues. She told them that she wanted to walk home, which was strange, but not unheard of. The cold had abated a bit that afternoon—the pillow snow wouldn't begin until that night—and it was only five kilometers to the kommunalkas and three more to town. Yulia set out. The departing bus passed her just outside the refinery gates, and a few people on the arriving bus—Ilya's mother's bus—saw her halfway to town, by the Tower, a cigarette in one hand and her cell phone in the other, and that was it. No one worried about her. No one called the police. She was missing for only a day before Mikhail Tukhachevsky felt her weight on his plow.

The picture of her was from her wedding day. She was in a white minidress, tight as a tourniquet, and white platform heels. Her legs were scrunched together at the knees like she was freezing cold, and a man's Adidas jacket was draped over her shoulders. Her hair was curled and piled on her head. A papier-mâché dove stuck out of it like a cocktail decoration. She had a shy sort of smile, but there was a gloss to her cheeks and eyes that suggested that she wasn't all that shy. She was pretty. *Pretty enough* was the thought that popped into Ilya's mind when he looked at her, though he felt guilty thinking it, because he wasn't even sure what he meant by *enough* and because she was dead. No one was in custody for the crime, and the police were pursuing all leads. Any information about the crime was to be reported to the Berlozhniki police department.

"Why would she walk home dressed like that?" Babushka said, when Ilya showed her the article.

"She wasn't wearing that when she walked home," Ilya said. "That's her wedding dress."

"Her wedding dress?! Case closed! You walk around in a dress that short and bad things happen."

"She didn't walk around in that," Ilya said. "She got married in it."

"Even worse!" Babushka said.

He asked his mother if she'd seen Yulia from the bus that day, and his mother had shaken her head and said, "She was a nice girl. But too dreamy. She served the golubtsy once and it was so frozen on the inside that Igor Zubkov chipped a tooth. She was a kid, you know. Into things."

Ilya didn't say anything. Since Vladimir had left, there was a new wistfulness to the way his mother spoke about kids, like the things they got into were inevitable.

In the communal kitchen, over the steam and bubble of their soup pots, the babki said that it was strange that she hadn't seen her husband in a year. They said it was strange that she'd been found so close to the Tower.

In the bathroom line, old men talked about how in winters like this one the spirits woke. They talked about the brothers who had jumped to their deaths off the top of Ilya's building, about how many prisoners hadn't been properly buried. They talked about how the snow had covered the crosses completely. They said the road was built on death and that ancient anger doesn't die. A spirit had killed Yulia, they said. A guard or a prisoner, depending on who was talking and whether their ancestors had been guards or prisoners.

Ilya read everything about Yulia that he could find. A later article reported that she'd been stabbed, that her cheeks had been slashed. The Berlozhniki police finally managed to get in touch with her husband—he'd been out on an ice ship for months and knew nothing of her death. All he could offer was that Yulia was a partier and had gotten into some stuff that he didn't approve of. After that, there were no leads and no new details released.

A week later a teenager was attacked by a bear outside of Syktyvkar, and there was an outbreak of listeria from some baloney sold at the Minutka, and the mayor began his reelection campaign. Posters of him were hung from all the light posts on the square, and he rode in circles around the kommunalkas, shouting into a loudspeaker about how Berlozhniki's time had come, about how Berlozhniki's youth needed to stay and procreate, and Yulia was pretty much forgotten.

"That girl?" someone might say. "The one who wasn't from here? Who knows what trouble she got herself into."

CHAPTER ELEVEN

On Ilya's third day at Leffie High, a sexting ring run by a student who posted under the alias Madame Grandedoix was discovered, and the school's collective attention shifted from Ilya to the Madame and didn't look back. Ilya's days settled into a pattern. He spent mornings and evenings online, compiling a list from the White Pages of all the Gabe Thompsons in America and checking the *Vecherniye Berlozhniki* site for news about Vladimir. He looked for news of other murders too, though he knew that the police would find a way of distancing any new murder from the ones for which Vladimir had been arrested just as they had initially insisted that the three murders were unrelated.

Days were devoted to school, and fortunately school in Leffie did not require much more from him than attendance. His science and math classes were remedial; home economics and gym were ridiculous. The English teacher was young and starry-eyed and obsessed with Chekhov, and he seemed willing to forgive any and all mistakes that Ilya made. Principal Gibbons had been right: American History was the hardest class. They were beginning the year with the Revolution, which was the driest revolution Ilya had ever heard of, mostly because it was discussed in such self-congratulatory terms, as though Americans had invented the concept of democracy. The Boston Tea Party. The Continental Congress. Dozens of noblemen in pastel coats and tights. Ilya did not care. Plus Mr. Shilling spoke in a soft drone, like his voice couldn't possibly project through the thicket of his beard, let alone inspire interest. It didn't help that Sadie was in the class. It was impossible to concentrate with her there, her skin lit by the projector's glow, J.T. constantly whispering in her ear.

Each afternoon, while Sadie was at track practice, Ilya trekked through a patch of woods that neighbored Leffie High to Bojangles', used his snack money from the Masons to buy a chicken-and-biscuit meal, and brought it back to the front office. He shared it with Miss Janet and then did his homework while she updated her online dating profiles.

The drives home with Sadie were the high point of his day. In the mornings, she was sleepy-eyed and slow to talk. She clutched a thermos of coffee between her thighs, scanned the radio with one hand, and rarely gave the road her full attention. But in the afternoons she seemed more relaxed, expansive. In the afternoons, she asked him questions—not about Russia, not about spies, or the KGB, or Putin, or vodka, which were the kinds of questions he got daily—these were simple questions about him.

"What do you like to do? For fun, I mean?" she asked one afternoon that first week, when they were driving home in a drizzle. The windshield wipers flicked across the glass, and the car had the damp, stuffy smell that his winter coat used to get when he left it on the radiator to dry.

Ilya thought of Michael and Stephanie. He knew that listening to them would not be anyone else's idea of fun and that his dependence on them was definitely strange and probably unhealthy. Still, it was the closest thing to a hobby that he had. "I listen to tapes," he said.

"Like music? Like Radiohead?" she said.

"Sort of," he said, making a mental note to find a way to listen to Radiohead. "Do you know Kolyan?" he said.

She shook her head.

"He's a rapper. From Russia. Very cool. He has white hair—like yours—and he wears these contacts that make his whole eye white, and he has these tattooed fangs."

"Mama Jamie would love him," she said. Most Americans spoke with this upward lilt, as though every utterance were a question, but Sadie had this deadpan sarcasm that reminded him of home.

"What do you do for fun?" he said.

"I draw."

He nodded. "I saw you drawing in history."

"My secret's out," she said.

"What do you draw?"

"Portraits," she said. "You want to see?"

He nodded, and at the next stop sign she pulled a tiny red note-book out of her backpack. A pencil stub, well chewed, was jammed in the silver spiral. Ilya flipped open the cover. Papa Cam looked out at him from the first page with a sleepy innocence, a vulnera-bility that Ilya saw, now, from the way she'd drawn his eyes, was the essence of him. There was a half-finished sketch of Mama Jamie next, and then a finished one, and they were both of just her face, but still there was this energy to her, this thrust of optimism to her expression that was just right.

"These are good," Ilya said. "The best I can do is a man with a line for his body and a circle for his head."

"A stick man," she said.

"Exactly," he said. He flipped the page again, and there was Marilee, her face a study in scrutiny.

"She hated it," Sadie said.

"But it's her. She looks like she's about to correct you," he said, and Sadie laughed.

He flipped the page again. The next drawing was of him. In history, in that moment when he'd frozen at the front of the class. He glanced over at Sadie, but she was watching the road, fiddling with the windshield wipers. Ilya looked at his face. The lift of his eyebrows and gauntness of his cheeks suggested fear, and he had been afraid, he remembered, but there was also this kinetic quality to his eyes, as though somehow she'd been able to bottle all their infinitesimal movements.

"Do you like it?" she said. "I don't mind if you don't. No one ever likes their own portrait."

He ran a hand over the page, could feel the dips and divots where she'd pressed hard with her pencil. It was him, but it looked like Vladimir too, and no one had ever seen Vladimir in him before. "I do," he said.

It took Aksinya a week to write back and say that she had no fucking clue why the police had taken Gabe Thompson, that the police were not exactly forthcoming, especially not with her. A few days later, Ilya completed his list of all the Gabe Thompsons in America. There were close to a thousand. A hundred in California alone. They all had addresses, and most had phone numbers as well. Ilya imagined himself calling Gabe, or stealing the Masons' car and arriving at his door. What would happen when Gabe opened it? Of course he wouldn't confess outright, but surely Ilya would be able to tell something from his reaction. Seeing Ilya wouldn't mean much to him if the police had booted him out of town for drinking or drugs, but if he'd committed the murders, Ilya and his Russian accent would mean everything.

Ilya had already found a database of Mormon churches online and that night he began the slow process of cross-referencing the addresses and towns with churches within sixty miles. An hour drive would be the limit, even for a zealot like Gabe, Ilya guessed. If there was no church within sixty miles, he crossed that Gabe off the list. He tried to go through ten Gabes a night, tried to make incremental progress the way he used to with his book of American idioms, and once he'd finished doing this and making his usual checks of VKontakte and the *Vecherniye Berlozhniki*, he'd email Vladimir.

I know you didn't do it, he'd write. The same thing every night, and when that started to feel rote, he began to add things about his day: that he'd played American football in gym, that they ate their fries with ketchup here, that American girls never wore high heels to school, that Mama Jamie had a crush on Sting, that Papa Cam drank beer that had purposely had the alcohol removed. Vladimir would not be allowed to check email, Ilya knew, and so before long these emails took on the tone of a diary. He told Vladimir about Sadie, about how in moments it seemed that she liked him but in other moments it seemed that she was completely indifferent to his presence—to *everyone's* presence. He told Vladimir about J.T., about how he was preternaturally developed and looked exactly like Sergey Fedorov in his prime, and how the fuck, he wrote, am I supposed to compete with that? He told Vladimir about the sexting ring, about Pastor Kyle and the way he sometimes made the pulpit seem like a strip pole. He attached the picture of himself that Papa Cam had taken on that first morning of school, looking terrible. *It's hard to sleep here*, he wrote, and what he meant was, it's hard to sleep without you.

Listening to Michael and Stephanie would have helped, but Ilya kept thinking of all the nights when he'd lain in bed and listened to them instead of Vladimir, when Vladimir and his stories had seemed unimportant, an interruption. So Ilya didn't ask the Masons for new batteries, and the tapes gathered dust on the dresser. When he did finally fall asleep, his dreams were horrible. There was Babushka washing the blood off Vladimir. There was the doctor touching Ilya's leg just where he'd cut Vladimir's. He dreamt of the Tower too. Of Lana's hair—those pink streaks—and the way they'd snaked around his face when she kissed him. He saw the grove where she'd been killed, with the crosses nailed into the molting birch bark and the flowers that someone had planted inside an old tire. There was Vladimir, opening up his pencil case and pulling out their mother's silver sugar spoon and holding a lighter under it. There was the stove in the Tower, the flames burning a strange blue, and next to it, Vladimir and Aksinya were fucking, both so high that they'd forgotten shame, and Ilya would wake up sure that he was still there, that he'd never left. Sometimes, in the heights of his nostrils, there was this acid burn as though somehow he'd actually breathed the Tower's air. But bad as the dreams were, he craved them, craved sleep, because they gave him Vladimir. Vladimir's face bent over the spoon. Vladimir's face bent over Aksinya's. Vladimir's face bent over his, saying, "*This* is not for you, bratishka."

Sometimes he managed to sleep through the dreams, to wake up with his pillow reeking of sweat and the light slanting through the deck supports onto that pile of abandoned bicycles. But most nights the dreams would wake him, and he would get out of bed and let his forehead cool against the sliding glass doors until he felt tired enough to try for sleep again.

He was standing like that one night, his forehead slick against the glass, when he saw the shadow of someone climbing down the deck stairs. The silhouette of calves and bare feet. Then Sadie walked past the pool, sat on the alligator wall, and lifted a knee to tie one shoe and then the other.

Ilya opened the basement door. He meant to say her name, but when she didn't turn at the sound of the door, he stayed quiet. She slid off the wall and into the neighboring lot, and it wasn't until he was at the wall, his hand on the bricks where she'd sat, that he realized he was going to follow her. She was a hundred meters away now, small enough to fit in his palm. He jogged after her, the sawgrass stinging his ankles, giving him the shallow, cross-woven cuts that Sadie's ankles had had that first night in America. He tried to be quiet and keep a safe distance. He thought of Jackie Chan, who always stepped toe to heel, and Jean-Claude Van Damme and the way that, despite his bulk, he moved with such stealth.

At the end of Dumaine Drive, a house had been abandoned half built. Tarps were draped in place of walls, the slick plastic shuddering in the dark like an organ, like something that shouldn't be exposed to air. Sadie stopped in the shadow of the house and pulled something out of her pocket. Ilya had assumed that she was going to meet J.T., but as she gripped whatever it was, it occurred to him that it could be drugs. A syringe or a pipe. He waited to see her creep into the half-built house. He thought of Lana high in the Tower. The way her lips had parted, the pink bud of her tongue between them, and how his dick had pulsed at the sight of it. He'd felt a weird sort of power looking at her, an awareness that he could touch her, that he could reach out and hook the hair back behind her ear, that he could go further, even, open her mouth a little wider and push his tongue deep inside it, and he'd wondered if all boys—all men—came upon these sudden pricks of violence in their fantasies. Maybe he was only different from the man who'd killed Yulia and Olga and Lana by a degree, and by the fact that he'd felt powerless, not powerful, knowing that the white puffs of her breath might simply stop. He could already see Sadie's face the same way, and he could feel the same mix of lust and fear and helplessness gathering in him, and he began to walk down the slope of the lot. He didn't know what he'd do, even as the distance between them collapsed, and then whatever she'd pulled from her pocket began to glow. Ilya stopped. It was a phone or an iPod. Her thumb twitched over the screen, and she pulled loose a tangle of headphones, stuck one in each ear, and kept walking.

Ilya gulped the hot, wet air, and let her gain some distance. She took Dumaine Drive to its end, cutting the corner it made with Route 21, and he followed her: past the old fireworks stand where a giant red rocket leaned on one haunch; past a plantation house that floated, gray-blue, down a dirt road; past the hot sauce plant that even at this hour made the air burn, made Ilya's nostrils sting and his eyes water.

She walked the white line religiously, like a child might. Tankers rushed by at steady intervals—the time between them the time it took to fill them—and as each approached, she stepped onto the shoulder and froze and the hair twisted up off her head like pale snakes rising up out of a basket. None of the truckers honked. She and he were too small; it was too dark for them to be anything but an aftersight, something to make the truckers rub their eyes and wonder.

They were headed south. It was the only direction Ilya knew in Leffie because the refinery was at the town's southern edge, and its light grew brighter and brighter as they walked, and even though he knew the light's source, even though it was the one thing here that was completely familiar, his brain kept tripping on the fact, telling him that it was morning already and that they should turn around before Papa Cam and Mama Jamie woke up and found them gone.

Soon it was so bright that if she turned, she'd see him. *Plain as day*, he thought, which was an expression Mama Jamie used that he was still trying to figure out. Sadie did stop every once in a while to change the song on her iPod, but she didn't turn. Then the refinery was right before them. The moonscape of it looked just the same as it had in Berlozhniki, and a memory caught Ilya: his mother holding him at their apartment window, telling him what each constellation of lights was—the high, flashing signal lights; the cluster of the cooling tower; the bright pool of the parking lot; the dim scatter of the administrative buildings; and the fires of the stacks, which from afar looked like crowns.

"That's where I am," she'd said. "There. *Tam*." Her finger had moved along the glass, tracing the low line of lights that was the cafeteria.

He wasn't the sort of child to miss her when she was gone, but still he'd find himself at the window every once in a while, separating lights from the glow. *Tam*, he'd think. Tam.

As they got closer, Ilya saw that the lights were configured differently here. Then they were close enough that Ilya could see the structures themselves: the cooling tower, and the guard booth with the dark blotch of a face inside it. He could see the motion of the fire that plumed from each stack, could see that it didn't look like a crown at all because its shape was always shifting.

Just before the refinery gate, Sadie turned onto a street of trailers. Some seemed permanent, with foundations and concrete walks and flowerbeds and swing sets and Christmas lights, though it was only September. Others seemed like they could be hitched to a truck and moved the next day. The refinery fence stretched behind them, higher than their roofs by a story at least. Plastic bags were caught in the fence, and they glowed like jellyfish in the purple-blue glare.

Sadie had slowed down, and Ilya matched her pace. When she stopped completely it was at one of the few trailers with a light on. This trailer had become part of the landscape against its will. A meaty vine enveloped one wall. The cinderblocks that held up each corner had sunk unevenly into the dirt yard, so the trailer listed slightly toward the refinery, as though taking a knee. J.T. would be inside, he thought. Or else it was a neftyanik—a roughneck, they called them here—with muscles and stubble and hands big enough to encircle Sadie's waist.

There was a path through the dirt yard, shiny as a scar, that led to the door, but Sadie stayed on the sidewalk, her hands in the pockets of her sweatshirt, her eyes on the window. Whoever was inside stayed inside. Ilya wasn't close enough to see into the window, and so he crept past Sadie on the opposite side of the street, trying to keep to the shadows of spindly trees and parked trucks. He hunched next to a car under a portico. Sadie was completely still, standing there in the shadow of the trailer. He wanted to see her expression, to know what this was. A vigil, he found himself thinking, and he could smell the wax on Babushka's fingers, could hear the crack of her knees that meant she'd spent the day at the church, lighting candles for Dedushka and Papa and Vladimir.

Ilya kept waiting for the door to open or for a car to pull up, but after thirty minutes—or maybe it was longer, maybe it was an hour; the light made it hard to measure time—Sadie left. She walked back the way she'd come, and Ilya crossed the street and stood in the spot where she'd stood and looked in the window just as she had.

A woman was sitting inside on a couch. She looked a little like Yulia Podtochina, with her blond hair and her wide-set eyes. Or maybe it was just her air of hopelessness that reminded him of Yulia. She was braless, her breasts tiny, nipples aggressive and pressing at the thin cotton of a tank top. Her feet were tucked up under her, and she was watching something on TV that made her smile in a wry sort of way, like she'd been in the characters' shoes, knew just what sorts of problems they were facing, and knew too that they didn't stand a chance.

Hanging askew behind her head was a poster of a woman standing over a vent, her white dress blowing up to her crotch. A pack of cigarettes rested on the arm of the couch. The woman smoked one, letting the ash get long. She hunched forward, out of Ilya's view, and for a minute all he could see was the top of her head, and then she reclined again with a pink glass pipe in her hand. She put her lips to it, lit it, took a hit, then another, all the while keeping her attention on the show. Her face relaxed. It lost the wryness and the hopelessness, and, as Ilya watched, the drug animated her. It brought a beauty to her wide mouth, a flush to her cheeks, and glitter to her eyes.

He was about to go when he heard the woman's voice.

"Come on," she said, in a croak that gained strength. "Come the fuck on."

She stood and stepped toward the window, and for a second Ilya thought that she'd seen him and was about to confront him. He stumbled back into the street, just as she reached out and gave the TV a thwack.

"That's what I thought," she said, with a tone like she'd wrangled an especially difficult child into submission.

Ilya was back at the Masons' an hour later. The house was quiet and dark, and he wondered if Sadie was sleeping or awake and thinking of the woman. Who was the woman to her? He thought of the drug and the way it had seemed to bring her to life; he thought of Sadie's empty room, the black cross over her bed, her nails bitten to nubs, the pages and pages of portraits. He knew that it should not have come as a surprise to him that Sadie had secrets, but his own secrets had made him myopic, made him forget that the world, even America, was a tangle of lives, all twisted and bent.

CHAPTER TWELVE

M aria Mikhailovna's building was on the square, one of the new ones that had gone up along with the refinery, when it seemed as though Berlozhniki's time had finally come. It was tall and slim in defiance of the squat practicality of the kommunalkas, and it was the only building in Berlozhniki with an elevator. When Vladimir and Ilya were young, before Ilya knew a word of English, they would lurk outside the building. If the custodian left the service door propped open after his afternoon smoke, they'd sneak in and ride the elevator. What a thrill it was, to press a button and see it light up, to hear a whoosh and feel the ground move under your feet. Usually they'd have five minutes, maybe ten, before the custodian kicked them out, calling them little thugs or golovorezy, which did not have the sting he intended because Vladimir and all of his friends wanted, badly, to be gangsters.

One afternoon, when the custodian seemed to have disappeared altogether, they snuck in and pressed a button with *PH* on it. The elevator climbed and climbed and then it dinged and the doors parted to reveal another door made of thick, brushed metal.

"Where's the hall?" Ilya had asked.

"It's the penthouse. Some badass has the whole floor," Vladimir said. He reached out and touched the door. "Bet you anything it's bulletproof."

The elevator hesitated there, shaking slightly, and then it dinged and the doors slid shut, and it descended again. In awe over the revelation that one individual might own an entire floor, they didn't immediately realize that the L button was glowing and that the elevator was not descending of its own accord. It had been summoned. The floors whizzed by, and this was usually Ilya's favorite part of the ride, when it seemed like the elevator could not possibly stop in time, and a delicious terror would fly up his spine. But the terror was not delicious this time. Vladimir began madly pressing buttons, trying to pick a floor that they hadn't already passed, but the elevator was quicker than him. Then it slowed, its cables smooth and silent, and stopped. The L above the door lit up. The elevator dinged once more, this beautiful impassive note, and the doors opened.

Ilya saw the man's shoes first—slick and pointy and dark green, like they had been made with the skin of some fantastic jungle snake. On each there was a thin metal buckle shaped like a bone. He was in a suit, an anomaly in Berlozhniki, and an overcoat. Ilya did not see his face—there wasn't time, because as the man stepped into the elevator, Ilya darted past him and ran for the door. Vladimir was behind him for a second, but the man must have caught him, because by the time Ilya yanked open the service door, he was alone.

"Vlad!" Ilya yelled, just as Vladimir staggered out of the elevator.

Ilya heard the man say "Scum," softly, and then the doors slid shut.

Under Vladimir's eye, blood pearled from a long cut, and as they pushed through the door and out into the snow, the blood began to roll down his cheek in fat droplets.

"He hit you?" Ilya said.

Vladimir winced and wiped at his cheek with the cuff of his sweatshirt. "He had this fucking ring on. With this fat diamond."

Ilya had never seen Vladimir hurt before, not really, and his anger was sharp and sudden, a pain in his belly as though the man had cut him there. "Let's get him back," Ilya said. "Put shit in the elevator, or—"

"Nah," Vladimir said, "let's go."

Once they'd rounded the corner and the building was out of sight, Vladimir squatted down so that his eyes were level with Ilya's. He turned and showed Ilya his cheek. Up close the cut was messy, the flesh snagged, the skin around it fattening. "Clean me up," Vladimir said. "I don't want Babushka freaking out."

So Ilya melted snow in his palm, wet the cuff of his sweatshirt, and dabbed the blood away as gently as he could.

"You know what?" Ilya said.

Vladimir shook his head.

"He's probably still in the elevator. You pressed every fucking button."

"It'll take him an hour to get to the top," Vladimir said, smiling. Somehow he'd decided that the man lived in the penthouse.

That had been a decade ago, but as Ilya pressed the button to call the elevator, he had the strange sense that the man would still be in it, the panel ablaze, every button lit, as though he'd been trapped there in life just as he had been in Ilya's memory. The *PH* button *was* still there, and Ilya was tempted, but he pushed the 7 for Maria Mikhailovna's floor. The button lit up, the elevator whirred and lifted, and Ilya felt a bit of that old thrill, or he remembered it, which was not so different.

"I'm making macaroni and cheese," Maria Mikhailovna said when she opened the door. "And french fries and apple pie. To celebrate. I had to use syr though, and the Americans use American cheese, so it won't be quite authentic."

"American cheese," a voice said behind her. "That's got to be an oxymoron."

Maria Mikhailovna smiled and stepped aside to reveal a small, fair man—barely bigger than she was—with glasses identical to hers. Her husband was a policeman, Ilya knew, but he didn't look the part. From the way Vladimir talked about policemen, Ilya had assumed that they were universally terrible, that they lived to spoil fun and besmirch human rights, infractions that Vladimir gave equal weight, but Maria Mikhailovna's husband had this lively expression, his cheeks high and bright, like they were readying themselves for a laugh.

"Dmitri Ivanovich," he said, and he held a hand out, and Ilya shook it.

"The cynic," Maria Mikhailovna said. She had a glass of wine in her hand, and there was a shine to her voice that it didn't have in the classroom. Ilya wondered if it was because he wasn't used to hearing her speak Russian or if she was truly that excited to have him here.

"I know you two would rather be speaking English, but mine's no good," Dmitri said.

"No," Maria Mikhailovna said, "it's worse than no good. It's hopeless. He only knows the words he shouldn't, Ilya. I've tried to teach him, but he has such trouble paying attention."

"It's true," Dmitri said. "When I was young, English was just a liability."

Maria Mikhailovna ushered Ilya inside. Her apartment was not much larger than Ilya's, but it was much nicer, and only she and Dmitri lived there. In the living room, there was an enormous single-pane window with a view down Ulitsa Lenina so clear that it was as though the glass did not exist. Windows in the kommunalkas were often papered over in the winter, rags stuffed in the gaps in the sill, and still the cold seeped in, but Maria Mikhailovna's apartment was warm. There was the whoosh of central air, like they were inside a living, breathing lung, and the light had this rich, amber glow that came, Ilya realized, from lampshades.

Dmitri was putting a CD into a stereo flanked on all sides by bookcases. The CD clicked and the sound of some stringed instrument floated into the air, and the notes were so clear and singular and free of static that they made Ilya feel as though he were hearing music for the first time. Their tree was already up for New Year's, the branches drooping with tiny glass snow maidens and wooden stars, and its lights were doubled in the window.

Ilya imagined Vladimir taking all this in—the tray of radishes and bread and butter, the tiny bowl of caviar, the pretty light, and the kvass that Maria Mikhailovna was handing him now, in a glass that looked like it was made of crystal. Vladimir would mock it all, no doubt. He'd want something stronger to drink; he'd ask if they had any rap or punk or club music.

"It's so hard for me to believe that you two haven't met," Maria Mikhailovna said. She took her husband's hand, and Ilya could see that for a moment she wanted to take his hand too. Her generosity had been a part of his life for so long that he hardly thought about it, and it occurred to him now that perhaps he gave her something too. She and her husband looked small under these high ceilings, and he wondered if they had wanted children of their own, whether that was something they'd had to give up on.

"I've heard a lot about you, Ilya Alexandrovich," Dmitri said. "You've made Maria very proud."

"I hope I do as well as she expects," Ilya said.

"You'll do wonderfully," she said. "I have a surprise tonight— besides the macaroni and cheese—I've gotten the surname of the host family." She waited a second, her eyes bright. "The Ma-sons."

"Ma-sons," Ilya said.

"It's spelled like 'ma' and 'sons' put together."

"What are their given names?"

"Cam and Jamie. Only I can't figure out who's the man and who's the woman." Maria Mikhailovna giggled.

"Come-on jam-eee," Dmitri said. "There are no patronymics?"

"No, sweetheart," she said. "That would certainly make it easier, wouldn't it?"

"Jamie has to be the man," Ilya said. "A diminutive for James. Like James Bond. King James."

"Maybe, but 'Cam'? It's manly for a woman, no?" Maria Mikhailovna said. "And they have three children."

Ilya had tried over and over to imagine what his host family might be like. Sometimes he pictured Michael and Stephanie waiting for him in the airport. Stephanie would be holding a picnic basket, her breasts as pointy as ever in her sweater, and she'd suggest that they go to the beach for the day, and Michael in his glasses would agree. Sometimes it'd be Jean-Claude and his girlfriend from the unlabeled VHS, their lives happily domestic now that Jean-Claude had defeated the mob boss. He'd never imagined kids, though, and he didn't know whether the idea thrilled him or terrified him.

"What are the children's names?" Ilya said.

"They didn't say."

"Probably equally ugly," Dmitri said. "Are you hoping for girls? Full immersion, right?"

Ilya's cheeks prickled at the thought of living in a house with an American girl and all the intimacy that entailed: eating off the same plates, showering in the same shower.

"Dmitri," Maria Mikhailovna said. "He's not there to meet girls."

"Of course he is," Dmitri said.

In the kitchen, a buzzer sounded, and Maria Mikhailovna leapt up and ran for the stove.

Dmitri leaned toward Ilya and put a hand on his thigh, and his posture reminded Ilya of pictures he'd seen of politicians in the thick of deals. "I bought us frozen pelmeni," he said, "just in case the macaroni doesn't work out."

Ilya laughed. "Whatever it is will be better than what my mother makes. She cooks everything 'til it's carcinogenic."

"That sounds like my mother, which is probably why she has cancer. That or the cigarettes," Dmitri said. His expression was the same: still that jolly, cherubic look that made Ilya feel in turns relaxed and like he was somehow a source of amusement. "You know I'm from here too," he said, "not like Maria, not a cultured city kid."

"You were born here?"

"Born and bred." He hummed a few notes of "My Berlozhniki" with false bravado, but Ilya could tell that his voice was good.

"I still had to leave people behind though. That's a fact of life now. Simple. Some people are dead weight." He made a "plop" with his lips, like a rock dropped in a pond. "I went to School #17. It was a better school back then, only there were no teachers as beautiful as my Masha."

"Stop it, Dmitri!" Maria Mikhailovna yelled from the kitchen.

With a start, Ilya realized that Dmitri was the reason Maria Mikhailovna's voice was different. They were in love, these two. Truly in love, and maybe that was why the air and the light felt like they did. Ilya finished his kvass, and Dmitri filled his glass with beer. It was bubbly and tart on his tongue, and his chair was incredibly soft. It seemed to have molded around his buttocks and spine, like it was meant for him. He imagined getting under the covers at home that night and having Vladimir smell the alcohol on his breath the way he'd smelled it on Vladimir dozens of times, and a sort of sprightly pride came over him. He had not felt so good since the day Maria Mikhailovna had told him about the exchange. In this chair, he could forget that Vladimir had not been home for more than a month. He could forget krokodil and the way his mother and Babushka looked at the door like dogs sometimes, hoping for a knock, for Vladimir to come home spun or sober or however. He felt like he was in a different world already, like the happiness he felt here was a preview of America. For dinner he had two helpings of macaroni and cheese, and enough beer that he lost his shyness and began to talk without thinking first.

"How did you meet?" he asked them, and maybe it was the drink, but he thought he could actually see the love seep into their faces the way morning light seeps over the horizon.

"Skating," Maria Mikhailovna said.

"How Russian," Ilya said.

Dmitri cackled.

"At the Winter Festival," Dmitri said, "if you can believe that. She is lovely, beautiful, brilliant, of course, but she is not so good on skates. In fact, her skating is a disruption of the peace."

"Luckily Dmitri was there, in uniform. And for the safety of others he removed me from the rink."

"So the Winter Festival is your anniversary," Ilya said. The Winter Festival was three and a half months away. That was when Maria Mikhailovna planned to announce the exchange as long as Ilya passed the boards.

They nodded. "It's been too many years to celebrate," Maria Mikhailovna said.

"Isn't that when you're supposed to celebrate?" Ilya could feel himself glowing. It was silly, he knew, but he felt the same sense of accomplishment talking with these two, in this apartment, in this light, that he felt when he perfectly translated a dictation or when he understood a whole conversation between Michael and Stephanie without having to pause and rewind.

"Exactly," Dmitri said. "And, between us, she says this—'No, no, I don't want to celebrate, no presents, no flowers'—but I'll be sleeping at the station for a week if I don't plan something."

Maria Mikhailovna smiled, and a small silence settled over the table. It was comfortable, calm, the sort of silence that could never exist in his apartment. He thought of Babushka's endless murmurings, his mother's rants, the neighbors' fights, which were audible enough to follow like soap operas. He had no memories of his mother and father together, but he could feel in his marrow that they had not been like this, and for a long second he let himself imagine that he was the Malikovs' son. It made him feel guilty, of course, to imagine that, and he wondered—not for the first time— if everyone was as traitorous in their daydreams, if Babushka wished she'd married Timofey when they were young enough to have a different son, one who survived. Maybe his mother longed for children who were nothing like him or Vladimir, maybe she longed to leave them all behind and go to America herself. But he could tell that these two, at least, did not regret each other.

Later, when Maria Mikhailovna was in the kitchen cutting the apple pie, Ilya asked Dmitri if he was a detective.

"Yes." Dmitri laughed. "But it's not so glamorous as you make it sound. Mostly I patrol for the refinery."

That explained the apartment. That explained why Maria Mikhailovna was the one teacher at School #17 who did not have a second job at a kiosk or café. Fyodor Fetisov probably paid Dmitri more than his salary from the police force.

"Did you hear of the woman on Ulitsa Gornyakov?" Ilya knew that Dmitri had heard of Yulia, and what he meant was, do you know anything?

Dmitri nodded. "It's sad, no? She was poteryana." Lost, he'd said, and Ilya didn't know whether he meant that she'd been lost when she died or in general.

"My babushka's scared," Ilya lied, "because my mother works the same job."

"She doesn't need to be scared," he said. "Your mother should take the bus to be safe. And stay away from the Tower. The woman was not so innocent."

"Did she die at the Tower?"

Dmitri looked at him, and narrowed his eyes. "You know how when you roll over a log there are worms and zhuki and slugs all grubbing around in the muck?" Ilya nodded. "The Tower is like that, only there are getting to be too many bugs. They're not staying under the log."

Maria Mikhailovna set the plates of pie on the table. "They need jobs," she said.

"Of course they do," Dmitri said. "Welcome to the new Russia." He sounded proud, because he had done just fine in the new Russia, but there was this tightness in his face that spread the way a crack spreads across ice. Maria Mikhailovna saw it too. She put a hand on his arm. Still he went on, "It's not even their fault. They have nothing, and they have nothing to hope for. At least before, we had a big idea, with big flaws, sure, but now what have they got? Is it any wonder they're killing themselves?"

Yulia Podtochina had not killed herself, but Ilya knew there was no point in saying so. Dmitri was grandstanding the way Vladimir sometimes did, connecting dots until he could condemn the whole world and make himself feel like he was somehow outside it. Only Vladimir *was* outside it, and Dmitri was profiting from it.

"That's why we teach them," Maria Mikhailovna said. Her voice was soft but firm. She had understood that for Ilya the conversation was more than ideological.

"Teach them to leave?" Dmitri said, lifting a hand toward Ilya. There was a bubble of spit on his lip that he didn't seem to notice. He was drunk, Ilya thought, or getting there.

"They leave and then maybe they come back."

Dmitri laughed. "Sure," he said.

"OK," Maria Mikhailovna said. "Pie."

"Pie. Yes. Sorry, pie and coffee too." Dmitri smiled at his wife and then at Ilya. "And no more politics."

"Yulia Podtochina was pretty," Ilya said. He knew he should drop the subject, but he wanted to say the *pretty* without the *enough*, and he had the feeling that Dmitri had slandered her somehow.

"To pretty women," Dmitri said.

He raised his wineglass and drank the dregs, and they all ate their pie, which was studded with raisins and not as good as Babushka's apple dumplings. Ilya reminded himself to tell Babushka this. "Shush," Babushka would say, "who's competing," but she would be flattered.

They ate in front of the enormous window, and from the seventh floor, the snow was beautiful as it fell. They were too high to see the slush, the streaks of oil, the yellow spots where dogs and drunks had pissed.

Dmitri offered to drive Ilya home, and Ilya demurred, but Dmitri insisted. He wanted to do a patrol of the refinery road anyway, and the kommunalkas were on the way. It was late enough and cold enough that Ilya said yes. In the elevator, Ilya looked at Dmitri's boots. They were shiny, without any trace of snow or salt. They seemed to be brand-new, and Ilya wondered if he and Maria Mikhailovna had lived here a decade ago and whether it could have been Dmitri who had kicked Vladimir and him out of the elevator.

"Who lives in the penthouse?" Ilya asked.

"The penthouse?"

Ilya nodded.

"It's been empty for a decade. Fetisov owns it. I go up a couple times a year to make sure the heat works and the pipes haven't frozen. But he's here occasionally with the new pipeline project." Dmitri ran a hand lightly down the elevator panel. "Almost all of them are empty. They built them for the bigwigs, but then the bigwigs didn't want to live here. They'd rather live anywhere else—fly in, fly out, not even spend the night if they can help it. So they've got no one who can afford the apartments, and they had to start cutting the prices. Ours is a perk of the job. But as you can see, the job never ends."

"Of course," Ilya said.

The elevator let them out in a garage. Somehow Ilya had not expected Dmitri to drive a patrol car, but there it was: the siren, the blue stripe, the MILITSIYA across the hood. There was not a flake of snow on it, the door was barely cold to the touch, and this was a marvel to Ilya.

"Maria is going to miss you, you know. She cares for you," Dmitri said, as they pulled out of the garage. "She thinks of you like family, which means you're family to me too."

Ilya nodded. He knew that he should say something more—that he cared for Maria Mikhailovna too, or that he wouldn't forget her—but he'd let the silence go too long.

"You want me to turn on the lights and sirens?"

"No," Ilya said with a smile.

"I figured you were too old for that."

On the corner of Ulitsa Tsentralnaya and Ulitsa Lenina, Dmitri hit the endless traffic light, the krasny beskonechnyy, which seemed to never be green, no matter what direction you were coming from. Dmitri groaned, and Ilya looked out the window and saw two figures sitting on a bench. Their shoulders were dusted in snow. They were looking down at their laps. Bare fingers flashing above their knees. They were gloveless, rolling cigarettes, and Ilya recognized the motion of Vladimir's hands before he recognized his face. On his lap was the little pouch that their mother had given him eons ago to hold pencils and pens and erasers and that he had only ever used for tobacco. A lighter sparked in his hands, and in the glow, Ilya saw that it was Sergey sitting next to him. Vladimir lit his own cigarette, as straight and even as a factory-made. It bobbed between his lips as he said something to Sergey that Ilya couldn't hear. The heat was blasting in the car and the windows were up, and Dmitri said, "You want to know a secret?"

Ilya nodded, his eyes on Vladimir.

"They programmed this light to be red for double the usual time. So people would run it and the traffic cops could pad their pockets, but of course here I am, waiting and waiting." He went on complaining, saying that they had all spent lifetimes waiting at lights like this even though there weren't any other cars in sight.

On the bench, Vladimir lit Sergey's cigarette. Their hands cupped around the lighter. Their heads dipped toward each other. Their noses might have touched. There was ease there and symmetry. They stayed that way for only a moment, but it was a long moment for Ilya. He had always believed that some cord, some twine of genes and history and proximity, held him to his brother and held his brother to him, but he could feel the cord—or his belief in it—slacken as he watched them. He had the sense that he wasn't looking out a window but at a screen, at a character whose fate he was invested in but powerless to change. And he had this feeling that he'd been getting more and more recently, that each time he saw Vladimir might be the last.

Sergey looked up at the car, smoke rolling up over his cheeks. He elbowed Vladimir. Vladimir stuffed the pouch in his pocket, and they both stood. Two shadow shapes cut out of the snow. Ilya thought they would walk away, but instead they headed toward the car, and Ilya could feel Dmitri stiffen beside him.

"Look at these two," he murmured.

Vladimir and Sergey cut across the street a few meters in front of the car, moving slowly, like they thought that might make them look innocent. Dmitri's headlights caught the stripes on the track

pants that Vladimir wore day in and day out. Then the traffic light
turned green. Sergey didn't notice, but Vladimir stopped and looked
toward the car. He can't see me, Ilya thought, the headlights are too
bright, but Vladimir squinted and stared.

Ilya saw him mouth, "Ilyusha?" and he hoped that Dmitri had
not understood.

"Is this fucker really going to test me?" Dmitri said. He dug his
palm into the horn and blasted it. Sergey was past the car, but he
stopped now too. Sergey, who was always ready for a fight, looked
back at them, his face wild with anger. Then he raised a hand and
lifted his middle finger and jabbed it in the air.

"Run!" Sergey yelled just as the car jolted forward.

The tires shimmied on the ice—Dmitri had pressed hard on
the gas—and the tail twisted out so that the car was almost side-
ways in the street. Dmitri cursed. Vladimir and Sergey were moving now, running sloppily, but gaining distance nonetheless. They
were half a block away. Sergey tripped once, caught himself on
one hand, and was up again. And then Dmitri righted the car and
gassed it, more gently this time, so that it glided smoothly over
the snow, gaining on Sergey and Vladimir until the bumper was
only a few meters from their feet. The bottoms of Vladimir's
shoes—ancient sneakers, with no treads—rose like shadows in the
headlights. His boots were at home, by the door, under the picture of their father in the red plastic frame that Babushka liked to
touch each time she left the apartment, but of course Vladimir
wasn't wearing them. Ilya shut his eyes. He was sure that Vladimir would fall, that he would hear the thump, thump of his body
under the tires.

"Urody," Dmitri said, which was the word for freaks, but also for
babies born with something wrong, for black sheep, for imbeciles.

Dmitri's face was thrust forward over the steering wheel. His tongue moved over his lips. "Fucking urody."

They were almost at the corner, the turnoff to the kommunalkas, and as Vladimir ran into the intersection, sinking ankle-deep into the crisscrossing mounds of snow left by the plows, Ilya managed to say, "Here. Right here. This is my turn." As though Dmitri were just driving him home.

Dmitri glanced over at him, and then he twisted the wheel right, and the back tires shot out from under them again. Ilya could hear him breathing through his mouth, as though he too had been running. Then he started to laugh.

"Can you believe them?" he said. "They were too high to even think of running out of the road."

The kommunalkas were ahead of them, a cluster of darkness blocking the refinery's light.

"Like ants, right? Too stupid to break the line," Dmitri said.

Ilya didn't say anything. Dmitri could easily turn the car around—Vladimir was still only a minute away, probably standing in the middle of the street, rehearsing the story with Sergey between jagged breaths. And Dmitri had power over Ilya too, over his whole future, over America, and Ilya thought that if he could just hold himself incredibly still and silent, he could protect it all.

"Not a word of this to Masha," Dmitri said. "You hear me?"

Ilya nodded.

"She's a pacifist," he said. "She's meant for a better world. That's why I love her."

Ilya nodded again.

"Listen," Dmitri said, as he pulled up to Ilya's building. His hand was on Ilya's thigh again. "Those two will be fine. Maybe even better for this. Maybe I scared them sober, right?"

Ilya could feel his leg shaking. He knew that Dmitri could feel it too. This wouldn't be over, he wouldn't be released, until he said something. So he smiled at Dmitri and managed to thank him for dinner and the ride home, and then he got out of the car and watched Dmitri drive over the bridge and down the road until his lights merged with the refinery's.

That night Ilya waited for Vladimir for a long time, pacing the stretch of carpet between the TV and the couch. He knew that Dmitri was right, that Vladimir had been too high, too stupid to just run off the road, to run up into the square, into the trees where the car couldn't follow him. And though he knew that that was beside the point, though he could hear the thump of Vladimir under the car so clearly that he had to remind himself that it hadn't happened, he was angry too. Vladimir was always in these sorts of situations. Vladimir was always the one out until two a.m., the one sneaking out of school, sneaking in the back door of Dolls; the one never, ever doing what he was supposed to, and it was infuriating to always worry that his latest mistake might be the one that was too big, too deep and stupid for him to escape. Ilya burned the beer off pacing. Eventually he burned his anger off too, and there was just this acidic film of fear on his tongue, lining his stomach. He lay on the couch. He was tired. He felt young. He wanted to tell Vladimir that he'd been in the elevator, that he'd seen one of the apartments. He wanted to tell him that no one even lived in the penthouse. He waited and waited, but of course Vladimir didn't come home.

Chapter Thirteen

Sadie didn't go to the trailer by the refinery the next few nights, and Ilya began to wonder if he'd inflated the importance of the woman. Maybe there was some simple explanation. Maybe it was J.T.'s house, and they'd arranged to meet, but his mom had been home and foiled their plans. Then in history one day, Sadie began a new portrait, and as it took shape, he realized it was the woman. Sadie spent five minutes shading under her eyes and at the corners of her mouth, somehow capturing her exact lassitude.

"Who's that?" Ilya whispered, as Mr. Shilling handed out a quiz on the key battles of the Revolution.

She shrugged. "This woman from church."

J.T., who sat on the other side of Sadie, leaned across the aisle, draped one arm behind Sadie's back and his other over the drawing, and said, "Next weekend at the Pound, y'all. It's my birthday." He was grinning like a child, and Ilya felt a pang of jealousy at how easily he touched Sadie.

"You're obsessed with your birthday," she said.

"Of course I am," he said. "Ilya? You coming?"

Ilya looked at Sadie, and Sadie nodded. "We'll come."

At the front of the room, Shilling said, "There's a Peppermint

Pattie in my drawer for anyone who gets all ten battles in chrono-logical order."

"What battles?" J.T. yelled.

A girl in the front row said, "What if more than one of us does?"

"Then I would be shocked," Shilling said, "and you'd split the patty."

J.T. shielded his mouth with a hand and whispered, "Who the fuck wants a Peppermint Pattie? Do they even make those anymore?"

Peppermint Patties had been one of the most coveted candies at the Minutka. Vladimir used to steal them with regularity. "I want it," Ilya said, and J.T. and Sadie laughed.

After class, Ilya stayed to receive the patty.

"Well done," Shilling said. "Although you're lucky that, as a rule, I ignore spelling."

The patty looked as though it had been in Mr. Shilling's desk drawer for a decade at least, but it tasted delicious, the filling minty enough to make the inside of Ilya's mouth snap, to remind him of the way the air tasted in Berlozhniki, on the days when the wind was blowing the refinery's smoke away from town. He ate the whole thing in a few ferocious bites, and as he dropped the wrapper into the trash can, he saw Sadie's drawing crumpled at the bottom. He pulled it out. The creases gave the woman a mild harelip and a scar that sliced one eyebrow. Ilya smoothed it as best he could and pressed it between the pages of his history text.

At church that weekend, Ilya scanned the crowd for the woman, but she wasn't there. He hadn't really expected her to be; she hadn't seemed like a churchgoer. As Pastor Kyle preached—a sermon about forgiveness that somehow tied in to an extended golf metaphor—Ilya closed his eyes, hoping for another clue or, at the least, to be transported back to the Tower like he had been during that first Star Pilgrim service, when he'd heard Vladimir's voice, the exact gravel of it, as though Vladimir were there next to him. He'd been in America for two weeks, and he'd crossed seventy Gabe Thompsons off his list—almost all of the Gabe Thompsons in the state of California—but there were still hundreds left.

On one side of him, Sadie picked the paint off her sneakers, scattering silver flakes on the floor. She was singing softly, practicing whatever the choir was performing later. On the other side of him, Papa Cam's eyebrows knitted in fervent prayer. His meaty hands were clasped between his knees, and Ilya wondered what he could possibly want or need. Babushka would say that that was not what praying was about, that God didn't listen if you talked to him only when you needed something.

In the middle of each of the church's glass walls were fragments of stained glass. They were clustered in abstract patterns like the inside of a kaleidoscope, but still they reminded Ilya of lying on the bed his mother and Babushka shared, looking at the light streaming through the pictures that Babushka had taped over the glass. The pictures from Gabe's pamphlets. They were still there, he thought, and Babushka had probably kept the pamphlets too, and maybe inside was the name of Gabe's church.

That afternoon, he called his mother from the Masons' kitchen. Her voice, when she answered, sounded very faint, as though she'd been swallowed by some larger creature and was calling out from within its belly.

"You heard," she said, and he could tell from her voice that it was nothing good.

"Heard what?" Ilya said. He tried to keep his own voice steady.

Around him the Masons' predinner preparations raged. Mama Jamie chopped celery with vigor, Marilee whined about setting the table, and Molly did somersaults across the den carpet. Only Sadie seemed to have sensed the import of the call. She was watching him from a stool at the counter, her pencil poised above an algebra equation, her head propped in her palm.

"The arraignment is set. Four weeks from now. In Syktyvkar."

In four weeks Vladimir would have to enter his plea, and given his confession he would likely plead guilty.

"Can you go?" Ilya said. "Have you gotten to see him?"

"No," his mother said. "They still won't tell me where he's being held. No one will talk to me, except for Dmitri Malikov."

"What does he say?"

She was quiet for a second, and he got the sense that she was gathering herself. Her voice, when it came, had gone up an octave. "He says that I should focus on you. That you're our hope. Although sometimes I think I've done that for too long already." She meant this as a reproach to herself, but Ilya couldn't help but feel the sting of it, as though her hope was a limited commodity that he'd intentionally cornered. "And sometimes I wonder why he confessed at all—"

"Mama," Ilya said.

"He was on drugs, Ilyusha. If he did do these things, it wasn't *him*. Not really. Do you remember? How he looked?"

Ilya did remember. He remembered the ammoniac stench of Vladimir's crotch. He remembered his mother trying to find a vein in the minefield of Vladimir's body. He had been pitiful, disgusting. *If he did do these things*, he thought, and he said, "Mama, he was practically dead."

Next to him, Mama Jamie speared a hunk of pork and dropped it into a hot skillet. Droplets of grease splashed Ilya's arm and left pinpricks of pain.

"I know," she said. "I just keep thinking about him as a baby. He always wanted to be held. Cuddle, cuddle, cuddle. All the time. If I put him down, he stretched his arms up to me, and of course I was always having to tell him no. No, Mama has to work. No, not now, Mama has to cook. I think of that and then this, and I just don't know. . . . How am I supposed to know? What could I have done—" She was choking on the words. Each one like something sharp dragged up her throat.

At the table, Sadie mouthed, "You OK?" and he realized that he'd been staring at her without seeing her.

"Listen," he said. "I need you to do something. I need you to send me one of those pamphlets from the American missionary. Babushka cut the pictures from them for the windows."

"Why?" his mother said, and her voice was clear again, and hard. "Don't you dare get involved. You hear me, Ilyusha? You are there, you are safe. You leave this behind, OK? That is the most important thing."

"He might have—"

"Keep your head down. Do you understand me? Do you know how easy it would be for someone to say you were both involved?"

"OK," Ilya said, and he did understand her. He knew that her fear was ingrained. He and Vladimir magnified it, of course, but it had existed before them; her parents had given it to her like an inheritance, something to help her survive the world. But what he wanted to say was: you're doing it again. Putting me before him. "It's just a year, Mama," he said. "Less than that now."

"Listen to me. I want you to study, work hard. I don't want you coming back here ever," she said. "Ilyusha, I have to go. I'm at work."

The dial tone flooded the receiver. His mother was crying now. She'd hung up so he wouldn't have to hear her, but he could hear her anyway. And he could picture her: in the cafeteria's dank break room, where the lockers had all been painted primary colors to boost morale. She was sobbing, dabbing at her face with her apron, eyes on the door, because her boss had caught her like this too many times already.

Sadie was still looking at him over the counter, her eyes a question. He made some approximation of a smile and held the phone to his ear until the dial tone broke into a pulse loud enough that he was afraid Mama Jamie would hear.

"Tell me you're hungry!" Mama Jamie said, when he hung up.

"I'm hungry," he said. *If he did do these things*, he thought.

Mama Jamie fixed him a plate, and he ate it while Papa Cam talked about a new hire, an engineer whose wife he thought Mama Jamie would like, but whose son was a little off.

"Please pass the rice," Molly said. Ilya passed the rice. He thought, *If he did*.

"How's school, Ilya?" Papa Cam said. He must have asked it more than once, because when Ilya said, "It's fine," they were all looking at him, the grown-ups and Sadie with concern, Molly and Marilee with amused curiosity, like he was a toy that had short-circuited.

If he did, he thought. His mother was back in the cafeteria by now, spraying cleaner on the long metal tray tracks that Vladimir and Ilya had loved to run their toy cars down the few times she'd brought them to work. She sprayed and wiped. Her cheeks were splotchy, but she'd washed her face, and it was not so obvious that she'd been crying. Spray and wipe. She had not been caught this time. That was a good thing. Spray, spray, wipe. She wished she'd asked him more about America—what the mother fed him, what school was like, whether he was the smartest there too. She wondered if that other mother thought of her, thought that maybe she was smart like Ilya. Spray and wipe. She did not think of Vladimir. She had given up.

Later, Sadie found him in the basement trying to read an espionage thriller from one of the dusty boxes that lived under the Ping-Pong table. It was the time he usually spent on the Gabe Thompson list, but the phone call with his mother had demoralized him. If he couldn't convince his mother of Vladimir's innocence, what were the chances that, even armed with evidence, he could convince the police? Maybe it was hopeless, maybe it was even cowardly, he thought, a way of hiding from life. He thought of all the years he'd spent with the Delta headphones clamped over his ears, of all the times his mother or Babushka or Vladimir had said something to him, and he'd pretended not to see their lips moving. He had liked to think that he was being transported, but maybe he'd just been hiding then too.

"Hey," Sadie said.

He dog-eared his page when she sat beside him, though he'd only read three pages.

"What's wrong?" she said.

Ilya shrugged. He'd told her that his brother was dead, and it had proved an easy lie to defend. With the exception of that horrible moment at Star Pilgrim, the Masons had tiptoed around his grief, and he'd become sickly comfortable with the duplicity. But now he couldn't think of any way to explain his mood without revealing that lie.

"J.T.'s party is tonight," she said. "I was going to go in a little."

Ilya ran his hand over the cover of the book. A man was holding a pistol. It was aimed at the reader, and the letters of the book's title exploded from its barrel. He thought of his mother's tiny voice on the telephone and wondered if he'd sounded the same to her.

"It's no big deal," she said. "I'll tell him you can't go."

"No," Ilya said, fast, because suddenly the idea of being left down here, of watching the light fade between the deck supports, seemed unbearable. "Let's go."

Sadie told her parents that she was taking Ilya to the movies in Alexandria, and the Masons seemed thrilled, especially when Ilya told them that there wasn't a movie theater in his town, and that he'd never actually seen a movie on a big screen.

"Well, this will be a cultural experience for you," Mama Jamie said. "Take some moolah from my purse, Sadie. Make sure Ilya tries the popcorn."

"Do the IMAX," Papa Cam said, which sounded like complete gibberish.

As they backed out of the driveway, Ilya said, "What if they ask about the movie?"

"Say we saw *The Fast and the Furious*. I saw it with J.T. It's like one long car chase. And then the good guy wins at the end." It sounded like something Vladimir would love. "And tell them the acoustics were amazing. My dad's obsessed with the acoustics at the IMAX."

Star Pilgrim and Leffie High were in opposite directions on the same road—Route 21—and they marked the dimensions of Leffie in Ilya's mind. Now Sadie sped past the high school and into the unknown. Ilya rolled down his window. The air was hot, but Sadie was going fast enough for it to have a cooling effect. She scanned the radio, then settled on something with a cowboy twang. A woman sang about scratching her ex's car with a key.

"Is it far?" he asked.

"The Pound? Not too far. It's an old impound yard." She told him that it was a place where cars used to get crushed for scrap metal, but that it had been shut down for a decade, ever since the owner ran away with the football coach's daughter. Kids from all different schools partied there, and she said there'd even been a guy who lived there for a winter, in the back of an old semi. That would be Vladimir, he thought.

She turned off of Route 21 onto a smaller road cupped by trees. Every once in a while, back in the woods, windows glowed high up, like they were in treehouses. This wisp of a memory drifted through his mind. A childhood story of fairies living in trees. "What are those lights?" he asked. "Why are they so high?"

"It's trailers up on stilts." Sadie said. "We're close to the bayou— it floods a lot."

They passed a clearing, and Ilya saw one of the trailers now, a box of light over a box of shadow. A handful of cars were parked under it. A spindly ramp climbed to the door, which was open. Ilya stared in-side. It was empty as far as he could tell, but he thought of that other trailer, of the woman Sadie watched, and then the trees took over again. The blacktop gave out to a rutted dirt road, and Ilya couldn't see the water, but he could sense that they were near it. The bugs' chant got denser, and there was a new salty stickiness to the air.

The Pound sounded like the Tower, and when they got there, Ilya could see that it was. Oil-drum fires were scattered among cars

in various phases of decay. Faces flared above the flames. There was
an enormous school bus, spotted like a banana with rust. Its windows were filled with silhouettes. There were kids on the edge of
the party too, and they looked like nothing more than dark on dark,
the suggestion of movement, like creatures swimming in the deep.
Sadie parked next to an enormous black truck. Its doors were flung
open, the stereo roared, and a girl in the truck bed twisted and
writhed to the music.

Sadie led him toward the bus, stepping over spare tires and a
rogue engine and bumpers that had been crushed and splintered,
their sharp ends glinting. J.T. was standing by a keg, wearing a hat
that said RISE UP. Three other guys sat in beach chairs with girls on
their laps.

"No way!" J.T. said, when he saw Ilya. "You came. Now that is a
birthday honor. You want a beer? Or I got some vodka for you.
That's like the national drink, right?"

"Sure," Ilya said.

"Lady Sadie?" J.T. said. He put an arm around her shoulder and
kissed the top of her head, and Ilya looked away.

"I'll have a beer."

"Prudent as always," J.T. said.

J.T. gave Ilya the vodka in a tiny paper cup, the kind Marilee and
Molly used each night to rinse their mouths after brushing their
teeth. The vodka was warm and singed Ilya's stomach, but he managed to drink it with a straight face and say, "Tastes like water."

"Damn straight," J.T. said. He handed Sadie a beer. "So you're
drinking tonight? What would Papa Cam say?"

"He'd quote Corinthians at me," she said.

Ilya and Sadie found vacant beach chairs and for a while they sat
and listened to J.T. and the other guys—all basketball players, Ilya

learned—talk about the various perversions of their coach. At one point, Sadie leaned over and said, "What did your mom say on the phone?"

He wanted to tell her the truth. He needed someone to know. Needed her to know, he realized, but the conversation had lulled and J.T. was looking at him like he was the punch line of a joke.

"Nothing really," he said.

He took another shot and another, and then he drank a beer so light and flat that it actually did taste like water. He'd been drunk twice in his life before this: the night at the Tower and the day he flew to America, and in all three instances the accompanying sense of depersonalization was both terrifying and calming.

"In Russia on your birthday someone has to yank your ears," Ilya said, after someone had sung J.T. "Happy Birthday." It was the sort of detail about home that he was normally loath to share.

"Yank my ears?"

Ilya nodded. "How old are you?"

"Sixteen," J.T. said.

"Then your ears get yanked sixteen times," Ilya said. "Plus one more for good fortune."

Two girls Ilya recognized from gym class were filling their beers at the keg, and J.T. said, "Can I get them to yank something else?"

Ilya looked at Sadie, wondering if this sort of talk would upset her, but Sadie was talking to another girl. Suddenly the other girl stood and grabbed Sadie by the hand, and Sadie said, "We'll be back," and they walked off toward the pickup truck.

J.T. had started talking with the girls about whether they'd rather bone Mr. Shilling or Principal Gibbons. Someone passed Ilya the vodka bottle, and he took a sip and passed it on. A wave of nausea crested in his gut whenever he tried to focus on the conversation. He stood, thinking motion might help, and managed to make it to the thicket behind the bus before vomiting. He retched until his stomach felt tight and empty and his vision cleared.

As he straightened, something glinted in the trees. A cool, lunar glow. He walked a few meters farther into the brush, thinking of the fairy story again, of lights leading some woeful soul into a bog. When his shoes sank into mud, he stopped and stared and eventually the silvery patch resolved and gained dimension: it was the pipeline, bending and twisting, catching the faint light of the moon wherever it emerged from the overgrowth.

Ilya stepped closer, the mud releasing his feet with a slurp that sounded like Timofey sucking down the last of his soup. The pipeline was higher than he'd thought it would be. He had to reach up to touch its belly. He put a hand against it and felt cool metal. This was a surprise too. He had thought it would be warm, like a vein, he guessed, with a hot gush of oil inside. Behind him, there was a honk, a scream, laughing. He tried to block it out. He cocked his head and listened, and at first there was nothing but the static inside his head, and then he heard it: a sound like a wave as it crashes over you, a sound that seemed to gain strength as he listened until it was a roar. He pulled his hand away, took a quick step back, and slipped in the mud. He landed on his back. A root jabbed him in the ribs, and his side pulsed with pain, and his arm—the one he'd held up over his head—quivered. He wasn't sure whether the pipeline had shocked him or just scared him, but as he trekked through the mud back to the party, he had the ridiculous but distinct impression that touching it had been bad luck.

J.T. wasn't at the keg any longer, and someone else was sitting in

Ilya's beach chair. Ilya looked up at the bus. A black guy was behind the wheel, and when he saw Ilya, he pulled the handle, and the door creaked open.

"Russia," he said. "Welcome. Have a seat." He smiled and stuck his tongue out, and there was a diamond nestled in the wet center of it, like an enormous pill he was about to swallow.

Ilya found a seat in the back, where it smelled less strongly of piss. The brown pleather seat had been slashed. Stuffing fluffed out of the cuts. The same stuff they used at the House of Culture to make fake snow for the New Year's performance. Ilya pulled at it, let it fall and pile on the floor.

When he looked up again, Sadie was coming down the aisle toward him. She held out a cup of beer.

"Want this?" she said. "I don't really drink."

Ilya shook his head. "Papa Cam doesn't allow it?"

"More like Mama Jamie," she said. "But that's not why."

"I don't drink much either. I was just sick in a bush." He waved a hand toward the brush behind the bus.

"Is that why you're all muddy? 'Vodka is like water,' huh?" She laughed and set her beer down on the seat next to him. She ran a finger down the cut he'd emptied of stuffing and plucked at its edge, and he had this feeling, like his future was close, like it was idiotic that he had not already scooted over to make room for her, and that if he did, there would be this tiny, celestial click and things would unlock between them, but instead he stayed where he was and said, "My brother isn't dead. He's in prison. For murder."

Her hand stopped moving. That was the only sign that she'd heard. Her face was shadowed enough that her eyes looked identical, that tiny imperfection erased. "Shit," she said softly, and then, "Did he do it?"

Ilya shook his head. He was so grateful for the question that tears clotted his throat and welled, hot and hard, behind his eyes. He looked up at the bus's ceiling. Someone had graffitied it with swooping letters that looked more Cyrillic than Roman. He bit the inside of his cheek until he could feel the lump of tears loosen and dissolve.

"No," Ilya said. "He did drugs. He stole. He was bad. He confessed even, but no, I still don't think—"

If he did, his mother had said, and Ilya forced himself to follow the thought to that curve in the road where the snowplow had turned up Yulia Podtochina's body, to the alley where Olga Nadiova had been dumped, to the clump of trees where Lana had died, and again he could not see Vladimir there. He shook his head. "He didn't do it," he said.

"He's an addict?"

Ilya nodded, and she was quiet for a long time. Her curiosity was strange, but he liked it better than pity. Outside a string of headlights made their way down the levee road and the Pound was washed in light and for an instant it looked just as sad as a face under fluorescence. Car doors slammed. Someone—it sounded like J.T.—yelled, "Can we change the fucking song?"

"The thing is," Ilya said, "when we were little, we used to talk about coming here together. It was stupid. I mean Vladimir thought he was going to play hockey for Severstal too. Be a big star. Or an oligarch like Fyodor Fetisov. Just stupid things kids think of, but it turned real for me." Just saying it made his gut burn with the need to vomit again. He swallowed. "And it's one thing to have him home and me here, but to have him be in prison and me here..."

"It's too much," Sadie said.

Ilya nodded. "It's too much."

"Can you help him?" she said. "I mean, if he didn't do it, there's someone out there who did, right?"

"I don't know," he said. "When I first got here, I thought I found a clue." He told her about the picture of Lana wearing Gabe's hat. He told her about the list he'd made from the White Pages, about cross-referencing it with Mormon churches, and checking VKontakte and the newspaper.

"Will you show me the picture?" she said.

He nodded. He thought he'd fallen in love with her that night in the kitchen when she'd told him to stop being an asshole, but the feeling was suddenly different. It was bigger and painfully urgent and held within it was the knowledge of the loneliness she might erase. He scooted over, and she sat beside him.

The door to the bus squeaked open, and a boy boarded with a semiconscious girl riding on his back.

"That'll be twenty-five cents," the kid with the tongue piercing said.

"Shut the fuck up, Tyrese," the boy said, and as he walked down the aisle, the girl roused herself and began nibbling his ear.

"I wondered what you were doing in the basement every night," Sadie said. "My parents think you have a girlfriend that you're always emailing."

"No," he said. "No girlfriend."

The boy walked past them, his hands gripping the girl's thighs so tight that she squealed. He flopped her into a seat behind them and then lowered himself down on top of her, and Ilya looked away.

"I thought you'd be angry that I lied," he said.

"Promise not to do it again," she said in a voice that was mock stern.

"I promise," he said.

Then Sadie said, "You know the Masons aren't my real parents."

"They aren't your parents." He said it slowly, hating the way English sometimes made him sound like a dim parrot, repeating what she'd said.

"Nope. Do I look like them? Don't say yes." She smiled.

"No," he said. "Not at all. Are your parents dead?" His inflection must have been off because there was a twitch of hurt on her face.

"I don't know," she said. "I don't know anything about my dad. My mom's alive. She gave me up for adoption. She got pregnant in high school, and Mama Jamie worked at the school then—as a guidance counselor or spiritual adviser or something—and she convinced my mom not to have an abortion. And my mom didn't, and Jamie thought that was it. She'd saved one soul and one life. I'm sure she felt pretty smug about it. Only I guess my mom must have sucked at being a mom, because when I was four she found Jamie and basically blamed her for my existence and begged her to take me. I got this from her—" Sadie pointed at her eye. "She wasn't aiming at me or anything. She wasn't that bad. She just threw a bottle and missed the trash can." She spoke fast, smoothly, with this hint of metal in her voice. And something in the story—the laziness, maybe, of that missed throw—made it clear to him that the woman in the trailer was Sadie's mother.

"So you're like Durashka. You're a rescue," he said, which was a word the Masons had taught him.

She laughed. "That's not really a word you use with people. But yeah, I guess I am. And you are too." She was quiet for a second. "We should go soon. Just in case they check the movie times."

She didn't move and neither did he, and then she turned, and he thought she was going to say something else, but instead she leaned in and kissed him. Her teeth hit his—there was this tiny click—and the back of his head bounced against the seat. He felt the warm melt of her mouth. For a second there was just the sensation of it. For a second his mind was blank, and then he became terribly aware of his hands. They felt feverish, bloated, and he had no idea where to put them. And his tongue. Hers had touched his, and he did not know whether to reciprocate or whether to let it lie in his mouth like a slug. His lips, thank God, seemed to move of their own accord. The drunk girl moaned audibly behind them. Sadie smiled— he could feel it, not see it—and as quickly as it had begun, the kiss ended. She pulled away. Ilya closed his mouth. Blood had rushed to his lips and his dick and the rest of him was limp and possibly paralyzed. She was still smiling, a lasting sort of smile that he hadn't known she had.

"I've been wanting to do that," she said, and she grabbed his hand and led him back to the car.

She drove home a different way, on a road that followed the pipeline. There was a fence now, the pipeline unfurling behind it, and Ilya thought of his arm and how it had quivered. He imagined the pipeline curling toward him, a long silver finger, and he felt another jolt of fear, but then it curved away from him across a flat stretch of water.

"That's Weeks Bay," she said. "Cam took me fishing out there when I was little. You can't go now 'cause of the pipeline."

The refinery was on the other side, its lights long on the water, and Ilya imagined the fish, swimming all night long in the brightness. He wondered how they'd adapt to it, whether their eyes would shrink from the light until they'd turned into a different species entirely.

It wasn't until they'd pulled back into the Masons' driveway that Ilya thought to ask, "What about J.T.?" and as he asked the question, he imagined J.T. watching them kiss through the bus windows. He imagined J.T. at school on Monday, marching down the hallway toward him.

"What about J.T.?" she said.

"I thought he was—"

"He's my cousin. My actual cousin. He's the only one that knows about my mom besides the Masons. And you."

"That's good news," Ilya said, and Sadie laughed and this time he leaned in and kissed her.

That night his email to Vladimir was a long one. Ilya told him about the party, about kissing Sadie, about her adoption and her mother and that J.T., that miracle of high school muscle, was her cousin and nothing more. He asked Vladimir what it would be like tomorrow, whether he could assume that she would kiss him again, or whether it might be a discrete occurrence. Any suggestions, he asked, for where to put my hands when we kiss? And he smiled because he could hear what Vladimir's answer would be: *Down her pants, durashka.* He told Vladimir about the pipeline, about how he'd actually touched it and that the oil had sounded like blood does in your temples. His whole body was throbbing with the night, with the excitement of it, and then there it was again: the blinking cursor, Vladimir's life. *I heard about the arraignment*, he wrote. *Please*, he wrote, *please don't say you did something you didn't.*

CHAPTER FOURTEEN

In Berlozhniki that last winter, birch trees slashed the horizon. Wind coaxed the snow into twisters, and Babushka murmured about snow children and snyeg demons and what it meant when the sun didn't appear for seven days straight. Babushka seemed to be the only person who had not forgotten about Yulia Podtochina. Some nights, she claimed to feel Yulia's spirit slipping under the door and whispering in her ear. Some days she said that Yulia left her handprints on the mirror in the bathroom.

In theory, Ilya had everything to be happy about. He'd be in America in less than a year. He'd taken practice boards with Maria Mikhailovna and scored close to perfect. The actual boards were only a month away, and that should have been all he thought about, but he kept picturing Vladimir on that bench with Sergey. The two of them leaning toward each other. Vladimir holding the lighter and Sergey the cigarette. The gesture old and practiced, like they were bratya, like they were actual brothers, and Ilya was nothing to them at all. And he kept seeing Vladimir running in Dmitri's headlights. *What if he'd slipped?* he thought, over and over, panic bubbling in his gut until he'd replayed the night to its end: Dmitri turning into the kommunalkas, his headlights shining on nothing but the snow falling as endlessly and innocently as ever.

One day he came home from school to find Babushka crying on the couch. Timofey was sitting next to her, looking small and a little lost. He patted her knee and murmured, "Tchoo, tchoo," which was exactly what Babushka used to whisper to Ilya and Vladimir when they skinned their knees or needed garlic in their ears to get rid of an ache.

"What is it?" Ilya said, though he knew: Vladimir was hurt. He'd broken something, had wound up in the clinic or prison or dead.

"We were robbed," Babushka said.

The apartment looked as it always looked: clean but cluttered. His mother and Babushka were neat, but they could not bear to throw things away, and so every surface—the counters, the kitchen table, the top of the TV—had the feeling of space about to be engulfed. Ilya looked at the door. The lock was cheap—it would pop out with one knock from a hammer. But it was in place.

"What did they take?"

"The samovar, your mother's spoon, her rings, your grandfather's medals, the vouchers—" She stopped, and Ilya thought a new wave of tears might come, but she swallowed and was quiet.

Timofey patted her knee. "They left the TV, though," he said, "and the stove and the space heater. The important things."

"Those are not the important things," Babushka said. "They were probably too lazy to carry the TV down the stairs."

"It's true," Timofey said. "Even thugs are lazy nowadays."

The medals were his grandfather's—"For Distinguished Labor" and "Veteran of Labor"—and Babushka had kept them in a tiny felt satchel inside a box of Q-tips in the drawer by her bed. His mother's silver spoon—with the unknown initials carved in the handle—lived in a dusty depression above the kitchen cabinets along with the vouchers that they'd been given during perestroika without ever being told how to exchange them. The samovar was nestled in the depths under his mother and Babushka's bed, hidden from the world by a warren of shoeboxes full of pictures and newspaper clippings and socks that needed mending and summer clothes that they never ever wore. Everything that had been stolen had been precious and nearly impossible to find.

Ilya dragged his crate out from under the couch. His clothes were all still there. His textbooks and exam prep books, his skates, and the decade-old New York City travel guide that he'd found at the bookshop and bought himself for his birthday were too, but his tape player was gone, and the Delta headphones, and all of the *Michael & Stephanie* tapes.

"Did they take anything of yours?" Babushka said.

Behind her legs, he could see Vladimir's crate. It had been completely emptied.

"No," he said, because she looked so forlorn. "Everything's still here."

"That's a relief," she said. "They probably wouldn't know what to do with a book if it hit them in the nose."

Ilya stood. His chest was tight. It must have taken Vladimir a half hour to catalogue exactly what they had that was worth taking, and to gather it all, and at the thought Ilya could feel blood pumping in his hands, as though they were growing rapidly, and he wanted desperately to use them on something, to punch the wall or splinter the door, the way men did in movies. "I'll go ask if anyone saw anything," he said.

"No," Babushka said, with enough force that Ilya understood that she suspected Vladimir too. "We don't want the police mixed up in this. It's not worth it. You hear? Ilya?"

Ilya nodded.

"Will you put on the kettle?" Babushka said.

Ilya filled the kettle from the pitcher on the counter and lit the stove. He watched the flame, and after a minute he could feel his hands relaxing, shrinking back to normal.

On the couch, Timofey said, "At least they didn't take the kettle."

"Pravda," Babushka said. "We have the kettle."

Weeks passed. On New Year's, Medvedev gave his speech, with the Kremlin ablaze behind him. Babushka kept saying that at least they still had their TV, that at least they got to watch the speech.

"Right," Ilya's mother said, "what luck," and she disappeared into the bedroom, and then Babushka fell asleep, and Ilya muted the TV and listened to the sound of fireworks cracking in the sky.

Ilya didn't see Vladimir in town anymore, and sometimes he wondered if he'd left Berlozhniki entirely. He imagined Vladimir and Sergey clinging to the back of one of the semis that braved the roads all winter. Sergey claimed that his older brother had done that once, though his brother had been in Berlozhniki for as long as Ilya could remember, working at an auto shop, father to three kids who'd all inherited his and Sergey's skin, which was as patchy as a rotten potato.

The more Ilya thought about Vladimir, about the stolen tapes, about the fact that he had mustered the energy to rob them but had not bothered to try to see Ilya in almost three months, the larger his hurt grew, and over time he found that he could cook it into hatred.

He should have hated Vladimir, of course, but it was hard to hate someone whom you never saw, so instead he hated his mother. He hated the way her eyes turned down at the corners. The noisy way she ate. The fatness of her ass. The skinniness of her legs. She couldn't say his name without it sounding like a plea. He hated her blind hope and stupid trust. There were other mothers, he knew, who helped their children with schoolwork, who did not stink of yeast and sleep all day. Grigori Alexandrov's mother had written out a five-year study schedule as soon as his talent in math had become apparent; Ilya's mother did not even know the date of the boards, though that did not stop her from applying pressure that Ilya didn't need. And there was the way she had picked him as the smart one and defined Vladimir by default: the idiot, the failure, trouble through and through. In more rational moments, he remembered the folder of math homework, the term card filled with 1s, the fact that Vladimir had said he would try and had not. He remembered that Vladimir had left of his own accord, but what sort of mother *let* her son leave? Why had she not gone to find him? And would she have if Ilya and his promise had never existed? At the hot center of his anger was a fact that he tried his best to ignore: Vladimir had not been home since the night Maria Mikhailovna had told them about the exchange. Vladimir had not wanted to be left, and when Ilya thought of that night, he hoped that he had looked his brother in the eyes, that he had at least considered not abandoning him, but of course that wasn't the case. He'd said, "Yes," more loudly and clearly than he'd said those first words of English nearly a decade before.

When his mother was at work, Ilya sassed Babushka instead. Babushka who, it seemed, could never keep her fingers still, could never just do nothing. Babushka who saw portent in everything, who, one day, when she was making gogol-mogol, cracked open an egg and saw that it was yolkless.

"It could be good," she said. "Or it could be very bad."

"So it could be anything," Ilya said, without looking up from his book. He was reviewing advanced algebra because a quadratic equation had been the only thing to trip him up on his last practice test.

"No yolk." Babushka thrust the bowl under his nose, and he looked down at the egg white. It was perfectly clear except for a few milky particles. "Maybe he'll come home."

"I doubt it," Ilya said. His voice came out sour, exactly as he'd wanted it to.

"You don't miss your brother?" she said, and when Ilya shrugged, she said, "Maybe you're missing your yolk."

That winter, his mind was like a fire heap, doused and fumy with gasoline. He lived for any insult, any slight or spark. He slammed his book shut so that the table wobbled and his chair wobbled and the egg white wobbled in its bowl. His coat and scarf and hat were bundled on the couch, still thawing from his walk home from school, and he grabbed them, shoved his feet into his boots and stomped out of the apartment. Halfway down the endless stairs, he paused. He had nowhere to go. Five flights above him, three below. It was freezing. Here, and everywhere else in Berlozhniki. He'd forgotten his mittens, and his fingers were already tingling, halfway to numb. His breath stung with the cold. He'd have to be gone for an hour at least. If he went home any sooner, Babushka's smugness would be unbearable. He'd skip dinner. He'd stay silent for the rest of the night. Maybe he'd stay silent through the winter, through the summer, until he said good-bye and left for America.

He was on the korichnevy floor, the brown floor, the worst floor, and it smelled of onions and cat piss. Every time Ilya climbed past this floor, babies were wailing and women were yelling and men were slamming doors—it had the general feel of humanity at war—but the long hallway was silent now. Across from Ilya, a door opened. A dumpy woman emerged from the bathroom in a robe with damp spots in terrible places.

"What are you lurking around for? Thought you'd sneak a peek?" She said it like she wouldn't mind if he had snuck a peek, and he was terrified that she might whip open her robe and make him look at her.

"I wasn't," he said. According to Vladimir, middle-aged women— especially ugly ones—could be aggressive. "But you could do worse," Vladimir had told him once, "if you're in need of an education."

"Which floor is . . . " He stalled.

She rolled her eyes, and her mouth stiffened with impatience. "All your life you've been living here and you don't know the floors. I thought you were the big brain."

Ilya backed away from her and ran down the stairs.

"Seems like your brain's shrinking!" she yelled after him.

He tucked his hands up inside his jacket sleeves and walked fast to the Internet Kebab on the square, where Vladimir had shown him his first porno over a stuttering, stalling connection. All those pauses, the endless buffering had been both painful and delicious.

"It's tantric porn," Vladimir had said. "A Berlozhniki special."

Ilya gave Kirill, the horny Chechen who ran the place, thirty kopeks. He wanted to see if he could find out a little more about his host family, or the town at least, which Maria Mikhailovna had told him was in the south, in the state of Louisiana. First he had to wait for the homepage—the *Vecherniye Berlozhniki*—to load, and as it did, he felt Kirill hovering behind him.

By the time a third of the page had loaded, Ilya recognized the picture on the screen. It was Olga Nadiova. Everyone in Berlozhniki knew her. When she was little, she'd been an ice-skating phenomenon. She'd gone to an athletics compound in Sochi at seven. She'd been an Olympic hopeful. For years her likeness had been carved in ice at the Winter Festival. She was put on a pedestal right next to Father Frost and Yeltsin. She'd been headed for the Goodwill Games, but then at twelve, in the second spin of a triple jump, she'd sliced through her Achilles tendon with the toe pick of her other skate, and that was it. She moved back to Berlozhniki. She taught skating at the rink, started drinking, and gave impassioned, nonsensical speeches at the House of Culture, and now here she was on the screen, a child again, in full skating regalia. The headline said she was dead. She'd been murdered two nights earlier. Stabbed, just as Yulia Podtochina had been.

"Fuck me," Kirill said, and Ilya knew it wasn't out of sympathy. Olga Nadiova had split her salary between booze and the Kebab. Ilya had seen her here, plenty of times, watching videos of her best performances.

Panic set in after Olga's murder, and it became hard to separate facts from rumors, to untangle the truth from the articles that ran in the *Vecherniye Berlozhniki*—which, after all, was edited by the mayor's brother. The *Vecherniye* didn't bring up any connection between Olga's and Yulia's deaths. Instead, it printed picture after picture of Olga in her red and yellow spangles, ice spraying off her skates. Olga midair, midaxel. The Pride of Berlozhniki, they called her, and they dredged up details of her skating career, her eleven medals in the Russian Youth Olympiads, her tragic injury. The articles always closed with a brief line about how her body had been found: "at 4 a.m. by a vagrant next to one of the trash bins behind the bazaar," and there was an accusation implicit in this description that wasn't lost on anyone. The trash bins. The vagrant. What had she been doing behind the bazaar at four a.m.? Nothing good.

Olga's parents lived in the kommunalkas, across the courtyard from Ilya's flat, and everyone brought candles and visited them, everyone listened to them insist that Olga had not done drugs—she had been a drinker, yes, of course, but never *drugs*—just as everyone had listened to them brag when Olga left Berlozhniki for the athletics compound in 1987. Olga's parents said that she had been stabbed, just like Yulia. They had seen her body in the morgue and said that each cheek had been slashed, just like Yulia's. They said that Olga had managed to call her mother while she was dying, but that her mother had been asleep and hadn't answered. The message was nothing but static broken by two thumps. They said that she had been about to turn her life around.

Late at night, people gathered in the kitchens, poured shots of vodka, and talked about the details. Some said that Yulia and Olga had the same number of stab wounds. Some said that the killer had taken each of their ring fingers. Some said that both had been raped and others said that neither had been. There was talk of a serial killer, and a few even speculated about his identity: Anton Solomin, who'd been caught masturbating outside the school a decade earlier; Maxim Grinkov, who never made eye contact; Roman Rochev, who had come back from Chechnya with this shattered look in his eye, who could no longer even manage to lift a hand and say, "Privyet."

Police cars appeared, sharking around the kommunalkas and the square. They trolled up and down the refinery road, where Yulia's body had been found. Occasionally, walking home from school, Ilya saw Dmitri in his patrol car, his eyes scanning the horizon like he might happen upon a murder-in-progress, and if Dmitri saw Ilya, he would lift a hand and smile so heartily that it was easy to forget the few minutes Ilya had spent in his car.

The Minutka stocked pepper spray and knives and bullets and padlocks. Those who could afford to had iron bars installed over their wooden doors. Women walked everywhere in pairs. And of course some said that Olga and Yulia were to blame. That they had not been smart, that they had not been sensible. As though of course men with knives were lurking at the fringes of life, waiting for any woman foolish enough to step out of bounds. Even the grown-ups knew, now, of the new drug. It's called krokodil, they said, because it makes you vicious, makes you violent. Krokodil, because it turns your skin to scales.

CHAPTER FIFTEEN

The boards were on a Saturday, and the day before, Maria Mikhailovna sent Ilya home early with pelmeni wrapped in foil. It was January, the clouds so low and heavy that the flag outside the school disappeared atop its pole.

Vladimir was leaning against a trash can, in the same spot where he used to meet Ilya for the walk home. He was waiting for Ilya as though it were the most natural thing in the world, as though the last four months had not happened.

Vladimir pointed at the pelmeni. "A present," he said. "You didn't have to do that."

"They're not for you," Ilya said. He'd meant to sound cutting, but he sounded childish. "Maria Mikhailovna made them." He didn't want to look at Vladimir, so he looked toward the school, hoping that Maria Mikhailovna might come out, but her classroom was aglow. She was still at her desk, grading papers, her fingertips turning white from holding her pen so tightly.

"Of course she did. She still have a thing for you?" Vladimir said.

Ilya shrugged.

"So, America?" Vladimir said. "Were you gonna leave without saying good-bye?" His voice was soft, and when Ilya did look at him, his face was full of some emotion that Ilya had never seen on him before—whether sadness or envy or regret, Ilya wasn't sure.

"I don't go until August. If I pass the boards," Ilya mumbled, and then, because he would hate himself if he didn't say anything at all, he said, "I thought you'd left."

"Left where? Berlozhniki? Where the fuck would I go?" Vladimir laughed, which was what he did to break awkward moments and make them better. "Plus I've got my hot-ass girlfriend here. I've got my man, Ilya. And I've got this new place," he said. "Come on, I'll show you."

Ilya closed his eyes and tried to find the anger that had been so huge in him all winter. It was there, but it was small compared to his relief. You've been waiting for this, he thought. You've wanted this. He looked up at his brother and smiled. "You still want me to hide you in my suitcase?"

"America is not fucking ready for *this*!" Vladimir flicked both hands against his chest. "*This* cannot fit in a suitcase!" He was grinning, and Ilya found himself grinning back. That was Vladimir's charm: to make you feel like you'd been living in a dark corner, unseen, until his light swept over you.

"Let's go," he said. Ilya smiled, feeling a rush inside himself, a melting sort of happiness that stung the back of his eyes and made his throat go narrow. He thought of what Babushka had said about his missing yolk. See, he thought, as he followed Vladimir down the street toward the square. See, he wanted to tell her, nothing's missing.

Aksinya was waiting in her car outside the Minutka, the beams of her headlights giving up against the snow.

"You found him," she said to Vladimir. As Ilya climbed in the backseat, she said, "What's up," in that dry, angry way of hers that Ilya had learned over time did not actually mean she was angry.

"I have your coat. The one with the fur." He'd stuffed the coat in the back of his mother's and Babushka's closet, and now he saw that it was creepy to have taken it in the first place and to have been imagining ways he might get it back to her. "Maria Mikhailovna was going to throw it out," he added.

"She's the worst. She's hated me since Basic."

Ilya almost told her that Maria Mikhailovna didn't hate her and that she'd called her smart, but Aksinya was smiling grimly, like Maria Mikhailovna's hatred was hard-earned and worth preserving. She had a black stocking hat pulled down over her ears and eyebrows, and it made what was left of her face look stark. It was the first time he'd looked at her and not thought her beautiful. With the dome light shining down, he saw that Vladimir looked like her in the way old people look alike, as if they've all shrunk down to fit one final mold. His chin had gone sharp. His arms like birch branches. And he'd rolled the elastic of his warm-up pants at the waist.

Aksinya pressed the gas and the car sprang forward. The snow was dry and thick, the sort of flakes that lived long enough to be examined on your palm. Vladimir produced some Imperia from the footwell and handed it to Ilya, and the rim of the bottle was so cold that it numbed Ilya's tongue before he could taste the vodka. He took a small sip, thinking of the boards the next day. He had planned nothing for this evening but to go to bed early after a final practice test that he did not need to take. The car sped out of town, shaking to the Kolyan that Vladimir had cranked. At home, Babushka would be beginning dinner while Timofey read aloud to her from the paper. His mother would be waiting for her turn in the shower. Neither knew the boards were the next day. He had not told them, had not wanted them hovering, worrying, feeding him excessively and making him nervous.

Ilya took another small sip and handed Vladimir the bottle. Soon they were past the kommunalkas and across the Pechora, which was nothing but a dip in the snow. The refinery was big and bright, its lights cast long. Looking at it, Ilya felt the same wash of wonder that comes with a spectacular sunset or a moon, huge and full. Like the refinery could trip some primal recognition of beauty, like it could convince him that it had its own gravity.

Vladimir said, "How's Mama?"

"She's crazy. She's on a diet competition with Nadya Radeyeva and they've both gained a kilo and gotten bitchy."

"Typical."

Aksinya pushed the gas through a patch of ice, and Ilya felt the tires twist under them, then straighten. "You two don't know a thing about being a woman," she said.

"I know my way around a woman," Vladimir said.

"Asshole," she murmured. She had the bottle between her thighs, and she took a swig. She thrust the bottle toward Ilya again and said, "Cheers."

This far out of town there wasn't much except for the refinery. A lumber mill. Some old, wooden houses that had belonged to the heads of the camp when it had been operational. The camp itself, whose buildings were clustered to the right, just the same gray as the sky, and beyond them the Tower, which marked the northern end of the prison yard. Somewhere along this stretch the plow driver had found Yulia Podtochina, and Ilya scanned the snowbanks for the pink flash of a bare foot.

Ice curled around the corners of the windows like filigree. In the passenger seat, Vladimir scraped at it with a fingernail. His giant gold watch drooped almost to his elbow. It was supposed to look like a Rolex, like the one Michael Douglas wore in *Wall Street*,

and when Aksinya had given it to him, it had fit his wrist perfectly.

"Are you coming back to school?" Ilya said.

As soon as he'd said it, he knew that it was a terrible question.
He was sure that school was the last thing these two thought about,
but Aksinya answered evenly, "Yeah. Eventually."

"A lot of people are gone."

She looked over at Vladimir, and Ilya felt them agreeing not to
talk, then her phone bleated and lit up in the cup holder. Vladimir
flipped it open. "Lana's there," he said. "She's on board."

Ilya hadn't seen Lana in months, not since the morning he'd run
into her and Sergey outside the school. Lana with the pink hair,
who wasn't as pretty as Aksinya, but wasn't as brittle either. Lana
bit her nails sometimes. Sometimes Lana didn't know what to say.
"On board with what?"

Vladimir turned to Ilya. "Congratulations, tovarishch. This is a
big night for you."

Aksinya cackled.

"A big night?" Ilya said, wondering if it was a coincidence that
the boards were the next day, whether this big night was Vladimir's
way of forgiving him for America, and at the thought, Ilya felt himself forgive Vladimir everything: his jealousy, his absence, the robbery. Everything.

Aksinya slowed, parked on the side of the road and looked back
at him. "What's that?" she said.

Ilya looked down and realized that he was still clutching the
packet of pelmeni from Maria Mikhailovna.

"Pelmeni," he said.

"Perfect. We don't have anything for dinner," she said, and she
took the pelmeni from him and handed him the vodka bottle.

The Tower was a square, concrete building not any different in shape from the kommunalkas or the school or the old office buildings that framed the arbat. Each floor was a string of a dozen rooms. A few had rusted stoves and cots with sagging springs. Other rooms were totally bare: four walls, a drain in the center of the floor, and the feel of a cell. On the roof there was a crow's nest, where the guards had stood, eyes narrowed, scanning the horizon for escapees. When they were young, in the summer, Ilya and Vladimir and Sergey would come out to the Tower, pry loose tiles from the showers, pitch them off the roof, and watch them shatter on the ground.

Once, when they were crossing the field that had been the prison yard, a woman had flagged them down. She was in nice clothes, city clothes, the high heels of her boots sinking in the mud. She'd asked them where the graves were. The graves were unmarked and everywhere—babushkas found bones in their vegetable patches—but Sergei had demanded five hundred rubles for information, and then pointed the woman toward a pile of stones at the edge of the field. The woman thanked them, her voice clotted as though she might cry, and then she'd picked her way toward the stones, which were the remains of an outhouse. Sergei had bought some comics and an enormous cake with the five hundred rubles, and they'd all eaten it until they felt sick.

Ilya had never liked the Tower much. It was a hike from the kommunalkas—a place where you could yell and hear it echo, but places like that weren't hard to find in Berlozhniki. That night, though, the place seemed to have a spirit, a sort of throb. They walked into a giant room—the mess hall, Ilya remembered. There

were no lights, but Vladimir had brought a flashlight, and the
beam lanced the air and showed snatches of sloppy graffiti and
glass crushed so fine underfoot that it looked like snow. Vladimir
and Aksinya wove through the room, and Ilya followed them to a
set of stairs that smelled of urine. They climbed up two flights, or
maybe it was three. In the dark it was hard to tell. There was music
playing somewhere, punctuated every once in a while by a shout or
groan. Vladimir pushed aside a curtain and led them down a long
corridor. Ilya looked into each room as they passed. Figures huddled by a stove, which gave off the smell of things that shouldn't
burn. In one room, a girl sat on a mattress staring at a phone. In
another, two guys were wrestling. Their necks flashed in the light,
and Ilya couldn't tell if they were joking or serious until one yelled,
"Mercy!" and the other started to laugh. Ilya gripped the vodka
bottle, glad to have something to hold, and from time to time he
took a sip so that he didn't have to look into any more rooms. As
they neared the end of the corridor, Aksinya tilted her head back
and called, "Lana!"

Lana poked her head out of a doorway and closed her eyes
against the flashlight's glare. "Hi," she said. "Hi, Ilya."

"This is us," Vladimir said, and he led them into a room with
four folding chairs in a circle around a pile of blankets. A rug hung
over the window, and a poster of Sylvester Stallone was tacked to
one wall. Ammo rounds were draped around his neck and machine
guns weighed down each of his arms. On the opposite wall, Putin
smirked in a suit, with a marker-drawn cock in his mouth.

"What do you think?" Vladimir said. He opened the stove door
and poked it with a stick. A weak wave of heat hit Ilya.

"Cool," Ilya said, though what he felt was closer to incredulity.
Vladimir was homeless. Worse, he had chosen this over home. The

vodka gnawed at Ilya's mind. The floor pitched a little. He sat heavily in one of the chairs.

Lana sat next to him. Her hair had grown in—the pink streaks began below her ears now. She'd lost weight, like Vladimir and Aksinya, only she had had some to lose, and she looked better for it. She reached for the vodka bottle and took a long sip.

"How's school?" she said. She was drunk, and it made her voice even softer and sweeter than usual.

"It's school," he said. "You know."

Aksinya laughed. "Like you don't love it," she said.

"Like you weren't little miss bookworm in primary," Vladimir said.

"Yeah," Aksinya said, "before you came along and fucked up my life." She picked up one of the blankets, shook it, and spread it out again. In the corner, there was a heap of Vladimir's clothes, a paperback with the cover torn off, a pink plastic bag, and a pair of red high heels.

"I just got a headache every time I walked through those doors," Lana said, sounding mournful. Ilya believed her. For all her sweetness, she had never been smart.

Aksinya folded another blanket into a pillow and laid it on the ground too. Then she nudged Vladimir and said, "We need to find Sergey."

"Bottoms up, tovarishch," Vladimir said. "Be back in a bit." He and Aksinya backed out the door, and Ilya could hear the echo of Aksinya laughing.

Ilya looked at Lana. There was this acid burn in his throat, and his stomach felt boggy, and he wanted to ask her if she felt the same way when she drank, but he knew better.

"You live here now? The three of you?" he said.

"Sometimes. Aksinya and I usually stay at her sister's," she said. She pushed up the sleeve of her sweater and scratched at the edge of a scab on her arm. "It's not as bad as it seems."

"It doesn't seem bad," Ilya lied.

Lana laughed, leaned back in her chair, and stretched her toes out toward the stove. She handed Ilya the bottle again, and he drank a gulp big enough to make his eyes water. He could hear the wind breaking itself against the walls. He could hear it seeping through the concrete. He scooted his chair closer to the stove and wondered what time it was, whether his mother and Babushka had started to worry.

"You know, I'm shy too," Lana said. "Not like those two." She waved a hand toward the door. "They'd talk a rock into moving. And Sergey. He never shuts up. Aren't men supposed to be the quiet ones? Between him and Vladimir, Aksinya and I can't get a word in."

She stood, and grabbed one of his hands. "Come here," she said. She had a loose sort of grin, and when he stood he could see that her eyes were glazed, and he wondered just how much she'd had to drink, or whether she was high too.

"I'm cold," she said. She took his other hand. He tensed despite the vodka, and she could tell. "That means you should hold me," she said.

He swallowed, nodded, and did not move.

"Here." She arranged his arms around her waist like they might begin slow dancing. He'd seen Babushka and Timofey dance like this once, when Muslim Magomayev had come on the radio and they'd thought Ilya was asleep.

"Better, right?" she said.

He nodded, and she pressed her hands against his thigh. He guessed she was aiming for his crotch, and it didn't really matter that she'd missed. His dick prickled and warmed, this feeling of gathering tension that surged as she repositioned her hand and began to rub him. He was shorter than her, and when he tried to kiss her, his lips didn't meet hers. They landed on her jaw instead, and so he kissed that. He kissed her shoulder, where her bra strap edged out from under her shirt. It was see-through, like a thin strip of plastic wrap, something he would have wondered about at any other time, but she took her hands off of his crotch long enough to direct his lips to hers. She tasted like vodka, or maybe that was him, and he couldn't tell if the swimming, spinning feeling in his head was from kissing, from the way her tongue was dipping into his mouth, or whether he was drunker than he'd thought.

She swayed a little, giggled, her lips vibrating against his.

"Let's lie down," she said, lowering herself onto her knees, with her hands still on him. Together they slumped down onto the blankets like some sort of clumsy, lame beast. And just as he thought how glad he was that the blankets were there, that they didn't have to lie on broken glass, he realized that Vladimir and Aksinya had planned this, that Aksinya had made this bed of blankets for just this purpose. The thought terrified him, and he twisted, looking for the door. Lana pressed her lips into his ear. "You're going to America, huh?" she whispered. "Hot shot. Big hot shot."

She tried to pull his sweater up over his head, but it caught on his ears long enough for him to say, "It's too cold," and pull it back down.

"You don't want to show up a virgin, do you?" she said. Behind her, people walked past the doorway. Just smeared silhouettes. One paused, a dark shadow that seemed to take them in.

"Let's shut the door," he said, but there was no door in the frame.

"We burned it," she said. Then she saw his face, saw that he was imagining a bonfire, girls dancing, things sacrificed. She pointed to the stove in the corner. "There," she said, laughing.

She leaned in and sucked at his earlobe, flicked her tongue against it.

"Lana," he said. "I don't feel good."

"How about now?" she said, as she grappled with his jeans, searching for the zipper, and his dick swelled at the prospect of escape.

"Stop," he whispered. "OK. Stop."

She let her hands drop. "What's wrong?" she said.

"Nothing," he said. He couldn't see much of her face, just light and dark, dips and curves.

She considered him for a moment and said, "Fine, let's stop, but you've got to tell your brother we fucked."

He nodded, and she kissed him again, but more lightly this time, like he was something very fragile. "You know, you're cute," she said. "You don't have to be so nervous." She kissed him one more time. "That was just for you. On the house," she said. "I might see you there, you know."

"Where?"

"America," she said, and Ilya was trying to parse the implication of this as someone began shouting in the corridor.

"It's Sergey," Ilya said.

"Fucking Sergey the drama queen," Lana said. She smoothed out her shirt and tucked the one bra strap back under the fabric. "Stay here," she said, and disappeared into the corridor.

He followed her as far as the doorway. It was dark, but he could still see figures huddled a few doors down, and as his eyes adjusted, he picked out Vladimir and Sergey and Lana and Aksinya, and someone else lying on the floor at their feet. It was one of the guys Ilya had seen wrestling earlier, only he wasn't smiling now. His jaw was slack and there was blood trickling out of his nose. Then Sergey said, "Pizdun," and kicked the guy. The guy groaned, and Sergey kicked him again.

Aksinya put a hand on Sergey's arm. "He's not going to pay if you knock him out," she said, sounding more tired than alarmed.

Ilya took a few steps toward them, and something sharp and metal tripped him. He caught himself with his hands, and felt glass and rocks dig into his palms. The group turned at the noise.

"Ilyusha?" Vladimir said.

Ilya was silent for a second, like that might make him invisible, and then Vladimir said, "Give me a minute," as though he were finishing up in the bathroom or jamming the last blini in his mouth before they left for school.

"Tomorrow, you hear me?" Sergey said to the guy on the ground.

Ilya turned back into the room. He held his hands out by the stove and brushed the grit off them. He wanted a glass of water, badly, or at least a handful of snow, but the idea of finding his way outside was dizzying, so instead he took another drink from the vodka bottle.

When Vladimir came back, a cigarette glowed in his mouth. Lana and Aksinya were with him. Sergey had gone to meet his girlfriend.

"So," Vladimir said, toeing the nest of blankets on the ground.

"Don't be nosy," Lana said. Ilya was quiet, and Lana reached out, took his hand, and swung it in hers. "It was good," she said softly, and from the way she said it, he could tell that she meant it, at least a little.

"Of course he was fucking good," Vladimir said. His words came out thick. He needed the doorjamb to stand. "He tell you about America?"

"*You* told me about America," she said, but Vladimir went on.

His eyes stretched past them, past Lana who was wrapping a blanket around her shoulders, past the smoking stove and Sylvester Stallone and the walls and wind.

"He's gonna be a fucking mobster. You think this is big-time?" he said, swooping his cigarette through the air in a gesture that could have meant the room, the Tower, or the whole of Russia. "Selling teenths and handling a whore or two? Ilya. Ilya's gonna go to America. There are Russians galore there, managing shit. Then he's gonna—"

"Come back and run this whole machine." Lana and Aksinya said it just as Vladimir did, and Vladimir pointed at them.

"Exactly," he said. A long tail of ash dropped off his cigarette. Ilya stared at Vladimir. He'd said this—all this gangster America shit—before. He'd said it enough for Lana and Aksinya to memorize it. It was ridiculous, of course, but still this sweet sort of warmth grew in Ilya's belly.

Ilya reached for Vladimir's cigarette and took a puff. "You and me. We'll run shit," he said.

Lana looked over at him, as though he'd only just now come into focus, or just now slid out of it. She licked at her lips, and he could feel them, damp and pillowy against his own. "Why the fuck would you come back?" she said.

"He comes back," Vladimir yelled, "for his brother!"

"Enough already," Aksinya said.

"Are you getting antsy?" Vladimir said. He hooked a finger through one of Aksinya's belt loops, pulled her close, and looked over her head to Ilya.

"Ilyusha, I think the ladies are ready for the next phase of the evening."

They all sat on the blankets, and so Ilya did the same. Vladimir pulled his pencil case out of his backpack, and then, out of the case, came their mother's silver spoon. Vladimir's eyes met Ilya's for a second, and then Vladimir stuck the spoon in his mouth, smiled around it, and dug a vial and a bottle of what looked like eye drops from the case.

After the robbery, Timofey had gone to the two pawnshops in town and found Dedushka's medals and their mother's rings and the samovar, and he had presented them to Babushka as though they were precious samizdat, *The Gulag Archipelago* or *The White Book* hand copied, and Babushka had acted as though it were the loss of the things that had broken her heart, as though it could be mended by their return. Timofey hadn't been able to find the vouchers or the spoon, and Ilya hadn't ever told him about the *Michael & Stephanie* tapes or the player. As Vladimir shook a mound of powder into the spoon's dip, Ilya wondered whether he'd sold them too, whether some other kid was listening to Michael and Stephanie right at that moment. Vladimir squeezed a few drops from the bottle on top of the powder and the powder let out a weak hiss as it turned liquid. Aksinya was sitting next to him, and she held a lighter under the spoon. She and Lana and Vladimir all watched the liquid, and Ilya watched them and wondered whether their concentration had ever been so complete. Their faces looked like the faces of the men who'd first made fire and had stared at it with a hunger and happiness they couldn't hide.

Lana went first, and when Vladimir filled the needle and held it over her arm, Ilya closed his eyes and thought of blank paper, just as he did before vaccines and after nightmares.

"There," Vladimir said. Ilya opened his eyes and watched Lana's shut. Looking at her felt like a violation. Her mouth went ajar and he could see her tongue perched there on her teeth, as though she were about to speak. Vladimir slipped the needle out of her arm, wiped the tip on his jeans, and turned to Aksinya. Aksinya had pulled a hair elastic up her arm and was doing hand curls and squeezing her fist.

"Gotova," she said. She straightened her arm. There was a vein, fat and gray as a grub, at her elbow, and Vladimir poked the needle into it without a bit of hesitation.

"You always get the ladies high first," he said. "Common courtesy."

Aksinya sighed and slumped back so that one of her arms was pressed against Ilya's. Somewhere in the depths of the Tower he heard a boy yell, "Marco!" It echoed, and then a girl called back, "Polo!"

"You ready for this?" Vladimir said. Vladimir was sucking the last of the liquid into the syringe. Ilya was terrified. He didn't know what it was, exactly, but the girls seemed to be unconscious or close to it—Lana was making a sort of purring sound—and they had presumably done it before. He thought of the rumors at school. How you could die from one hit, how it turned your skin to scales. But Vladimir is here, he thought. Vladimir will take care of me. Ilya pushed up the sleeve of his sweatshirt. Vladimir was tapping the syringe.

"Ready," Ilya said.

Vladimir looked at him. "Are you fucking kidding me, Ilyusha? Finish the vodka, but none of this. OK? This is not for you."

It was a relief; it was embarrassing. Ilya's arm was still outstretched, and so he grabbed the bottle and took as big a swallow as he could manage.

"It's krokodil?"

Vladimir nodded. He was tying himself off with a bandana, his teeth on one end, and Ilya thought—too late—that he should have offered to help. "We don't really call it that, though. We don't really call it anything." There was a warmth to his voice. It was a tone he only used with Ilya, when he told Ilya things about the world, about women, about music, about how to act. He would make a good teacher, Ilya realized, though of course that would never happen.

"What does it make you feel like?"

Vladimir laughed. He ran a finger down the length of his arm, where there was a bruise that stretched from his bicep to his forearm. Ilya couldn't see any of his veins, but Vladimir stuck the needle in anyhow.

"It's funny," he said. He was moving the syringe around, fishing in his flesh for a vein. "Mostly it makes me remember."

"Remember what?"

"Stuff," Vladimir said. He pushed the plunger down. "Do you remember the time Papa took us to Leshukonskoye?"

Ilya shook his head, though there was something about it that rang a bell.

"You were little, I guess. I don't know—four or five, maybe. We were supposed to go visit a friend of his, but there was something wrong with the Lada. It was guzzling petrol, making this thumping sound, and Papa kept joking that he'd kidnapped Stalin and stashed him in the trunk. It took us forever, even to just get to the end of Ulitsa Lenina. We had to stop at every petrol station along the way for gas and to see if there was a mechanic in. Papa would get a beer at each, and so then we were stopping for him to piss every half hour."

Ilya laughed.

"He was a wonderful drunk, though," Vladimir said, "which is where I get it."

"Clearly," Ilya said.

"You were being a bitch, of course. Complaining about being hungry all the time and carsick, and Papa just turned the music up loud, so we couldn't hear you or the car thumping, and I remember wondering why he wasn't worried about how we were going to make it to Leshukonskoye, let alone back home, but he wasn't. So I didn't worry about it either," Vladimir said. "I can count the number of days I spent with him. On one hand."

Ilya nodded, and Vladimir leaned back so that his head was nestled against Aksinya's.

"Then the petrol gauge was low again, and we rolled into this station with these bright yellow pumps and a wind chime dangling above the door. Papa went inside to pay. He told us not to move a muscle, and so we didn't. For ten minutes. Twenty. And then you had to pee, so I took you out and let you pee on the shoulder. It was hot in the car, so we sat outside instead, and wrote our names in the dust on the pumps. And there was this old cat with a goiter on its stomach that dragged in the dirt, and we found sticks and were playing this game where you got a point if you poked its goiter with a stick. Of course the cat got pissed and then it got desperate, and it was running for the road, and you were following it. Fucking toddling along after it, not a care in the world except that you wanted points, you wanted to win, and I can see this truck coming. Flat out. Fast as it can go. You were screaming at the cat, and then you tripped over your stick and fell into the road. And you were just lying there, whining about a scrape on your knee, in the middle of the road, and the truck is basically on you, is honking so loud, and I was so fucking scared, but I ran out there and pulled you to the shoulder and the truck swerved and the cat—splat."

Vladimir clapped his hands softly.

"No way," Ilya said.

"Swear to God," Vladimir said. "Swear on Papa."

Ilya lifted an eyebrow. Vladimir had lied in their father's name before and, when called on it, said, "What does he care? He's dead."

Vladimir shrugged. "It's the truth," he said. "I practically shat my pants. I thought you were toast. I was so scared I made you hide under a blanket in the backseat with me for a full hour, sweating our balls off. And when Papa finally came out, he was even more wonderfully drunk, and he'd bought us slingshots and candy."

Ilya remembered the slingshots, the smooth birch handles, the cradles made of strips of tire rubber that smelled singed. They were strong enough to shoot a rock from their balcony all the way across the courtyard. "I kept waiting for you to say something about the truck. I wanted to know if he'd be proud of me for saving you or if I'd get in trouble for letting you in the road in the first place, but you didn't say a word, and he slept it off. We ate the candy, and the next time you had to piss I made you do it in a bottle. Then he woke up and drove us home. Like he'd forgotten all about Leshukonskoye. Like he'd never meant to get there in the first place."

"That's what you remember?" Ilya said, because aside from the slingshots the memory didn't seem to hold much that was good.

"It's the farthest from home I've ever been," Vladimir said. "Halfway to fucking Leshukonskoye." His eyes were drooping, and next to him, the girls' faces had gone pale, like faces under ice.

"But you could remember it anyway," Ilya said, and he could feel himself getting shrill.

"I know, but it's more than remembering. It's like it's all happening at once. Like I'm there and like I'm holding it at the same time. And then there are the times that aren't so good."

"What happens those times?"

Vladimir smiled at Ilya, a melting sort of smile. "This time's going to be good. Look—" He held his hand out to Ilya and opened his fist as though there were something in it that might explain, but his palm was empty.

They were just taking naps. That's what Ilya told himself over and over. When he couldn't convince himself of that, he told himself that they were all having the good high, the remembering kind. And it seemed as though they were. Aksinya laughed twice, said her sister's name, and then called for someone named Yuri. Once Vladimir started to hum, but Ilya did not know the tune. He watched them for a while, and then he began to look for his tapes. They were in the pink plastic bag in the corner, stuffed underneath a camouflage sweatshirt of Vladimir's. Ilya counted them. All ten were there. He read each of their titles and ran his finger down their spines. The tape player was in the bag too, and this was a mystery to Ilya. Vladimir could have sold the player in an instant—the pawnshop was filled with more worthless items, with the flotsam of the Soviet years—but he hadn't. There was a glimmer of decency in this, a tiny promise of restraint, and so Ilya put the tapes and the player back into the bag.

It took Aksinya and Lana an hour to come to, longer for Vladimir, and Ilya gathered that, chivalry aside, Vladimir had given himself a little extra. They were quiet when they woke, with sour faces. They drank more of the vodka, and ate Maria Mikhailovna's pelmeni, which had congealed into a cold lump.

The boards were the next day, in twelve hours. Ilya hadn't forgotten, but still he took the bottle whenever they handed it to him, and when Lana said, "Let's go dance," he agreed. As they walked down the corridor, he nudged Vladimir with his elbow.

"Was it the good high?" he asked.

Vladimir smiled. "Yeah," he said. "I saw you there."

People had flooded the mess hall while Vladimir and the girls were high. It was so full that as Ilya moved through it he felt his feet leave the ground, like he was suspended in that crush of bodies. It smelled of yeast and smoke, and more than once, Ilya was jabbed with the burning tip of someone's cigarette. Lana was a good dancer, better than Aksinya, who could never quite lose her stiffness, and Ilya just copied Vladimir. He shuffled his feet, tried to roll his shoulders to the beat. He bummed a cigarette, and then another. He smoked his way through a Michael Jackson song and then some skinhead music from St. Petersburg and U2 and a Eurodance song that Vladimir rolled his eyes at and that Sergei flat out refused to move to.

"If you're not going to dance, take a fucking photo," Aksinya said. She jammed her phone in his hand, and Sergey pressed back against the crowd to get an angle on them.

Ilya put his arm around Lana, and tried to think why he had not let her unbutton his pants. The phone was flashing at them, over and over.

"Not your best angle, Aksinya," Sergey said.

The girls held out their fists and flicked Sergey off. Lana kissed his cheek, just as Gabe Thompson shouldered through the crowd. His face was shadowed by a black baseball cap. He bumped into Sergey, and Sergey said, "Watch yourself," and for a second Gabe's eyes seemed to take in Ilya with Lana's lips against his cheek.

"You've got competition, Ilyusha," Vladimir said, as Gabe disappeared into the crowd.

Sergey flipped the phone shut, and the song ended.

"Thank you Jesus," he said, and the bass started up again, these deep plunging notes. A rap song, Ilya thought, and Vladimir must have recognized it because he started to cheer, and then they were all dancing.

Chapter Sixteen

It was strange watching Sadie look at the picture from the Tower: at his brother, Lana, and Aksinya. At him.

"You look different," Sadie said. "Happier."

He did look carefree, but he hadn't been. He had been worried about Vladimir for months by then.

"And that's Vladimir?" She pointed at him, and Ilya nodded. He expected her to examine him, to lean in and see if the truth was written on the planes of his face, and Ilya wouldn't have blamed her—that was what he wanted to do with Gabe Thompson—but she just said, "You have the same eyes."

She pointed again, at Gabe this time.

"That's him," Ilya said.

She hunched close to the screen and zoomed in on the picture just as Ilya had a few weeks earlier. Gabe's cheeks bloated and his eyes fattened, the hat and that bear looming over them.

Outside, there was a splash, then a shriek. Marilee and Molly were swimming with Papa Cam, and Mama Jamie was sitting on a beach chair, her laptop propped on her thighs, organizing a Halloween costume drive for needy children. Sadie had told them that she and Ilya were working on a joint history report on the Founding Fathers.

Ilya clicked over to the photo of Lana on the bed in Gabe's hat.

"It's the same, right?" he said, and she nodded.

"Maybe the bear's a mascot," she said. She traced its outline on the screen. It was jagged with pixels.

"What's a mascot?" Ilya said.

"Like a symbol for a team or a club or whatever, and if we knew what team, it might tell us where he's from. Leffie High's mascot is the Gators. Louisiana State's the tiger," she said, "so somebody from New York's probably not going to be wearing a hat with the LSU tiger on it."

"Of course," he said, thinking of Vladimir's Severstal jersey with the eagle diving across one arm. He felt this tiny lift in his chest, a loosening of his lungs. If they could narrow down his list to a state or even a region, then there was a chance of finding Gabe before the arraignment. And even if Vladimir did plead guilty, maybe it wouldn't matter if Ilya could prove that Gabe had actually committed the murders.

Sadie opened a new browser window and searched for "mascot" and "bear," her fingers flying across the keys. That turned up hundreds of people prancing around in bear suits, so they narrowed the search to "NFL mascot" and "bear," and then "MLB mascot" and "bear." They searched hockey teams, basketball teams, college teams, high school teams, debate teams, and they found lots of bear mascots, but none were like the one on Gabe's hat: fangs bared, tongue splayed, and a rabid roll to the eyes.

"I guess it could be anything—an emblem, a character, a logo for some company," she said. "Have you tried Facebook or Myspace?"

Ilya shook his head. "I don't have an account. I checked VKontakte, but he wasn't on there."

Sadie logged in to her Facebook account and typed in Gabe's name. The results loaded endlessly. There were seventy Gabe Thompsons, and again Ilya felt this lightness in his chest. It wasn't just the possibility of all of these faces—it was Sadie's hope too, the way it amplified his own.

They combed through the profiles one by one, eliminating anyone over forty and under eighteen, anyone who wasn't white, anyone with brown or black hair, anyone who had been anywhere but Berlozhniki the previous year. After an hour they reached the Facebook dregs: the profiles that hadn't been updated for years, the ones with a John Doe silhouette where a picture should be or else an anonymous, grainy shot. Of a blue sports car, in one case, and a droopy-eared dog with bloodshot eyes in the other.

"I'm sorry," she said. She turned and faced him, leaning against the desk. They hadn't touched since the night before at the Pound, and he had the feeling that the longer he waited, the harder it would get.

"Don't be," he said. This was a phrase that he'd heard her say to someone, and though he loved the quick rhythm of it, the meaning had mystified him at first. *Don't be*. A command against existence.

He reached out and touched her hand, and she looked out the glass doors. They could see only one corner of the pool, and Marilee's head rose out of it, a dark splotch, like a seal's, above the water.

"My parents would freak out," Sadie said.

"Because I'm Russian?"

"No," Sadie said, "'cause of my mom. They live in fear that I'm going to have a baby any second."

Ilya went quiet at the implication of all that pregnancy entailed, and Sadie leaned over and kissed him again. Her lips were chapped and a little rough, like winter skin.

"So we just have to be careful," she said, "and they'll keep assuming you have a girlfriend in Russia." She clicked out of her account and closed the browser, and the picture of Lana was waiting there behind it, her freckles scattered across her nose like birdseed.

"Was she your girlfriend?" Sadie asked.

"No," he said. He thought of Lana kissing him. Maybe a little part of her had wanted to, but mostly she'd been fulfilling her end of the deal with Vladimir. He'd understood that when Vladimir gave her the krokodil. "I guess I had a crush on her. She was the only one of Vladimir's friends who was nice to me, really."

Sadie nodded. She moved one of her legs so that it rested against his knee.

There was a knock at the glass doors, and Sadie and Ilya both whipped around. Molly was standing under the deck in her swimsuit, a pair of goggles pulled torturously tight across her eyes.

"Come swim!" she yelled. "Mom says you're going to get vitamin deficient if you don't get outside!"

Sadie looked at him.

"OK," he said. He clicked the X in the top corner of the picture, but it took a second for the image to disappear, and in that second Lana's expression seemed clouded with disappointment.

After church the next day, he and Sadie worked on the list of Gabe Thompsons, starting with Colorado and Utah, where, Sadie said, there were the most Mormons. They found two matches, and Sadie must have seen the excitement on his face because she said, "I think *everyone* is Mormon there. Not that one of these isn't him, but just so you know."

Ilya stared at the two numbers, which he'd circled in red ink. "I don't think I can call," he said. "My accent—I don't want him to know I'm looking for him. Or at least not until I'm there to see his face."

"I'll call. What should I say?" Sadie said.

Ilya had thought of this. All those nights when he'd compiled the list, then begun crossing Gabes off it. "Say you're calling for Mr. Gabe Thompson because he left a personal item on his flight." Ilya was especially proud of that quintessentially American phrase, "personal item," which had been used dozens of times on his own flight to the States.

They told the Masons that they were taking Durashka for a walk and sat on the stoop of the half-built house at the bottom of Dumaine Drive. Durashka curled at their feet resignedly, as though she'd known all along that the walk was a ruse. Sadie punched the first number into her cell and cupped the phone to her ear. Ilya was expecting to have to wait, because nothing about finding Gabe Thompson had been easy thus far, but a voice answered before the first ring had even finished.

"Howdy," the voice said.

"Hi," Sadie said, "I'm calling for Mr. Gabe Thompson."

"You got him." It wasn't him. Ilya was almost positive. The man sounded like a cowboy, like John Wayne in the few westerns that Vladimir had allowed in his VHS collection.

"I'm calling because you left a personal item on your flight."

"My flight?"

"Yes, sir," Sadie looked at Ilya, eyes wide. This was as far as the script went.

"Darling," he said, "I wish I'd been on a flight recently, but I think you've got the wrong guy."

Ilya shook his head, and Sadie apologized and hung up.

"OK," she said, "take two," and she dialed the second number they'd found.

This time the call rang and rang, the sound just like that blinking cursor. Sadie was in another of her enormous T-shirts. Her collarbone jutted through the fabric like a shelf, and he thought of his own snapping at birth, and he was suddenly terrified to let her have anything at all to do with Gabe Thompson.

"Hang up," he said.

She shook her head.

"Please," he said. He reached for the phone, just as the last ring was cut short by the static of a message machine: "You've reached Gabe Thompson. Leave a message if you'd like. Have a blessed day!"

The voice was wrong. Ancient and rickety and nothing at all like Gabe Thompson's, which had been confident on his better days, but more often sullen and curt, as though he meant for his blessings to sting. Ilya ended the call, and Sadie looked at him.

"No?" she said.

"No," he said.

She rubbed Durashka's belly with the toe of her sneaker, and the dog rolled onto her back and lifted her feet up to the sky. The refinery was small on the horizon, looking, from this distance, like a castle sending out an endless smoke signal. Above them, the tarp covering the second floor ballooned with wind, then flattened again with a sigh. Somewhere inside the house, water was dripping.

"I followed you once," Ilya said. "When you went to see your mom."

He had been wanting to tell her this since the night at the Pound. She didn't know everything about him—she didn't know about the boards, didn't know that he'd kissed Lana—but he wanted her to at least know everything he knew about her.

Sadie tucked her hair behind her ear. "So you saw her," she said. "She's a wreck, huh?"

"I've seen worse," Ilya said. He turned and looked at her. It was almost dinnertime, and the last of the light pinked her skin. She squinted into the grass like she was looking for something in the blades. "Why do you go?" he asked. "Why do you watch her?"

She shrugged, and he thought that was it. He stood up, and Durashka did too, her collar jangling. Then Sadie said, "For the same reason you're doing this." She lifted the phone in her hand, but kept looking at the ground, and he realized why her room looked the way it did. Uninhabited. Like there was a suitcase just out of sight. Like she was ready for flight. She'd been the Masons' daughter for over a decade, but she was still waiting for the moment when her mom might call, might toss a bottle at her window, might want her or, at least, need her.

The sun went down, and Durashka barked as though in response. She began to chase her tail, her feet springing, the white fur on her haunches flashing. She looked like one of the chechotka girls, twirling on the stage.

"What an idiot," Sadie said, and together they walked back up the hill to the house.

Chapter Seventeen

Ilya woke in one of the folding chairs with Vladimir's jacket draped over his chest. Lana was gone, and Aksinya and Vladimir were intertwined in the lump of blankets. All Ilya could see of them was the point of an elbow, the coil of Aksinya's ponytail, and a stray foot, the sock a holed disgrace. The room was hazy. It was dark enough that it could have been early morning, that there could still have been time for him to flag down a bus headed for town, to sprint from the square to the school, to slide into his desk so quickly that its legs shrieked against the linoleum. Maria Mikhailovna would be angry, furious, but she'd forgive him when his scores came back. She'd still drive him to the airport in Leshukonskoye as they had planned. He'd still get to go to America. For a minute he let himself lie there and believe that that was what would happen. Then he got up and lifted a corner of the rug that had been hung over the window.

The sun was ridiculously high. It was almost noon. Ten, at least. The snow was electric with light, and the sight of it made blood surge at his temples. A car flashed by on its way north to the refinery. Dmitri Malikov, he thought, no doubt looking at the Tower with the same scorn that had surfaced when he talked about it. He could hear the grind of a lumber saw in the woods somewhere, and the noise drilled into his head until he could feel it in his teeth.

Behind him, someone sighed. Ilya froze, terrified that Lana had reappeared. He had no idea what to say to her. They had only kissed, but it occurred to him that he might be the sort of boy a girl regrets kissing in the morning. When he turned, Vladimir was up, pulling on his jeans with a hand against the wall. He had always been skinny, wolfish, the sort that babushkas live to feed, but there was something wrong with him now. He looked like the photos of the camp prisoners that Daniil Chernyshev showed anyone who was unlucky enough to end up in his apartment. For a dumb moment, Ilya thought, *He's sick*, then Vladimir turned, put a finger to his lips, and tipped his head toward the door. Ilya stepped over Aksinya. Sleep had drained the drugs from her face, and she looked peaceful again.

Outside, the daylight was torture. Ilya could feel his brain constricting from its brightness. "Where'd Lana go?" he asked, as they trudged across the prison yard.

"You want to get back on that horse, huh? I don't blame you. She's got that X factor. Je ne sais quoi. Every time she opens her mouth, I'm like, please don't talk, but still there's something about her. I couldn't send you to America a virgin, could I?"

"America," Ilya said. "Right."

Vladimir stopped, and Ilya was afraid that something in his voice had given him away, but Vladimir knelt in the snow and yanked at the laces of his boot, which were snarled in an icy knot. When he stood, he pointed toward a telephone pole, one of dozens strung along the road.

"They found that woman over there," he said.

"Yulia Podtochina?"

"I don't know her name," Vladimir said, with a world of impatience in his voice. "The dead one."

"Oh," Ilya said, and the day before he would have been fascinated, he would have corrected Vladimir, asked him *which* dead woman, but he was thinking of the boards. Of Maria Mikhailovna. He wanted to know the time with a sudden urgency, needed to know exactly how long it had been since she'd sat at her desk with the pale green booklet in front of her, how long since she'd ripped it in two, put on her coat, locked her classroom, and walked home. He knew that he'd made his decision the night before, when Vladimir passed him the bottle of Imperia, or when Lana wrapped his arms around her, or when he'd danced with all of them, but in those moments he'd convinced himself there was still this chance that he could make it. The chance had grown dimmer and dimmer as he slept, like a dying star, and for some reason it was crucial to him that he know how far he was from that moment when it had disappeared entirely.

"What time is it?" he said. They were almost to the telephone pole, to the mound of plowed snow that shouldered the road. It was January, and the mound was at its tallest, shoulder-high and streaked with dirt and oil.

"You got somewhere to be?"

"Nah," Ilya said.

"Good. Let's go to the Internet Kebab. We'll let the girls sleep it off. Maybe hit up Dolls. You can get back to studying tomorrow."

Once they'd made it to the snow heap, Vladimir fished his watch out from within his jacket. "It's almost twelve," he said.

It was completely over then. He was three hours late. He had never been three hours late for anything. He had missed fewer than three days of school in his entire life. Next to him, Vladimir was breathing hard, and Ilya could smell the tang of his breath. Then Vladimir put his hands on his knees and vomited into the snow. Nothing much came out, and Ilya winced at the thought of his ribs—the cage of them—heaving. They stood with their backs to the heap, waiting for a bus, Ilya thought, but when one came, and he began to scramble up, Vladimir stopped him.

"Don't you want to go?" Ilya said.

"Use your head," Vladimir said. "Mama's out."

Their mother's shift ended at twelve. She'd most likely gotten the 11:47 bus, which usually ran late enough for her to catch it, but sometimes, if the 11:47 was on time, she had to wait for the 12:17. They sat down, and the bus passed them in a wet whoosh that made Ilya's ears pop. They waited until their asses were numb and the bus was long, long gone, and Ilya wondered how many times Vladimir had done this and whether it was for their mother's sake or for his own and whether he'd ever climbed the snowbank at just the wrong time and looked up to see her looking down at him. It was fifteen minutes, maybe twenty, before they heard the hiss of another bus. Ilya stood, too fast, and his head spun a bit, and he thought he might vomit like Vladimir had. This time it was not a bus, though. It was a black SUV, cutting down the road so fast that it seemed almost to fly.

"Did you see that?" Ilya said. It had been going fast enough to miss.

"Fyodor Fetisov. Here to count his billions," Vladimir said, and Ilya couldn't tell if he was bitter or just tired.

They chanced the 12:47 bus, and it was empty except for a few neftyaniki in their coveralls, who were electric with Fetisov's visit. The bus driver was not. He took their rubles, then said, "If either of you vomits on this bus, you're not getting off until it's clean."

"Fair enough," Vladimir said, and they sank into their seats. Vladimir seemed to fall instantly asleep. His shoulder bobbed against Ilya's once they hit the potholed roads in town. Ilya's hangover grew with the motion of the bus until his headache seemed to eclipse all rational thought, to give him the attention span of a gnat. He couldn't focus on the boards, on the possibility that Maria Mikhailovna had gone straight to his apartment and that his mother and Babushka were sitting at the kitchen table waiting for him in a fury usually reserved for Vladimir. He couldn't really think of anything without a sharp, frontal lobe pain that forced him to shift his attention, and with this realization came an understanding of Vladimir and how he lived his life, sloughing through the hangovers so he could get to the highs. Dolls tonight, and what tomorrow?

Ilya shut his eyes, not really expecting to sleep, and when he opened them again, they were stopped on the square, right by the traffic light where Ilya had seen Vladimir and Sergey the night Dmitri drove him home. The bus was empty, the driver standing on the curb smoking a cigarette and drinking something out of a paper bag.

"Sweet dreams?" the driver said, as they clambered off.

Vladimir snorted, gripped the waistband of his jeans, and loped down the block toward the Internet Kebab, and Ilya followed him.

Vladimir shouldered open the door. "Hey pervert," he said to Kirill as Kirill poured water on the grill. It hissed, and a cloud of steam plumed around them. The monitors had all been set to the same screensaver—a tennis ball bouncing in eternal blackness—and they were all somehow in sync. A dozen balls hit the lower right corner, then drifted toward the middle of a dozen screens. "Ilyusha, can you spot me?" Vladimir said.

Ilya had a thousand in his wallet—name-day money that he'd

planned to exchange for dollars in Leshukonskoye. He had imagined that transaction for months—the gray-green of actual dollars in his wallet—but there was a triumph in this too: handing the thousand over to Kirill, paying for his brother, two lamb combos, two Fantas, and a computer for fifteen minutes.

Vladimir trawled VKontakte—his "business," Ilya guessed—while Ilya inhaled his shwarma. His stomach felt instantly better, like its gravity had been restored, and his hangover ebbed to a general fuzziness.

Aksinya, with her car, had beaten them to a computer. Her sister had one, Vladimir explained. It was a gift from a client, and in return, Aksinya's sister had to send him naked pictures every night. Aksinya had posted a photo of all of them to Vladimir's wall. Their faces were whitewashed and bright as snow, their eyes as shiny and black as a bird's. Lana's fist, her middle finger, took up much of the foreground, but he could see his own fingers on her waist. Aksinya had tagged herself and Vladimir, and as Vladimir scrolled the mouse across the picture, Ilya saw that he'd been tagged too.

"What bitches," Vladimir said, his voice full of affection. Vladimir clicked to the next photo—he'd been tagged in a few more from other nights: dark rooms, white faces, cigarettes, the flash hugging the curves of a bottle. Vladimir sopped the last bits of lamb juice off his plate with a hunk of pita.

"Go back to the other picture. The one with Lana," Ilya said.

"You want to see that one again, huh?"

Ilya nodded. It wasn't Lana that he wanted to see, though. He looked so happy in the photo that he barely recognized himself. His smile, like it might break his face in two. When had he last smiled like that? he wondered. Or was this the only time?

"Don't fall in love, Ilyusha."

"Why not?" he said, but he was thinking that it wasn't Lana he was in love with. It was himself, there, in a picture with Vladimir.

"Because you're leaving, for starters."

Kirill called out the one-minute warning, and Vladimir logged in to his email. He didn't have anything except a one-liner from Aksinya saying, "Dolls tonight?"

"I don't want to go."

"To Dolls?"

"No. To America."

"What do you mean you don't want to go? Are you afraid you're going to get homesick? You're going to miss all this snow while you're lounging on the beach?"

America is not one big beach, Ilya was tempted to say, because he knew that in Vladimir's mind the whole country was *Miami Vice*—girls in string bikinis and men in pastel suits.

"You going to miss sleeping with me every night?"

I already do, Ilya thought.

Vladimir pulled on his coat, and Ilya followed him out the door. The sky was purple with the last of the sun's light, and it had begun to snow.

"You going to miss getting five hours of sun and having a waste of space for a brother?"

"The boards were this morning," Ilya said.

He didn't see Vladimir's hand until it had already hit him. Then there was a flash of pain in his cheekbone and a deep throb in one eye. It had been something between a slap and a punch, sloppily executed. Ilya's eye began to sting and drip, and he pressed a hand to it.

"I thought you knew," Ilya said, and this was true. Somehow he'd thought that Vladimir had known; he'd thought that, in his way, Vladimir was asking him to stay.

"I *knew*? Are you fucking kidding me? I don't even know what day of the week it is."

"Saturday," Ilya said.

"Shut up," Vladimir said. Ilya looked up, ready for Vladimir to berate him or to hit him again, but Vladimir's eyes were slim and far away. He sucked his lip between his teeth and began chewing on it feverishly. It was a look of determination, a look as rare as a rainbow for Vladimir.

"It's only a year," Ilya said. "The America thing. It's not like—"

"Only a year. Fuck you. Do you know what people would do for one year there?"

"Don't worry about it," Ilya said, something Vladimir had said to him millions of times, and he tried to sound as casual as Vladimir always did, but of course he sounded as stung as he was: he had missed the boards for Vladimir. It was a penance of a kind, a way of making up for how happy he had been to leave.

"Shut up, Ilya."

Ilya's other eye began to sting, and he shut them both. If Vladimir could tell that he was crying, he didn't show it. When he spoke again, his voice was tough, each word hammered out like a nail hit perfectly: "Listen to me. Do not tell anyone else that you didn't show. Not a fucking soul. Do you hear me?" Vladimir's eyes were darting across Ilya's face, and sweat pearled above his lip. "I will kill you if you fuck this up," he said, and then in a voice that was almost a laugh, "Ilyusha the smart one. Ilyusha the big brilliant brain." His hands were clenching and unclenching, and it wasn't just from anger. It was time. Vladimir needed a hit. Angry as he was, he was only half here now, and the stupidity of it all hit Ilya. He could stay here, he could go to America. Either way he would lose Vladimir.

Ilya stopped crying. He could feel the skin tightening on his cheeks. "I don't know why you give a shit," he said. "This has nothing to do with you. You're going to be at the Tower no matter what, right? In that—" he searched for a word that would encompass the decrepitude of Vladimir's room there, but Vladimir spoke before he found one.

"But I could have had you *there*," he said. He smiled. It was this strange, jerky little lift of his lips that was in no way happy. "I'm going to fix this. I'm going to see Maria Mikhailovna and fix it," he said, and he walked away, past the kiosk, which was lit up like a beacon, past Gabe Thompson's bench, which was covered in new snow.

Vladimir was almost at the corner. He was limping. Just a little, one shoulder dipping down lower than the other. Had he been limping all day? Ilya wasn't sure. *Who cares*, Ilya thought, but he did. Vladimir was only a block away. Ilya's face still hurt; he could feel his eye starting to swell. He was angry—at Vladimir, at himself—but still he had to resist the same old temptation to follow Vladimir, to catch up.

CHAPTER EIGHTEEN

The cheerleaders were stacked in a pyramid on the basketball court. The smallest one perched on top of the stack, gripping her stocky leg by the ankle, toes pointed in an ecstasy of school spirit.

"Leffie Gators!" she screamed, and the pyramid deconstructed in a flash of fluorescent orange bloomers. The girls rearranged into two lines that spanned the gym, and the football players ran through a gauntlet of shaking pompoms, while a male of murky sexuality yelled their names and numbers through a bullhorn.

It had surprised Ilya that Leffie High was not so different from School #17—as though institutional style had been an addendum to some international accord—but the gym was the exception. The gym at School #17 was a remnant of a concrete factory, with one wall of windows so old that each pane thickened at the bottom. The glass was barred against errant balls, so that the light coming through plaided the plank floors. Leffie High's gym was window-less, trapped in the center of the school, with a smell that reminded Ilya of the opening gasp of a time capsule, of air held captive for centuries.

He was sitting at the top row of the bleachers. Directly beneath him a couple seemed to be having sex or something close to it. He and Sadie had done nothing but kiss. It had been a week of him and Sadie as a thing now, as something joined by an "and," and his body wanted what came next as badly as his mind feared it. Vladimir had told him plenty of lewd stories and shown him a few pornos at the Kebab, but still Ilya felt completely unprepared to navigate anything beyond kissing, so he was taking breaks from the overwhelming pep of the pep rally to peer between the bleachers' slats at the progress below. The boy had the girl pressed up against a wall, and his hand was down the front of her jeans. His mouth was on her neck, which was arched, her eyes closed in an expression that shifted continually from boredom to ecstasy to annoyance, and the mercurialness of her experience terrified Ilya.

On the basketball court, the last football player was announced. Ilya couldn't find Sadie in the crowd. The entire student body was in Leffie High colors: fluorescent orange and lime green. The combination made the gym look like the confluence of two terrible chemical spills, and Principal Gibbons strode into the center of it with a microphone and began to wax poetic about the football team. Below the bleachers the girl's pants were halfway off now, obscured by an overpour of upper thigh flesh. The boy's head was bent, his hands at his own crotch. Ilya wasn't sure what he was doing—whether he was working on his zipper or putting on a condom—and as he tried to puzzle it out, the girl looked up, and her eyes met Ilya's.

"What the fuck," she said, as though she had been copulating somewhere private and Ilya had intruded.

The boy followed her eyes and glared. "Fuck off," he said, and Ilya slid down a row and over, toward a clot of kids playing some sort of fantasy card game. Below them, the marching band stood, their feathered caps shaking, a conductor waved an arm, and cymbals crashed. Ilya's heart was racing from the girl's yell and the boy's glare, and so it took him a long moment to notice Sadie, who had just come in through a side door. Her ponytail whipped over one shoulder as she turned, scanning the crowd. He could tell that she was looking for him, and the knowledge of it calmed him, made him feel warm and full. Bread belly, he and Vladimir had called that feeling when they were little and happiness was as simple as eating too much.

She saw him and lifted a hand and ran across the basketball court. As a rule, Sadie was composed. Soft-spoken. Almost every conversation between Mama Jamie and her began with her saying, "I'm right here. You don't have to yell." He had never heard her say anything in public that might be overheard—Babushka would love this about her, her natural discretion—but as she took the stairs two at a time, she began to call his name. The kids playing the card game froze and looked at her. Her cheeks were splotched. On the court, the cheerleaders cartwheeled. Principal Gibbons began to sing the school song just as Sadie reached Ilya's row and sidestepped past the gamers.

"Look," she said. She was holding a piece of paper that was shaking in her hand.

"He wrote me back," she said. "Gabe Thompson."

"Back?" Ilya said.

Sadie nodded. "I wrote them all—all the outdated profiles. I figured it couldn't hurt."

She handed him a printout of a series of Facebook messages, and Ilya read them from the bottom up, from the first message Sadie had sent:

Hi,

I'm a high school sophomore doing a report on Russia, and I got your name through the LDS community. I just have a few questions about what it's like there after communism and was wondering if you might be able to answer them. Thanks for your time and God bless!

Sadie

Sadie,

I'm willing to talk to you about Russia, although I've got to say that God threw a lot of problems my way there. Honestly, before I saw your message I'd been trying to forget that part of my life, and I was this close to deleting it without responding, but I wonder if this isn't God's way of saying that forgetting is not the path to forgiveness, that I need to look the past in the eye in order to move forward. Honestly, your message feels like fate to me. I'll help however I can. Who gave you my name again? Not sure where you're located, but we could meet up or you could give me a call whenever.

God be with you,
Gabe

A phone number appeared under his name. "It's him, right?" Sadie said. "It has to be. 'God threw a lot of problems my way there.'"

Ilya thought of Lana and Olga and Yulia dying in the snow.

"'Forgetting is not the path to forgiveness,'" Sadie said.

Everyone around them was standing now, in response to some cue from Principal Gibbons that Ilya had missed. The marching band had removed their hats and were tucking their clarinets and trumpets and bassoons into velvet-lined cases.

"Let's go to the library and look at your list. The area code here is for western Pennsylvania, so if we check all of those, the Pennsylvania ones . . ." She trailed off, seeing something on Ilya's face.

Feels like fate to me, he was thinking, and it did feel like fate, in the best and the worst way. They had found Gabe, and somehow this solidified the connection between Gabe and the girls, between Gabe and Vladimir. It felt certain now, real and concrete, something only dreamt made manifest, and the certainty was terrifying, like seeing a monster slip out from under the bed, each scale just as he'd imagined it. They had found him. It was a good thing, but what Ilya kept picturing was Gabe in western Pennsylvania—wherever that was—staring at Sadie's face on a computer screen. His hands were just barely touching the keys. He took her in, every bit of her, her jagged pupil, her white-blond hair, and then slowly, deliberately, he began to type.

"You're mad," she said. "I should have told you."

The bleachers were almost empty now. Beneath them the couple was gone, and one of the boys from the fantasy game was searching for a dropped card.

"If we found him, he could find you too."

Sadie smiled. It was this terrible, invincible, American smile. She didn't think it could happen to her—the clothes ripped, the knife against her cheek, the blood in the snow. But *he* could see it all happening to her just as it had happened to Lana, and he would be responsible for it because he had opened a portal between her world and his.

"I didn't use my profile," she said. "I made a fake one."

"With a different picture?" he asked.

She nodded. "A different picture and a different last name," she said, and the anger drained out of him and left just the fear, because finding Gabe Thompson meant seeing Gabe Thompson.

There was only one Gabe Thompson in western Pennsylvania, in a town called Warren. The home phone number was on the list, and the area code was the same as the number Gabe had included in his message to Sadie.

"I bet one's the landline and one's his cell," Sadie said, "which means he might not actually be in Warren." She pulled her phone out of the front pouch of her backpack, and Ilya shook his head.

"You're not calling," he said.

"OK," she said. She tapped the phone against the palm of her hand for a second, and then she said, "What about J.T.?"

J.T. seemed like a gossip and a flake, the sort of person who would use Ilya's life for conversational gain without thinking twice, but when Ilya told Sadie this, she said, "He's known about my mom all this time and he's never told anyone. Not a single soul."

They found J.T. at his mom's apartment on Leffie's old main street, which, Sadie said, had been the center of town way back in the day before Route 21 enticed Leffians east with a Super Walmart and a Cracker Barrel. J.T. sat on his stoop, wearing a gray sweatshirt and smoking a cigarette.

"Sick day," he said, when Sadie asked why he hadn't been at school.

He finished that cigarette and then another as they told him about Vladimir and Gabe and the girls.

"Fuck," he said, "that is some fucked-up shit," and for a second Ilya thought that this was his way of saying that he didn't want to be involved, but he pulled his cell out of the front pouch of his sweatshirt. Ilya had written Gabe's home phone number on his palm, and he held it out to J.T., and J.T. dialed and put the phone on speaker mode.

"So you think this guy murdered people," J.T. said, as the ring tone sounded.

Ilya nodded and Sadie put her finger to her lips and J.T. rolled his eyes.

It rang three times before a woman answered.

"Hey," J.T. said, "I'm calling for a Mr. Gabe Thompson."

There was a thick pause. The woman's voice, when it came again, was weary. "He can't come to the phone right now."

J.T. looked at Ilya, and Ilya nodded, and J.T. continued with the script: "I'm calling because Mr. Gabe Thompson left a personal item on his flight."

"Oh," she said. "OK. You need our address then?"

"Well is Mr. Gabe Thompson there?" J.T. said.

"He is—" she said.

"Who is it, Ida?" another voice said in the background. It was a man, older, and audibly aggrieved.

There was the stethoscopic *thwump* of a hand covering the receiver, but they could still hear Ida, her voice like the buzz of an insect in the heat. "The airline," she said. "Gabe left something on the plane, and they want to send it to us."

"The plane?" the man said. "His flight was six months ago."

Ilya could feel the skin tighten at his temples. Lana's body had been found in March.

"What does it matter, Frank." The woman sighed. "They just want to mail it to us."

"Fine," Frank said. "Has he had lunch yet? He's saying he's—"

"They're still on the *phone*, Frank. I'll give him lunch in a second."

The hand was removed from the receiver, and the woman's voice was clear again as she gave J.T. the address that Ilya had read in the library a half hour earlier.

J.T. thanked her, and just as he was about to hang up, she said, "Wait a second." She lowered her voice to a whisper, but still Ilya could feel the hunger of the question: "What was it that he left?"

J.T. hesitated. "A hat," he said, fingering the brim of his own hat, which featured the fluorescent outline of a naked, supine woman.

"A hat?" the woman said. "What kind of hat?"

"It'll be in the mail tomorrow, ma'am," J.T. said, and ended the call.

"Those were his parents," Ilya said. He had not expected Gabe to be living with his parents, but it was a stroke of luck. This meant that Ilya did not necessarily have to be alone with Gabe.

Sadie nodded. "Frank and Ida," she said.

"Can I borrow your car?" Ilya said, and in his mind he was already in the car, was pulling up at the house. He could see Gabe at the door, standing between his parents, and when Gabe saw him there would be a look of recognition, of anger, hatred, a look like the one he'd given Ilya through the glass at the Minutka.

"Do you even know where Pennsylvania is?" J.T. said.

Ilya did not, but soon they were crouched around J.T.'s laptop, tallying the time it would take to drive through the five states between Leffie and Warren. It was nineteen hours away.

"So basically a day with stops," J.T. said. "What are you going to tell Cam and Jamie?"

Ilya had not thought of this—the enormity of finding Gabe had eclipsed whatever punishment the Masons might dole out for Sadie and him going missing—but apparently Sadie had.

"I'm going to Kayla's for the weekend, and Ilya's going fishing with you at your dad's camp. A real bayou experience."

"A bayou experience," J.T. said. "Shut the fuck up. Like you're not bayou to the bone."

"I'm telling you, they'll eat that up," Sadie said. She was laughing, but Ilya's body felt suddenly clammy, as though fear were a virus he was coming down with.

"Will you come too?" Ilya asked J.T., because he could imagine Sadie following him into Gabe's house, refusing to stay on the sidelines. J.T. wouldn't let her—he hadn't ever told a soul about Sadie's mom; he would protect her.

Sadie looked at J.T., and J.T. shrugged. "I'll drive you fools, but I'm not going in a fucking murderer's house. Haven't you all ever seen a horror movie?"

"I guess we should talk about the plan," Sadie said.

Ilya had had plenty of time to think about what exactly he'd do if he ever found Gabe Thompson: he'd imagined peering in a dingy window to a room papered with pictures of Lana and Yulia and Olga; he'd imagined digging through Gabe's drawers and finding the knife, the knife that he and his mother had asked the police about over and over, the knife that they *knew* had not been in Vladimir's possession at the clinic; he'd imagined finding Gabe doing something so completely sane—mending a gutter or washing his car—that it would be instantly clear that he was insane, for how else could one person contain such disparate selves? But none of these imaginings were realistic. They were the sorts of things that happened in movies, so that people could feel the satisfaction of a story stitched shut. And life was not like that. Life was a constant unraveling. "Neither of you is going into his house," he said. "I'll go alone, and I'm going to ask him what he knows about Lana and see what he says."

That night, after dinner, Ilya dug his tape player and his *Michael & Stephanie* tapes out of the dresser drawer where he'd stashed them when he first arrived. He wanted to record Gabe, hoping to get something concrete enough that he could use it in court. The tapes were coated in a fine layer of dust. He picked up the player, his hand curling around its familiar heft. It was still missing its batteries, courtesy of the Leshukonskoye baggage department. He popped the battery slot open and pressed a finger against one of the springs, felt the tiny insistence of the spring pushing back. The batteries had been Russian 286s. It seemed unlikely that the United States and Russia might have reached some agreement on battery size when they could agree on so little else, but perhaps, Ilya thought, there was an exact translation.

Upstairs the den was abandoned. As Ilya searched between the couch cushions for the TV remote, he heard the murmur of voices in Papa Cam and Mama Jamie's bedroom. Light from beneath Sadie's door fanned the hallway. She'd told him that she drew before bed. She said it emptied her out, made it easier for her to sleep, and he could almost hear the scratch of her pencil, could see the way her tongue sometimes traced her bottom lip. Ilya reached under the couch, and his hand closed on the remote. He popped open the back. Four batteries slid out. They clacked, cool as stones in his palm, and he could feel that they were right.

Back downstairs, he opened up the player and took out the tape, which was the first one, Level I, Volume 1. He hadn't listened to the tapes since Vladimir had stolen them from his crate under the couch, since he'd found them in Vladimir's room at the Tower. He'd have to record over one of them, but he didn't want it to be this one. Vladimir might have listened to this one, and so he wanted to save it, wanted the chance to listen to it and hear the same words that Vladimir had, as though this might allow him to be there with Vladimir in that moment. Ilya closed his eyes and plucked a tape off the pile on the dresser. It was Level II, Volume 4, in which Michael and Stephanie tackled prepositions and their usage. As Ilya clicked the player shut, there was a light knock on the basement door.

Mama Jamie had not come down into the basement since she'd given Ilya the tour of the house. Or at least she had not ventured into the basement while Ilya was home. When he returned from school each day, there was evidence of her presence: laundry folded and stacked on his bed, plump rolls of toilet paper pyramided on the back of the toilet, and, occasionally, the water inside the toilet bowl glowed a fluorescent blue. But now she was padding down the stairs in her slippers and her jeans and a magenta shirt that brought out the piggish undertones in her skin, but that he knew was her favorite because she wore it every other day. She was holding a white paper package in one hand. It was the shape of a small pillow and had torn in a few places to reveal its pulp.

"This came today," she said, handing it to him.

His name was inked on the outside above the Masons' address. It was his mother's handwriting, and he could imagine her double-checking the Roman *F*s in "Leffie," the half-moon *D*s in "Dumaine Drive," and the simple slash of the *I*. The package felt like a book, and he didn't know what he'd been expecting, but his heart sank a bit because a book was most likely from Maria Mikhailovna, some new text or translation that she'd wanted him to have.

"Are you excited for your trip?"

For a moment, Ilya stared at her, and then he remembered that he was supposed to be fishing with J.T. this weekend. He nodded.

"I'll pack you guys a cooler," she said. "Sandwiches and some chips."

"Thank you," he said.

"J.T. gets into trouble sometimes," Mama Jamie said. "But I trust you to stay out of it."

Ilya nodded.

"He has a phone—you can call me whenever. You know that?"

He nodded again, and she did too. "Get some sleep," she said, "'cause I know you won't be getting any tomorrow."

Once she'd shut the door behind her, Ilya tore the top off the package. It was not a book at all, but a stack of papers, and he was still thinking that they were from Maria Mikhailovna, some stiff, formal English-with-a-capital-E exercises that would be entirely useless now that he was here and immersed in the disaster of the language itself, but as he pulled out the stack, he saw a picture of Jesus. His robe the color of butter, a halo flaring over his head. It was one of Gabe Thompson's pamphlets. There were a half dozen in the package, with titles like *The Plan of Salvation* and *The Restoration* and *Chastity*. Some of the pages were hollow in the center, like empty frames, the pictures still pasted to the windows at home. Ilya didn't need the pamphlets any longer—he knew where to find Gabe, and it was a good thing because they gave no trace of him: no address, no church name, but still Ilya's heart thrummed as he flipped the pages. It wasn't just that Gabe had touched them; it was the fact that his mother had sent them. He could imagine how terrified she'd been to bring them to the post office, to write that American address. She'd been too terrified to include a note, or a return address. She'd taken a risk, and there was desperation in it, and permission too. Permission to find Gabe, to help Vladimir. For the first time that Ilya could remember, she was putting Vladimir first.

Ilya collected the pamphlets in a neat stack and put them in his duffel along with the tape player, printouts of the photos from VKontakte, a change of clothes, and a pocketknife that Timofey had given him. The hinge was rusty, and the blade was not much larger than Ilya's pinkie, but still it was better than nothing.

CHAPTER NINETEEN

V asili Vasilyevich was at the sink in the bathroom at the end of the hall, his face covered in shaving cream. The razor shook in his hand. "Takes me two hours to shave now," he said.

"Oh," Ilya said, because Vasili was a talker and Ilya did not want to encourage him. Ilya's eyes were gritty, and he could still taste the Tower's chemical haze in the back of his throat. He needed to talk to Maria Mikhailovna, but he needed a shower first. He'd spent the walk back to the kommunalkas imagining all of the terrible things Maria Mikhailovna would say to him. He'd blown his chance at America, but she might want to keep him out of university altogether. She might kick him out of School #17. Or maybe, he thought, his mind clenched around the hope, maybe, maybe Vladimir would somehow fix the situation, persuade Maria Mikhailovna to let him take a makeup test or go the next year.

"If you're going to shit, give me some warning," Vasili said. "I may be old, but I can still smell." When Ilya didn't laugh, he said, "You're a bit sour, aren't you?"

"No," Ilya said, sourly.

Ilya peed, and Vasili listened and then lamented his own flow, which was, he said, more like a leaky faucet. Ilya brushed his teeth, and Vasili asked him if it hurt to hold such a terrible expression for so long.

"Does it hurt your tongue to talk so much?" Ilya said.

He looked at Vasili in the mirror, straight into his dull blue eyes. Normally he wouldn't have had the nerve to make eye contact, let alone to insult the man, but he felt a new sort of recklessness that came, he guessed, from not having much of a future. Vasili paused, the razor trembling by his wattle. Ilya expected him to be stung, but he said, "Molodoy chelovyek," which meant "little man," and his voice was warm, familial even, as though Ilya were a grandson whose attitude was a source of gentle amusement. "Whatever it is that has you so upset, it will pass. Trust me. I'm ancient. I've lost two women that I love, and each time I thought I wouldn't survive, and yet here I am, shaving my beard because my third wife doesn't like stubble scratching her pussy."

Ilya blushed and mumbled something about a stomachache, and after his shower, he walked to Maria Mikhailovna's apartment so slowly that his toes tingled and went leaden in his boots. He pressed the buzzer. No response. He pressed it again. No response, and he was about to press it a third time when the custodian—old now and stooped, but the same one who used to kick them off the elevator all those years ago—told him to fuck off. Halfway across the square Ilya looked back. He had the sense that the custodian might be following him, might want to keep scolding him just for the sheer pleasure of it. The old man *was* watching him from the lobby, with an expression of grim determination. Seven floors above him, Maria Mikhailovna's apartment was dark, but way up at the top of the building, the penthouse was ablaze. Ilya could see a figure inside, silhouetted against the glass. It was Fyodor Fetisov, he guessed, and for a moment it seemed as though Fetisov were watching him, but then he stepped away from the glass, and Ilya told himself that he couldn't be seen anyway. He was invisible in the darkness of the square, just another patch of shadow on the snow.

Ilya trudged on to the school, not really expecting to find Maria Mikhailovna there. It was a Saturday, after all. But he could see the light on in her classroom from a block away. She was at her desk, as always, with a stack of graded papers on her right and a stack of ungraded papers on her left.

He stood outside the window for a long moment. He wanted her to sense him and look up, but she did not. When he knocked on the glass, her head snapped toward him. She had to walk halfway across the classroom before she recognized him, and then she nodded, and he walked around the school and met her at the front doors.

She did not say her usual "Hello! How was your weekend?" to which he was expected to respond in English and at length, even though his weekends were always the same, blocks of studying punctuated by Babushka reminding him to eat. Instead she led him down the hallway, past the dark rooms, in silence. Once they were in her classroom, she locked the door.

"I thought you were hurt. Or worse," she said, her voice barely above a whisper. "What happened?"

The answer was simple: he had wanted Vladimir back. He'd thought that he could choose Vladimir, but now he saw that he'd built that choice on a false premise, because Vladimir being gone had nothing to do with him, and nothing he did could change the fact of it. This idea was like a little spur of bone lodged in Ilya's chest, something he had to breathe around.

"Ilya, what happened?" She reached a hand out and touched his brow bone where Vladimir had hit him. Her eyes were huge. She thought something truly terrible had prevented him from taking the boards. Vladimir had said that he would try to fix the situation, but Vladimir's plan was half-assed in the way of all Vladimir's plans: Ilya had no idea if he had seen Maria Mikhailovna, no idea what he might have told her, or how to corroborate it, and so he just told her the truth.

"I was with Vladimir," he said. "At a party at the Tower."

"The Tower." She paused, her brain taking a moment to process the unlikely combination of Ilya and the Tower. "Was he in trouble? Did he need help?" Ilya hesitated, and she said, "He forced you, didn't he? To miss the test. Is that it? He wanted to sabotage you?"

Ilya was about to shake his head, and then he thought better of it. What in the world did Vladimir have to lose? "Yes," he said, his voice small.

He looked at the empty hook on the wall where Aksinya's coat had hung. He looked at the "Look Where English Can Take You!" posters that marched across the wall. Big Ben. The Statue of Liberty. The Sydney Opera House. The Wild West. He looked out the window to the hall, which was tiled in a yellow that was the color of butter, of winter sun.

She looked to the hall too, and then she spoke in a rush: "Listen," she said, "I took them for you. I couldn't not. Not after all the work you've done—all the work *I've* done." She let out this strange little snort. "I sharpened five pencils. I even set the timer for myself. For each section. I didn't give myself an extra second. I just did the best I could. And you know the thing that made me the saddest?"

Ilya was stunned. She would be fired. Arrested. She was insane, taking a risk like that. Of course she was insane, he thought. How else did someone from Moscow wind up teaching in Berlozhniki?

He couldn't speak, couldn't even shake his head. And then, as if she knew he was thinking she was crazy, her eyes went glassy.

"What made me so sad—*so* angry—was the fact that you would have done better. You would have done perfectly."

And then America burst into his brain like something held too long underwater, and with it the same huge hope. Her hope. His hope. His hands began to sweat. He could feel his heart beating in his palms, his pulse like something trying to escape him. It was absurd to be given such a chance twice; it was a sign of a universe completely lacking in logic. He felt sick, betrayed almost, like when he'd first learned that languages have as many exceptions as they do rules. He shook his head. "You shouldn't have done that," he said.

Maria Mikhailovna pulled her chin back into her neck. Her look was still incredulous, but it was no longer sympathetic. "Did you want me to let you fail? You want to spend your life drinking at the Tower? Puking in the snow? You know there are other kids who are smart. They might not be as smart as you, but they're smart enough to be grateful."

Ilya thought of Grigori Alexandrov with the doughy crescent of flesh that hung over the waistband of his jeans. He had been taken under the wing of the math teacher, but he was proficient at English too. He worked hard. Sometimes, walking home from school after a long session with Maria Mikhailovna, Ilya would sense Grigori walking behind him. He wouldn't turn around, though, nor would Grigori say hello.

"It's not that," Ilya said. "It just doesn't feel fair. It's never felt fair."

"Fair."

"That I get to go."

"It's not fair," she said. "It's unfair. It's terrible. But you don't help anyone by spitting in the face—" She took a breath, tried to calm herself down. "Do you know that your brother came to me?"

A tiny bubble of something—hope or trepidation—shot up Ilya's spine. Vladimir had kept a promise. He'd come to see Maria Mikhailovna, and he'd made her take the test. He'd made all of this happen.

"After I came to your house and told you about the exchange, he came to me, and he begged me to let him go. To America. He said that he would change, that he would turn it all around. He wanted to be the one. He said that you would succeed no matter what, that you'd get to go to university for sure, but that this would be the closest he'd ever come to an opportunity like this." She took a breath, then looked at Ilya as though aiming at him through a sight. "I had to tell him that he wasn't close at all."

That was why Vladimir had not come home, Ilya realized. That was why he lived in that terrible room, and Ilya didn't know if he felt more guilt or anger at the knowledge.

"Did Vladimir come to see you today?" Ilya asked, his voice so tired and sure of the answer that it didn't come out sounding like a question.

"Today?" she said. "No. Why would he?"

"No reason," Ilya said.

"He doesn't know, does he? Ilya? No one can know."

"He won't tell anyone," Ilya said. He thought of Vladimir begging Maria Mikhailovna to come to America. He had never heard Vladimir beg for anything, and he wanted to know what his voice had sounded like, and if it had happened here, where Ilya was standing, and whether Vladimir had been serious enough about the plea to stay sober. He didn't need to know what Vladimir had done

when Maria Mikhailovna had told him that he wasn't close at all—
he could already imagine that.

"Let's hope he doesn't," she said, and then she sat heavily in her
chair. The school was completely quiet, so quiet that the air felt like
it was made of cotton. Maria Mikhailovna blinked and rubbed at
the spot on her nose where her glasses dug into her flesh. Then she
pushed a stapled packet across the desk. "I made a copy. Just in
case. So you know the questions, and what you answered."

The board results came with unusual speed. A week of snow, a
week of no Vladimir, a week of memorizing the test that Maria
Mikhailovna had taken, and then she presented Ilya with a gray
envelope from the Ministry of Education in Leshukonskoye.

"I thought you might want to open it at home, with your family,"
she said, with this lightness to her voice that made it seem far away.
This was how she spoke to him now. "I have a copy as well."

And though Ilya had always thought he'd open the letter at this
desk where she'd tutored him, the desk with the tiny moon and
stars etched in the upper right corner and the slight list that meant
a pencil always rolled off the left side, he walked home with it, in-
tending to do what she'd said and open it at home with his mother
and Babushka. But when he got to the kommunalka, there was a
cluster of boys—younger than him—smoking in the stairwell, and
he didn't want to murmur "Izvinite" and listen to them go quiet as
he edged by them. Instead, he kept on walking toward the Pechora.

There was a slick path cut by cross-country skiers that followed
the river for twenty kilometers and then circled back, across taiga
to the south side of town. To his left, the Pechora was frozen solid,
a blank strip of snow flanked by birches. Ilya slid along the path for

a kilometer or so until he was sweating inside his coat and he'd found a spot that seemed both beautiful and desolate enough for such an occasion. He sat on the frozen ridges of the path and opened the envelope.

Maria Mikhailovna had scored in the ninety-second percentile. As he knew from the copy she'd given him, she'd done perfectly on the multiple choice. She'd lost all of her points on the written section. He'd read her essays and dictations and knew just the things that had tripped her up: the plural possessives and habitual aspect. Ilya's personal information was clustered at the top of the page. His name, his birthdate, his school and address and identification number. That was it. Most of the page was empty. There was no "Congratulations!", no personal note at all, and this reassured him. No one was looking too deeply into this test. The State had more important matters to attend to.

He walked home as the light was faltering. The boys were gone. When he showed his mother and Babushka the results, they both started to cry and then to laugh.

"I thought you were better at the written than the multiple choice," his mother said, and then she said, "Listen to me, looking a gift horse in the mouth." She kissed Ilya. "You're my brilliant boy," she said.

"Your papulya would be thrilled," Babushka said. "He'd be yelling in the halls."

"He'd be drinking," Ilya's mother said, but without the usual scorn, and she pulled down a bottle of vodka and insisted that they all—even Babushka, who only drank on religious occasions—have shots.

Then they borrowed the neighbor's Lada and drove it to the place on the square that served pizza on red and white checked tablecloths and catered to the refinery apparatchik and the rare tourist. The one with the faded photo of Gabe Thompson eating pizza in the window. His mother ordered mushroom pizza for all of them, and Ilya did not even try to protest. He had never seen her so happy. Even when she called Vladimir's cell—a cell that he hadn't answered in weeks, that Ilya was sure he'd traded for drugs—the smile stayed on her face.

Just as the pizzas arrived, there was a knock at the window behind them, and they turned to see Maria Mikhailovna and Dmitri standing at the glass. She smiled and lifted a hand. Ilya stared, wanting so badly to thank her and to apologize. Then his mother was tugging at his sleeve.

"Get them to join us, Ilya," she said. "Go, go! Our treat!"

By the time he was out the door, they were past the restaurant, giving Gabe Thompson and his bench a wide berth.

"Maria Mikhailovna!" he called. "Will you join us? Please?" He said it like he was saying sorry. He *imagined* that he was saying sorry, and she must have heard that in his voice, because her face took on this soft look that was the look his mother got when she thought of Vladimir, like all she wanted to do was forgive him.

"We'd love to," she said. "Another time—Dmitri's been working so hard with these cases. He needs rest."

She meant Yulia and Olga. The police had not made progress on either case, and Ilya could see the wear of them on Dmitri's face. There were rings that fully circled his eyes, like another set of glasses, and his skin was sagging in a way Ilya did not remember.

"Of course. Another time," Ilya said. He and his mother and Babushka had never been to the pizza place before, but it seemed suddenly possible that they might go there again, that after America, eating out on the square might become a regular thing.

"Congratulations are in order," Dmitri said, and there was this tiny snag to his voice as he said, "Congratulations," and Ilya wondered whether Maria Mikhailovna had told him about the boards.

"Spasibo," Ilya said, and then Dmitri ducked into the restaurant and beckoned to a waiter.

When he came back out, he kissed Maria Mikhailovna on the top of her head. "I ordered the ladies a bottle of wine. Surely they've earned it," and again Ilya wondered if Dmitri meant something else by what he was saying, but Maria Mikhailovna smiled at him and said, "They have."

Behind them, Gabe Thompson coughed—a terrible sound—and when they turned to look at him, he said, "Fuck off."

Maria Mikhailovna looked at Dmitri, and Ilya did too, expecting the same anger he'd seen in him the night he'd chased Vladimir in the car, but Dmitri just said, "I'm off duty tonight, myshka," in this tired voice. And then to Ilya, "Even the Americans have their problems. Remember that," and he led Maria Mikhailovna away.

His mother and Babushka were thrilled with the wine, and with each glass his mother alternated between saying that she'd never, ever imagined this and that she'd known all along that Ilya would succeed—from the moment she'd first held him, his head huge, his eyes alert to the whole world—that through hard work he would create great opportunity. Babushka was adamant that Jesus was involved, and she swore over and over that Jesus would be thanked like he had never been thanked before.

Ilya winced when the waitress brought the bill. Just the pizza cost what his mother made in a week, and she'd gotten them all hot chocolate too. His mother saw his face and said, "Don't worry, golubchik, there will be only three mouths to feed soon."

Two, Ilya thought, and normally his mother and Babushka would have thought the same thing, all of them acknowledging Vladimir in a beat of silence, but they were too happy or too drunk to think of Vladimir that night.

"Unless Timofey Denisovich moves in," his mother said.

"Please," Babushka said, blushing. "That old fart."

"More like old flirt," his mother said.

By the time they left it was close to eleven, and the borrowed Lada wouldn't start. It was sixteen below freezing, and the battery had gotten too cold. Ilya's mother tried, and then Babushka tried, though she hadn't driven in a decade. Their neighbor kept hot water bottles in the glovebox for just this situation, and they brought them into the restaurant and begged the waiter to fill them, and then they wrapped them around the battery the way Babushka wrapped them around her knees at night. When the water cooled, they filled them again. Once, twice, and the waiter began to charge for the hot water. On the third try, the ignition sparked, and his mother ground the gas pedal to the floor, and the car groaned to life. His mother and Babushka cheered and the sound of them filled the square, which was empty and bright. Even Gabe Thompson had found somewhere warmer to be.

CHAPTER TWENTY

On Friday morning, they parked Sadie's car at the Walmart near Leffie High and piled into J.T.'s truck, which was not as inconspicuous as Ilya would have liked, with the matte black paint job, the enormous tires, and the flame decal that sprouted from the grille and licked at the windshield. As they sped north, sugarcane fields filled the windows, electric green in the sun, and they went over the details: Ilya would be the one to knock on Gabe's door. He'd have the tape recorder running inside his duffel, and he'd have Sadie's cell on him so that he could call J.T. or the police if worse came to worst.

They all went quiet at this last statement. The asphalt unspooled ahead of them, gray and smooth. Roads like this were rare in Russia, and its very perfectness seemed to convey a sort of expectancy, as though it had been waiting here, in the middle of nowhere, to carry him from past to future. It was a ridiculous thought, Ilya knew, sprung from a hope that he'd let grow too large, and as a way to reduce his hope, to turn it into something useful, he reminded himself of all the ways this might go wrong: Gabe's parents might not let Ilya see him. Gabe might admit nothing, might show nothing. He might slam the door in Ilya's face.

Up ahead one of the fields was burning. Smoke ribboned up from the rows of cane, giving the air the taste of burnt sugar. Ilya had succeeded in making his hope smaller; it was a tight knot between his lungs, something he could almost ignore. They passed a sign, and Ilya read the letters, which would have seemed an incomprehensible combination except that he'd teased out the tangle of their syllables the day before when they'd planned their route.

MISSISSIPPI, it said, WELCOMES YOU!

They drove all day and into the night. J.T. and Sadie took turns behind the wheel and napping in the truck's tiny backseat. At five a.m., on a highway skirting Pittsburgh, under a blur of fluorescent signs, Sadie took a hand off the wheel and reached for Ilya's.

"Are you scared?" she said.

He nodded. J.T. was snoring lightly in the backseat, and Ilya lay down with his head on Sadie's thigh. He could see the point of her chin and that delicate triangle of skin that bridged her jawbones and that quivered each time she breathed. She put a hand on his cheek, then on his forehead the way Babushka did to check for fever, and he felt safe just as he had with Babushka, as though his existence was simple, was reduced to the spot where their skin was touching.

The sun, bright on his face, woke him. They were at yet another Walmart, identical in every way to the one in Leffie. J.T. was standing in the parking lot smoking. Sadie sipped at an enormous coffee.

"We already drove by. It's just a couple blocks away," she said. "And they're home."

Gabe's parents' house looked like a poor man's dacha: dark-stained wood with blue trim, a tiny screened porch, and a vegetable garden surrounded by more wire than a camp. There was a loved, labored-over feel to the place—in the potted herbs that lined the steps, in the rocking chair on the porch, which had been painted to match the trim. There was a truck in the driveway and from somewhere inside Ilya could hear the churn of a washing machine.

As Ilya climbed the steps to the front door, he turned and looked at J.T. and Sadie, who were parked on the other side of the street. The duffel was on Ilya's back, the tape player inside, already recording. Sadie lifted a hand and J.T. nodded, and Ilya pressed the doorbell.

For a second the sounds inside did not change, and then he heard Frank's voice, just as it had sounded on the phone, say "If it's that lady again, I'm going to—"

"Just let me get it," Ida said. She was whispering, but they were somewhere close to the door, or the walls of the little house were thin enough that Ilya could hear every word. "I don't know why you get so worked up about it. She just wants to see how he is."

"She wants to gawk is what she wants," Frank said, and scared as he was, Ilya was comforted by the ordinariness of their bickering. There was the clatter of one plate against another, and then brisk footsteps, and then the door was open.

Ida had a resolute smile in place for whatever lady she'd been expecting. It stayed there, evolutionary baggage, for the second it took her to examine him, then it was replaced by an expression of gentle skepticism, as though she knew he was here for no good reason, but she hoped that he might prove her wrong.

"May I help you?" she said.

This was a line straight out of *Michael & Stephanie*, one that Ilya had never heard an actual American say. He knew that she didn't mean "help" literally, but he needed help so badly that for a moment he was stunned by it.

"I'm looking for Gabe," he said. "I'm from Russia."

"Russia?" she said.

Ilya nodded. In the shadows behind Ida there was a shift in the light. Frank was standing behind her.

"He lived in my town," Ilya said. He tried his best to minimize his accent, which he knew surfaced most with the letter *o*. He tried to smile, because Americans smiled constantly, and to make his voice open and warm, like Mama Jamie's. He tried to hunch so that he seemed shorter than Ida, who was remarkably short, tried in every possible way to broadcast that he was not a threat. Though of course he was, and Frank sensed it immediately, or else saw threats in everything, because he stepped between Ida and Ilya and said, "What do you want with Gabe?"

"He told me to come visit him. Once I'd arrived," Ilya said. "I don't know anyone else in America, and he—"

Ida put a hand on Frank's arm.

"Come in," she said, and she ushered Ilya into the kitchen. The table was covered in newsprint, which was speckled with bits of balsa wood, tiny trees, and cars. There were tiny pots of paint and jars of a shimmering white powder and brushes with bristles thin as eyelashes. "Excuse the mess," Ida said.

Ilya nodded. "Where is Gabe?" he said.

"Sleeping," Frank said. "He sleeps half the day now."

Ida cleared a patch of table, and Ilya sat, and as she poured them glasses of iced tea she said, "We'd love to know about Russia, about his time there."

Ilya tried to think of his first memory of Gabe, but he kept picturing Gabe on the sidewalk, staring into the Minutka, and the way that Anatoly had gripped the shovel. "It was two years, I think. I can't remember exactly when he came."

Ida nodded.

Frank was standing at the sink, holding a glass of water under the tap, and as Ilya watched the water began to overflow the glass.

"He was there on a mission, right?" Ilya said. "Your church sent him?"

Frank turned the water off, set the glass down on the counter, turned, and said, "What did you people do to him?"

"Frank," Ida said. "Please."

"He left here at eighteen. So happy. So excited to spread God's word, and when he comes back, he's like a different person. And the doctors say that he has—" Frank made an ugly noise in his throat, and tears flooded his eyes.

Ilya looked at the table. There was a row of tree trunks drying on the newspaper. They'd been painted the exact silvery gray of birch trees.

"—the doctors say that he has gangrene on his foot. *Gangrene.* It's a miracle that he could even get on the plane. That he could get back to us. So you tell my wife whatever she wants to know, and then I want you to get out of my house."

Frank walked outside, and the screen door slapped behind him. He'd forgotten the glass of water on the counter. Ilya's hands had begun to shake. He pressed them between his knees. He saw Vladimir on the floor in the kitchen, saw the way his leg had rotted. He had known that Vladimir would die if he didn't get the drug, that he would die if he kept getting it.

Ida sat at the table next to him, and her feet barely touched the floor. She put a hand on Ilya's arm, just as she had with Frank a few minutes before. "Gabe won't talk to us about it, about Russia," she said.

I'd been trying to forget that part of my life, his message had said.

"There has to be something you remember—you knew him there," she said. There was this ache in her voice again, the same ache it had had when she'd asked what Gabe had left on the plane, the same ache his mother's had had whenever she asked Ilya if he'd seen Vladimir at school, in town, anywhere. Gabe had been lost to them, and here Ilya was, a gift.

"If you let me see him," Ilya said, quietly.

Ida nodded. "OK," she said.

"Americans don't come to our town," he began. "It's far from everywhere. And cold. So he was special, exciting. Everyone paid attention to him. He got an apartment on the square. The pizza place put his picture up in the window."

Ida smiled.

"And then he started giving out the pamphlets. He handed them to anyone who walked past." Ilya thought of all the stoves stoked by those pamphlets, all those angels and prophets burning. He thought of the windows in Babushka's bedroom, papered with Gabe's saints. "He'd preach all day about angels and a mine where they dug up dreams, and everyone was patient with him, but no one paid any attention. No one wanted to be converted, and maybe that was why he started to drink. He would sit on this one bench and drink vodka, and then samogon, which is cheaper—it's homemade, sort of—and can be stronger. And he got angry, and he said the same things he'd always said—'It's not too late to find God,' or 'Give me a minute to show you the way'—but it started to feel like he was cursing us. He was sober less and less and more and more crazy, and then last winter this new drug came."

"What's it made of?" Ida said. "Is it heroin? Crack?"

Ilya shook his head. "It's like heroin," he said. "But it's not the real thing. It's made of cheap stuff. Stuff they could get when the trains stopped running."

Ida closed her eyes at this.

"He'll be OK here," Ilya said. He didn't know if that was true. He thought of Vladimir in the bed at the hospital saying that he would kill for a hit. His eyes had been fervent with the belief, and Ilya wondered how long it took the want to leave you, or whether it ever did.

"I hope so," Ida said. She slid forward on the chair so that her feet were flat on the ground and hesitated there for a moment. "I'll wake him," she said, and she disappeared down a dim, narrow hall.

On the wall above Ilya was a picture of Gabe as a little boy, kneeling on a grassy field, a soccer ball propped on his knee. He had a cowlick at his hairline and the wide-set eyes and freckles of a cartoon character. There was a picture of Frank and Ida in front of a lake, looking impossibly young and happy. Below it was another picture of Gabe, in a white collared shirt and a plaid tie that Ilya remembered him wearing daily. His arm was around another boy in a matching tie, this one dark-haired with an enormous, squinty-eyed smile. They were seventeen or eighteen, necks chafed from shaving and from their stiff collars, and behind them was the Hermitage, robin's egg blue, the Russian flag flapping above its golden cupolas. There were footsteps again, and Ilya looked up, expecting Gabe, but Ida had come back alone.

"He says no," she said. "He says he didn't tell anyone to visit him."

There was a silence. More than a silence, it was a feeling of listening, like Gabe was listening in his room down the hall, and Frank, somewhere out in the yard, was listening, and inside the duffel the tape player was listening, the silence spooling across the ribbon, writing over Michael and Stephanie, erasing all of their beautiful, English words.

"Please," he said. It had been the first word that Maria Mikhailovna taught him. He opened his duffel. The tape player cast a weak red light on the canvas, and he dug beneath it for the pamphlets. "Show him these," he said, thrusting them at Ida.

Ida fingered a sharp edge where Babushka had cut. She looked at the pamphlets in the way you look at something you love that has betrayed you, and he could see that she had lost her faith over this, over her lost son. "Fine," she said.

This time Ilya followed her down the hallway, and when they reached a door at its end, she put a hand up to stop him and disappeared behind it.

"He brought these," Ilya heard her say, without emotion, and Ilya could hear nothing from Gabe. He put his hand on the knob. Ida had not locked it. He could twist it, push it open, have a moment to see Gabe's face—but then the door opened of its own accord.

Gabe was sitting on a couch. His hair had been shaved, and he'd gained weight. Fat wreathed his face, his features gathered in the middle like a herd huddling for protection. He was in sweatpants and a stained T-shirt and his foot was swaddled in an enormous bandage. The room was hazy, the blinds pulled, the light like a video with poor resolution. A TV was on, but muted, its colors dancing on the shiny skin at Gabe's temples. The pamphlets were in his hands. He'd grasped the top one between his thumb and forefinger as though he were still by his bench in Berlozhniki, ready to hand it to the next passerby.

"Here he is," Ida said, and Ilya did not know which of them she was talking to.

"I'm from Berlozhniki," Ilya said. "Ilya."

Gabe nodded.

"You're OK?" Ida said, and Gabe nodded again, and she turned and disappeared back down the hallway.

Ilya wanted to make her stay. He wanted to know exactly where J.T.'s truck was and how long it would take him to run to it. Sunlight pulsed at the edges of the blinds. He'd gotten disoriented inside the house and wasn't sure whether the truck was outside one of Gabe's windows or in a different direction entirely. He catalogued his talismans: Sadie's phone was in his back pocket, Timofey's knife was in the front pouch of his sweatshirt, and he'd worn both of the saint medals that Babushka had given him although he believed in neither of them and neither was specific to this occasion, to confronting a murderer.

"You kept them," Gabe said. *The Path to Salvation* was on top. That was the one he was holding. "Did you read them?"

He should have, if only to know Gabe better, but he shook his head, and Gabe laughed, this short, shallow sound.

"No," Ilya said. "They were my grandmother's. She cut out the pictures." His English felt thick and slow, was suddenly something he was conscious of again, like his fear had tripped some crucial neural circuit.

"At least she didn't burn them like everyone else," Gabe said. He set the pamphlets next to him on the couch and said, "Why are you here?"

Ilya had meant to ease into the subject of Lana's murder, to try to catch Gabe off guard, but the directness of Gabe's question had caught him off guard, and so he said, "I'm a friend of Lana's."

When he said Lana's name, Gabe stiffened. He hunched forward, his back coming off the cushions, and there, in that one movement, Ilya saw what he'd come for. Gabe knew Lana, and he knew something about her death. His eyes settled on Ilya's face, reading it, wondering at Ilya's intent. Ilya had not noticed his eyes at first, but they were blue and bright even in the dimness of the room, bright enough that it seemed to Ilya that they *could* read his intent, that Gabe understood that Ilya was working up the nerve to ask if he had killed Lana, was trying to force himself to say that word "kill," was wondering why Maria Mikhailovna had taught him it, how she had divined that it would be necessary and made him conjugate it just as she had thousands of other, more innocent words.

"Lana," Gabe said. He slumped back against the couch, and there, in the defeat of that one movement, Ilya saw that he hadn't killed her, that Gabe had never killed a soul.

"You knew her?" Ilya said. He had the pictures in his duffel. He could prove that Gabe had known her, but he didn't need them, because Gabe was nodding.

"Yeah," he said. "We went out together a couple times. To the Tower. To Dolls once. Sometimes we hooked up."

"What happened?" Ilya said, and Gabe didn't seem surprised at the question. He seemed relieved by it, in just the way that Ilya felt relieved to hear Gabe talk about the Tower, like by saying the things that came to them in nightmares they might rob them of their power.

"We would meet in the polyana. To hook up," he said. It was the word they'd used for the grove of trees where Lana's body had been found. A local word, one that Lana must have taught him. "Or to get drunk. Or high, if we had anything. It wasn't a regular thing. Not like she was my girlfriend." Gabe laughed suddenly, and then just as suddenly he stopped. "We could understand like ten words the other one was saying. I wouldn't even know how to say 'girl-friend,' but I liked her. At least I think I did." He rubbed a hand across the top of his head, then let it drop in his lap. "I was sup-posed to meet her there the night she got killed, but I didn't want to go 'til I scored. She wouldn't have wanted me there 'til I scored." He said this like there was a clear logic to it, and there was, Ilya guessed. The same addict logic that Vladimir had used when he'd stolen their stuff and sold it at the pawnshop, when he'd asked Lana to sleep with Ilya in exchange for the krokodil. "And there was this guy at the Tower who usually hooked me up. Either him or your brother."

"My brother," Ilya said, trying to keep the surprise out of his voice. He had not planned to tell Gabe that he was Vladimir's brother. Vladimir had been accused of the murders, and whether Gabe was guilty or innocent, Ilya's relationship to him was bound to put Gabe on edge.

"Vladimir, right? He talked about you all the time, about how you were coming here," Gabe said. "You look a little like him."

Ilya nodded, ignoring the vision of Vladimir flooding his mind: Vladimir, in the thick of a drug deal, bragging to an American about how his brother was moving to America, about how he'd come home and run the whole machine. "Sergey's the other one that would sell to you?" he said.

"Yeah," Gabe said. "He seemed to be the boss, or at least a little more sober. Sometimes he'd give me some. To be nice, I guess. Or maybe to keep me hooked."

"Did you find them that night? At the Tower? Did you find Vladimir?"

Gabe nodded. "Yeah, around midnight, I think. So I got high. Got drunk. I hadn't forgotten about Lana, but it wasn't serious like that. She'd stood me up a few times. So it was almost morning when I made it over there. Four or five a.m. It was so dark that it was hard to tell." He paused. His story had seemed smooth up until now, like something he'd gone over in his mind enough times that it didn't hurt him to say it aloud, even the parts he was ashamed of, but as he went on, his voice tightened, gained this quality that made Ilya think of the way ice shrieked before it shattered. "I knew right away that she was dead, even before I saw her neck. It wasn't that she wasn't moving—" He paused, grappling with something ineffable, some quality in the dead that was instantly recognizable to the living, and Ilya thought of the snowplow driver and how he'd known that Yulia was dead the moment he'd seen her leg. Ilya nodded, not because he understood, but because he needed Gabe to go on. "I could tell she was dead, and I didn't know what to do but pray. I'd never talked to her about God or whether she believed. I knew better than to bring it up, with her or anyone else at the Tower. By then it was like there were two of me: the one who had faith and the one who'd lost it, or I guess that's what I liked to think, but of course it was just the one me. Drunk off my ass and praying for her because I didn't know what else to do. There was blood all around her. The snow was so bloody, and I remember that I was careful to stay in the white snow. I didn't want her blood on me. And then at a certain point I got so cold that I started to feel warm, hot, even, like I could stay there forever, and I thought it might be a message, like God was telling me that I was doing the right thing, but another part of me knew that I'd die if I stayed. So I left her there. And as I was walking away, it hit me: she'd chosen the grove, she'd convinced whoever killed her to go there, because she'd thought there was a chance that I might come in time. That I might save her. And when I realized that, I couldn't leave her. I turned around, and just as I did, a car passed me on the lumber road, and a minute later, somebody got out of it and walked into the grove."

He must have seen the excitement on Ilya's face because he shook his head. "All I could see was a flashlight. Moving around in the trees. For a couple of minutes. Maybe five. And at first I was relieved, not scared, because she wasn't alone anymore, and because I wanted her to be found. So the whole next day I'm waiting to hear something, and there's nothing. And the next day and the next. Whoever it was had seen her—she wasn't hidden, there was no way to miss her, not with a flashlight—but still he wasn't saying a word, and so I knew that I couldn't either. I was scared then, for those weeks. Things got bad then."

"You don't have any idea who it was? What about the car? What did it look like?"

Gabe shrugged. "It was dark, and I was out of my mind."

That was it, Ilya thought. A flashlight bobbing through the trees, an impossible lead, and maybe Gabe could feel the force of Ilya's disappointment, because he said, "Believe me, I wish I knew who it was too."

"But you don't think it's my brother?"

"No," Gabe said. "I don't think it's your brother."

And it didn't matter for Vladimir what Gabe thought, but still it was a relief to Ilya that this would be on the tape, that he would be able to listen to Gabe saying it again and again.

"How'd you get back here?" Ilya asked. "I heard it was the police?"

Gabe nodded. "I went on a bender one night. The last thing I remember is walking home from the Tower—like I had a million times before—and then I wake up in the back of this SUV. At first

I thought I was gonna get killed. I kept thinking of the car passing me and the flashlight in the woods, and I'm sure that whoever it was had seen me and thought that I'd seen him. But the guy tells me that he's a cop and that he's taking me to the airport. He'd packed my bag, gave me withdrawal meds and everything. When we got to the airport, he kissed me on the forehead and told me, 'Don't ever come back,' and he handed me over to some thug who looked like a bodyguard, and he told the bodyguard to get me home 'cause the last thing he needed was a dead American on his hands."

"The policeman was a short guy? With glasses?" Ilya asked, though he knew the answer. He could see Dmitri in all of it, especially that kiss on the forehead.

Gabe nodded. "He saved me."

"Lucky you," Ilya said, his voice catching on the hypocrisy of it. Here they were, the saved ones, and the air in the room seemed suddenly unbearable—sharp and sour, and he had the sense that there was some message gathering in the shadowed corners, in the dark slit of the closet door, the way clouds mass into a storm. He didn't want to look at Gabe anymore, didn't want to see him sitting there on the couch, hollow-eyed but saved, looking like a teenager home sick from school. Ilya turned. There was a desk behind him, and it was covered in the same tiny detritus as the kitchen table. Miniature buses. Miniature telephone poles. Tiny slabs of wood. A red car the size of a button. It was a Lada. The license plate precisely inked with the Russian flag.

"What is all this?" Ilya said.

Gabe pointed to a coffee table on the other side of the room, and even in the dimness Ilya recognized what Gabe had built. There were the kommunalkas, the curve of them like teeth scattered along a jaw. There was Ilya's building, the closest to the road, with a dozen paper-thin balconies and dental-floss laundry lines. There was School #17, and the wooden church, with a sloppy little cupola, and the Minutka, and the square, with its empty pedestal. Maria Mikhailovna's building was all shining glass, the police station a slab of concrete, the clinic crowned with its tiny red cross. Gabe had covered the town with snow—that sparkly white powder on the kitchen table—so that cars were half buried and the benches on the square lost their legs and looked like driftwood in a sea of white. The Tower was a tiny gray box, innocent at this size, edging a field of snow ridged like the roof of a mouth. Tiny toothpick crosses speckled the snow. Ilya's breath caught in his throat when he recognized the polyana, a scattering of birch trees, but the snow was clean and white there too, no trace of Lana's blood. On the model's edge Gabe had begun to build the refinery with a few centimeters of screening for the chainlink fence and silver-painted straws for the pipes.

"It's exactly right," Ilya said.

"You think so?" Gabe said, and Ilya nodded.

He leaned close, counted the floors in Building 2, and then the windows, until he found his apartment. He peered in, half expecting to see his life there as it had been—Babushka cooking, Vladimir splayed on the couch, his mother dressing for work, and him at the kitchen table practicing his English—but the windows were opaque, made, Ilya could see now, with squares of wax paper the size of his fingernail.

It was a wonder, all of it, every tiny component speaking of a larger love. "How did you end up in Berlozhniki?" Ilya said. "Were you assigned there, for your mission?"

Gabe shook his head. "We were assigned to St. Petersburg. My best friend, Austin, and me. The church assigns you in pairs." Ilya thought of the squinty-eyed boy in the picture. Their matching ties. "We were there for a month—not even—three weeks, and then he died in his sleep. I guess he had a heart defect, had always had it, and his heart just stopped."

"I'm sorry," Ilya said, and Gabe smiled weakly.

"He's with God," he said. "The coordinator there wanted to send me home, give me some time to grieve, but Austin had wanted to go to Russia so badly, so much more than me. He was always saying stuff like, 'We leave our family for two years to bring other families together for eternity.' He didn't care if people ignored us, when they cussed at us or flicked us off or tossed their cigarette butts at our feet. I'd get angry, so angry, but he was invincible because he believed completely.

"And after he died, going home felt like giving up, so I got on a train instead. I had a couple hundred bucks, enough to keep paying the conductor every time we stopped, but I had no idea where I was going. I was on the train for two nights, almost three days, and then I'm in Berlozhniki. The last stop. End of the line. It was September, and it was snowing, and the sky was huge and gray with these clouds that looked completely ominous, and it seemed right, like a place that needed the Gospel." Gabe smiled this rueful smile. "I thought you all needed me. Ridiculous, right?"

It was ridiculous, of course, but there was something in Gabe that wasn't. A humility, maybe, that made Ilya point at the pamphlets and say, "My grandmother put the pictures up in our windows. She thought they looked like stained glass."

"Stained glass," he said. "I like that."

Down the hallway a door slammed, and Ilya could hear Frank's

voice, its rising notes, and Ida's lower, like an undertow. They listened for a moment, and Gabe said, "You should go. He's fucking
desperate to blame someone besides me."

Ilya nodded, and then Gabe said, "You know, I went to see your
brother at the clinic. Or I tried to, but they'd just arrested him. To
be honest I was looking to score—I thought he might have a stash
somewhere, and I could help him sell it and split the money or
something. But the nurse told me to get out of there unless I wanted
to get arrested too. And then she gives me this plastic bag that I'm
supposed to give to you—his personal effects, she says—and I took
it, thinking there might be drugs in it, but there weren't. And then
I didn't want anything to do with it, not with Lana dead and Vladimir arrested, so I just left it in his room at the Tower. I should
have found you," he said.

"What was in it?" Ilya said, though he knew. He could picture
the pink plastic bag sitting in the center of the room like an offering.

"Tapes," Gabe said. "These tapes for learning English. But I didn't
think you'd need them. You were coming here, after all."

CHAPTER TWENTY-ONE

H e didn't do it," Ilya said, as J.T. turned the truck around in the gravel cul-de-sac at the end of Gabe's street. He told them the story that Gabe had told him—how he'd found Lana's body and prayed over her in the snow, the car passing him on the lumber road, the flashlight lancing the trees.

"It could be anyone," he said.

"Not anyone," Sadie said. "Vladimir doesn't have a car, right?"

"No," Ilya said, "but he has a flashlight." Vladimir had gripped it as he'd led Ilya through the Tower. The light had snagged on glass, swept over graffiti, and, at the end of that long hallway, it had found Lana's face.

Anger grew, hot, in Ilya's stomach. He was angry at Gabe, of course, for not being the one. He was angry at whoever had killed the girls. He was angry at the girls, even, for their vulnerability. But most of all he was angry at Vladimir, for becoming the sort of person who got addicted, convicted, who confessed to things he hadn't done, because no one would believe the truth from him. He was angry at the millions of mistakes Vladimir had made—large and small. He was angry for Vladimir's sake, and for his own. What had Dmitri Malikov told him? That you can't change people who don't

want to change themselves? The solution was easy: let Vladimir confess, let him plead guilty, let him go to jail if that was what he wanted.

They were passing the last of Gabe's town: a grocery store with
one cart stranded in its lot; a balloon man bending and snapping in
the sky over an auto dealership; then the high school, its marquee
announcing the score from the previous night's football game.
Above it was the bear from Gabe's hat: orange, with rabid eyes, its
fangs bared. The last piece of the puzzle—but the picture it formed
didn't help Vladimir, didn't really include him at all.

That afternoon, exhausted, they stopped at a campground for the
night. It was an old-growth forest, the shade of shadows like home to
Ilya. A copper creek rushed through its center, the water whitening
with the current. J.T. went on a food run, and Ilya and Sadie wandered down a trail that followed the creek. The light was brindled
and beautiful, and it was hard for Ilya to believe that the day could
contain this moment and Gabe's house. He wondered what Gabe was
doing now, whether he had fallen back to sleep or whether he was
working on the refinery, gluing together the tiny panels of its fence,
painting its lengths of silver pipes. What would he do with himself
when the town was complete? And, as if in answer, Ilya could picture
him painting the trees of the endless forests that surrounded it.

Sadie held his hand as they walked. They passed a few tents close
to the trailhead, bright flags between the trees, but after a while, the
sounds of the highway faded, and the woods got quiet. The air was
laced with this fungal tang, and Ilya thought of the terrible painting
at home over the couch, of the mother and daughter mushroom
hunting in the forest. Babushka had told them that she hated that
painting, hated the smug smile on the little girl's face, hated the

suggestion that all was right with the world. And Vladimir had said, "But that's why I like it," and then, because there wasn't any place for earnestness in their world, or maybe just because Vladimir was perpetually horny, he'd added, "That and the mama's titties."

"You know what I fantasize about sometimes?" Sadie said. The sun was behind her; her profile carved the light.

Ilya shook his head.

"Burning my mom's place down. Not when she's home or anything. I just want it to be totally destroyed. All her shit charred. I want to see her face when she finds it, and I want her to know it was me. Then I want her to leave, to go somewhere where I don't know where she is." She walked faster as she talked, as though she knew what was at the end of the trail and she wanted to get to it. "I tried it once. When I was eleven. I had a newspaper and some matches and was so fucking pissed."

"What happened?"

Sadie laughed, this harsh, little sound. "I was crouched in the bushes beside her house, trying to light a match forever. But I almost threw up thinking that she'd be gone, that I wouldn't know if she was alive or dead or high or what. Then a neighbor found me and called Mama Jamie. And of course Mama Jamie was in hysterics. Crying for days, asking me what she was doing wrong, why I was turning into a delinquent. Like I was turning into my mom. I could see how scared she was on her face. Never mind that I hadn't actually *done* anything. I couldn't even get the match lit."

They reached the end of the trail, which was nothing but a cluster of logs that bordered the creek. He reached into the water, felt the cold more in his bones than in his skin, and his hand closed on a rock. A perfect slingshot rock, he thought, and he slipped it into his pocket.

"But that doesn't mean I don't wish I had. Every day," she said.

"Until you came." He looked at her. Half of her face was in the light, the other half in the shaking shadow of some leaves. She smiled. "Now I just think about it every other day."

He laughed, and they kissed, and he could still feel it—that happiness for him was like a dog chained to a stake, that whenever he let it run, he'd be yanked back, but still he let it run for a second and tried not to brace himself for the pull of the chain.

When she unbuttoned his jeans, he said, "I've never done this before," and it didn't occur to him until afterward that that was something Vladimir would never say, that inexperience was something Vladimir never admitted to, and it didn't matter anyway, because she said, "We're not doing that. I've got something else in mind."

Ilya was home in time for Sunday dinner and opened the door to the usual chaos. Molly and Marilee were tussling over what to watch on TV. Papa Cam was whipping open a new trash bag, the plastic ballooning as Mama Jamie sang along to Sting and pounded a chicken cutlet to the beat. Sadie had come home in her own car an hour earlier, and when she saw him in the doorway, she said, "Hey! How was the fishing?"

At the sight of her, the woods came back to him, made his dick swell with the memory of her hand on it, of her mouth hot on his stomach.

"That good, huh?" Papa Cam said. "You look like you're a convert."

Ilya nodded. "We caught gar," he said, which was what J.T. had told him to say.

"Well, where are they?" Papa Cam said. "We were counting on you for a fish fry."

"J.T. kept them all, didn't he?" Sadie said. "He's literally the most selfish person on the planet."

"Did you miss me?" Molly asked, which was something she had started asking him every day when he got back from school, and Ilya felt this sudden ache for these people, for their patterns, for how willing they had been to take him in, and for how little he'd given them in return.

"Of course," he said.

"After dinner let's watch the sermon," Mama Jamie said. "So you all can see what you missed."

Ilya's eyes met Sadie's over the table. She had predicted this punishment, and she was grinning at him now, as she said, "Can't wait. Were the testimonials especially juicy?"

The testimonials were wedged between the hymns and the sermons at every Star Pilgrim service. They were awkard allegros of shame or expansive expressions of guilt, depending less on the severity of the transgression than on the character of the transgressor.

"Don't mock it 'til you've tried it," Mama Jamie said. She was always begging the girls to give testimonials, but Molly was too shy, Marilee too self-righteous, and Sadie too private. "But since you asked, no, they were not especially juicy. It was Margaret Joy again."

Sadie groaned and, as they set the table, she told Ilya the story of Margaret Joy, whose favorite cat had been accidentally poisoned by a neighbor whom Margaret Joy now tortured in tiny, mostly inconsequential ways. "She'll turn her neighbor's hose on so it's just barely running all night long, or cut the roses off her bushes before they bloom."

Ilya laughed, and Sadie said, "Bet you can't wait to hear what she's done this time."

Later, after dinner, after they had watched the service and Margaret Joy had confessed to allowing another cat of hers to urinate on her neighbor's lawn furniture, once he was alone in the basement, Ilya played the tape he'd made at Gabe's house. He listened to Gabe's story over and over, with his eyes closed so that he could see it all. Lana and that halo of bloody snow. The redheaded nurse shoving the bag of Ilya's tapes into Gabe's arms. Austin with his perfect faith and his wide smile and the plaid tie. There was Gabe roaming the Tower, looking for Vladimir and Sergey and krokodil. *What did you people do to him?* Frank asked, over and over, and Dmitri Malikov was kissing Gabe's forehead, and the train was pushing through the snow to Berlozhniki, the end of the line, and Gabe stepped off it, looking small under the faded banner that proclaimed, BERLOZHNIKI MINES RUSSIA'S FUTURE!

Ilya listened until the parts of the story seemed dissociated from the story itself, until they were rendered nonsensical, then he clicked open his email and wrote another message to Vladimir. He wanted to tell him everything that had happened with Gabe. He thought that Vladimir might see something in it that Ilya could not, but the police would be reading Vladimir's email. He didn't tell Vladimir about Sadie in the forest either, because he was afraid that Vladimir would somehow divine the feeling that had come upon Ilya afterward. It was not quite contentment, but something akin to it. Like he'd compartmentalized his fear, his worry, like he'd somehow compartmentalized Vladimir himself. He had known that it was a temporary containment, a pill he'd swallowed, the membrane thinning, the drug soon to hit him again, hitting him now, as he wrote the same, tired message. *I know you didn't do it*, and then, because he wanted Vladimir to feel his desperation, he wrote, *but I don't know how to help you.*

That night, for the first time, he dreamt of Sadie instead of

Vladimir. He was sliding his hand into the waistband of her jeans. They were in the forest again, and he was too terrified to actually put his fingers inside her, so he rubbed at the cotton of her underwear until it dampened. That was right, he knew, and so he pulled her underwear down and touched the hot, damp pulse of her until she arched her neck and her body tightened. Her nails dug into his arm and he kept going, afraid to stop, until she pulled his hand away. She smiled at him, an embarrassed smile, and then they plucked leaves and pine needles off each other's clothes and hiked back up the trail to the campsite, where J.T. waited with burgers and beers and a knowing look.

He woke up throbbing, and as soon as Sadie had turned off Dumaine Drive toward school, he started to kiss her, and they found a lot behind the discount grocery store, and then it was all happening again, as it had in the dream, and in the forest, and it wasn't until Ilya got to school—and saw that every locker and door, every millimeter of wall space, had been papered with posters for the Homecoming Dance, which was on the same day as the arraignment—that Ilya thought of Vladimir.

The next week was like that. Ilya managed not to think of Vladimir for longer and longer stretches. A half hour here. An hour there. It was easiest when he was with Sadie, but he started to throw himself into his studies too. Into the thick of quadratic equations, the joy of isolating and solving for x. Into the components of a cell: the mitochondria and villi and endoplasmic reticulum, each with its own tiny, vital function.

It rained that week, and there was a comfort in sitting next to Miss Janet in the front office, in listening to the clack of her keyboard or the quiet rasp of her nail file. To avoid the rain, he skipped his usual Bojangles' chicken box in favor of cookie packets from the vending machine, but that Friday the weather cleared a bit, and he trekked through the soggy woods. The woman at the register—Sharice, her nametag read—treated him with the same disdain she doled out to all the Leffie High students, who made out in the booths and left ketchup smeared on the tables, pee on the toilet seats, and more work in general for Sharice. At first Ilya had appreciated being included in her curled-lip nonresponsiveness, but over the weeks it had worn on him. He'd thought of his mother, endlessly plating pirozhki for the neftyaniki, wiping trays and spraying floors, and he'd wondered if she gave them the same face that Sharice gave him. He'd tried to treat her with extra politeness. He'd used every greeting from *Michael & Stephanie*, every expression from their unit on small talk, and Sharice had only ever responded with an unwelcoming "Welcome to Bojangles'. What's your order?"

But maybe he'd worn her down after all, because that Friday, Sharice said, "The usual?"

Ilya was almost unable to respond both from shock and noncomprehension, and by the time he'd parsed her meaning, her eyebrows had clenched together in the same old scowl, and when he said, "Yes," and then added, "It has rained all week," she gave him nothing but a grunt.

As he took his receipt and turned to wait for his order in the sticky eddy by the fountain sodas, he bumped into a slight woman with a mass of blond hair that smelled like the front pocket of Vladimir's jacket, where he'd kept old cigarette butts for when he got desperate.

"Excuse me," Ilya said.

The woman ducked her head and walked up to the register. Ilya wouldn't have paid her another second's attention, except that Sharice said, "You bring your wallet this time?," which was another break from her script. The woman produced a five-dollar bill from her pocket and passed it across the counter. It wasn't until she'd ordered and turned to wait next to Ilya that he recognized her.

She was high, he could see that, and as they waited she seemed to become more so. Her neck slumped a bit, and she took a few steps backward, searching for support from the wall, but her elbow hit the soda machine, and Dr Pepper sprayed down her arm and onto the floor.

"Fuck," she said.

At the register, Sharice rolled her eyes.

The woman looked at Ilya, and the shape of her eyes, the way they canted upward, toward her temples, was the only thing of Sadie that he could see in her. "You gonna get me some napkins, or you just wanna stare?" she said.

Ilya pulled a wad of napkins out of the dispenser and handed them to her, and she snatched them and said, "They treat me like shit here."

She dabbed at her elbow, ignored the puddle of soda on the floor, and then stuffed the dirty napkins into a metal bucket of creamers.

"Me too," Ilya said. "But I thought that was because I'm Russian."

She laughed, a little too hard, then said, "Russia? What the fuck?" to herself, as though Ilya were an especially juicy hallucination.

Sharice slid Ilya's chicken box across the counter, and when Ilya reached for it, she said softly, "I'd ignore her if I was you."

Ilya nodded just as, behind them, Sadie's mom stepped into the puddle of soda and slipped. She caught herself, but not before her spine hit the edge of the counter. Ilya saw the pain pierce her high. For a second, she stayed still, her knees bent, hand gripping the counter, and then she straightened.

"OK," she said softly, and again Ilya had the sense that she was talking to herself. She stood up, hitched the strap of her tank top back onto her shoulder, raised her voice, and said, "This place is a dump. Clean the fucking floors once in a while, before I sue your asses."

The Bojangles' went silent. A group of boys whom Ilya recognized as some of J.T.'s basketball buddies froze, their chicken fingers poised above various dips. A man—Sharice's boss, Ilya guessed—appeared, as though expelled from the bowels of the Bojangles' at any threat of legal action.

"Can I help you, ma'am?" he said, and Sadie's mom turned and walked out the door. "Get the mop," he said to Sharice, and he disappeared back past the deep fryers and into the bowels once more.

Behind Ilya, the basketball players erupted in laughter.

"Did you see her face? It's not like she's going to say no," one of them said to some suggestion that Ilya had not heard.

Sharice slid another box across the counter toward Ilya. "You want her chicken?" she said.

Ilya nodded, stacked it on top of his own, and followed Sadie's mom out into the parking lot.

She was sitting on a crumbling concrete bumper at the head of a parking spot, with her arms draped over her knees and her hands dangling. It wasn't just her eyes that were like Sadie's—Ilya had been wrong about that—her hands were like Sadie's too. *Piano hands*, his mother called them, with this note of regret because she had had them too but had never played a piano. Ilya set the Bojangles' box by her feet.

"Did King send you?" she said. "It's not like I've got anything." She lifted her head and spread her arms as though Ilya might pat her down.

Ilya shook his head. He didn't know whether she meant drugs or money, or who King was. "I just thought you might want this," he said, holding out her meal.

"It's not even real chicken," she said. "Did you know that? It's like some mashed-up cartilage and shit."

He nodded.

"Where you from again?" she said.

"Russia," he said.

She smiled and shook her head. "What the fuck are you doing here?"

"It's an exchange program," he said. "You remind me of someone from home." That wasn't true. She didn't remind him of Vladimir at all. Her personality seemed to hinge on self-pity, and Ilya had never known Vladimir to feel sorry for himself. Vladimir was an optimist, even when optimism seemed an impossible attitude to sustain.

She looked up at him. "I heard Russian women are good-looking," she said.

"Sometimes," he said, thinking that sometimes Russian women looked like her, like they were hanging on to life by a dirty, painted fingernail.

"Listen, if you ever need help, if you ever want anything—to stop—or anything, call me."

It was easier to say than he'd expected, and the ease of it stung because it was the sort of thing he'd thought of saying to Vladimir a million times but had never managed to.

"Oh please," she said, with a snort, and she opened up the box and began to pick at the manufactured chicken. "Now I know King didn't send you. You religious or something?"

Ilya shook his head. He was groping inside his backpack for his history book, and when he found it, he pulled out the drawing that Sadie had done. In person, the likeness was even more profound.

The coarseness of her hair, the way her nose ended in a shiny little knob, the grooves that cupped her lips like her pout was an offering. Ilya wrote the Masons' number on the back and held it out to her.

"Sadie drew this," he said.

He dropped the picture onto her lap. She didn't say anything until she'd stared at it for a few seconds. "My Sadie?" she said.

He nodded.

"It's not bad," she said. She looked up at Ilya. "You know as a kid she was like that. Artistic. I could give her a couple crayons and she'd be so good—just coloring for hours. You could forget that she was there." She had a memory in her eyes, he could see that, could see her watching Sadie color, a crayon clutched tight in her hand, before the commercial break ended, her show resumed, and she forgot Sadie all over again.

"My number's on the back," he said.

She flipped it over and the grease from her fingers turned the paper translucent.

"Did Sadie send you?"

"No," he said.

"And not King either? For real?"

He shook his head.

"Then fuck off," she said softly, and he walked back into the woods. Before long he was out in the open of the soccer field. Up a rise, the track ringed the football field. Sadie was up there some-where, running, her white ponytail whipping back and forth be-tween her shoulder blades. He thought of the soda dribbling down her mother's arm, of the silence she'd inspired when she yelled, and he decided not to tell Sadie about it. If he did, she'd start a pilgrim-age to the Bojangles' too, and eventually she'd see a scene like the one Ilya had today.

CHAPTER TWENTY-TWO

R az, dva, tri," the gym teacher, Ekaterina Borisovna, counted.

It was the end of class, and Ilya was the last in the row, stretching, reaching his fingertips toward his toes, toward the floorboards, which had been scrubbed with lye so often that the smell of them made Ilya nauseous.

"Lana Vishnyeva was killed," a girl said loudly, as though she needed everyone to hear it.

Her friend nodded. "I know," she said.

Ilya stood up, and his vision went black and then cleared.

"What?" he said.

The girls turned, their hands still dangling at their toes, their rumps high in the air. Their ponytails dusted the floor. He had never spoken to either of them before.

"They found her yesterday," one girl said. "But she'd been dead three weeks at least."

Ekaterina Borisovna pointed a finger at Ilya and then at the ground, and Ilya bent back into the stretch. He could feel Lana kissing him. Their teeth hitting, her tongue darting into his mouth. "Don't worry," she'd said. "You were fine."

"She was killed?" he said, thinking of her overdosing, of how thin she'd been.

"Her throat was cut," the girl's friend said.

"And stand," Ekaterina Borisovna said.

They all stood and crossed their right arms over their torsos and began to count. They had been doing the same series of stretches for ten years.

"So not exactly like the other two. But she had the slashes on her cheeks. And apparently the knife was the same."

"They were stabbed thirteen times," her friend offered.

"No," she said. "Twelve."

Ilya skipped math for the first time in his life and went to the Internet Kebab to read the article in the *Vecherniye Berlozhniki*. It was short and formal. This time there was no picture. The girls were right: Lana's throat had been cut, and she had been dead for three weeks before her body was found by a group of kids playing in the grove of trees behind the kommunalkas, only two kilometers from Berlozhniki proper. A two-minute walk from Ilya's apartment. One minute in the summer. When Ilya was little, kids had used those trees as hiding spots in tag, crouching among the trunks until they were flushed out.

Most of the article was devoted to a self-satisfied explanation of how the police had calculated Lana's date of death. Snow, the article explained, could serve as a chronological record in the same way that sediment layers did, and Lana's body had been preserved under a layer of ice that rested beneath a half meter of snow. The ice was formed during a deep thaw and flash freeze that had occurred four weeks before. Her family had not reported her missing.

"She was living with a friend," her mother was quoted as saying, "because we had argued about her lifestyle."

It was impossible to read the tone in this—whether it was said with regret or reproach. The article said that Lana did not appear to have been robbed and that the motive may have been sexual. It closed with a list of what she had been wearing when she was killed—jeans, a parka, and a pink T-shirt—and a plea for any information that might aid the police in their investigation. Ilya read this last line over again, sure that he'd misread or imagined. She'd been wearing a pink shirt that night in the Tower. Four weeks and a day earlier. He remembered the pink of it with the pink of her hair; he remembered wanting to ask her if she liked to do that, to match her clothes with her hair, but he'd been too afraid.

He looked up the weather in Berlozhniki from the past month, which was a flat line punctuated by one deep dip, like a heart giving one last twitch. The thaw had been the night after the boards, the night after Ilya had kissed Lana. He tried to think when he had last seen her at the Tower, whether she'd left the mess hall with all of them or whether she'd stayed and kept dancing, but all he could remember was that she'd been gone when he woke up.

Ilya walked home so fast that his lungs were burning when he got to the grove. It was just a thin cluster of birch trees that had grown around some long-departed spring and that, for some unknown reason, the loggers had spared. The police had marked off the entire area. The slim gray trunks were banded together with police tape like a bouquet. The police were not there, though, and Ilya could not tell the exact spot where Lana had been found, whether she'd been leaning against a tree or lying in the snow between them. There were crisp packets and plastic bags and cigarette butts everywhere. All the usual garbage. High up in the branches of one tree, a bra dangled. It had been there for years,

fading from red to pink, and a tiny icicle had managed to find purchase on one of its straps.

Yulia Podtochina's and Olga Nadiova's deaths had been met with
shock, but Lana's was met with resignation. Look at where we live,
people said, gesturing, vaguely, toward the camp and its crosses.
Should we expect anything different? And yet defensive preparations were made. Lana was blond like Yulia and Olga, and so women
started darkening their hair. Dye rimmed the sinks in the bath-
rooms and the communal kitchen, and the women—who went
everywhere in pairs now—took on the look of actresses poorly cast
as sisters.

When the police tape was taken down, the grove became a shrine.
People left teddy bears and plastic bouquets and laminated postcards
of Jesus and Axl Rose, who had been Lana's idol. Ilya hadn't known
this. He hadn't really known her at all, he reminded himself, and
when he thought of her death, it was with wonder rather than grief.
Someone he had touched had died. Someone he had kissed. Someone
young. He had the feeling too that her death was a portent of worse
things to come—whether for him specifically or Berlozhniki in general, he couldn't say—and he found himself desperate to get to
America, to leave before whatever happened next.

He drew a grid on an enormous sheet of newsprint, numbered
the days until he left, and crossed off each one with a red X. One
hundred and fifty-two. One hundred and fifty-one. If Babushka
and his mother resented his eagerness, they didn't show it. Babushka bought him supplies: a new sweatshirt and jeans, a watch
that was also a calculator, a pair of Adidas knockoffs with four
stripes instead of three, a St. Nicholas medal to wear when he flew,

and a St. Sergius medal for after he landed. She washed the clothes and folded them, and Ilya stacked them carefully in the crate under the couch, and tried not to think of Vladimir and all of his tapes in that pink bag in the Tower.

At the Internet Kebab, Kirill took his passport photo. Babushka had given Ilya a fresh haircut, and he wore the shirt with the collar reserved for the Winter Festival and the official announcement of the exchange. He looked good, he thought, but Kirill was not impressed.

"Stop smiling," he said.

Ilya thinned his lips and tilted his chin up like Vladimir did for photos.

"Now you look like a mole," Kirill said. "Just relax." Ilya tried to, but Kirill put the camera down and came over and unbuttoned the top two buttons of Ilya's shirt. "Better," he said. "Way better."

He took three photos and the flash made Ilya jump each time. They printed instantly, and Kirill murmured over them approvingly. "I should charge for styling," he said.

"I look like a thug," Ilya said.

"Exactly," Kirill said. "You can thank me when you don't get jumped as soon as you get to America. It's the fucking wild west there."

"I'm going to Leffie, Louisiana," he said. "It's in the south." The name of the town had been the latest tidbit from Maria Mikhailovna. She had stopped tutoring him, but sometimes after class she'd ask him to stay a moment. She'd told him that the Masons' children were girls—three girls. One day she'd handed him a plastic envelope with his plane tickets inside, and, thinking of Vladimir and the way he'd robbed the apartment, Ilya had asked her to hold on to them for him. "Of course. Of course," she'd said, embarrassed, as though it were insensitive of her not to have anticipated the request.

"When do you go?" Kirill said.

"One hundred and fourteen days," Ilya said.

Kirill laughed. "We'll miss you too, you fucker," he said. "You want to see some young-but-not-too-young pussy? On the house." He spread a hand and gestured grandly toward the computer monitors.

"Save it for Vladimir," Ilya said. "Next time he comes in."

"That thug," Kirill said, with affection. "Nothing's on the house for him."

Ilya hadn't expected there to be many people at the Winter Festival—not after Yulia and Olga and Lana—but the square was packed, and there was a feverishness to the crowd, as though they were all taking a risk being out, and they were determined to make it worthwhile. Women walked in tight groups, their hair—light or dark—hidden under fur caps, their eyes skidding toward the edges of the crowd, the shadows, the places that might hide a killer. They laughed too loudly, sipping at the kvass that vendors sold with pirozhki and shashlik. A few fights had broken out, and the police, who were normally patient enough to let things peter out as long as no weapons appeared, had carted the men off immediately.

Ice sculptures were scattered around the square, glowing under the lights strung up from the larches. A stage stretched from Gabe Thompson's bench all the way to the Minutka. It was laced in bunting that must have been silver a decade earlier, but had faded to the color of slush. The stage was empty. Later, Ilya would stand up there as Fyodor Fetisov announced the exchange. Later still, girls from Ilya's school would dance the chechotka and the Komis would spin in circles, their elbows and feet flying, and inevitably some drunkard in the crowd would get too excited doing a barynya and fall off the stage. For now, though, classical music blasted from speakers as Ilya, his mother, Babushka, and Timofey let the crowd press them from one sculpture to the next.

The theme of that year's festival was "Wind & Fire," and it was announced on banners that dangled from every lamppost in Ber-lozhniki, but most of the sculptors seemed to have ignored it or interpreted it liberally. There was a life-size ice replica of a Toyota Land Cruiser, with one door propped open and the steering wheel wrapped in leather and a real gearshift ripped from some less fortu-nate car. The line to get your picture taken in the driver's seat wound past the stage and all the way to the Internet Kebab. There was an enormous television set with antennae so thin they seemed as if they might crack at any moment. A blue light glowed and flick-ered inside it. There were the traditional statues too—Leda and her swan and Pushkin and Yuri Gagarin standing in front of a mini Monument to the Conquerors of Space. Timofey stared at each sculpture as though he were at the Hermitage examining master-pieces. He liked the sculptures that had taken physical risks—the spider web with its thin filaments, the top-heavy St. Basil's, Barysh-nikov perched on his big toe.

In the center of the square, the most coveted spot, Gazneft had sponsored an enormous replica of the refinery. It was shot through with multicolored lights that flashed and pulsed, and it was encir-cled by a red velvet rope. It was entirely unnecessary—the refinery itself was visible from the square, as were the gray columns of its smoke, which had not been replicated—but Fyodor Fetisov did not normally attend the Winter Festival.

"Don't tell Fetisov, but they forgot the cafeteria," his mother said.

"It's a gift to him, from him," Timofey said, fingering the velvet rope. "Heaven forbid we touch it."

"Don't talk that way," Babushka said. "It's an honor Ilya will meet him." Babushka hated Fetisov more than any of them, but not as much as she feared any disrespect of authority.

"I'm just shaking his hand," Ilya said. Maria Mikhailovna had told him that it would be entirely transactional: Fyodor Fetisov would detail plans to expand the refinery, he would announce the exchange, the handshake would occur, and that was it.

They wandered over to the amateurs' section, to a Snow Queen whose ice nipples jutted through her fur coat like a force of nature. Her face had been so crudely hacked that it looked manly, and at some point her chin had melted and refrozen into a Lenin goatee.

"What are you grinning at?" Timofey said.

"The cross-dressing Snow Queen," Ilya said, and Timofey laughed.

"Ridiculous," Babushka said. She looked at the little card that listed the sculptor. "And it's Mikhail Kolchin. He just gets worse and worse every year. Remember the bear?"

Ilya's mother started to laugh. "It was the skinniest bear ever. It looked like a weasel."

"A demented weasel."

The next lot seemed to be empty. His mother and Babushka strolled past it, but Ilya stubbed his toe on a ridge of ice. He bent and dusted snow off the ridge with the sleeve of his jacket. The ice was curved into a long, low hump, and Ilya swiped more snow off until he'd uncovered the whole thing. A crocodile. It was poorly done. It looked more like the pedestal for a statue than the statue itself, but the primitive shape was there: the tapered snout, the bulbous eyes and bulging body, the long, ridged tail. Half of the creature had been gouged with crude scales before the sculptor had lost interest.

Ilya stared at it, remembering how Vladimir had said, "We don't really call it krokodil. We don't really call it anything." Still, it seemed to Ilya like more than a coincidence. It seemed like a sign. A declaration. The crowd was still by the Land Cruiser and the refinery. Babushka and his mother had joined a line of women to get their pictures taken with a bust of Vladimir Mashkov. They yelled Ilya's name and waved at him, and he waved back before leaning over and brushing the snow off the card by the crocodile's snout. It was blank.

A half hour later, Fetisov arrived in a cavalcade of sirens, and the loudspeakers announced that the speeches and performances would soon commence. Ilya's mother ushered Babushka and Timofey to a bench by the stage, and Ilya waited in a sort of holding pen between the portable toilets and an ice cream cart. A ten-year-old girl in an orange tutu and too much makeup waited next to him. She was dancing the solo from *The Firebird* for Fetisov, she told him, with no small amount of pride. Every few minutes she twirled spontaneously, kicked one leg into the air, and wiggled her toes up by her ears.

The mayor took the stage as the anthem was played. He announced Fyodor Fetisov, and a half-dozen enormous bodyguards surrounded the stage. Two more flanked the man himself, so Ilya could only see a sliver of him. He was shorter than Ilya had expected, but with a meaty neck that was incredibly tan, as though he'd been somewhere tropical just hours before. He was known for his terseness—brevity, was how people put it when they were being diplomatic or were afraid of being overheard—and he dispensed with thank-yous altogether and in a quiet monotone announced that the refinery would soon be expanded to accommodate supply from a new pipeline.

There were cheers from the crowd, and one boo that required the attention of one of the bodyguards.

"And I'm pleased," he said, sounding far from pleased, "to announce that this marks the inaugural year of an exchange between Gazneft and EnerCo. This year's Gazneft Academian is Ilya Alexandrovich Morozov."

The crowd cheered again—with less enthusiasm than they had for the refinery expansion, but still it was paralyzing. What if someone knew that he hadn't taken the boards? What if Maria Mikhailovna decided that *this* was the moment for a crisis of conscience? Why did he even need to go up there at all? His name had been announced. That was enough, wasn't it? But Fetisov extended an arm into the empty space to his right, and the ballerina nudged Ilya's elbow, and Ilya managed somehow to climb a small set of stairs and cross the stage. Fyodor Fetisov gripped his hand. A camera clicked wildly, the flash spasming. And as Fetisov dropped his hand, Ilya felt the sharp edge of something against his palm. A thick, gold ring, studded with an enormous diamond. Ilya looked at Fetisov's shoes. They were pointy, slick, expensive.

"Congratulations," Fyodor Fetisov said.

Ilya nodded. Fetisov's lips thinned. Ilya was supposed to thank him, but he couldn't muster it. He was back in the elevator, all the buttons glowing. He was running for the service door, and Vladimir was staggering out of the elevator, his face bloodied, and Ilya wondered if Vladimir was in the crowd somewhere, if he could see Fetisov and had recognized him also.

In the end, Fetisov left the stage before Ilya. He trooped off with his bodyguards, and the mayor ushered Ilya back to the holding pen and said, "You're Berlozhniki's best and brightest?" as the ballerina tiptoed out to the first tiny, teasing notes of *The Firebird*.

It was close to midnight when they walked home, but dancers were still twirling on the stage, their skirts a red blur. The road out to the kommunalkas was filled with people too belligerent to let cars pass, so the cars joined in the procession, horns honking, the windows rolled down, the music from their radios mixing with the music from the square.

Ilya was the first up the eight flights, and so he saw Vladimir first. He was sitting with his spine curled against the door and his head on his knees.

"Vlad," Ilya said, and he could hear it echo down the stairs behind him, could hear his mother reframe Vladimir's name as a question. Vladimir didn't move. There were fast steps on the stairs behind Ilya. Then Babushka said, "What is it?" and Ilya's mother was pushing past him, saying Vladimir's name again and again, and still Vladimir didn't move until she was kneeling in front of him, lifting his head up in her hands.

"You locked me out," he said. Then he retched, and nothing came out but a bit of frothy spit. He tried to stand and couldn't, and even in the dimness of the hallway Ilya could see that something was wrong with one of his legs and that he was covered in blood.

"Oh God," Timofey said from behind Ilya.

"I'll call an ambulance," Ilya said. He could hardly breathe, and the words rose up his throat like stones.

"No," his mother said.

"He's sick, Mamulya," Ilya said, his voice sounding high and afraid, though he had meant to be firm.

"They'll arrest him," she said.

She wrapped her arms around Vladimir and pulled him up, and Babushka opened the door behind them. Vladimir closed his eyes. His skin looked like marble. Ilya could hear the sound of Babushka turning on the stove in the apartment, and all he could think was that she was cooking blini for Vladimir the way she had cooked it for them when they were little and something had happened to make them sad. His mother dragged Vladimir inside, into the light, and the blood, which had looked like shadow in the darkness of the hall, turned bright red.

"Get more hot water," Babushka said to Timofey. Timofey nodded, but Babushka had to say, "Now," before Timofey ran for the kitchen.

"Shut the door, Ilya," his mother said. "I need you to hold his head up and talk to him. Try to get him awake."

Ilya sat and pulled Vladimir's head into his lap. Vladimir's skin felt like marble too, and somehow this was a comfort to Ilya because the cold was a familiar threat. He's just cold, he thought. He just stayed out too long in the cold. He rubbed at Vladimir's cheeks. He said his name over and over, as his mother pulled off Vladimir's jacket. At the stove, Babushka had both teakettles whistling. She poured them into the enormous roast pan that was reserved for the New Year's feast and filled them again from the jug of water on the counter. Ilya's mother unbuttoned Vladimir's shirt. He was even thinner than he'd been in the Tower, with deep shadows between his ribs. There were scabs at the crook of his arm, marching along the veins all the way to his hands, and their mother must have noticed them, but she just said, "Thank God," when she saw his chest, the skin intact, the heart fluttering under it.

"Ilya," she said, "wake him up. And if he vomits again, turn his head. Make sure he doesn't choke on it."

Ilya pinched Vladimir's cheeks and red bloomed on his skin, then faded in an instant. "Wake up!" he yelled. "Wake up, wake up!" He slapped Vladimir, felt his own cheeks burn in apology, but Vladimir's head just lolled to the side, and his lips parted and let out a gasp of bitter breath.

Timofey was back with two kettles of steaming water, and Babushka pointed to the roast pan and said, "More," and he poured the water into the pan and ran for more.

Their mother had Vladimir's shoes off. His socks were filthy, crusted brown with blood. His mother rolled them off, and Ilya could see that the pockets of skin between his toes were oozing. When his mother pulled at Vladimir's jeans, Vladimir's eyes flashed open, and for a second, Ilya thought, He's OK. He's awake, and he's OK. But then Vladimir screamed, his body jackknifing, his head smashing into Ilya's chin. He twisted onto his side and vomited again, and again nothing came out.

Ilya's mother let out a sound that was something like a sob, though she wasn't crying. She put her hands on her knees and bowed her head, and he thought that she might give in and call for an ambulance, but after a moment she lifted her head and said, "I need scissors," and Babushka brought them from her sewing kit.

"OK," his mother said. "Vova, can you hear me? I'll be gentle, but we have to get your pants off. We have to get you clean. OK?"

The pain had woken Vladimir, and his eyes were narrowed on a spot on the carpet just past his nose. His face was slick with sweat, and Ilya could see that he did not have it in him to respond, let alone fight her. She began to cut, very slowly, very gently, along the seam of his pants. On one leg, the fabric fell away, but on the other, it stuck to the skin and so she cut even more slowly, millimeter by millimeter. Timofey brought water again, and now the roast pan was full and steaming, and his mother had cut Vladimir's pants all the way up through the waistband.

"Ilya," she said, "you need to really hold him now."

Ilya put his arms around Vladimir's head, so that his fingers laced under his chin, and Babushka pushed a spoon between his teeth.

"This will hurt, Vova, but I'll be quick," their mother said. She had never talked to Vladimir so softly before, had not used his nickname since they were children. Always she said "Vla-di-mir," the syllables a scale of disappointment.

The spoon clattered in Vladimir's teeth, and Ilya couldn't tell if he was nodding or shaking. He groped for Ilya's hand and found it, and Ilya thought of war movies, of all those glorious deaths in the Great War, when it had seemed so clear who the enemy was and who the hero. Vladimir yanked at his hand, feebly, and spit the spoon out of his mouth. He wanted to say something—and this was like the movies too, Ilya thought, his heart racing. Vladimir had some last words, some assertion of love or apology, something for them.

"Pocket," he said, his voice sounding full of sand. "Coat pocket."

"Mama?" Ilya said.

His mother closed her eyes and nodded, and it was from her

expression—that calm defeat—that Ilya knew what was in the pocket.

There was a vial and a syringe. The syringe was visibly dirty, the needle crusted with something yellow. The vial had a pathetic amount in it. Less than a teaspoon. Less than a lick, already mixed, with gray sediment at the bottom.

"Do I have to cook it?" Ilya said, thinking of the process he'd witnessed at the Tower, knowing that he couldn't replicate it, that he hadn't been watching it with the right sort of desire.

Vladimir shook his head. Ilya wiped down the syringe and sucked the liquid into it. He pressed the plunger down to get the air out because Vladimir had told him a story about a man, three floors down, who had filled his insulin syringe with air and pushed it into his veins in '98, when the currency crashed.

"Mama," Ilya said again.

She took the syringe from him, held it out, and started to cry. "I don't know how to do this," she said. "I don't know how to find a vein."

Vladimir's eyes were clearer, now that the syringe was in sight, as though he could already feel the drug working. "It doesn't matter," he said. "It doesn't have to be a vein."

So she stuck the needle into the bare skin of his thigh, in a spot that looked vaguely blue, and Vladimir leaned back onto Ilya's lap and opened his mouth, and Ilya put the spoon back between his teeth though his jaw was too slack to hold it. Once she'd pushed the plunger down, his mother handed the syringe to Babushka, and Babushka opened the door to the balcony, disappeared into a gust of cold air, and came back without it.

"The water's getting cold," Babushka said.

His mother nodded and gripped the edges of his pants where they were stuck to his skin.

"Ready?" she said.

Ilya nodded and gripped Vladimir's hand, and Vladimir's mind was far away, gripping whatever memory it had found, and when their mother ripped the fabric away and bits of his flesh came too, he did not yell or move.

The leg was ruinous. The skin, where it remained, was the color of onions cooked in grease, and below the knee there was a crater where his shin should have been, and in the muck of flesh and blood and pus, there was the clean white flash of bone.

Ilya would remember the horror from this night. In America, he would dream of it, but he would remember this too: how his mother and Babushka had moved in concert, each seeming to find strength right when the other had lost it.

It was his mother who had ripped the fabric off, who threw up at the sight of Vladimir's leg, but then looked again anyway. It was Babushka who spread a towel under Vladimir and bathed him with the water from the roast pan, which had been their tub when they were babies. Her hand plunged into the water over and over, as endlessly patient as an oil pump dipping into the earth.

"He'll have to go to the hospital," she said, when he was clean.

"I know," his mother said.

Timofey sat at their table with his head in his hands. "It's gangrene," he said softly, then, "How the hell did he get gangrene?"

His mother brought her makeup kit from the bedroom and began to dab makeup over the puncture marks on Vladimir's arms, between his toes, everywhere except the bone-deep sore on his leg.

Her fingers shook as she put it on. The makeup was the wrong color—too orange for Vladimir's skin—and the scabs made his skin look like rocky soil. It was ridiculous, but she couldn't stop herself and neither Ilya nor Babushka tried to stop her. She was writing her hope out on his skin. Hiding the drugs so that he wouldn't get arrested, blacklisted, or sent to a narc clinic, which was worse than prison. They dressed Vladimir in a sweater of Timofey's and a pair of Ilya's sweats—a respectable outfit for Vladimir—and still the nurse at the hospital took one look at his face and said, "Any idea what he's on?"

They were all silent.

"We'll need to know to treat him," she said, sounding infinitely patient in the way of the disinterested. She had tiny gold crosses in her ears, and she tucked her hair behind them.

Ilya looked to his mother for permission, and she shrugged.

"Krokodil," Ilya said, and then, "I think that's what they call it."

The nurse looked up at them then. Her face was full of pity. "How long has he been using?" she said, though for a second it seemed that what she wanted to say was that she was sorry.

CHAPTER TWENTY-THREE

Across the street from the clinic there was a medical supply store that did a thriving business, and Ilya and his mother went there on a bright, cold morning, armed with a list from a nurse of what Vladimir would need. For three days, the nurses had not let them see him. "Today is not good. You don't want to see him today," they'd said, and, "He's coming off it. Tomorrow will be better," and, finally, "Tomorrow. Tomorrow will be good. Here is a list. Bring all of this, tomorrow."

They loaded Vladimir's old army duffel with a set of sheets, two IV bags, coils of plastic tubing, five papery polka-dotted hospital gowns, a bedpan, tape, ointments, and a plastic satchel of gauze that weighed nothing, that on a different day Ilya would have been tempted to throw into the air just to see how high he could get it.

Babushka was sitting in the clinic waiting room with an enormous container of marrow broth wedged between her knees. An old man slept in a corner chair, his fly gaping open and a tuft of underwear poking out. He woke up briefly upon their arrival and said, "My son," and Babushka shushed him. Before long he was snoring again—a gurgle, wheeze, gurgle, wheeze that made Ilya wonder if he shouldn't be admitted.

They waited, and they waited. Occasionally a nurse with too strong a jaw and a red braid as thick as a boa emerged from the door, marched over to a clipboard, squinted at it, squinted at them, and squinted at the old man, before disappearing back into the clinic's bright white light. Ilya's mother had given him an envelope of cash to tuck in the clipboard's grip, and the nurse had taken it, but still they waited. Aksinya's name had been on the visitor's list, and Dmitri Malikov's too. Maybe he'd been visiting his mother, Ilya thought, because he remembered Dmitri saying something about her being sick.

Ilya's stomach rumbled. His own hunger did not seem like something he could mention, and so he eyed Babushka's broth. He could see the paleness of the ox bone through the liquid.

Around noon, a young woman came through the front doors, so pregnant that her spine curved backward. Babushka looked at her as though she were about to give birth to Jesus.

"It's a girl!" Babushka said.

The woman rolled her eyes, but Babushka no longer cared about the nuances of expressions, and she kept on, undeterred. "How far apart are the pains? That's a low baby. Let me feel."

Babushka began to get up, arms outstretched, but the woman said, "No," loudly enough that even the old man stirred. She turned to her husband, a thin man who had been entirely obscured by her generous silhouette in the door, and said, "You have the money?"

He nodded, looking terrified, and when the nurse appeared, he handed her a thin pile of rubles—straight from the ATM—and murmured, "Soon, please."

The nurse put her palm over the money in his and squeezed his hand. "Don't worry," she said. "Getting the baby out's the easy part.

It's the next twenty years that will be hard." She smiled, showing one long, gray tooth in a line of white ones.

"That's the truth," Babushka said.

The pregnant woman grunted and sank into a chair. "A room, please."

The nurse smiled again, but without showing her teeth this time. "Be patient. I can tell from your face that you're not even three centimeters."

"It helps to pray," Babushka said. "I prayed through my labor."

The woman moaned, from annoyance and agony, and Ilya wanted badly to plug his ears. The idea that a baby was moving through her, would soon emerge from her, made his stomach seize, and he eyed Vladimir's bedpan, thinking he might vomit. Then the doors to the clinic swung open again. It was a doctor this time, in a white coat that was too short in the sleeves, with a tiny stain of what appeared to be blood on the collar. The nurse started and strode toward her clipboard.

"Vladimir Alexandrovich Morozov," the doctor said, as though it were roll call, and Vladimir would raise his hand.

You have Vladimir, Ilya wanted to say. His mother jumped up from her chair. Ilya gathered the supplies, and as he was helping Babushka with the broth, he heard the doctor say, "We weren't able to save the knee."

Ilya had his back to his mother. He could not see her face. He eased Babushka down into her chair and turned. His mother's neck was bent, her arms slack at her sides, and the doctor was looking at her kindly, sadly, but with a little embarrassment too. Then the doctor's eyes met Ilya's.

"You're his brother?"

Ilya nodded.

"You can't all see him. Only one of you. You brought all of the supplies?"

"Yes," Ilya said.

"Good."

Ilya's mother's face had gone the gray it went when she had the flu, when Vladimir had kept her up all night with worry, but she managed to say, "Where did you cut?"

The doctor held a hand to Ilya's leg, halfway between his hip and knee. "There," he said. Ilya's mother made a small, choking sound. Later, she would rant about the doctor, about how strange, how cruel it had been that he had demonstrated on Ilya's leg and not his own. But Ilya thought it natural that the doctor could imagine taking another's leg more easily than his own since that was exactly what had happened. And for weeks after, when Ilya thought of Vladimir, he would feel the pressure of the doctor's fingers in that spot, and it would make him feel close to Vladimir. There, he'd think. Right there.

His mother was not crying, but Ilya could see that she would be soon—crying or yelling or both—and so he said, "I'll go see him."

The doctor shrugged, and in the silence, the pregnant woman gave her husband a shove forward.

"Izvinitye," the husband said. The doctor looked at him, and then at his wife.

"How bad is the pain?" he asked her.

"Right now, not so bad, but—"

"Good," the doctor said, "because it will be a while. The rooms are full. Your brother"—he looked at Ilya, with an expression both kind and pointed—"is not the only one to lose a limb. These kids are willing to die, to rot. Over what?" The doctor was shouldering through the doors now, and Ilya glanced back at his mother and

Babushka. His mother had her head on Babushka's shoulder, and Babushka was whispering in her ear, and Ilya knew what she'd be saying.

"Tchoo, tchoo. Tchoo, tchoo." A nonsense word that she used for scraped knees and spilled tea and for this now too.

Vladimir looked healthier than he had in months. His eyes were clear, the whites like snow, and the bruised skin under them had faded to a respectable gray. His leg was bandaged in so much gauze that it was easy to ignore; it was easy to forget that there was not actually a leg under there but a stump. His room was halved by a curtain with a repeating scene of wild animals picnicking—a lion, an elephant, a zebra, and a tiger plopped down around a basket as though they'd all decided to ignore their baser instincts for a day and share some cucumber sandwiches. Ilya could see nothing of the patient on the other side but a pair of tiny, filthy sneakers under a chair.

Ilya's tape player was in Vladimir's lap, the Delta headphones around his neck, and when Vladimir saw him he lifted the player up and said, "OK if I borrow it for a bit?"

Ilya nodded. "Learn some English," he said. "I brought you a bedpan. And polka-dotted gowns."

Vladimir grinned. "Did you see the hot nurse?"

"The one with the red hair?"

"Yes. That braid is made for tugging. She comes in here to help me pee. She said if I ever lose my arms, she'll hold my dick for me."

"In your dreams." A male voice came from the other side of the curtain, high and wheezy.

Vladimir rolled his eyes and pretended to take a swig from a bottle. "It's none of your business what happens on this side of the curtain, Tolya."

"That's not what you were saying last week. Screaming for me to put you out of your misery."

Tolya began to laugh, and Ilya looked away from Vladimir's face.

"Does it hurt?" Ilya asked.

"It's numb. I don't feel anything there—no real leg, no ghost leg. People are going to think I'm a vet. Tolya and I are going to make a killing panhandling."

Ilya put the duffel in a chair in the corner and handed Vladimir the magazine he'd gotten him at the Minutka. On the cover, a girl in an ushanka, lace underwear, and fishing waders posed in a river. Vladimir nodded without much enthusiasm, and Ilya wondered if he'd already seen this one, or if it was too tame, if Ilya could not even pick the right kind of nudie magazine.

"How is Mamulya?"

"She's fine. She'll be fine."

"And you're going?"

Ilya nodded.

"When?"

"August."

"That's good," Vladimir said. "Don't fuck it up again, OK?"

"I won't."

Behind the curtain, Tolya's cough grew rough, like he was dredging up something awful from his sternum.

"Tolya?" Vladimir said.

Tolya was silent.

"Is he OK?" Ilya said.

"Are you OK?" Vladimir said.

"I'm dying," Tolya said.

"Don't be dramatic," Vladimir said.

Tolya coughed again, and Ilya could feel the pain of it in his own chest. The lights flickered overhead, and for a moment he and Vladimir just listened to Tolya coughing. A phone was ringing somewhere down the hall. Then there were footsteps and the nurse appeared pushing an empty wheelchair, her braid tick-tocking behind her. She looked at Vladimir like he was an especially tough tea stain on her counter and said, "You're about to get a life lesson. Have you ever seen a baby born?"

"You're shitting me," Vladimir said.

"I am not. And this woman does not seem like the friendly type—not that any woman is when she's being ripped stem to sternum—but you might want to shut your trap for once."

"What about me?" Tolya said.

"You're out of here," she said, pulling back the curtain.

Tolya had the body of a ten- or eleven-year-old and the face of someone much older. His cheeks were speckled with scars the size of kopeks and there was something strange and sucked-in about his lips. He did not have any teeth, Ilya realized, and as the nurse lifted him out of the bed Ilya saw that he did not have any legs either.

"Jealous?" he said to Vladimir as the nurse hugged him to her and carried him to the wheelchair.

The nurse made a noise between a snort and a laugh. "You have two minutes," she said to Ilya.

As she wheeled Tolya from the room, he looked back over his shoulder at Ilya and said, "You're the one going to America?"

They were gone before Ilya had a chance to answer, but he heard Tolya's voice, fading down the corridor, saying, "In America, they eat this shit up. Thirteen and a double amputee. They'd have me on ten reality shows at once. Jerry Springer would be interviewing me every fucking day."

They both stared at the door. "He took it too?" Ilya said.

"Yeah."

"Did you know what it would do?"

"I'm not a complete idiot," Vladimir said. *Then why*, Ilya thought, and his face must have shown the question, because Vladimir said, "I can't explain it."

"You said it makes you remember. That's what you said that night"—he was going to say the night Lana died, because that was how he thought of it now, but instead he said, "in the Tower."

"Yeah. It makes you remember . . ." He trailed off and plucked at the edge of the gauze on his leg.

"Is it worth it?" Ilya said.

Vladimir looked down at the magazine on his lap.

"If you'd brought some, I'd take it again," he said. His voice was quiet and frank, and then it took on a harder cast: "I'd kill you to take it."

"No you wouldn't," Ilya said.

"You don't have any, do you?" Vladimir said, and he was joking now, but Ilya still thought he might cry, and so he concentrated on Tolya's bed. The rumpled sheets with the yellowish shadow where his body had been. His sneakers were still under the chair, and Ilya wondered how long they'd sit there before someone noticed. Down the hall, he could hear the pregnant woman coming. "Don't touch me!" she bellowed, at her husband no doubt, and Ilya stood up.

"Thanks for this," Vladimir said. He picked up the magazine. "I have a feeling it's going to be a dry spell for me for a while. Aksinya is pissed at this gimp situation."

"Will you come home? When they let you out?" Ilya said, and he wondered why he hadn't ever asked this before, why it had seemed like something he couldn't say. "They're going to be lonely once I'm gone."

"You kidding me? Those two are going to live it up. Put up a disco ball. Get themselves a boom box."

"Yeah," Ilya said.

Vladimir was smiling, but there was this toska in his eyes—a sadness that Maria Mikhailovna had once told him didn't have an English equivalent, like it belonged only to them. Ilya thought of telling Vladimir this, but instead he smiled back.

"Later, Vlad," he said, and Vladimir said, "Yeah, come again, will you?"

And as Ilya walked down the hall, past the pregnant woman who had propped herself against a wall, Vladimir yelled, "And bring Fanta next time and a kebab. Tell Babushka no more nasty broth!"

Their mother had to go back to work, but Ilya and Babushka spent every day of the next week in the clinic waiting room, begging to see Vladimir. Every day they gave the nurses more money, and every day they were told that the rooms were too full for visitors.

After a week of waiting, the nurse with the red braid took pity on them. She came and squatted by Babushka's chair so that their eyes were level. "They took him in yesterday," she said.

"Took him where?" Babushka said.

"He's lucky he had time to heal here first," the nurse said.

"He got off the stuff. He was clean. Ilya said he was clean. He didn't need to—" Babushka said.

"Not detox. Jail," the nurse said. "And not for the drugs, either."

Babushka kept her face completely still and in her ice voice said, "You're mistaken."

The nurse must have been the sort of woman who was sick of tears and sobs and moans and could only be softened by toughness, because she said, "He was not smart, that's for sure, but I agree. He didn't seem like the type to kill anyone. More a Don Juan. But he confessed."

"Confessed?" Babushka said.

"To the murders. Of those women."

Babushka nodded stiffly, and gripped Ilya's hand, and they sat like that, on the bench, for a long time. Then Babushka patted his arm, rose on her own, and together they walked across the square to the bus stop.

Chapter Twenty-four

Papa Cam had heated the pool so that it was as hot as Babushka's tea, and a layer of steam formed between the water and the October air that made it look like an enormous cauldron. Since he'd come to America, Ilya's swimming had improved, and he and Molly and Marilee took turns diving, and Mama Jamie and Papa Cam ranked their scores as though they were in the Olympics. Sadie floated on the water's surface, and every once in a while, Ilya used his dives as an excuse to swim underneath her, to twist like a seal and look at the way the water fanned her hair and blued her skin.

He had a biology quiz the next day, and so it wasn't until he'd memorized the steps of photosynthesis that he got into bed and listened to the tape from Gabe's house. He'd listened to it so many times that it was hard to actually pay attention, and his mind drifted to Sadie, as his mind did more and more recently. That afternoon she'd asked him if he'd want to stay for longer than a year. Her shirt was off—they were in the back of her car in the parking lot behind the defunct fireworks stand—and his hands ran down her ribs, her skin so smooth it made it hard to think, but even if he hadn't been touching her, he would have nodded, would have said yes.

On the tape, Gabe was saying *stained glass* and *personal effects*, and Ilya was saying yes, and kissing her neck and then her chest, and he was slipping down one strap of her bra and then the other, and then Gabe said, *Tapes. These tapes for learning English.*

Ilya sat up. *Only I didn't think you'd need them*, Gabe said, and he was right, of course. Ilya didn't need them. Why would he need them here, in America? But Ilya had brought them anyway, had brought them though he knew them by heart, because when he'd found them in the Tower it had seemed like a message. When Gabe told Ilya that the nurse had asked him to give them to Ilya, Ilya thought that he'd understood the message: the tapes were Vladimir's way of apologizing for stealing them in the first place, for everything, or else they were his way of saying good-bye. Vladimir had known that Ilya would want the tapes even in America—Vladimir, who had spent years of his life plucking the headphones off Ilya's ears so that he could call him a loser or a brainiac or tell him that dinner was ready or ask him if he wanted to go find some cardboard and sled down the concrete ramps under the bridge.

Ilya rewound. *Tapes*, Gabe said. *I didn't want to be involved.* Ilya could imagine the redheaded nurse thrusting them at Gabe, telling him to get them to Vladimir's brother. Clearly she'd been doing Vladimir a favor—she'd taken the tapes from him instead of giving them straight to the police—but she hadn't wanted to wait to give them to Ilya and Babushka, who came to the clinic almost daily. The only explanation that Ilya could think of was that she'd gotten scared, as though they were contraband, a pack of Marlboros or three stolen pounds of rye, something that, back in the day, would earn you ten years without the right of correspondence.

Ilya pressed stop. The other tapes were stacked on the dresser. The one on top was the one that Vladimir had left in the player, the first installment of *Michael & Stephanie*. Ilya's hands were shaking so much that at first he couldn't get the tape in, couldn't get the player closed, and then he finally did, and he pushed play and Michael said, *"Unit One: Hello, How Are You?"* and Stephanie introduced herself, and Michael did the same, and Ilya forced himself to repeat back everything that they said, to pay attention to each syllable in just the way he had when he was six, sitting on the carpet reading the lips in Vladimir's movies. Each side was an hour long. He started the third tape at midnight, and soon afterward, Sadie crept down the deck steps. Ilya hit pause and slid the door open.

"Hey," he whispered.

She froze at the edge of the pool, then squinted down at him in the shadows below the deck.

"You almost gave me a heart attack," she said, as she picked her way past the rusty bicycles toward him.

He told her what he was thinking, how he kept picturing the plastic bag sitting there in the Tower, how it had seemed alive, almost, the bright pink of it against all that concrete.

"I'll listen with you," she said.

"You're not going to go?" he asked. He thought of her mother on the Bojangles' parking stump a few days earlier, and wondered what shape she might be in.

Sadie shook her head. "I'll go tomorrow."

They lay on his bed, and he pulled the headphones out of the jack, and Michael's and Stephanie's voices poured into the basement. He had never listened to them like this—out loud, with another person, in America—and he could sense how shabby they were, how stilted. It felt something like the time his mother had shown up at the school for a talent show, her hairnet forgotten on her head.

Michael and Stephanie were at the train station, buying tickets, checking the time, finding their seats. Sadie was quiet, listening.

"It's old-fashioned, isn't it?" he said. "No one says, 'Is this seat taken?'"

"I like it. They sound like you," Sadie said.

"I sound like them," Ilya said.

On the B-side of the third tape, Michael and Stephanie went to the zoo. They fed peanuts to elephants and bread to ducks. Stephanie listed her favorite animals. Giraffe, tiger, lion, snake. She was talking about their habitats, about the savannah, when Ilya fell asleep.

He woke as the sun was coming up over the rim of the alligator wall. Sadie was asleep beside him.

"Did you figure it out?" she said as she woke.

"Not yet," he said, and she snuck out the sliding doors and back into the house undetected.

That morning he feigned illness in order to keep listening to the tapes, and Mama Jamie was so concerned for his health that she brought him mug after mug of chicken soup, bowls of crackers, and bottles of a liquid called Powerade that looked like antifreeze but that she claimed would keep his electrolytes in balance. Halfway through the tapes, he told her that he needed fresh air, and he moved out onto the patio by the pool. He stationed himself on a beach chair, with the Delta headphones over each ear. The heat had relented, and above him the oak leaves shimmied in a breeze. Clouds chained the sky, and in the brilliance of the day, the idea that a message might be embedded in the tapes, that they might hold anything beyond Michael's and Stephanie's clear, vacant voices, seemed ludicrous. But there was planning and effort in the fact that Vladimir had asked the nurse to get the tapes to him, and Vladimir was not a planner, was not one to make an effort.

He was on the A-side of the seventh tape. There was only one tape left plus the tape he'd recorded over, and this was a thought that he was avoiding. What if he'd erased Vladimir's message with Gabe's story? It was too horrible an idea to entertain.

Michael was discussing the days of the week as a way of practicing the future tense. *On Monday I will drive to the market. On Tuesday I will cook dinner. On Wednesday I will clean the house. On Thursday I will—*

There was a thick silence. Before he noticed it, Ilya's mind had completed the sentence. *On Thursday I will get a haircut.* He could picture the workbook image that accompanied this statement: Michael smiling while a barber pointed a pair of scissors at his neck. Then there was a muffled sound, a cough, and a faint Russian voice said, "Thank you," and "Shut the door."

Ilya sat up and pressed the headphones to his ears, trying to bring the voice closer.

"You want one?" the voice said.

There was no answer but a staccato thwacking.

"Light?" the voice said, then, "Don't tell your mother." A few seconds passed, and the voice said, "I'll begin recording."

"Da," another voice said. It sounded like Vladimir, though the word coming from Vladimir was usually a lazy, drawn-out thing, and in this case it was clipped, nervous.

There was a light click, and Ilya thought that that might be it, but the first voice came back, full of bravado, so loud and clear that Ilya dropped his hands from the headphones.

"This is Officer Dmitri Malikov, interviewing the suspect, Vladimir Alexandrovich Morozov, at fifteen hundred hours, at the Berlozhniki Medical Clinic. Can you confirm your identity for the record?"

"Yes," Vladimir said, and his voice was clearer now too. "It's Vladimir Alexandrovich Morozov."

"And can you tell me how you knew Lana Vishnyeva?"

"We were friends. Friends since primary. And her best friend is my girlfriend."

"Your girlfriend's name for the record?"

"Aksinya Stepanova."

"And where were you on the night of the twenty-third of January?"

There was a pause. "Which night is that?" Vladimir said.

A note of annoyance crept into Dmitri's voice. "The night Lana was murdered."

"Aksinya wasn't with me," Vladimir said.

"OK," Dmitri said. "Who was with you? Lana?"

"Yes. Lana," Vladimir said.

"And," Dmitri said. The annoyance had ceded to encouragement.

"I killed her," Vladimir said.

There it was. He'd said it. And just as Ilya was beginning to wonder if that was the message, if this was Vladimir's way of saying that he'd done it, no matter what Ilya believed, Dmitri asked, "How?"

"With a knife," Vladimir said. "I stabbed her."

"You mean you cut her throat? It was Yulia Podtochina and Olga Nadiova that you stabbed."

"Oh," Vladimir said. "OK. I cut her throat."

"Where did you get the knife?"

"A store," Vladimir said.

"You don't remember which one?" There was a pause, and then Dmitri said, "I need you to make a verbal answer."

"No," Vladimir said.

"And what did you do with it after you stabbed Lana?"

There was another pause. Dmitri cleared his throat. It was a tic of his, Ilya remembered, from that dinner at the Malikovs' apartment.

"I threw it off the Bolshoi Bridge, into the river."

"Walk me through the whole night," Dmitri said. "When did you meet up with Lana?"

Vladimir began to talk again, but Ilya was picturing him up on the Bolshoi Bridge. It had been the thick of winter when Lana was murdered, and the river was frozen solid. Nothing could be thrown *into* it.

The whole confession was like that—Vladimir making missteps and Dmitri correcting those he caught. Vladimir got the location of Olga Nadiova's murder wrong. He described a struggle with Lana, though the newspaper had reported no signs of a struggle after her autopsy. He guessed wildly at the number of times he'd stabbed Yulia Podtochina, and Dmitri said quietly, "Try again," and then, "Again."

By the end of the confession, Vladimir's voice had gone hoarse and thick.

"Why did you do it?" Dmitri said.

"I don't know," Vladimir said.

"Because of the drugs?" Dmitri said.

"Because I felt like it," Vladimir said. This had been a refrain of his for much of their adolescence. "Why did you break the window?" their mother would ask. *Because I felt like it.* "Why would you say that to her?" *Because I felt like it.* "Why did you steal the cigarettes?" *Because I felt like it,* and his mother would say, "How nice it must be to always act the way you feel."

"OK," Dmitri said. "Enough."

There was a click, and Ilya waited a second for Michael and Stephanie to resume, but that was the end of Dmitri's recording, not Vladimir's.

"So the deal," Vladimir said. "This confession and Ilya gets to go, and not just for a year. I want him to stay there. A permanent exchange."

"Yes," Dmitri said. "That's the deal."

"And the murders?" Vladimir said. "What if there are more murders?"

"I'll make sure there are not," Dmitri said. "Maybe prison will be good for you. At least you won't lose any other limbs."

"Can I have a minute—for a cigarette?" The recording was threaded through with static, but still Ilya could hear a new clarity, or force, in Vladimir's voice here, as though this question were the only thing he'd said that mattered.

Dmitri didn't seem to notice. He scoffed and said, "Take five if you like."

His footsteps faded, and the muffled sound returned—the microphone against bedsheets. There were footsteps again, and then a woman's voice said, "Hurry up," and Ilya understood why the question had mattered. The tape clicked. For a moment there was silence, pure silence, the kind you'd hear in outer space, between worlds. Then Stephanie's voice replied to something Michael had said, and Ilya could picture Vladimir, stuffing the tape player back into the pink plastic bag and handing it to the nurse, whose courage hadn't yet deserted her, and she'd hidden it somewhere—in a wastebasket, or a food cart, or a bundle of dirty bedding—while Dmitri took Vladimir away in handcuffs.

Ilya remembered standing in the square with Vladimir after the Tower, after he'd admitted to skipping the boards. His cheek stinging from Vladimir's slap. Snow melting fast on him like anger was heat. Vladimir had said he'd take care of things, and Ilya hadn't believed him, hadn't thought him capable. But this was Vladimir taking care of things. It was idiotic, terrible. It was amazing. It was Vladimir.

Vladimir hadn't known that Maria Mikhailovna had taken the boards for Ilya, and he hadn't had anything to barter with except for his terrible reputation, so he'd become Dmitri's fall guy. But did that mean that Dmitri had done it? How else could he ensure that there were no more murders? Or would he just make sure that any more murders weren't connected to the original three? Surely if Dmitri had been killing the girls, Vladimir would have hinted at that in the tapes?

Ilya didn't know. He could see Dmitri Malikov over dinner, with a snifter of vodka in hand, talking about the Tower, about the people who went there like they were an infestation. Ilya thought of Maria Mikhailovna. Her thick braids. Her glasses. The way that she looked at him sometimes as though he were a work of art that she was grateful to have framed. And then he thought of Vladimir. He imagined Vladimir strutting out of the prison gates like he owned the whole world. If he got out, his smugness would be intolerable. "They should make a movie of me," he'd say. "A whole fucking series. I'm like the love child of Jason Bourne and Jackie Chan." Ilya could feel a smile on his face. The big, hurting kind, like the one he'd had in that picture in the Tower.

CHAPTER TWENTY-FIVE

Ilya called Maria Mikhailovna from the phone in the kitchen. The house was empty except for Durashka, who was staring out the sliding glass door at a bird perched on the deck railing. Somehow Maria Mikhailovna must have known that it was him, because when she picked up, she said his name instead of "Hello."

"Zdravstvuyte," he said.

"Why are you talking to me in Russian? I want to hear your English! All those Americanisms! They haven't corrupted your grammar, have they?" The excitement in her voice was almost enough to make him hang up, but the tape was in his hand. He had the sense that if he let it out of his grasp it might disappear, and it was sickening to him how light and small it felt, given how much it contained: the ridiculous confession, the months Vladimir had spent in prison and all the miseries that must have entailed.

She said his name again, cautiously this time, as though she could sense his anger fortifying. Then she switched to Russian and said, "Are you all right? What is it? Are they mean to you, the family? Tell me." Ilya thought of Mama Jamie and the way her face relaxed when she prayed, of the way she held Molly sometimes and stroked the hair back from her forehead, of the notes she left in his lunch bag, each one signed with a string of Xs and Os.

"Nyet," he managed.

She said, "Is it Vladimir? Is he OK?"

"Are you alone?" he asked.

"I'm alone," she said, her voice lifting at the end like it was a question.

"I know Vladimir came to see you before the boards—I know he wanted to come here—but did he ever come after the boards?"

"Yes," she said quickly, as though she were relieved at the ease of the question. "Once."

"He wanted to help me, right?"

"Yes," she said again. "Why?"

"What did you tell him? Did you tell him that you'd taken the boards?"

"No. I just said that he needed to keep his mouth shut. I wasn't about to tell him, not after he'd taken you to the Tower—"

"And did you tell Dmitri that he'd come to see you?"

Ilya had never interrupted her before, and he could hear the sting of it in her voice when she said, "Of course I did. Dmitri was worried that someone would find out. Fetisov or the mayor or who knows who. *Has* someone found out?" she said. "Is that what's wrong? Someone there?"

He was quiet for a moment. He could understand, now, how Dmitri had threatened Vladimir, what he had used. It had been Ilya, here, in America.

"Ilya," she said, "please tell me."

But Vladimir had not known how much Dmitri loved Maria Mikhailovna; Dmitri never would have kept Ilya from coming to

America because that was what she wanted. That December night in their apartment, Ilya remembered thinking that the Malikovs' love had been palpable, strong enough to change the quality of the light, the air. And then, after Dmitri had chased Vladimir with his car, he had asked Ilya not to tell her. He had said that she was too good for this world. He was right, and Ilya knew that if there was anyone who could hold Dmitri accountable, it was her.

He told her. About the tape that Vladimir had made and about how Gabe had found Lana and about how Dmitri had driven Gabe to the airport and told him never to come back.

"Are you saying he killed them? The girls? I was with him the night Lana died. I'm sure of it—if it was the night before the boards. There has to be another explanation." Her voice was incredulous, defensive, but not scared, not yet. She didn't know what came next, and he hated her for that in the same way that he hated Lana in that picture in the Tower, the assumption in Lana's pursed lips, her angry eyes, that life would continue as it always had.

"I have the tape," he said. "I could send it to the TV stations."

"To the—" She made this small, choking sound. She understood now. Now she was scared.

Once, when Ilya was eleven or twelve, Babushka had called Maria Mikhailovna a saint. His mother usually resisted Babushka's effusions, especially those of a religious nature, but in this case, she'd agreed, and agreement between them was like a warm, cloudless day in Berlozhniki—rare—and Ilya had soaked it up, thinking, *She isn't just a saint, she's mine. My saint.*

He said, "If anything happens to Vladimir, it'll be on every news channel, in every paper in America. Tell him that."

She was quiet for a long moment, and Ilya felt, suddenly, the distance between them: the thousands of miles of line slicing the sky and sea. Then she said, softly, "But you haven't done that yet?"

"No," he said. "I wanted to give you a chance—to give him a chance—to get Vladimir out."

"Then I guess I should thank you for that," she said, and she hung up, and he felt like he might vomit.

It was nighttime in Berlozhniki, and he could see her standing at that enormous window. She was tiny against the inky darkness pressing at that one, perfect pane. He could see her, banging a fist against the glass. It didn't break. It wouldn't break no matter how hard she hit it. The night Ilya had come for dinner, Dmitri had told him that the window was reinforced, bulletproof, that nothing could shatter it, not ever.

Ilya found Sadie up at the track. Practice was over, or at least she was the only one still there, crouched in the blocks on the far straightaway. She didn't see him at first. Her eyes were on the spot where the track started to curve. She hit a button on her watch. Raz, dva, tri, he counted, and she started to run.

He'd only ever known Sadie to move with a nonchalance that was almost lazy—even when they were together in the back of her car—but as he watched her now, the laziness fell away and the nonchalance too, and there was a naked urgency there. Pure want, he thought, or maybe pure fear, and he wondered if Lana had had a chance to run the night she'd been killed and whether her eyes had looked like Sadie's did, like they wanted to leave her body behind.

She slowed when she saw him and lifted a hand.

"Is it good or bad?" she said. She put her hands on her hips and hung her head for a second to catch her breath.

"Both," Ilya said. And as they walked around the track, he told her about the confession, and that he'd called Maria Mikhailovna.

"And what will she do?" Sadie said when he'd finished.

"She'll get him out," he said.

Sadie shook her head. "What if you'd never listened to them?"

"I know," Ilya said. He'd imagined the tapes still sitting in their plastic bag in the Tower; he'd imagined them stolen in transit, just as the batteries had been; he'd imagined the redheaded nurse dropping them into a trash can; or Gabe searching the bag for drugs and, finding none, leaving it in the snow by his bench; and with each way Vladimir's plan could have gone wrong, his stomach seized.

Sadie squeezed his hand. "What's the bad? You said it was both."

He told her about the boards.

"You never took them at all?" she said.

He shook his head. Vladimir, in his bravado, had thought that if he could just get Ilya to America, the *how* would not matter. A *technicality*, Vladimir would say, because he did not understand the rigidity of American morals. In Russia, you paid the nurse for the chance to see your brother; in Russia, a bribe was how you got your foot in the door, the starting point of negotiations. But not here. What had Principal Gibbons said to Ilya on that first day of school? *Hook or crook*, with a nasty emphasis on the *crook*.

"Will they send me back? If they find out?" he said. He'd asked her the same question that first night, and he felt, suddenly, the weight of all the lies he'd told the Masons, and he wanted to be rid of them.

Sadie was quiet for a second, and then she said, "Do you want to stay? I mean, if Vladimir gets out, would you still want to stay?"

He could sense, under the question, her fear of being left. He could feel how hard it had been for her to ask it lightly, to keep her own want out of it.

He nodded. "Yes," he said. "I want to stay."

She smiled at him. "OK," she said, "then we find a way for you to stay."

The next day, Ilya heard nothing from Maria Mikhailovna or Dmitri. He checked his email between classes and then, when that became unbearable, he skipped his classes altogether and sat at the computer in the library refreshing his email over and over.

"Time's up, Ilya," the librarian said, and Ilya swiveled in his chair to find the room empty, the lights dimmed. The last bus was pulling out of the parking lot, and the librarian was giving him a look of concern.

He nodded, hit refresh one more time, and watched his inbox blink, then reload, still empty. He walked to the Bojangles' more out of habit than hunger. At the register, Sharice failed to greet him.

"Has that woman been back?" he said. "The one who fell." He gestured toward the soda machine.

"You think that was bad," Sharice said. "She slept in that booth half the day yesterday. I swear she comes here just to haunt me."

"She seems worse?"

Sharice nodded, then gave Ilya a long look and said, "What are you creeping on her for? *You* are the last thing she needs."

"I'm not creeping," Ilya said.

"Sure," Sharice said. "You want more chicken or not?"

That night Ilya could not sleep. Midnight came, then one a.m., then two. He was hoping that Sadie might go to see her mother, that he could walk with her, get his mind off everything, but by three a.m. it was late enough that he knew she wouldn't go.

He pulled on his sneakers and slid open the door and hiked down the hill to Route 21. He broke into a run. At first to warm himself—it was finally cold at night here—and then because the motion felt good, made him optimistic. With each step he took, the refinery bobbed on the horizon. He could feel his lungs, the wet curves of them drying with each inhale. He wondered how long it had been since Vladimir had been outside. He wondered if there was a window in Vladimir's cell. He tried to send patience through the air to Vladimir like it was a wish. Sweat stung his eyes. He was close now. The air was cut with chemicals, so burnt and acrid that he couldn't breathe deeply. Vladimir and Sergey used to say that you'd get superpowers if you breathed the refinery air, like Superman did from living on Krypton. Lap it up, they'd tell him. Stop holding your nose. That had been when they were young enough and the refinery was new enough that they noticed the smell.

The lights were on in the trailer, and from the sidewalk Ilya could see Sadie's mom sleeping on the couch. She looked peaceful enough, but still he wanted to know that she was breathing. He couldn't get what Sharice had said about her haunting the Bojangles' out of his head. There was a bush in front of the window, dry with neglect, and even when he pressed himself into its bristles, he couldn't see the rise and fall of her chest.

Over her head, one corner of the poster of the woman in the white dress had come unstuck. Trash covered the coffee table—an empty tissue box, a jug of juice, a couple of cans, a wadded T-shirt. The pink pipe was nestled among them, and next to it was a syringe.

Ilya's sweat turned cold, and his skin tightened. She was completely still on the couch. Too still, he thought. He reached down, grasped one of the bush's branches, and broke it off. He rapped it against the window. Once, twice, three times. Nothing.

No, he thought, imagining Vladimir's bone, all that blood. No.

He crouched and groped on the ground until he found a rock, half embedded in the hard-packed dirt of her yard. Before he could think better of it, he took a step back and threw the rock. It hit the trailer's plastic siding, and the noise of it was enormous. Across the street a motion light flashed on. A dog barked. And on the couch, Sadie's mom sat up and yelled, "What the fucking fuck?"

By the time she got to the window, he was running again, back down Route 21, wondering why he hadn't just knocked on her door.

CHAPTER TWENTY-SIX

Ilya sat on the steps of the Berlozhniki police station, watching the square wake up. Kirill yanked up the metal grate to the Internet Kebab, grunting each time the grate snagged in its rusted tracks. Anatoly opened the Minutka, and a man selling pirozhki from a cart steered it through the slush, calling out the day's choices: "Cabbage! Egg! Beef! Cabbage! Egg! Beef!" Every once in a while, he added "Jam!" to the list, but with less conviction, like it was his least favorite filling. At eight, a few secretaries in high-heeled boots picked their way from the bus stop to the station. They teetered up the stairs, toting purses and thermoses, and did not look at him.

"That's it," one said. "That was the whole date. And then he expected a fuck." The others laughed, and the sound was suctioned off by the door shutting behind them. Eventually the policemen trickled in, but not Dmitri.

As the sun inched up to the tops of the birch trees, a babushka poked her head out the station door and said, "You should wait inside. You'll freeze. Come, come."

She held an arm out and bent it as though Ilya's shoulders were already wrapped in it, but he shook his head. He wanted to talk to Dmitri alone, knew that Dmitri would be more apt to listen without an audience, and, besides, the idea of going into the station and announcing that he was Vladimir Alexandrovich Morozov's brother was too terrifying, too shaming, even though he knew that his mother came to the station every day to plead Vladimir's innocence and that she did it without shame.

The babushka sensed his degradation and did not like it. Her arm dropped and her face tightened. "Wait on the bench then." She pointed across the street to Gabe's bench, which was flanked by overflowing trash cans. "You're in the way."

So Ilya waited on the bench, and after another hour the babushka came out with a bucket of salt and began to scatter it on the station steps. The policemen left for lunch at the Kebab or Tepek, and each time they came down the steps the babushka skittered away from them. One policeman coughed, then spat, and his spit landed on the babushka's shoe, and she made no move to wipe it off until he was out of sight. Occasionally she looked up at Ilya and glared, as though his presence in her periphery were a burden even heavier than the bucket of salt.

It was well past noon, and still Dmitri had not arrived. Ilya began to wonder if Dmitri even came to the station at all. He patrolled the refinery, Ilya knew, and he knew that the refinery paid him on the side to keep the private road clear, to make sure that the miles and miles of fence were secure, that the pipeline was safely buried under its coat of snow. And Ilya was about to stand, to stretch his legs and begin to walk north past the Malikovs' apartment and then out of town, toward the Tower and the refinery, when he saw Dmitri round the corner of Ulitsa Lenina. He was in his valenki and pogony like all the other policemen, and they made him look anonymous and sharp. Ilya stood, and forced himself to think of the night when he'd eaten at the Malikovs', when Dmitri had said that Maria Mikhailovna loved him like family and that that meant that he, Dmitri, loved Ilya like family. He thought of this, and not of what had happened next—of Vladimir and Sergey running in his headlights—as he ran across the street.

"Dmitri Ivanovich," he said, when he was near enough that no one but Dmitri would hear him.

Ilya was not expecting Dmitri to be happy to see him—there was a chance that someone might recognize Ilya, might know that he was Vladimir's brother, and Dmitri could be tainted by association—but Dmitri smiled and made room for Ilya to walk beside him. "Berlozhniki's pride!" he said. "How long have you got left here?"

Ilya's chest cinched. "Berlozhniki's Pride" was what the papers had called Olga Nadiova in her heyday, when she had braids and could do a perfect double axel with her eyes closed. "A few months," he said.

"Good, good," Dmitri said, and then he stopped walking, and Ilya stopped too. "Listen," he said, "I'm sorry about your brother. Sorry that I had to be involved at all. And I don't believe what they're saying—that he was evil—all this shit. He was on drugs, and the drugs made him crazy. In a way, prison might save him. But I'm sorry—I know it's hard for you."

This was kind. Kinder, at least, than what any other policeman would say to him. Kinder than the things that had been spat at him and his mother in the kommunalkas. The mean things always made his mind turn to metal, made his spine straighten, but at this kindness tears banked up behind his eyes, and before he could cry, he said, "That's why I wanted to talk to you, Dmitri Ivanovich. I was with Vladimir the night Lana died. I went to the Tower with him, and I was there, with him, the whole time." This wasn't exactly true, but he figured it was a lie worth telling. "He was with me and Aksinya. Aksinya Stepanova. We were together the whole time. She will tell you—"

"Your brother confessed, Ilya. He knew things he could only know if he'd done it. If he was guilty."

"I know, but I was with him. It doesn't make any sense. He loved Lana. And the other two—he didn't even know them."

"Love can be like that. It can have two sides." Dmitri put a hand on his shoulder. "You're smart, right? This is what Maria is always telling me. That you have a *gift*. And that it is a gift to teach you, to see how a mind is supposed to work. Sometimes I'm jealous when she talks like that. Me, I'm a dolt. My mind is all rusty gears. Nothing's a gift."

It was true that Maria Mikhailovna said this about Ilya. She'd been saying it for four years, and it had always embarrassed him, made him feel like a fraud or an alien. "Maybe I'm not as smart as she thinks I am."

"There are different kinds of smart," he said. "And I'm sure that Maria's not wrong about you. But it is *not* smart, it is idiotism, to tell someone—even me—that you were at the Tower with a girl the night she was killed. Do you understand that? Do you know how quickly people could believe that it was you and your brother—or even the three of you? Aksinya too. That you all worked together?"

He was right. Ilya could see that, and he understood that he'd been naive to think himself above whatever trouble Vladimir had fallen into. A new sort of panic hit him with force. Not only had he been with Lana the night she'd died, he'd kissed her. He pictured himself holding her, leaving bits of skin and hair and who knew what other traces of himself.

"He's your brother. You love him," Dmitri said, and his voice was soft and level. "I know that, and I'm sorry, but there's not an alibi in the world that can help him. Not after he's admitted to it all." Dmitri sounded sorry, truly sorry, and his apology felt like a dead end, as final as a prison cell. Then Dmitri reached out and put his palms on Ilya's cheeks. He leaned in and kissed Ilya on the forehead. "Soon you'll be gone. Soon you'll start over," he said. Ilya looked over the epaulets on his shoulder. The babushka was staring at him. Then she turned and climbed the stairs back into the station, the empty bucket banging at her hip.

CHAPTER TWENTY-SEVEN

Two days after Ilya called Maria Mikhailovna, the news of Dmitri's suicide broke in the *Vecherniye Berlozhniki*. He had driven his car off the Bolshoi Bridge and straight into the Pechora, the same river into which Vladimir had claimed to have thrown the knife. It was a mild day for October, the paper said, so a number of people were out picnicking at the tables that lined the river's banks and had witnessed the crash. One man, who'd narrowly avoided being hit by Dmitri's car, said he'd never seen a vehicle move so fast. Another man said it had been flying. And the car must have been, at least for a moment, because it sailed almost entirely over the river before crashing in the muddy shallows and bursting into flames.

Suicides were not so uncommon in Berlozhniki, nor were violent deaths. After suggesting that the refinery pay city taxes, the former mayor had been stabbed in broad daylight in front of the statue of Iron Felix. His wife shot herself the next day. But Dmitri's death had been spectacular.

"It was like a meteor strike," one woman said, to describe the impact. There had been enough petrol in the tank that for a full minute it seemed as though the river itself were in flames. And perhaps because of the fire, it took a while for the reports to shift from one casualty to two.

For a sickening hour, Ilya feared that the second casualty was Maria Mikhailovna. He imagined Dmitri taking her down in the elevator, down into that cavernous garage, where her footsteps would sound so small, but another article soon took over the paper's home page announcing that the passenger had been Fyodor Fetisov, one of Russia's richest men, the majority owner of Gazneft.

Dmitri had been driving Fetisov from the airstrip on Berlozhniki's south side to the refinery—the newspaper explained that Fetisov made occasional visits to Berlozhniki and that Malikov was his driver—when Malikov lost control of the car, or, as bystanders claimed, drove it intentionally off the Bolshoi Bridge.

Ilya had noticed that Russia did not feature in the American news nearly as much as America featured in the Russian news, but evidently it was a drama-free day in America, because Fetisov's death made the American news almost instantly.

"You know this guy?" Papa Cam hollered down the basement stairs, and when Ilya came into the den and saw Fetisov's face, his eyes so big that they seemed to greedily take in the room, he knew. He could picture Fetisov hitting Vladimir on the elevator, the ring slicing Vladimir's cheek. He could feel the way it had snagged his skin when they'd shaken hands on the stage.

Then the picture shrank and was dispatched to a corner of the screen. A Moscow correspondent, a woman of unclear nationality with bright red curls and a face made fuzzy by makeup, said, "To give you a little background on Fetisov. He's an oligarch, on the *Forbes* 500. He's famous, even in his own set, for his decadence. . . ."

She went on, describing a maelstrom of champagne and caviar and fine art and prostitutes and private jets, all the decadence that Ilya and Vladimir and Sergey had imagined as boys, sitting damp-assed in the snow by the refinery fence. Then she paused and touched the mic in her ear, and Ilya saw that she knew now too.

"We've just gotten confirmation that Fetisov's death was likely a murder-suicide," she said, and she described a note left by Dmitri accusing Fetisov of three murders in Berlozhniki, the "Gulag Murders," as they were called by the American press for the hour they made the news, though the murders had had nothing at all to do with the gulag.

Online, Ilya found clips from Russia 1 on the story. The network summarized Dmitri's suicide note in depth. Apparently he had begun to suspect Fetisov because the first two murders coincided with Fetisov's visits to Berlozhniki, which were rare and brief. When Lana's body was discovered, the date of her murder coincided with a visit from Fetisov as well, but it wasn't until Fetisov asked Dmitri to get rid of a witness—Gabe, trudging along the lumber road at just the moment when Fetisov had returned to the grove—that Dmitri was sure of Fetisov's guilt. And Fetisov had not seemed to care if Dmitri knew. He didn't need to care, Dmitri explained, because he'd threatened to kill Dmitri's wife if Dmitri didn't take care of the witness and find someone else on whom to pin the murders. So the witness had been taken care of.

"Malikov doesn't explain *how* he took care of the witness except to say that he didn't kill anyone," the newscaster said. "And apparently a local teen was put in prison for the murders."

The newscaster paused. She was practically panting with excitement or horror. The wrong emotion, whatever it was, and Ilya wanted to throttle her weedy neck, to make her feel, for a moment, as trapped as Vladimir had been, as Dmitri had been. Then she gathered herself and said, "Unfortunately the final lines of the note are redacted. They were a last good-bye addressed to his wife, and she's chosen to keep them private."

As the news cycle wore on, Fetisov was linked to a handful of other murders in other refinery towns, to women stabbed in Ukhta and Krasnodar and Orsk. Other women who'd survived him came forward too—a waitress, an escort, a stewardess—to detail the abuses they'd suffered at his hands. The newscaster interviewed one girl with long brown hair and blue eyes, and for a moment Ilya thought it was Aksinya, or maybe her sister, but the newscaster identified her as Irina from Ukhta. Irina said that Fetisov had hired her for a week, and that all he'd wanted to do was to cut her cheeks.

"Why did you let him?" the newscaster asked. A stupid question made insulting by the way she tilted her head as if in commis-eration.

The girl did not seem to mind. "He paid me so much," she said. "It was a bad week, then a good year."

Vladimir, the "local teen," was never named, and Ilya worried it wouldn't be enough, that somehow Vladimir would be allowed to languish in prison, innocent, but a victim of bureaucratic neglect nonetheless. Then his mother called, and for a full minute she cried so hard that she couldn't get a word out.

"Mama," he said. "Mama, what is it?"

"They're letting him go," she managed. "A lawyer called. After the arraignment, they're letting him free. We're going tomorrow—to Syktyvkar—and we'll stay until he's out." She paused, and then she said, "How did you do it?"

Ilya told her about the tape, about calling Maria Mikhailovna. His mother paused, and he could feel her debating whether to tell him something.

"What is it?" he said.

"I saw her," his mother said. "She was standing on the square, right by the bench where that American used to stand, and for a second I thought that she'd lost her mind, that she was handing out the same pamphlets that he used to. The ones I sent you. I was too afraid to go over to her, but it didn't matter, because the letter was everywhere. In all the newspaper boxes. At every kiosk. In our mailbox. She taped them to the door of the House of Culture, the police station, every tree on the square."

"His letter?" Ilya said.

"Yes," his mother said, and Ilya imagined Maria Mikhailovna finding the letter on her pillow or on the kitchen table or on the chair by the window that had been his. She'd read it once, twice. With a thick marker she'd inked out the lines beginning with *Masha*, which only he had called her, and then she'd walked across the square to the school. She'd copied the letter on the ancient machine in the teachers' lounge, the one that was half the size of a car and smelled of burnt oil and that sometimes expelled papers with such force that they took flight in that tiny room. She'd watched each copy slip out of the machine, each one a promise, a hope that what had happened could not be ignored or denied. Each one proof of Vladimir's innocence.

Ilya was in the kitchen. The Masons were moving around him in the way water moves past an obstacle to which it's grown familiar, and it wouldn't be the worst thing, he decided, if they saw him cry.

That night, he asked them if he could give a testimonial.

"Of course," Mama Jamie said. She'd held him after his mother called, and there was still a damp patch on her shirt from where his face had been pressed against her. "I can call Pastor Kyle and let him know," she said.

"I want to do it now," Ilya said. "Here."

Mama Jamie looked at Papa Cam, and Marilee opened her mouth to explain that this was not how testimonials worked, that they came *after* the hymns and *before* the sermons, that it was not even Sunday, but Papa Cam did not give her a chance. He clapped a meaty palm over her mouth and said, "Of course."

So Ilya stood on the fire skirt, where he'd posed for the picture on the first day of school, and the Masons sat on the couch, close enough that he could have stretched out a leg and touched their knees with his toes.

Sadie smiled at him, and Mama Jamie said, "Remember, you're telling God, not us."

Ilya nodded, though he was not telling God, he was telling them.

He started at the very beginning: "I was six years old," he said, "when I learned my first word of English." He told them that it was the sort of word you weren't supposed to say, and then he said it aloud anyway because the whole point of this was admitting the truth. He told them how Vladimir had lifted him up onto the balcony rail and made him shout it out across the courtyard. And even now, a decade later, he still couldn't say whether it was a moment that he would undo, because everything terrible that had happened to him was rooted in it, but so was everything good.

He told about Maria Mikhailovna, and the books Vladimir had bought him at the shop on Ulitsa Snezhnaya, and of Michael and Stephanie, and the hours and hours he'd spent listening to them, and studying, and the way each hour had seemed to lay a brick in a wall between him and Vladimir. Telling his story, something strange happened. Time folded back, or else it split open. It seemed somehow less linear, so that he remembered yelling from the balcony, his body small enough that Vladimir could hold him with one arm, but in the same moment he could see Lana's birch grove with its wilting flowers and damp ribbons, and at the school, Maria Mikhailovna looked up, her hand poised above a test with his name on it. In the square, on his bench, Gabe Thompson cried out in his sleep. Vladimir was behind Ilya, propping him up, his breath hot on the back of Ilya's shirt, but he was in the Tower too, in that horrible room with the rug over the window and the tapes in their bag in the corner. He and Aksinya and Lana and Sergey, boney and desperate and doomed, dancing like children to some song from the '80s that no one in America listened to anymore. And Dmitri Malikov was in his patrol car, his face milky in the refinery's light, as he drove in an endless loop around the town.

It was a horrible story. He could tell from their utter silence, from the way even Marilee and Molly were still, mesmerized by the badness of the things people did to each other and themselves. Still, though, there was something beautiful in the telling of it. Vladimir had told him that krokodil made him remember, that it was like he was present in his memories and like he was holding them at the same time, and it was like that for Ilya now. They were all around him—Vladimir, his mother, Dmitri, Maria Mikhailovna—every version of them, the good and the bad, and he himself felt as though he were gaining dimension, becoming as solid and present as the stone he'd plucked out of the creek, which even in the hot damp of his palm had seemed endlessly cool, like it had a source of energy all its own.

He sped up as he neared the end—the forced confession, Dmitri's suicide, Fetisov's guilt, Vladimir's release. "Vladimir's not good," he said. "I know that. There's plenty he's done to be ashamed of. And there were so many ways that his plan could have gone wrong. So many ways. When I think of them, I'm so scared that I can't breathe. But then I remember why he did this—"

Mama Jamie was wiping at her wet cheeks, and Papa Cam was staring at him with an expression of frank wonder.

"So that I could be here."

This was the end, but somehow it gave him a feeling of vertigo, of running a step too far off a cliff. He thought of Sadie, and her nightly pilgrimage. He thought of Sadie's mother slumped on that couch. He thought of Vladimir, of his confession and the way that each word had sounded like a wound so that by the end he'd barely been able to talk. Ilya had earned the Masons' forgiveness—he could see that—but it wasn't enough.

He cleared his throat. "I know that I don't have the right to ask you all for anything," he said. "I don't deserve to be here, and you know that now—but still I have to ask: let Vladimir come here. Please. Let him come too."

In the quiet that followed, Ilya could hear the hiss of cars on Route 21. Somewhere far off a siren whined. Sadie was crying silently. This smile shook on her lips, and Ilya smiled back at her.

"Please," Molly said, as though Ilya had asked for a dog for Christmas and she wanted one too.

Marilee bit her lip and said, "Hmmm. That's a lot to forgive."

Next to her, Papa Cam reached for Mama Jamie's hand. Ilya did not know whether he was asking for permission or giving it until Mama Jamie nodded. "OK," she said.

CHAPTER TWENTY-EIGHT

Marilee and Molly made a new sign with Vladimir's name etched in deliberate letters, only this time Ilya helped them write it in Cyrillic, because, he explained, Vladimir really, truly didn't speak any English at all. Sadie sat next to him on the ride to the airport, and though she was careful not to touch him, he could feel that she wanted to, and that was enough.

Vladimir had called two days earlier. Ilya and the Masons were just home from Star Pilgrim, where Pastor Kyle had told a white-washed version of Vladimir's story after which the collection basket had bobbed down the rows, filling with money to fund his stay. Marilee had been the one to answer the phone, and after a moment she had looked at the receiver with exasperation and said, "I think it's a wrong number." She punched the speakerphone button, and Vladimir's terrible English had flooded the kitchen.

"Hello," he'd said, over and over, only coming from him the word sounded like "Yellow."

Ilya grabbed the receiver from Marilee and turned the speaker off just as Mama Jamie realized who it was and ushered the girls out to the deck, hissing something about privacy to Marilee.

"Vlad," he said.

"You better stop emailing me about this girl and seal the deal. Just once, Ilyusha, think with your dick instead of your brain."

"You got my emails," Ilya said.

"Of course I got them. One day in the life of fucking Ilya Denisovich." His voice was rushed, euphoric. There was no regard in it for the risks he'd taken. It was exactly as Ilya had expected it to be, as Ilya had wanted it to be, but still Ilya had to fight the urge to ask him if he was high. He wanted, so badly, not to ruin the moment.

"Are you home?" he said instead.

"At the Kebab, and Kirill the tight-ass motherfucker is the only one in this whole town not cutting me a deal so I have—I don't know—a minute left, but I'll see you soon, bratishka."

"Wait," Ilya said, wishing there were a way to keep Vladimir on the phone for the next two days until he saw him in person. "Tell me how you did it. How'd you get him on tape?"

Ilya had wondered this; he'd marveled at the planning it must have entailed for Vladimir to know that Dmitri was coming to the clinic and to record him.

"He came and threatened me," Vladimir said. "He said he wouldn't let you go if I didn't confess to the murders. And the boards—he said you'd have it on your record for life that you'd cheated, that you wouldn't be able to go to university, get a job. He said he was going to fuck you over so completely, and the whole time he's talking, I'm thinking, *I'm going to fuck you over, you fucker. I'm going to rip you apart.* That's the thing about everyone assuming you're an idiot—every once in a while it gives you the upper hand.

"So I told Dmitri I needed a couple days to think about it, and then I convinced that nurse to give me a little warning, and two days later, when he comes back, I stuck the tape player under the sheets. Right where my knee should be."

"But how'd you get the tapes?" Ilya said.

"Aksinya brought them. I'd been listening to them for a while. Like you," he said, sounding almost bashful at this confession. "I figured if I could just learn a little English then you'd find a way to get me there."

Someone called Vladimir's name in the background.

"I'm talking to my brother, asshole!" Vladimir shouted. And then he lowered his voice, so that it was just like it had been when they were little and would whisper in bed even though their mother was at work and Babushka was sleeping and no one was trying to overhear them. "You and me, Hollywood Boulevard, right?" he said, and the call ended.

Ilya and the Masons waited by the arrivals door for fifteen minutes, more even, until the people coming from the gates slowed to a trickle. The security guard stationed by the NO RE-ENTRY sign took out a pen, gave it a cruel click, and began to do a crossword puzzle. An airport employee pushed past him with an old woman in a wheelchair. Something was stuck in one of the wheels, making a ticking sound with each revolution. Surely the old woman was the last passenger, Ilya thought, which meant that Vladimir had missed the flight. He'd found some party in Moscow and had ended up using his tickets as roll papers. Or he'd never left Berlozhniki at all.

Sadie pulled her hair back, twisted it into a bun, and then let it drop again, which was something that she did when she was nervous. She saw him looking at her, saw him see her nervousness, and perhaps to make up for it, she took his hand and squeezed it. Mama Jamie noticed without understanding, and she gave Ilya this small, close-lipped smile. It was a smile meant to temper expectations, and it made Ilya's chest hurt.

"Maybe he missed it," he said, just as a figure appeared at the end of the corridor. He was silhouetted by a bank of windows, and far enough away that Ilya couldn't be sure. His first day in America he had conjured Vladimir in the back of the Masons' car, and he thought he might be doing it again. The loose-jointed walk. The laces of his boots dragging on the carpet. How slowly he moved! Had always moved, as though he had nowhere in the world to be. And often he didn't. He was meters from them now, but Ilya was afraid to look at his face, afraid it might disappear under scrutiny.

Papa Cam said, "Is that him?"

Marilee and Molly raised their arms over their heads, locked their elbows, and held the sign high.

The figure seemed to hesitate there, by the NO RE-ENTRY sign, by the chubby guard and his crossword puzzle. His face was bland and friendly. His eyes bovine in their lack of guile. He looked at Ilya with a mild disinterest that felt like a kick in the gut. And, of course, he had two legs, and Vladimir had only one.

"No," Ilya said.

Papa Cam and Mama Jamie left Ilya and the girls, and went to have Vladimir paged. That same terrible Russian blared through the bathroom's empty stalls, each of which Ilya checked and re-checked, hoping that somehow he had missed Vladimir, that he might be lost, hiding, as scared or hesitant as Ilya had been two months earlier. They got pretzels from the vending machine, took over a bank of chairs, and waited until the next flight from Atlanta had arrived and departed, until the security guard had finished his puzzle, and then his shift, and finally Papa Cam said, "Let's go, troops. We can always come back tomorrow."

There was a message waiting on the Masons' machine, and as soon as Ilya saw the flashing light, he knew what it would say. Or maybe he'd known sooner, when that other boy, that American boy, with his two perfect legs, had walked past them, and then out the door to the curb, where he'd stood and blinked in the light.

Ilya's mother's voice was detached, formal, as though the Masons might be able to understand her. Vladimir had gone to Aksinya's on his last night to say good-bye, only he hadn't come home in the morning. He'd taken krokodil again. They both had, and Aksinya had woken up with his arm around her, and his mother said that she had lain that way for minutes, because she hadn't been so completely happy in a long time, and then Vladimir's arm began to take on a strange weight, and he wouldn't answer when she said his name.

A month later, early in the morning, Ilya woke to the sound of splashing. The sun wasn't up yet. The sky was the color of slush. He pulled open the doors under the deck and climbed up to the pool expecting to find Papa Cam there, dredging leaves, or Mama Jamie swimming as part of her new exercise regime. There was something in the pool. It was moving, dark and fluid under the leaves that had fallen overnight. It swam more slowly than a person, though, and as Ilya stood there and watched, it did not surface for air. Could it be one of the girls, Ilya wondered, unconscious and drifting on some current? Only he must have known that this was not the case because he made no move to jump in. He was, in fact, backing up the stairs onto the deck. His fingers found the light switch, and he flicked it, and the pool shone, a turquoise brick cut out of the earth. Swimming in its depths was a crocodile. Its body was the color of mud, its shape impossibly prehistoric, yet it drifted with a slow grace that held Ilya there on the deck.

He knew from some long-forgotten textbook or nature program that crocodiles killed by drowning. That they grabbed you by a limb and pulled you down and held you there for the burning moments it took your lungs to empty.

The crocodile reached the steps and paused, its nose perched just out of the water. It was an invitation, Ilya thought, and he could see himself walking down to the pool and stepping carefully into the water. Even as he knocked on the glass doors and called out to the Masons, he could feel the slice, the tear, the pressure. Mama Jamie was running toward him, and even once she'd opened the doors and was holding him in her arms he could feel the heat in his lungs, the crush of them giving up, and the cold rush of water filling him.

"There's a crocodile," he said.

Sadie was at the door now too, and as Mama Jamie bent over the rail and peered into the pool, she hugged him.

"Breathe, breathe," she said, as though she understood that he was drowning.

Mama Jamie shook her head. "Ilya, honey," she said, "an alligator can't climb over that wall."

He spent that day sitting by the pool, in the same chair where he'd listened to Vladimir's confession. He wanted to keep an eye on the water, to keep an eye on the wall.

The Masons were gone—Sadie had track practice, which she'd wanted to skip, but he'd insisted that she go—and Mama Jamie and Papa Cam and the girls were shopping for Thanksgiving, which was

only a few days away. Durashka was curled in a patch of sunlight by
the grill, her paws twitching in some dream. The deck doors were
open, and when the phone rang, the sound was as clear as a bell
pealing. The dog cocked her head. Ilya ignored it. It stopped, and
then started again. It went on like that for ten minutes, and then
this thought formed in his head and sank like a stone to his gut:
Babushka had died. Or his mother. Because what else could that
terrible insistence mean? The phone had rung like that when they'd
been at the airport, waiting for Vladimir. They hadn't heard it, of
course, but Ilya had seen the ten missed calls. He had still not allowed Mama Jamie to delete the message.

The phone stopped. Ilya exhaled, careful not to break the silence, as though the caller might hear him and start up again. A
plane passed so far overhead that he could not hear it, then somewhere on Route 21 a tanker bellowed at some lesser car, and the
silence was pierced. Durashka licked her chops with wet vigor and
rattled her tags scratching at a patch on her belly. Inside, the phone
rang again, and Ilya stood and walked along the edge of the pool and
up the deck steps, and when he picked it up, the voice on the other
end was clotted with tears, which he had expected, but it was
speaking English, which he had not expected.

"It's me," she said. "You said to call."

It sounded like an accusation.

"Who?" he said, though her tone congealed into her identity as
he said it.

"I had a close call," she said. "Too fucking close. And I don't have
anybody. It was either you or the fucking bitch at the Bojangles',
and she would probably like to see me dead."

He couldn't tell if she was high or scared or both, but a story
tumbled out of her, of waking up in a ditch by an old racetrack on

Leffie's outskirts. She'd been half dressed, and that was all as bad as you'd expect, she said, but the really fucked-up thing was that when she'd pulled herself together, sat up, stood up, and started walking down the shoulder, something made her turn around. She'd looked back—for her purse, maybe, she thought—but she'd seen herself lying there, still in the ditch, her cheek on this weedy mound of gravel, her eyes open and drying out in the sun. She kept walking, she said. Running almost, but every time she looked back, she could still see her body. It was like that for half a mile, and she thought that was it, she'd killed herself and was a ghost now, and this was Hell or purgatory or whatever. When she'd gotten to the 7-Eleven in Latraux, a man had stared at her from inside his car, then locked his doors, and she'd been sure she was a ghost. Then the cashier had stopped her at the door.

"It wasn't 'til that fucker said, 'Uh-uhn. No way. You can't come in here after the way you was last night,' that I realized I was at least mostly alive."

"Where are you now?" Ilya said.

"At home," she said.

"I'll come there, OK?" he said.

"OK," she said.

"Turn on the TV. For company," he said. "And don't take anything."

"I got nothing to take," she said.

"OK," he said.

"OK," she said again.

He called Mama Jamie on her cell and told her what had happened, and she left the store and met him at Sadie's mom's house.

"Sadie's not coming?" Sadie's mom said, as soon as Mama Jamie walked in the door.

"No," Mama Jamie said. "Did you want her to?"

Sadie's mom shrugged, and Mama Jamie helped her pack a bag while on the TV a reporter in Hollywood interviewed an actress about her morning beauty routine. Ilya sat on the couch and looked out the window to the sidewalk and the street. It was so close. He imagined Sadie's face framed in it. How could her mom never have seen her? Maybe she had, he thought. Maybe she'd wanted to open the door and invite her in, but she'd known better. She'd given her up once, and maybe she didn't have the strength to do it again. A van drove past the window to the end of the cul-de-sac, turned around, and parked in front of the trailer. TOMORROW'S SUNRISE was printed in rainbow letters on the side.

"It's supposed to be good," Mama Jamie said. "Pastor Kyle recommended it."

Sadie's mom nodded. She had barely spoken since Mama Jamie had arrived. She had not cursed once. Something about Mama Jamie had turned her docile, and as she grabbed her bag and walked out the door, it occurred to Ilya that her docility was the closest she could come to saying thank you.

Once she'd left in the van, he and Mama Jamie drove home. "I'll tell Sadie tonight," she said. "Maybe it'll be a good thing for her."

"Maybe," Ilya said.

"At least she'll get some sleep for a while." Ilya looked at Mama Jamie. Her cheeks were so round and high that she looked innocent regardless of her expression. "She thinks I'd be mad. Be jealous, maybe. And I don't like the lying, the sneaking. But I'm proud of her. Proud of her heart," she said. "So don't break it."

"I won't," Ilya said.

They passed the fireworks stand, the old plantation, the hot sauce plant. They turned up Dumaine Drive to the house that still

did not feel like home. He saw Vladimir waiting on the stoop, stub-
bing a cigarette into one of Mama Jamie's potted plants, running a
hand through hair that had only just grown past the prison buzz.
He thought of Sadie's mom seeing herself in the ditch, and he wondered if it had been that way for Vladimir. Whether he'd seen himself lying there, with his arm around Aksinya. Their spine-studded
backs, her beautiful face, the drugs on the table, his clothes on the
floor. Why, Ilya wondered, had he not seen anything there worth
saving?

He and Sadie walked to her mom's place the next night. The landlord had emptied it already. The couch sat in the yard, soaked from
an afternoon storm. Her mattress slumped against the window,
blocking their view inside, but the door gave when they tried it.
The carpet was damp—it had been cleaned with some sort of
cleaner that smelled of rancid oranges—and because the furniture
was gone, or because the landlord had replaced the bulbs with fluorescent ones, there was an anonymity to the space that was alarming. It felt as though Sadie's mom were more than gone. It was like
she had never existed at all. Ilya remembered Sadie telling him
about burning down her mom's house, about wanting to walk
through the ashes, and he'd brought a lighter for her, just in case.

Sadie paused for a moment in the doorway, and then began to
walk carefully around the room's edges. She was counting footsteps, he realized. Some holdover from childhood, when these
walls had been the limits of her world. When she'd finished with
the living room, he followed her through an accordion door into the
bedroom.

"This was our room," she said. "I slept there." She pointed to a corner as blank as the other three. And then she saw her drawing, which her mom had tacked in the center of the wall. Her mom's penciled eyes looked out at them with a sad reproach that reminded him of saints' eyes in icons, as though she'd pasted it there to watch over her. Sadie looked at it for a second, saw the Masons' number written on the back, and her mom's greasy fingerprints on the edges.

He handed her the lighter, but she shook her head, folded the picture into a square, and put it in her pocket.

"Let's go," she said, and she took his hand.

CHAPTER TWENTY-NINE

When summer came in Berlozhniki, the snow thawed and things surfaced. Trash, mostly. Old issues of the *Vecherniye Berlozhniki*, their ink bled to a uniform gray, their stories erased. Scarves and mittens, dolls and books, dead squirrels and birds, perfectly preserved, their eyes like crystals. Sets of keys glinted patiently in the newfound sun, waiting for discovery. Rubles appeared on sidewalks, in gutters, on stoops. Cars emerged on corners where snowbanks had loomed the highest. Their windows were cracked from the pressure, their seats soggy, but sometimes their engines sputtered and caught, and their owners cheered and bought a bottle of Imperia and gathered friends to witness the miracle and before long they'd forgotten, all over again, where the fuck they'd left their cars.

Children stepped out of the kommunalkas, blinking, their eyes adjusting from the TV to the world as it was. They yelled. They ran. They remembered, suddenly, how full their lungs could get.

There was talk that the snow would melt and reveal another body. Multiple bodies. There was talk that Vladimir had killed others that winter and buried them in deep drifts. Sometimes Ilya was tempted to believe these rumors. As the snow grew patchy, he eyed the piles that were still big enough to hide a body, and he wondered if there might be someone in there. A victim with a clue that would absolve Vladimir: a chunk of the killer's hair gripped in a fist; the knife with fingerprints frozen on its handle; or a note, written in the throes of death, naming the killer.

By July the snow was gone entirely. The ground was swampy, and they'd all traded their felt boots for rubber ones. No more bodies appeared, and the *Vecherniye Berlozhniki* began to cover other news besides the murders and Vladimir's arrest. A twelve-year-old girl collected enough change in the melting town's nooks and crannies to pay her family's rent for a month. She smirked in the picture in the *Vecherniye Berlozhniki*, each hand hoisting a tube sock filled with rubles.

"What a ferret," Babushka said, slapping the paper down on the table. "She steals people's change, and they call her a hero."

"You're jealous you didn't beat her to it," Ilya's mother said. It was her day off, and she'd spent it watching *Simply Maria* and smoking cigarettes out the open window. Ilya was not used to her smoking—she'd quit when she was pregnant with Vladimir and begun again after his arrest—but he liked to watch her slim fingers pinch the tobacco into a neat row. She rolled a cigarette just like Vladimir did.

A week before Ilya left for America, he walked out to the Tower. It was empty. Daylight streamed through glassless windows. Puddles had collected in the dips in the concrete. It didn't seem to Ilya like a place he'd ever been before, and it took him a while to find Vladimir's room. The posters had been torn down and left in long strips on the ground. The blankets were gone, and so were Vladimir's clothes, but sitting there in the middle of the room was the pink plastic bag. Vladimir's camouflage sweatshirt was inside, and as Ilya pulled it out, he heard the familiar, plastic clatter of his *Michael & Stephanie* tapes beneath it.

Ilya spent much of that last week in the kommunalkas, on their tiny balcony. If he leaned over the rail a bit and looked to the right, he could see the polyana, where they'd found Lana. The police tape was long gone, but there were still these snatches of color from the photos people had left. Someone had painted a tire in rainbow colors and planted flowers inside it. Sometimes Ilya thought that if he stared hard enough he'd be able to see what had happened. He'd see Lana walk to the trees. He'd see who was with her. He'd see it all, and he'd know that it hadn't been his brother.

That was where Maria Mikhailovna found him. It was early morning, but already light. He hadn't slept, and he tried not to think of the only other time she'd been in their apartment.

"It's time to go," she'd said, in English, as always.

His mother and Babushka hugged him good-bye, and Timofey pressed a thousand-ruble note and a tiny knife with the hammer and sickle on it into his hands.

"It's a lucky one," he said.

Two hours south of Berlozhniki, halfway to Leshukonskoye, they stopped at a petrol station with faded yellow pumps.

"Two hours to go," Maria Mikhailovna said, and Ilya filled the car while she went inside to pay. It wasn't until the tank was full that he noticed a wind chime above the door. There was something familiar about it, about the hollow clatter it made when the door opened. And the yellow pumps. Ilya touched one, picked at a flake of paint with a fingernail. He walked toward the road. A truck was coming. A pale splotch on the horizon, far enough away that he could barely hear it. He could feel a memory growing like a bubble within him. He remembered running, laughing. Vladimir was chasing him, reaching out for him. Behind him, the wind chime made its rattle. The truck was close now, its horn blasting. In a second, Vladimir's arms would be around him. He waited, and he waited.

"Ilya!" someone called, and then a hand yanked him backward, and the truck passed, close enough that the pressure of it made his body shake. Maria Mikhailovna gripped his hand in hers. The sun was hitting her glasses, turning them into mirrors.

"Ilya," she said again, in this way that meant he was forgiven, and he forgot what it was that he'd been trying so hard to remember.

Acknowledgments

Thank you to Emily Cunningham and Samantha Shea for their passion for this project, their brilliant edits, and their calm guidance, without which both this novel and I would be lost. And thank you to Kate Griggs and Michael Burke for turning these pages into a book, and to Gail Brussel, Matt Boyd, and Grace Fisher for bringing that book out into the world.

Thank you to the Wallace Stegner Fellowship, the Wisconsin Institute for Creative Writing, the University of Michigan M.F.A. program, and the Elizabeth George Foundation for their generous support. And to Elizabeth Tallent, Tobias Wolff, Adam Johnson, Judith Mitchell, Michael Byers, Peter Ho Davies, Eileen Pollack, and Malena Watrous for their patience and insight.

To Austin, Brad, David, Helen, Juliana, Monique, Nicole, NoViolet, Tony, Shannon, and Lydia C. for helping me see what this novel might be.

To Karolina, for reading this not once, but twice, and for her expertise in editing and in all things Russian; and to Alex Raben for the late night spent in the labyrinth of transliterations.

To Hannah Tinti at *One Story* and to Linda Swanson-Davies and

Susan Burmeister-Brown at *Glimmer Train* for taking a chance on my writing.

To Svetlana Alexievich for her brilliant and heartbreaking *Secondhand Time*; to Ian Frazier for *Travels in Siberia*; to Johann Hari for *Chasing the Scream*; and to Donald Weber for the photographs in *Interrogations*, especially *Vorkuta* and *April 26, 2008, Vorkuta, Russia*, both of which I turned to time and time again for inspiration.

To Patricia, for being a "Bacca" to my girls every time I disappeared to reckon with this story.

Thank you to my families, the Fitzpatricks and the Davids, for your encouragement and enthusiasm. To Jan, for your endless faith in me. To my brother, whom I look up to even more than Ilya does Vladimir. And to my mother, for inspiring me every day, in every way. Thank you for all the books on tape we listened to, sitting in the car, in the driveway; and thank you for all of the adventures—especially the Russian ones.

To my grandfather, the first writer I knew, and to my father, who wanted to be a writer. I wish you could hold this book in your hands.

Thank you, with every bit of my love, to Margot and Win, who, in acknowledgment of themselves, have typed their names here. And to Grainger for all the moves, all those midwestern winters, for all the drafts you've read, and all the love you've given. How lucky I am to have you.

A PENGUIN READERS GUIDE TO

LIGHTS ALL NIGHT LONG

Lydia Fitzpatrick

A Conversation with
Lydia Fitzpatrick

How did you come up with Ilya and his life in Russia? Do you have any personal connections to Russia?

My mother is a Russian historian who lived and studied in Russia during the Cold War, and when I was little, my family hosted two Russian students, Olga and Tatiana. They were young—Olga couldn't have been older than six—and both were completely brilliant. Olga was a piano prodigy, and her stay with us culminated in a duet that she performed with master cellist Mstislav Rostropovich at the Kennedy Center. I remember her playing standing up because otherwise her feet couldn't reach the pedals.

When I was older, my family went to Russia for a summer. This was in the mid-'90s, in the long, chaotic wake of perestroika. We had a driver, Aleksey, whose life savings had amounted to a pack of cigarettes after the "shock therapy" economic reforms. I'll never forget him telling us this as he weaved through Moscow's hellish traffic, looking back at us in the rearview mirror to see if we understood, puffing on a cigarette that I couldn't help but think was from that fateful pack.

Ilya's story came about, in part, through my attempt to unpack these experiences, to tap into Aleksey's resilience and into that mix of trepidation and euphoria with which Olga and Tatiana took in my family, my world, and our version of America.

Very roughly speaking, the novel seems to tie Ilya's coming-of-age story to an unraveling mystery about his brother's culpability in a series of brutal murders. What inspired you to meld these seemingly disparate plotlines?

I love mysteries and coming-of-age stories, and when I began writing the novel (more years ago than I care to count), I wanted it to be both. I've always been obsessed with the structure of "The Gift of the Magi," and that was an early inspiration for the novel, though the "gifts" that Ilya and Vladimir exchange create an imbalance in their relationship—and the only way for Ilya to rectify this is to solve the murders.

I think, too, that in a way the storylines aren't disparate at all. Solving the novel's central mystery is the catalyst for Ilya's coming of age because it allows him a deeper understanding of Vladimir and Vladimir's love for him. To me, decoding that familial bond is what the book is about as much as it's about the murders.

Ilya's town and the people in it seem haunted by the past. How did you get a sense of the shadow communism and the gulag cast over their lives?

Through visiting Russia and by reading everything I could get my hands on about Russia in the '90s and '00s. *Secondhand Time* by Svetlana Alexievich was absolutely indispensable. It's a collection of oral histories from 1991 to 2012 that beautifully captures the complexity of Russians' view of communism and its collapse. Communism did cast a long shadow, but in the poverty and chaos of perestroika there was also a lot of nostalgia for it.

That said, Ilya and Vladimir are teenagers. History is all around them, but that doesn't mean they're always aware of it or sensitive to it. They're not above lying to a woman from Moscow about where the camp graves are, or rolling their eyes at their grandmother's paranoia. This is a long way of saying that it was important to me that their characters—their personal histories— took precedence over their national histories.

It seems that one of the biggest differences between American and Russian mind-sets in the book is that Americans are more optimistic, Russians pessimistic. Is that something you've found to be true?

Interesting. I think both the Russians and the Americans in the novel are optimistic, they just wear their optimism very differently. Ilya's storyline is fueled by hope—his own, his grandmother's, his mother's, his teacher Maria Mikhailovna's, and, most significantly, Vladimir's. And, of course, Ilya's own mission to get Vladimir out of prison is almost outrageously optimistic, given how thoroughly the cards are stacked against him.

Ilya and Sadie's bond seems formed in part out of what they have in common: traumatic pasts. What are the challenges that come with writing young characters who are dealing with such adult problems, or who feel out of place in typical teenage worlds?

Ilya is living with one foot in the past and one in the present. He's half in Russia, half in Louisiana, and the enormity and urgency of the problems he's dealing with don't leave him much time or bandwidth for typical teenage life. But life presses on—there's his burgeoning crush on Sadie, his first day of school, dinner with the Masons—and having Ilya engage with these less pressing concerns felt like an incredibly difficult balancing act, one that I had to reckon with in each chapter, paragraph, and sentence. Anthony Marra once told me that you need to make a reader laugh and cry on every page. I don't think I've ever managed that, but allowing some typical teenage life on the page felt key to achieving a tonal balance in the book.

This book is coming out at a time when the United States has a complicated—to say the least—relationship with Russia. Did any of that change how you perceive your book?

I think there's a risk that our current relationship with Russia will lead to a resurrection of Cold War stereotypes, and it's my hope that the novel challenges some of those stereotypes, that it brings to light a very different segment of Russian society, far from the intrigues of Moscow, but still very much subject to its politics.

QUESTIONS FOR DISCUSSION

1. Ilya arrives in Leffie and finds nearly everything about it foreign and strange, from the Masons' church to the swimming pool that's lit up at night. Have you had a similar fish-out-of-water experience in an entirely new setting? What specific features about your new surroundings seemed most strange to you?

2. One of the primary themes of the novel is the complexity of Ilya and Vladimir's relationship. What are the different forms that their brotherly bond takes, and what circumstances cause that bond to shift and change?

3. Berlozhniki and Leffie are different in so many ways. What are some ways that they might be more similar than it seems at first glance?

4. Very soon after Ilya arrives, he and Sadie find themselves to be kindred spirits. What do you think draws them together so strongly?

5. Gabe Thompson is an enigmatic supporting character in the novel. What do you take from his short-lived experience in Berlozhniki, and what do you make of the model he builds of the town upon his return home?

6. Their role in solving the murders aside, what role do you think *The Adventures of Michael & Stephanie* English-language tapes

serve in Ilya's life, first in Berlozhniki and then once he arrives in Leffie?

7. How would you describe the growth or change that Ilya undergoes during his first year in the United States?

8. Throughout the novel, Ilya experiences powerful feelings of homesickness for Berlozhniki, but by its end, he's come to think of Leffie as a kind of home as well. What do you think this says about what "home" means to us, and do you think more than one place can be a true home to the same person?

9. Mothers play a very large role in this story. How do you think the personalities of Sadie, Ilya, and Vladimir have been shaped by their mothers?

10. Vladimir's story ends with devastating finality, but Ilya's story is left open-ended. What do you think happens to Ilya after the novel ends? How about Sadie and her mother, or Maria Mikhailovna?

Book Recommendations
from Lydia Fitzpatrick

Remains of the Day by Kazuo Ishiguro
I was twelve or thirteen when I first read *Remains of the Day*, and
Stevens, Ishiguro's reserved, meticulous narrator, stole my heart.
Stevens is an English butler, the product of a society that is
crumbling around him, and Ishiguro brings him to life with wry
humor and a tough and tender touch.

Middlesex by Jeffrey Eugenides
For me, there's no truer pleasure in life than sinking into an epic,
sweeping, multigenerational saga. The longer, the better, especially
when the story's as energetic, digressive, and devastatingly funny
as *Middlesex*.

The Talented Mr. Ripley by Patricia Highsmith
Tom Ripley is one of the most compelling characters ever created.
A sociopath who manages to elicit not just the reader's sympathy
but his shaky allegiance, because who hasn't wanted to sink, just
for a moment, into another identity?

Lincoln in the Bardo by George Saunders
I love everything George Saunders does. This novel is narrated by
Willie Lincoln in the days after his death, along with a host of
other raucous souls in limbo. There's a palpable, contagious
delight to Saunders's writing, even as it delivers a portrait of a

father and son in mourning and a powerful meditation on the power of the past over the present.

Selected Stories by Alice Munro

Munro made me see the possibilities in writing short fiction in a way no other author has. She moves through time, through lives, with such brilliance, and there's this clean serenity to her prose that belies just how much is happening beneath the surface.